I0668549

THE ETERNAL ELEMENTS

THE BLOOD OF GOD

JASON JONES

ALL THINGS THAT MATTER PRESS

THE ETERNAL ELEMENTS

To my four lovely children: Scarlett Aurora, Caspian Elias, Eden Isabella, Juliette Rose. Every inspiration beneath my pen was fueled by my love for you.

To my wife Tara Bridget. Without your daily encouragement my hopes of success would be futile.

To all my family. Thank you always for your love and support.

1: BROWNIES

Thunder rolled through the heavens as rain slapped against the bedroom window. Killian waited eagerly for the next streak of lightning to rush through the night. Sometimes he imagined that they were branches of fire reaching out into the sky from some mighty monstrous creature. Or, that the thunder was the sound of the atmosphere splitting apart right above his head, allowing something magical to come through. Storms like these fueled his imagination with endless possibilities.

"Son, I told you it's not safe to leave these curtains open during these storms. Do you know how many people die from lightning each year in

Florida?" Jacob shut the blinds and pulled the star-speckled curtains closed.

"No, how many?" Killian asked, jumping into bed.

"Well, I don't know, either, but it's a lot." Jacob walked over to the bed.

"But Daddy, I love the storms here," Killian said as another burst of lightning lit up the edges of the window.

Jacob glanced at his son, who was pleading within a clan of stuffed animals crowded on the mattress. Jacob walked back to the blinds and cracked them. He maneuvered towards the bed, navigating through scattered toys littering the floor. He leaned over the bed to perform his nightly ritual. Each stuffed animal had its place, and Killian couldn't rest until they all surrounded him. The pile was getting so large Jacob wondered how Killian was able to sleep comfortably in this chaos.

Jacob kissed his son on the forehead. "Tomorrow is a big day and you're not staying up all night like you did last year. And don't even think about sneaking out and peeking at your presents while I'm wrapping, buster." He rustled his son's chestnut hair, kissing him several more times on the cheek.

"Tomorrow, I'll be five, right, Daddy?"

"Yep, you'll be a big boy," Jacob replied, tucking the sheets tightly around Killian. A few of the animals fell as he did this. He picked them up and placed them back strategically.

"Did you get me a puppy?" Killian asked, clapping his hands together.

"You know I wouldn't tell you either way," Jacob teased.

"Daddy, why is my birthday on Halloween?"

Jacob stared at him, his hand shaking. "Because . . . that's the day Mommy gave birth to you. But you don't turn five until ten-thirty-two tomorrow night, remember?"

Killian looked over at the picture of his mom on the nightstand, tucking a stuffed turtle under his arm. "But why is Halloween on my birthday?"

"Well, because you were born on Halloween, so your birthday and Halloween are on the same day. That makes your birthday extra special."

Thunder roared overhead as Jacob moved towards the door, placing his hand on the dimmer switch.

"But Daddy?"

Jacob waited, his palms sweating a little in fear of the question he knew was coming. A question he wished he had an answer for, a question he asked himself every night before he went to bed, and every morning when he woke.

"Daddy?"

"Yes, Killian."

"When is Mommy coming back?"

Killian's words formed an invisible knife plunging into Jacob's stomach. He waited a moment before he responded. "I hope really soon, son."

Killian glanced back towards the window as flashes of lightning highlighted the drapes. "I hope she's okay in this storm."

Jacob studied his son. His heart ached with the loss of his wife but hearing the sadness in his son's voice hurt even more. He dimmed the lights until they were off and said, "*Melinyel hildinya.*"

"*Melinyel taryo,*" Killian replied.

Jacob stepped out of the doorway, leaving the door ajar.

The rain beat harder upon the window with peals of thunder rolling overhead. The center of the storm was close now, but Killian wasn't afraid. He was getting more excited. Storms were one of his most favorite things in the world. Tomorrow was Halloween, his birthday, and he might get a puppy. Maybe, he'd even get to see his mom.

His eyes wandered over to the picture of her beside his bed, and the beaded necklace she had given him when he was born. Two tears trickled down his small cheek, and he turned away from her beautiful face.

A creaking noise came from the door, and Killian watched as it opened and then shut. This was quite peculiar because his dad never shut the door all the way. Maybe he was serious about wrapping his presents alone and didn't want to be disturbed. More rain pounded the window as the intensity of the lightning increased. Between rounds of thunder, Killian heard scratching on the wooden floors, faint at first, possibly in his room, perhaps in the hallway.

Maybe the puppy dad bought me escaped, he thought. Once again, he was wide awake thinking of what he was going to name his first dog: Rex, Lightning, or Spot.

This sudden burst of excitement was short-lived as his dresser drawer began to move. He froze, listening intently to the rough scratching upon the floor as small sounds of snarling came from the corner. Killian pulled the sheets tightly around him as another drawer opened and closed. The scratching grew as loud as the rain. He thought perhaps there was a rat in his bedroom, but he didn't think rats could open drawers or snarl.

The scratching stopped abruptly. As Killian looked towards the window, lightning plumed again, illuminating a shadow sneaking along the wall. Killian's entire body went rigid as the shadow disappeared in the loss of light. *What was that?* He wondered, terror gripping his little mind. *A monster? A shadow monster? A child-eating, stuffed-animal-killing monster?*

Lightning flashed again, and the shadow reached out for the edge of his bed. Two horns protruded from its skull with large tentacle-like hands reaching towards him. Killian stiffened, his breathing almost ceasing. He wanted to scream, but he couldn't find his voice. The sheets rustled, but Killian didn't move, he didn't flinch, he didn't blink. His hands were gripping the sheets so tight that his fingernails cut into his palms.

Then the sheets jerked within his grasp. Killian moved his head just high enough to see the edge of his bed. A small creature stood upright. He watched it intensely as it moved towards him. He whimpered in a release of the mounting pressure enveloping his chest. The beast whined back, mocking his fear. Killian held his breath as the creature moved closer. The sheets pulled from his hands as it crawled.

Lightning flashed once more. A crackling explosion burst outside his window. The creature jumped towards him, landing in the pile of stuffed animals. Killian took a deep breath as he turned towards the strange being.

A distant flash of lightning brought a glow into the room revealing two flamingo-pink eyes between two pink floppy ears protruding from a fluffy white face. The creature had a brace of small golden horns no bigger than Killian's pinky fingers, and it was shaking nervously. Killian

4

sat up. The beast dug into the covers to hide, but instead, more stuffed animals fell on it. Killian laughed, hearing his own voice echoed by the creature.

Moving the stuffed animals one by one, he found a trembling pink butt sticking up in the air. Killian chuckled, and his fear faded. He noticed the creature didn't have tentacles at all. Its arms and legs were wearing socks. Not just any socks either. They were Killian's socks, and none of them matched.

"It's okay little guy, I won't hurt you," he said, moving the last stuffed animal out of the way.

Without warning, a screech sounded from above, and a second creature jumped from the ceiling, falling directly into Killian's lap. He screamed from the sudden shock so loudly he felt his throat would burst. The small black creature screamed in response and threw its sock-covered arms in the air, shaking violently.

Jacob burst into the room, throwing on the lights. Killian glanced over at his dad in exasperation.

"Oh, no," Jacob screamed as the two little creatures burst into laughter, bouncing on the bed. "You guys were supposed to stay in the cage until morning!" he shouted.

The creatures continued to cackle as they bounced higher and higher on the bed.

Killian laughed, watching the little guys float up into the air then fall playfully back into the sheets.

"Until the morning?" he asked, staring at his dad curiously. Both of them watched as the black one grabbed the ceiling fan.

"Yes, these are your birthday presents. They're not a puppy, but I thought they'd be a little more interesting."

"But daddy, what are they?" Killian asked, as the black one crawled across the ceiling.

"Well, they're called brownies."

"Like the food?"

"That's just what people call them." Jacob rustled Killian's hair, sitting next to him on the bed. "They have a scientific name, of course. They're from daddy's work."

5

The white one jumped into Jacob's arms, emitting a sound somewhere between purring and humming. The black one followed suit, jumping again from the ceiling into Killian's lap.

"They're amazing, Dad!" Killian ran his fingers through the black one's soft fluffy hair, noticing a gold patch between its golden horns. In the blink of an eye, both brownies disappeared then instantly reappeared, swapping places. Killian gawked at them in utter amazement.

"Yeah, they can switch places," Jacob laughed. "They're kind of like living furry electrons."

"What do they eat?" Killian asked.

"They're vegetarians, mainly salads, fruits, and nuts. I guess sometimes they could have a cupcake or something. They can't talk, not yet anyways, I'm not sure if they ever will. They kind of just mimic sounds like a parrot does."

"Yeah, they laugh just like me," Killian said, watching them evaporate again. This time the white one ended up on the bookshelf and the black one hanging from the curtain. Killian giggled, "Are they always like this?"

"Yeah, they're super hyper and nocturnal. Sunlight will kill them, so you can never have them out during the day. I bought some special black-out curtains that we'll have to put up tomorrow to be safe because, as you can see, they're a little reckless."

As Jacob said this, the black one threw the white one into the bookshelf knocking over several of Killian's favorite classics. Jacob picked up the books as the brownies headed back for the bed. They bounced from one wall to the next, sometimes lightly touching items and sometimes knocking over entire bins of toys.

Jacob beamed from the sight of joy on his son's face. "So, what are you going to name them?"

Killian looked up at his dad, a smile drawn from ear to ear, but then confusion interrupted his happiness when he realized he had been thinking for months about dog names, and these were not dogs. He looked at them again. They were as tiny as most of his stuffed animals.

"Will they get any bigger, daddy?"

"No."

"Are they magical beings, like in Harry Potter and Narnia?"

"Sort of, they're not from . . . well, they're not from our world, exactly."

"Are they aliens?" Killian asked, excitedly.

"No, they're not aliens. At least they're not from Mars or anything like that. I'll explain those things to you when you're older. Can't you pick names for them without all the fine details?"

Killian shook his head, pondering this excruciatingly important decision. What to name his first-ever magical pets? Both brownies were now swinging from the fan, and the white one's socks flew off. The creature squealed in terror, popping in and out of visibility, rapidly collecting the socks. The black one laughed hysterically and fell to the bed.

"What do you think?" Jacob asked, scooping up the black one while the white one popped into Killian's lap, nestling gently against his stomach. His cotton velociraptor sock moved oddly on the brownies arm.

"Why do they like socks so much?" he asked.

"No one knows, but they can't stand for their claws to be exposed. So, they're always searching for something to cover their paws with."

"Hmm, what are they called again?"

"Scientifically, they are called Pauxillum Daemonium, but in ancient mythologies, people called them brownies."

"Like little living furry chocolate brownies?"

"Yep," Jacob nodded.

Killian studied them intently. "What's the name of those brownies you always make me?"

"You mean the Betty Crocker brownies?"

"Are those the ones with the marshmallows?"

"No, I think those are the Duncan Hines brownies."

Killian examined the white cotton-ball, watching the pink ears flop up and down. "I'll call this one Duncan," he said, and the brownie squealed with laughter. Instantly, the black one swapped places with Duncan jumping up and down eager to be named.

Killian took the black one up into his arms. "And I'll call you Crocker."

The little creatures purred in his lap.

Jacob stood up from the bed. "Now, what is the most important rule that we always have to remember?"

"No sunlight."

"Well, yes, but what is even more important than that?"

Killian put a finger to his mind, thinking. "Never, ever, tell people about daddy's work stuff?"

"That's right." Jacob walked back to the doorway and dimmed the lights. "Happy birthday, son. Don't stay up all night."

"I won't," Killian laughed as Jacob cracked the door.

Crocker and Duncan stared at their new master, their faces wide with expectation. A roll of thunder ripped overhead, and they jumped in Killian's arms. Killian laughed and laid back down in his pile of stuffed animals petting his magical birthday presents.

2: NEW JERUSALEM, PA

Jacob watched Anah as if through a shattered mirror, boarding the cerulean sailboat for the last time. The crew were busy as ants, sweat pouring from their brows under the midday sun. Waves slapped the side of the boat as an anchor burst up through the sea caps. Within an hour, they would reach their final destination.

A storm was brewing in the distance, and the taste of salt was heavy in the air. Anah's frustration mounted as she struggled with her wet suit, clinging to her like a black robe of death, sucking the life from her even now.

"Anah, we don't have much time," the captain said. "The forecast calls for a storm in three hours."

She nodded. "I need a few more pieces of the wreckage. You know what's at stake here."

The captain tilted his hat, blocking the sun. "Get those hooks secured and get back on this boat. That's an order."

"Aye, aye, skipper," she said with a laugh.

He gave her a thumbs-up as the boat stalled. She fastened her mask and fell backwards into waters of doom. The water was unusually warm for this time of year, and the turquoise void invited her into its arms. Gripping the swaying hooks, she attached each of them to her utility belt. Her hands moved along the sleek yellow propulsion device, checking the settings on her depth chart. Anah fired up the engine, and a mass of bubbles burst from the turbines, sending her plunging into the abyss.

Jacob screamed, "Anah, no, don't go." But that was all he could ever say, and she never heard him.

Within ten minutes, she was halfway to her destination. Jacob knew her mind was wandering from the way she bit her lip. Was she thinking of their son? Two years old and on the other side of the world, just a memory to her. He could remember their conversation that morning. Today would be her final dive. After this, she could go home and be with him and Killian for months, maybe years, until she was needed again.

Anah checked the depth on her piranha: one thousand feet. Kicking on the light, she illuminated the darkness around her, causing her to blink several times, possibly from the pressure, perhaps from the light. He watched her intently as drowsiness washed over her face.

Is it narcosis? Jacob thought.

She rechecked the depth chart: twelve hundred feet, but there was nothing there. She seemed nervous and discombobulated. *The oxygen tank must have had impure elements within it.*

The piranha plunged on, and she began to laugh. Jacob's fear momentarily halted as her sweet smile reminded him of the joy he'd once known, and the face he missed so much.

For the third time, she checked the depth chart: it read fourteen hundred feet. She'd never dived this far before, and she knew something was wrong. Killing the motor, she floated in the silent darkness.

Jacob slowed this moment to a crawl. Watching his wife float like an astronaut among the blackness of space. There was something in it. Something he couldn't understand. Something he was missing.

She gazed upwards, her face changing slowly, filling with some new emotion.

He looked up as well, still amazed by the spectacle even now.

Another mass of bubbles ripped through the water, and he looked away as terror swept over her face. She turned, soaring up through the water, and burst above the surface, flinging her mask into the air. There was no boat, no sun. She was alone in the dark.

Together, they peered into a blanket of stars. The constellations moved like cosmic dancers in an astrological opera. Individual specks flashed blue, red, white, and yellow. He gazed at her one last time, etching the moment again into his mind. Her grey eyes flickered as her pink lips parted. Then came those words, those awful words that had tormented him for years. Words he wanted to destroy as they passed over her lips: "Where am I?"

***

Jacob awoke, body slick with sweat, that vivid universe flooding his mind. For fifteen years, the same dream had haunted him, and for fifteen years, he had wondered what it meant. The university had passed on their condolences and told him a story about a shipwreck with no survivors. He could never accept that. He would never believe that.

Rolling out of bed, he glanced at his phone. The screen read three-thirty-three p.m. He had woken up early again. Rubbing the sleep from his eyes, he meandered towards the bathroom. Fresh mint filled his mouth as bristles ran across his teeth. He examined his low stubble and pulled out his new razor. With each stroke, he pondered his dream. *Could she have traveled to the other side? Or another dimension? Could there be a wormhole in the Red Sea?*

Jacob lifted his head to shave his neck, noticing something very peculiar. Wallpaper covered Mrs. Peterson's ceiling in a garish pink cupcake design. *That's odd*, he thought. He dried his face with a Popsicle rag and glanced around the unusual bathroom. The light fixtures were shaped like lollipops, the light switch like a piece of butterscotch, the shower curtain was speckled with jellybeans, and the commode covered in lace. He shook his head and turned back into the bedroom.

A brown suede suitcase opened its mouth, regurgitating its contents onto the bed. Jacob's usual attire lay scattered: a white collared shirt, blue jeans, a pair of brown boots, and an old leather jacket. Tying the last knot of his shoelace, he pulled a small briefcase out from under the bed.

A red light flickered as he placed his palm across the top metal plate. Several locks clicked, opening a false lid. Inside was a platinum-plated electronic necklace holding a silver-coated seashell, a golden phone with an unusual obsidian face, a pair of gold aviator glasses with frosted blue lenses, and a golden ring encapsulating a tigers eye. He plucked each of the items up and slid the case back under the bed.

He glanced in the mirror briefly. *Forty-eight, widowed, and no home for me and my son to call our own. Fifteen years traveling the world, one week after another, and for what? Was it all worth it? Will I ever find her?* He couldn't believe what life had dealt him and what it had dealt his son.

Shaking his head, he grabbed his brown fedora and left his reflection behind.

He walked into the hallway, noticing Killian's door still shut. A purple-flowered wreath hung from it crookedly. He thought about knocking but hesitated.

Killian is *growing so fast. He needs his rest. I'll wake him when I'm done.*

Jacob moved towards the stairs. Stepping quietly, he maneuvered down each step, attempting not to disturb Mrs. Peterson and her clan of cats. Unfortunately, the old wooden floor creaked at every level, making him cringe.

"Good morning, Mr. Gold," a voice rang out behind him. "How was your sleep last night . . . or should I say, throughout the morning?"

Startled, he twisted around, nearly falling down the remaining stairs. At the top of the floor stood Mrs. Peterson smiling at him with curious eyes. Her puffy blue hair eccentrically accented her rosy red cheeks. In each hand was a long-haired feline eyeing him suspiciously.

"Good morning, Mrs. Peterson. I slept wonderfully, thank you. The rooms here are quite exquisite, very, very nice. Thank you," Jacob replied, maneuvering to the first floor.

"Will you want tea, Mr. Gold, coffee, juice, breakfast?"

Jacob nodded as five cats raced up the stairs to the sound of their master's voice.

"Would you like the usual: steak, bacon, fruit, scrambled eggs, kidney pie?"

He recounted his options as he walked backwards. "Um . . . is it turkey bacon?"

"They make bacon out of turkey?" she asked.

Jacob put his hand to his temple. "Um, everything but bacon, and perhaps coffee first, if you don't mind?"

Decisions are best made after coffee, he thought.

"Absolutely, Mr. Gold, I made a fresh pot this morning, but I'm afraid I've drunk the last cup. I don't usually have visitors sleep in until afternoon tea, but you young people nowadays. I'll start a new one immediately. Have it out in a jiffy, make yourself at home, anywhere you please."

Jacob smiled and turned towards the cellar making his way down another flight of steps. He opened the door and shut it hastily. Light burst into the room as he turned on the cellar switch. Seven tiny voices rang out in immediate protest.

"What the feck man?"

"You blow-in!"

"Jeanie-Mac, Jeanie-Mac, turn that light off!"

12

Jacob reached the bottom of the cellar stairs and yelled, "Quiet," as softly as he could. "What is wrong with you, little monsters? Every day it's the same thing whine, whine, whine, complain."

Sitting down on a small stool, he counted seven little beings walking out from behind a pair of boxes. They were about two feet in height, with carrot-topped hair except for the eldest whose hair was white. Most of them wore suspenders with flashy clover green pants and sunshine yellow shirts, but despite their clothing, they all wore a grimace on their faces.

"Leprechauns you monkey, its leprechauns, not monsters, you overgrown gorilla, how many times must me tell ya, old man?" This deep-voiced, curly-haired leprechaun, was called Cornedbeef. He looked up at Jacob shaking his fist, a green plaid bonnet bouncing around his head.

Jacob shook his head at the mess of the group. Some belched loudly, as others twisted suspenders out of uncomfortable places. "You know, guys. I can mail you right back to Dublin anytime. You just give the word."

Tiny "boo's" filled the air with a hefty amount of stomping. "Feck, old man, why ye want to go and do a thing like that, Jeanie-Mac, you just startled us, that's all," Squeezie said, the smallest and thinnest of the bunch.

"Yea, stop acting the maggot, maggot," Cabbage added, running his hands through his slick orange hair.

Jacob looked furiously at the muscular, quick-tongued leprechaun, "I told you to stop calling people that. You guys have got to start learning some manners, or I'm sending you right back to the emerald isle."

"Er, force of habit, we can't help it, laddie," the eldest of the group replied. "We're angry little people. Always have been, always will be." His name was Murphy, and he had thick snow-white hair with a debonair goatee. Jacob liked him the most. He could be reasoned with.

"Aye, aye, aye," rang out from the party, along with several punches and a kick to each other's ribs.

A tug on Jacob's jeans caught his attention as two female leprechauns, folded their arms, and gazed up at him.

"Yes, Clover, Freckles, what is it?"

"Obviously, Jacob, the boys need their bangers and mash, or they're going to get way saucier than this. Personally, I feel it's this kip of a place. It's turning me scarlet just being here." Clover fixed her blue dress and primped her hair.

The smaller of the two was Freckles, and she nodded with enthusiasm, adding, "Feck, this place is manky for sure."

Jacob rubbed his temples. "You guys keep it down, and I'll see about scrounging up some breakfast."

Instantly, cheers went up, and food orders rang out.

"Make it a sambo and some gargle!"

"Get the black stuff!"

"Make sure there's afters!"

"Don't forget spuds and poke!" Everyone agreed with this statement, and they all started dancing and shouting, "Spuds and poke, spuds and poke, spuds and poke!"

"Shh …", Jacob hissed, and the voices died down to giggles. "Now, where's Smirk?"

They all shrugged, putting their hands in their pockets, except Clover and Freckles, who were still giggling.

"Guys, where's Smirk? And where's Pixel and Pixley? Did they go out last night?"

The leprechauns grumbled at this suggestion saying, "Yea, boyo is making bags of that, he's acting the maggot for sure, chancer, dosser—"

"Okay, okay," Jacob said. "I'll go upstairs and look for food, but no beer, it's too early for that, and no afters until the three of them are found."

Urgent protests went up as Jacob marched upstairs and closed the cellar door. He turned around to find Mrs. Peterson standing beside him, a cup of coffee in her hand.

"Creme, sugar, hot sauce?"

Hot sauce, Jacob thought, *what in the world is she talking about?*

"Um, just creme is fine, thank you. By the way, you wouldn't happen to have any pasta, would you?"

"Uh, no dear, I'm afraid not, but I just finished your eggs and steak. Is that still okay?"

14

"Definitely, I was … just … thinking of something for Killian when he wakes up."

"Oh, that sweet boy of yours, I'll cook him up something proper. Can't have guests in the house walking around hungry, they might steal the couch."

He looked at her, confused, wondering if guests have stolen furniture from her before. "How about any canned soups or potatoes?"

The older woman thought for a moment, an exceedingly long moment, Jacob thought perhaps she was in the onset of a stroke.

"Actually dear, I believe there are some Spaghetti-O's in the cabinet from the Smith's visit a couple of weeks ago. Would that do?"

He opened the cabinet and found two small cans. "Do you have a small bowl and a microwave Mrs. Peterson?"

"Certainly, Dear, above the stove to the left."

The microwave bell dinged, and Jacob grabbed seven spoons along with some bowls. He went back down the cellar stairs and handed out the silverware to the hungry little leprechauns.

"What in the bollocks of St. Patrick is this?" asked Lil McMan, smelling a spoonful of the O's.

"Do you want to starve to death?" Jacob asked, bending down to pick up the bowl.

"No," screamed everyone lifting their spoons in unison. Loud, hefty slurps rang out as they licked their lips, and their bellies growled. Cabbage belched, and the others backed away. They eyed each other for a moment, then burst out in cheers of approval, diving into the rest of the bowl.

Jacob left them to their meal. Mrs. Peterson laid the final plates on the dining room table and motioned for him to sit. He did so gratefully, looking at a feast of sorts. Mrs. Peterson sat down and placed two cats in her lap. Four others jumped into empty chairs with paws on the table.

"This is a lovely place you have here, Mrs. Peterson," Jacob said, filling his plate with scrambled eggs.

"Thank you, dear, after Alfred passed, I didn't know what to do with such a large home. Then Marjorie at Bingo night told me about this, Airbnb thing and I thought why not. I love entertaining guests, and it makes life so much more fun meeting gobs of new people from all over.

Of course, I don't know why anyone would want to come to New Jerusalem except for the leaves and the Crystal Cave. Is that what you and your boy are here to see?"

Jacob wanted to respond but at the moment, he was chewing a rather tough piece of steak. Swallowing and almost choking, he replied, "Yes, the leaves here are beautiful, very … unique."

"Not the leaves silly, they don't change for another three months. Crystal Cave, will you be visiting the ghosts there?"

Jacob peered over his cup of coffee. *Did she know something about the cave? Were there ghosts there? Is that the local disturbance he was sent to investigate, or was this just more of her crazy talk?*

"I've never heard of it, is it haunted or something?" he asked.

"Oh good gracious yes, local legend really, the white crystals speak sometimes, or so they say. I've never heard them myself, but my late Alfred said he did once when he was a boy. Of course, he was always a bit off in the mind, especially towards the end, you know. You have to take … what's your boy's name again?"

"It's Killian," a deep voice replied, coming down the stairs. "I could smell the food from my room." He surveyed the table. "Wow, this looks delicious."

Jacob examined his son. His chestnut hair looked like a rat's nest, and he was quite sure he'd worn that blue t-shirt for a week.

"Hungry, hungry teenagers. A good meal always drags them out of bed," Mrs. Peterson said, getting up suddenly. "Heaven's me. I forgot the jam, anyone for jam, marmalade, apple butter?"

"Sure," Killian said, shuffling scrambled eggs in his mouth.

"Sleep well?" Jacob asked.

"Yea, you?" Killian replied through a mouthful of kidney pie.

"Like a baby."

Killian glanced up at him and swallowed. "You were dreaming about mom again, huh?"

"What makes you say that?" Jacob replied, wiping his mouth, and turning towards the multitude of cats wandering into the dining room.

"You look like you just ran a marathon, and your eyes are red," Killian stated, matter-of-factly.

16

"That's just from dealing with the 'chauns this morning." Jacob stabbed another piece of steak.

"Right. Anyways, I told you, let me handle the 'chauns. They need a gentle, understanding touch, which you don't have." Killian took a spoonful of kidney pie and smelled it.

"Well, you'll get your turn for sure. Finish up here and get their bowls from breakfast. How's Duncan, Crocker, and Wendy?"

"Wendy splashed me this morning to wake me up. The boys are still asleep under the sheets." Killian carved the last piece of steak on his plate and eyed it like it was the most beautiful thing in the world.

Jars of jam whizzed by as Mrs. Peterson said, "Okay, we have blueberry, raspberry, boysenberry, gooseberry, and cherry. These are all made local. Mr. Carter has a fruit stand on Saturday mornings. He makes all of them at home. Oh, and here are some biscuits, my special recipe."

Killian grabbed two biscuits, splitting them in half and applying a different jelly to each side. The food was so delicious he thought about suggesting they stay here an extra week when they finished the job.

"How old are you, dear?" Mrs. Peterson asked, stroking a fat silver cat in her lap.

"Seventeen," he replied, a piece of biscuit hopping out of his mouth.

"Oh, are you a senior this year?"

"Um, no, I'm a junior."

"Oh, well, that's pretty good. What's your favorite subject?"

Killian swallowed another piece of egg and gulped down some pineapple juice. "Um, I liked Chemistry and Physics last semester, but I'm looking forward to Calculus."

"Wow, those sound very advanced, you must be a smart-one, what's the name of your high school?"

He lifted a spoonful of kidney pie, glaring at his dad, who chimed in quickly.

"Killian graduated high school when he was fourteen. He's in his third year of college right now. We travel a lot, so he does everything online."

"Only because you won't let me go to the University and stay on campus like a normal college student," Killian muttered, dangling a piece of egg on the tip of his fork.

17

Jacob glared at him.

"Oh my, college at seventeen. That is spectacular. Well done, very well done," Mrs. Peterson congratulated, beginning to clap. Unfortunately, the clapping sent a mad dash of cats running into the dining room from every direction of the house.

Killian watched the infestation of black, calico, ginger, white, and brown cats take over the table. Three of the cats snagged several pieces of bacon, and one got a bit of steak.

"Now Jingles, Snowflake, Dasher, you get down from there," Mrs. Peterson said, shooing them away unsuccessfully. Five more cats were on the table in an instant. The jams fell over, and three biscuits disappeared.

Killian stood up with his plate, shoveling food in his mouth before the cats could get it.

Jacob was already standing, plate in hand, finishing the kidney pie.

"This was delicious, Mrs. Peterson, best meal I've had in years, honestly, thank you so much," Jacob said, signaling for Killian to follow him into the kitchen. They finished the remaining morsels and placed their plates in the sink as Jacob looked at his phone: five-fifteen p.m. "I'm going upstairs to finish charging the equipment and pack the bags. You need to take a shower and get ready to go."

"Okay, I'm just going to check on the lads for a minute, and I'll be up," he replied, looking in the cabinets and the refrigerator.

"What are you looking for?" Jacob asked.

"Some after's—you know how they are."

Jacob threw him a pack of snack cakes from the counter.

"I told them no afters until we find Smirk, Pixel, and Pixley, but I guess that doesn't apply to your *understanding* with them."

Killian laughed, "Yea, eighty percent of why they love me is because I give them sugar. Did the pixies go out again?"

"Apparently. You tell those orange-haired squirrels that I said they better be ready to go in one hour, we have a lot to do tonight, and it's Sabbath I wanted to do Havdalah."

"Seriously?" Killian turned and stared at his dad with his head hung low and mouth wide open.

"Yes, seriously," Jacob replied, walking upstairs. "You know this week is the ninth of Av, and I want to do something special. One day you're going to wish you'd learned all the Hebrew liturgy when you meet a nice Jewish girl."

"And how am I supposed to meet a nice Jewish girl or any girl for that matter when we are never any place longer than a month?" Killian yelled.

Mrs. Peterson walked around the corner. Killian opened the cellar door and slid inside. He shut the door and popped his knuckles. He pulled out the Little Debbie snack cake and opened the package, holding it behind his back. The floor was empty except for seven bowls with seven spoons in them. Wondering what his dad had fed them, he cleared his throat and snapped his fingers twice. Seven tiny heads poked out from around the corner.

"Killian. My boy. My lad," bellowed through the cellar.

"What's up, fellas? Did you sleep well? Did dad give you something good for breakfast?"

"O's, O's, O's, O's," rang out from the excited group, pumping their fists in the air.

"O's?" he asked, wrinkling his nose.

"Your old man brought us something called O's with balls of meat inside and some magical red sauce. It's delicious," Freckles said, hugging Killian's barefoot.

"You must mean Spaghetti-O's, where in the world did he get Spaghetti-O's from?"

"I don't know, but they're smashing good laddie," Lil McMan slapped his belly.

"Well, you guys interested in some afters?" Killian pulled the snack cake from behind his back.

Cheers roared into the air with shouts of, "Afters, afters, afters, afters."

Killian broke the cake into seven pieces passing it around quickly. "Dad said we're leaving in an hour, so you guys better be ready and no noise when we go upstairs. This lady has about a hundred cats, and I bet they would all love a squishy little leprechaun chew toy."

"Feck, I'll kill a cat, let one try to touch me," Cornedbeef said, with icing painted all over his beard.

"I ain't afraid of no feline, bring it on," Clover yelled.

19

"No one is fighting any cats, but you have to get in the duffel bag when I get down here, okay, no arguing."

Eyes rolled, and mouths muttered as they finished up their snack cake. Killian picked up the bowls and spoons.

"It's just until we get in the van. I'll be down in a bit, be ready." Killian headed back up the stairs shutting the door quietly.

Neither Mrs. Peterson nor the pack of cats was around, but the table was left quite a mess. He laid the used bowls down and examined the leftovers. He found a few grapes, half an apple, some mandarins, and a piece of rye toast. He placed them on a plate and muttered, "This will have to do."

Opening his bedroom door, he slipped inside. Two furry brownies jumped on his neck. "Good morning boys, are you finally up? Are you hungry?" Killian asked, scratching the top of their heads. They looked at the fruit mimicking, "Hungry, hungry," several times.

Killian placed the plate on the bed and grabbed the small piece of rye. Walking over to his aquarium, he scanned the large sea castle, and bits of flora spread throughout the tank. Miniature glowing fish swam across the glass as bubbles blew out of a treasure box.

"Wendy, where are you? I brought you something to eat." He lifted the glass and swirled his finger in the water three times. A small face peeked out of the castle window, her purple hair flowing around her.

"Come on, Wendy, it's bread. You love bread." Killian tapped gently on the tank. In a flash, the mermaid popped out of the water and snagged the bread from his fingers. She sat on a tiny bay within the aquarium and nibbled the bread.

"What do you think?" he asked, looking at her admiringly.

"Dry," she said, taking another bite. "Very dry."

"Well, it's all we got for now. You'll have to wait until dad and I can go to the store. I'll pick you up some of those gummy worms you love and maybe some angel food cake, okay?"

Nodding with a scowl, she dove back in the water, circling the castle many times, her emerald green fins sparkling.

Killian stripped off his clothes and headed for the shower. Pulling back a curtain wholly covered with roses, he found a bathtub lined with poinsettias and daisies. *This is the weirdest house we've ever stayed at*, he thought, letting the warm water hit him in the face. Water always made him feel better and he faded into thought.

Boom, boom, boom, heavy beats sounded from the door.

"Killian, what are you doing? We need to leave in ten minutes," Jacob shouted through the bathroom door.

"I'm taking a shower, what does it sound like?"

"You've been in there for half an hour. My toilet started gargling the moment you got in. Hurry it up."

"Okay, okay, five more minutes."

"I'm putting everything in the van. Don't forget the 'chauns." Jacob walked out of the bedroom.

Killian finished his shower grudgingly and stood in front of the mirror with his towel wrapped around his waist. He flexed his muscles, making his abs rip across his torso. His pecks thumped triumphantly upon his chest. He grabbed his trusty hair clay and fiddled with his hair until it looked as though he had been sleeping for a week. He winked at himself and threw on his favorite red three-quarter-sleeve shirt, a dark pair of jeans, and his dad's specialty items: a seashell necklace, a gold ring, glasses, and a black-faced phone.

"Duncan, Crocker, don't you dare leave this room," he demanded. They waved sock-covered paws in the air, saying goodbye, and cackling. "And don't mess with any of my books, either." A sound like "ya, ya, ya," came from the two creatures as they began jumping up and down on the bed.

Shutting the door, he rushed downstairs into the cellar. "Lads get it together, everyone in the duffel, we got to go." Grumbling sounds spawned from the little minions, but they filed in line at Killian's request. Struggling momentarily with the bag, he heaved it over his shoulders. Yelps, cries, and curses flew around inside.

"Watch it maggot, that's my eye, feck, keep your feet on your side."

"You guys knock it off until we get to the van," Killian whispered. He opened the cellar door and peeked around the corners for any cats. They appeared to all be upstairs with Mrs. Peterson. He maneuvered the bag around dozens of pieces of antique furniture, nearly breaking a colorfully flowered vase. He opened the front door and slipped through it quietly.

He placed the duffel in the backseat, unzipped the bag, and found seven miserable creatures eyeing each other with distaste.

Killian jumped in the front seat, noticing the time on the dashboard: six-thirty-seven p.m. Jacob sat down in the driver seat as a voice sounded over the speaker system, "Hello, Mr. Gold, where would you like to travel this evening?"

"I need the fastest way to Crystal Cave in Kutztown, Pennsylvania, Karen."

"Yes, sir, checking the routing system now. The estimated time of arrival is seven-twelve p.m. Will you need to stop for food, there are three possibilities—"

"No, Karen!" Jacob shouted.

"Excellent sir, would you like to stop for gas, my tank is currently at a capacity of thirty-seven percent. Shall I schedule an appointment at the nearest—"

"No, Karen, we are just going to the caves, no more suggestions." Jacob sighed, glancing at Killian, who shook his head.

"Excellent sir, beginning route immediately, no detours." The steering wheel folded automatically into the dash as computer sensors throughout the car lit up. The automated driving system, Jacob had named Karen, began their departure as he unfolded a map of Crystal Cave.

Killian stared out the window, watching the large brick house fade out of view. Giant maple trees and ancient ash lined the road. Lifting the middle console, he pulled out a thin blue leather book. He turned it over, running his fingers across the silver emblazoned tree holding seven stars within its branches; the title read *The Silmarillion*.

"What chapter are you on?" Jacob asked, highlighting a significant section of the map.

"Eleven," he replied, thumbing to his bookmark.

"What's the name of that one again?" Jacob peered over, glimpsing the chapter heading, "Of the Sun and Moon and the Hiding of Valinor."

"That's a great chapter full of valuable insight. What have you learned so far? Does it apply to what we are doing?"

Killian shrugged, flipping a page here and there. "I don't know. I suppose the Valar are kind of like the creatures we find from other dimensions. They're lost trying to get back to Valinor, something like that."

"Possibly, or maybe this is Valinor, and they're trying to come back home, and we're the invaders."

Killian hadn't thought of that, but he supposed it was possible. *Are we the aliens on this planet? Did we migrate to Earth from some other sector of the universe? When does anyone stop being an alien?* He stared out the window, watching hills of trees roll into the distance. The sun was getting low, and the sky was changing to deep blues and oranges.

"Oh yea, don't forget we have to go find Smirk, Pixel, and Pixley when this is over," Jacob reminded him.

"Did you bring the tracker?" Killian replied.

"It's in the backpack with everything else," Jacob answered, turning the map sideways.

"In five minutes, we shall arrive at your destination, Mr. Gold," Karen sounded over the speakers. Jacob folded up the map and glanced over at his son.

"This should be the usual. Possibly a gremlin, maybe a goblin, nothing over a level six, I imagine, but just in case, you have your *Charleston*, right?"

Killian tapped his jeans pocket lightly, still looking out the window.

"And your ring?"

Killian lifted his hand, displaying the ring.

"I hope it's a goblin, I'm in the mood to smash something green," Cornedbeef said from the back seat, punching his right hand into his left.

"Well, you can punch Squeezie then because he's as green as you're ever going to get," Cabbage replied. They all looked over at Squeezie, who was swaying drunkenly in the seat with a complexion of pale green.

"It's his motion sickness, someone grab him a cup," Jacob shouted. The leprechauns searched around frantically.

"Oh, it's coming," Squeezie shouted.

"Lift him to the window, everyone hurry," Murphy yelled. They pulled Squeezie onto Cabbage's shoulders, then Cornedbeef got under him.

"Karen roll down the rear passenger window now," Jacob yelled.

"Right away, Mr. Gold."

The window crept down the door as Squeezie continued to sway.

"Steady boys, steady," Murphy screamed, as the window locked into place. Seconds later, Squeezie lost all his O's and meatballs into the wind. Cabbage and Cornedbeef lowered Squeezie onto the rug. The color was coming back to his face, but he was still holding his stomach.

"Give him some room, give him some air," Murphy bellowed, separating the crowd from Squeezie.

"You okay there, laddie? You gonna have another go or what?" Murphy asked, patting Squeezie on the shoulder. Squeezie gave a weak thumbs-up as the others sat down on the floor around him.

Jacob smiled at Squeezie with a nod. "That a boy Squeezie! We're very proud of you, aren't we, Killian?"

Killian didn't reply. He was still staring blankly out the window.

"What's wrong, son? What are you thinking about?"

"Nothing," he replied, but Jacob could see the anger on his face and hear the frustration in his voice.

"Come on, Killian, what's going on?"

Killian's hands gripped the book tightly as the pent up words of months of frustration tumbled out of his mouth. "You have this hope, Dad, hope that I don't have. Mom's not out there. She's dead; she's gone. I can't live my whole life, hoping she'll be back. I'm sick of hoping. I don't think she's in a place like Valinor or some other dimension. She's at the bottom of that godforsaken sea, and I'll never see her again. I know that's what you're searching for on all these missions. You're looking for Mom, dragging me across the world as you do it. I have no home, no chance at a girlfriend, and no friends, except a bunch of creatures I can't tell anyone about. This isn't living. This is torture!"

"You have arrived," Karen announced, parking the car.

Killian jumped out, slamming the car door shut.

Jacob looked in the back seat as shock and terror spread across the leprechaun's faces.

"You guys stay here while I talk to him, okay."

They didn't even nod. They just kept staring at Jacob with mouths wide open. Opening the door, Jacob moved towards the trunk where Killian was sitting. His face was tear-stained, hands still gripping the book.

"I'm sorry, son. You know I love you more than anything. You didn't deserve this, having your mother taken from you at such a young age. It wasn't fair. None of this was fair. Life isn't fair. It's unjust and savage. I've searched for a reason in all this madness for years, but I can't see any. I've done the best I can, not knowing what I was doing at all. Your mom always had the plan; I just went along with her. I have hope that I can't apologize for, but I also have a job. A special job. There are not many people qualified to do what we do, right?"

Killian placed the book on the trunk, exhaling with extreme frustration.

"We've had the chance to do something extraordinary with our lives, but if you want to stop all of this and move somewhere, make friends, live a normal life. I …" Jacob hesitated, breathing deeply. Killian looked up at him, studying his facial expressions.

"I thought, maybe when you turn eighteen, you could pick a university to attend. You could spend a year there. Finish up your Bachelor's and decide where you want to go for your Master's if that's what you want to do. Is that a bargain, something you would like?"

Killian eyed his dad suspiciously. "Are you serious? I can stay on campus. I can pick anywhere I want to go?"

Jacob sighed, "Sure, son if that's your wish. I mean, I guess I can do this job all alone. I'll have to change a lot of things without my main helper. I'll have to go on dangerous missions by myself. Find new and exotic creatures by myself, but if it's what you want, then yeah."

Killian jumped off the trunk and hugged his dad. "It's not that I don't love working with you, and it's not that I want you working alone. You'll have the 'chauns and Smirk and Pixel and Pixley when we find them. I just, I just …"

"You don't have to say it, son, I know. You want to try the world out on your own. Make friends and find that special girl. Every boy has the same dream. I'll be fine. I'm so proud of you and the man you're becoming. Your mother would be proud of you, too."

They hugged once more, and Jacob said, "Melinyel hildinya."

"Melinyel taryo," Killian replied, as Jacob took his son by the shoulders.

"You're the best son a father could ever ask for, and you're going to do great things. I want what's best for you, not for me. If you're ready, if this is what you want, we'll look into a campus this semester. I'm sure Mark can get me some connections for a quick enrollment somewhere, anywhere. This job does have some perks, you know."

"Thanks, Dad, I'm sorry for yelling, I was just—"

"You had to get it all out, that's all. I know. I understand. I used to be a ball of rage myself at your age."

Killian stared at him doubtfully. "Uh no, no, you didn't. You're cool as a cucumber."

"I wasn't always this way. I was quite the rebellious one in my younger years. That's what brought your mom and me together. See—"

"Yeah, this, I don't need to hear," Killian laughed.

"Okay, but I'm just saying, I was quite the hellion; don't be fooled," Jacob grabbed him around the head and ruffled his hair. They both laughed a hearty laugh.

Killian walked around and opened the passenger door; seven leprechauns screamed at the top of their lungs.

"Did you kill your father, Killian?" Freckles yelled.

"Oh my God, you did, you murderer?" Clover wailed.

"Say it ain't so laddie, say it ain't so?" Murphy whimpered.

Jacob opened the driver's side door, and screams flew out again. Squeezie passed out on the ground while Clover and Freckles fell into each other's arms.

"He's alive," Lil McMan shrieked, jumping into Jacob's arms. The others followed suit, crying pathetically.

"We thought it was the end for you, old man, maggot," Cabbage said, tears pouring into his beard.

"I'll never call you the dullest color in the rainbow again," Clover wept.

Jacob shook his head, and Killian laughed.

"All right, all right, I'm fine, get it together, we're going into the cave, remember. You lads gotta be on point," Jacob said.

Tears burst from the leprechauns as Cornedbeef screamed, "He said lads, he called us lads, finally, finally."

"I'm proud of you, old man." Murphy patted Jacob on the leg.

Jacob placed them all in the seat and crouched down until they were eye to eye. "Do you want to help us in the cave tonight?"

Heads nodded as Squeezie finally stood to his feet, joining the group.

"Okay, here's the deal. Clover and Freckles, you take the top of the cave when we get inside. Cabbage and Lil McMan stay on our left, Cornedbeef and Squeezie on the right, Murphy bring up the rear. We're trappers, not killers. Whatever is in here may be scared. We're going to talk to it, find out what it wants and free it if we can. Don't whip out your 'Care-bear Stare' unless I give the cue, understood?" Heads bobbled in understanding.

"And you know the rule. If I snap my fingers, I'm about to drop the Charleston. That means everyone back to the van. You'll have five seconds, are we clear?"

The leprechauns rubbed their faces dry and stood at attention.

Jacob glanced up at Killian. "Do you have everything?"

Killian nodded, hiking the backpack onto his shoulders.

"Then let's go."

The troop piled out of the van. Jacob shut the door behind them. There were no cars in the parking lot, and the doors entering the cave were closed.

"Murphy, can you take care of that," Jacob asked as they walked across the asphalt.

"Sure thing, old man," Murphy replied.

In a flash, Murphy was at the opening to the cave, and he had removed all the wooden planks blocking the entrance. The door swung open, and the pitch-black entrance to the cave was revealed.

Jacob took the special glasses out of his jacket pocket and motioned for Killian to do the same. They simultaneously turned on the night-vision apparatus. Measurements came pouring over the frosted lenses along with depth analysis, temperature readings, and vibration sensitivity. They stood before the door. Jacob turned on a silver box with numerous glowing dials.

"This place is darker than Guinness Stout," Cornedbeef said.

"I wish I had some Guinness Stout," Murphy replied.

"Aye, I miss the black stuff from the homeland," Lil McMan groaned as "Aye, aye, aye," rang out from the other little voices.

"Quiet guys, we don't know what's in here. Keep to your positions and follow my lead." Jacob stepped into the darkness, Killian at his heels and a clan of emotional miscreants at their sides.

3: CRYSTAL CAVE

They ventured deep into the cave, walking on an old, creaking, wooden boardwalk. An emerald glow surrounded each of the leprechauns as Killian traced Clover and Freckles' steps walking along the cave ceiling. Jacob followed the path with the aid of a faint, pearly glow pulsating in the darkness beyond. A low, chanting sound echoed through the cavern walls as Killian's heart began to pound deep in his chest.

"Get the interpreter out," Jacob whispered.

Killian released the backpack from his shoulder, unzipped it quickly, and reached inside. He pulled out a sleek silver pad with an array of knobs and buttons.

"Give me the gilgameter as well," Jacob motioned with an open palm.

Killian peered into the bag and grasped a large black box with two antennas. He handed it to his dad. Lights flickered from either side of the contraption as two electronic beeps indicated it was on.

"What's the reading? Is it a ghost?" Killian's voice shook.

Jacob didn't answer as he watched the gauges on the box move erratically.

"It's not finding the frequency. This thing's all over the place. I've never seen it act this way before," Jacob muttered.

Killian glanced over his dad's shoulder, watching the needle rise and fall. He swallowed, feeling the sweat on his palms.

"We should leg it out of here, boys. This isn't the dwelling of a goblin or a gremlin, not even a Pooka Puk. There's something seriously manky down here," Clover urged.

"We'll be fine," Jacob responded, banging the gilgameter with his hand. "As soon as we lock in on this creature's frequency, we'll know what we're dealing with."

"And if that contraption ain't working, we'll walk straight into it, whatever it is, then what?" Lil McMan bit his quivering lip.

Jacob didn't answer but continued moving the gilgameter around as if he was drawing figure eights in the air. "Stupid gadget," he complained, allowing the gilgameter to fall to his side. His nose perked up as a scent of flowers hung in the stifling hot air.

"Do you smell that?" Jacob sniffed.

Killian breathed in, allowing the perfume of roses and tea leaves to fill his nostrils. "Where is that coming from?"

Jacob wiped the beading sweat from his brow. "Maybe they put air fresheners inside the cave walls to make it a more pleasant experience."

"More like cover up this baking heat and humidity." Killian fanned himself to no effect.

They drew further into the cave, watching lights twinkle across a small body of water. The chanting grew deeper, sounding more and more like growling.

"Are you picking up the frequency? Can you get a read on the language?" Jacob asked.

Killian stared at the gilgameter, sweat dripping onto the machine. The salty sweat clung to the corners of his eyes as he wiped them roughly with his fingers. A thin layer of mist coated the touchpad blocking the buttons' response.

"Nothing," he whispered, cleaning the mechanism with his sleeve.

"My God, lads, get it together," Murphy hissed. "Feck, this isn't the usual holy show we're used to, I'll bet me buckets of gold on that."

The growling rumble stopped as they entered the central cavern. Killian and Jacob removed their glasses, beholding a spectacle few had ever seen. Ivory crystals pulsated with an inner light, illuminating the cavern. It was as if they were inside a living diamond, breathing in and out with every flicker.

"It's mesmerizing," murmured Killian, gaping with eyes wide.

"And you want to go to college and live a normal life?" Jacob teased, wiping another layer of sweat from his forehead.

"If there are girls there, I do," Killian replied, smiling at his dad.

Without warning, the cavern began to rattle. Pieces of stalactites fell into the pool. A booming voice echoed within the walls. Stalagmites shook like a dog's tail as the boardwalk vibrated and squeaked.

Killian's interpreting mechanism finally caught the growl's frequency. A robotic voice translated the monstrous snarls and said, "The time has come. The time is now. The time has arrived. Let me out."

Killian glanced at his father, banging the gilgameter again. The needle was stuck on max capacity.

Jacob tossed the mechanism aside, sliding the Charleston from his pocket. He pressed a key on each side, initiating the power sequence.

Killian followed his dad's lead.

The growling voice rumbled through the cavern again as the robotic voice took off, "Let me out, let me out, let me out!"

Killian shook.

Jacob grabbed the device from his hands. He pressed the orange translation button and began to speak. The device converted his language to that selected on the screen.

"Uh, good evening, this is Dr. Gold, I represent the Paranormal Investigation Field Unit for the United States Military. My superiors have identified your disturbance. I have been tasked to analyze the situation here. May I first ask how we may be of assistance to you, and what exactly you are?"

A raspy laugh resounded through the cavern as the crystal lights grew dim. Then the voice sounded again. Less angry, almost academic. "Has he sent a mage to talk to me, after all of this time, a mage? So be it. My name is Amazarak, the Archon, an ancient ruler of this realm, bound for seventy generations. But the time for the last prophet to arise is upon us, and when he is revealed, my chains will melt like wax upon these stones. Then my wrath will be like none this world has ever seen. How may you assist me, mage? Worship me, like the sorcerers of old in the days of Adam, before the worm betrayed us all."

Jacob tried to swallow, but his mouth was dry. At his feet, all seven leprechauns were shaking in terror.

The white lights pulsated again around the cave. Jacob didn't know what to do or say. He cleared his throat as one question came to mind.

Leaning down, pressing the orange button, he spoke into the interpreting device again. "I recognize thee, Amazarak, the great and ancient Archon, we are blessed to meet thee."

As he said this, he bowed low and motioned for Killian to do the same.

"Oh, great Archon, please grace us with your awesome countenance?"

Killian hit his dad in the shoulder, completely disagreeing with this request.

There was a long silence.

The leprechauns surrounded the gilgameter lying on the ground, noticing the stabilized reading at max capacity.

The tense silence evaporated as the growling voice returned. "No mortal can gaze upon me. I stand in the shadows between two worlds. Locked in chains of light. When the prophet appears, I'll be set free, and then the world will behold my glory."

Jacob smiled at Killian. "He says he's between two worlds. Do you know what that means?"

"Dad, no way!" Killian quivered, shaking his head.

"It'll be fine," Jacob replied, scooting the leprechauns over to Killian.

"Are you crazy? Go into the void? What if he can harm us or trap us in there?" Killian cracked his knuckles looking around.

"You're not going, only I am. I need you out here. I'll see what this creature is, and I'll be right back."

"Dad, you're not leaving me here. You can either take me with you, or you can stay here, but we're not splitting up."

"The 'chauns are right here, son. You'll be fine, watch over them. They need you," Jacob insisted, watching the leprechauns nod vigorously.

"Yeah, but so do you. How will I know if I need to come get you, save you if something goes wrong?" Killian pleaded.

"Listen to me," Jacob said, peering into his son's beautiful grey eyes, just like his mother's. "If anything goes wrong, I'll come right back. I won't go far. I'll stay in this area. Three minutes in and then right back, okay?"

Killian nodded, his eyes downcast and his hands fidgeting.

"Look, this thing could know something about your mother. Maybe something that could help us find her. I've encountered nothing like this before, and it's speaking." Jacob turned the interpreting device towards Killian.

Killian read the letters flashing upon the screen: ENOCHIAN.

Jacob slid the Charleston into his pocket. "Enochian was the lost language your mother was researching when she disappeared. She found the keystones that unlocked the ancient Sumerian text. Maybe this Archon can tell me something about the language. Its origin, its fall, something that will help us find her."

Killian nodded, looking down at the leprechauns huddled around him. He wanted to say something but couldn't find the words.

Jacob bent down, facing the leprechauns. "You guys protect him at all costs, no matter what happens, stay with Killian."

"You got it, old man."

"Aye, we'll take care of him."

"Aye, aye, aye," they replied.

Jacob smiled, staring into Killian's eyes. "*Melinyel hildinya,*" He pressed the center of his platinum seashell necklace.

Killian stared at the blank spot left by his father and said, "*Melinyel taryo.*"

***

Jacob breathed in the ice-cold air of the shadow world, a veil between two dimensions. He peered around at the oddly shaped cavern rising thousands of feet into the sky. The cave was colorless and vague, but the creature standing before him was breathtakingly visible.

"How have you come to this place, magi?" Amazarak's eyes burned with a golden flame.

Curiously, Jacob could understand him without the interpretation device. The being towered thirty feet above him with four flaming cardinal wings.

Jacob bowed slowly and said, "I've come here through the ways of science."

"Science? Is this a new form of sorcery?" Amazarak asked, his face glowing with a long flowing crimson beard.

"Maybe … maybe in your time, in ancient times, it would have been seen as sorcery, but now we call it science." Jacob gazed in awe at the silver horns protruding from the being's skull. It was then he noticed the chains of light the creature had spoken of—one around his neck, two around each arm, and three around each leg.

"Who has done this to you, Amazarak?" Jacob asked, motioning to the chains.

"The Senate," Amazarak replied as cobalt flames shot through his horns like electricity.

"What Senate?" Jacob asked.

"The Senate of this Galaxy. Guardians of Creation. Commanders of the Heavens." Amazarak growled.

"I'm sorry, your greatness, I am not familiar with these entities or these titles." Jacob bowed again.

Amazarak's demeanor lightened. "They are ancient beings of the first era: Mikael, Gavriel, Rafael, Uriel, and Heylel."

"You mean like the angels? Like the Archangels Michael and Gabriel from religious lore?"

"I know nothing of religion or lore, but the commanders are not archangels, they are Cherubim. Rulers of the species," his face tightened with anger.

"How long have you been here?" Jacob asked, surveying the prison.

"Since the great flood of the Annunaki, many cycles ago."

"You mean the Annunaki in Sumeria … from Mesopotamia?" Jacob smiled, almost leaping.

Amazarak's brow contorted, "I do not know these words, these titles."

"They're …" Jacob paused, thinking. How could he describe a place to an ancient being whose familiarity with this world was from another time? Then he thought of something that might give them both a point of reference.

"Where was Eden, Amazarak? The old garden of Eden? Where was it in the world of your time?"

"The garden was the center of Pangea before the prism broke. Once the lands separated, it was difficult to know."

Abruptly, the Archon seemed intensely angry. "Why would you bring up that forsaken island? What is your true purpose in coming here, son of Adam? How did you get here? Are you the prophet I've waited for millenniums? If you are, set me free, and stop this imprisonment at once!" The Archon's wings blazed scarlet as his eyes flashed with flame.

Jacob bowed low, apologizing earnestly. "I am no prophet, great Amazarak, and I have no means by which to set you free. I am a son of Adam, that may be true, but I have no power to free you from your bonds of light."

"Do not lie to me, mage," Amazarak shouted.

The air around Jacob gripped him tightly, making it difficult to move.

"You may be of the bloodline of Adam, but your mother is Lilith, and your seed will be stripped of this world. If you will not release me, then melt before me." Amazarak burst into a fury of flames.

The heat seared Jacob's clothing, engulfing him in smoke. He tried desperately to reach the center of his seashell necklace, but the Archon seemed to be manipulating the atmosphere.

The great being smirked at the puny mortal's struggle. "You're right. You are no mage." Amazarak sneered.

Jacob wrestled against the being's power with all his might. His skin felt as if it was melting off his bones. He thought of Killian and Anah. He thought of Killian's laugh and his mother's eyes. With every ounce of energy, he plunged his hand toward his throat. His forefinger grazed the center shell transporting him into the darkness of the cavern.

"Dad," Killian screamed, watching smoke rise from his clothing. "What happened, are you all right?"

Before Jacob could respond, tremors shot across the cavern walls. The cavern's crystals that were blazing with light shattered by the dozens. Jacob got to his feet as darkness filled the room.

Killian grasped his dad's arms, but they were ice cold.

"We've got to go," Jacob screamed over the crashing walls.

They ran, glancing behind them sporadically as the stalactites fell from the ceiling, destroying the cavern.

"Lads, you gotta help us, use your Lucky Charm," Killian hollered.

Beams of colored light pierced the darkness, bursting stalactites into a million pieces. Colors of red, orange, yellow, green, blue, indigo, and violet channeled through the leprechaun's eyes, and within minutes, they were free of the cave racing across the parking lot.

They jumped in the van as Jacob screamed, "Go Karen, go, back to Black Crow Drive, now!"

"Good evening, Mr. Gold, setting course for 2210 Black Crow Drive. New Jerusalem, Pennsylvania. Journey's duration is nineteen minutes." The van shifted into reverse and crept out of its parking spot.

Killian turned, watching a full implosion of earth shoot clouds of smoke into the air.

No one spoke as they sat rigid on the seat, trying to catch their breath. Killian's pulse relaxed, and he glanced at his dad. Jacob's eyes were shut as if he was praying or in a trance.

"Dad," Killian said, but there was no response. "Dad," he hollered. "Are you okay, do we need to go to a hospital?"

"What? No, no hospital. I'm fine. I'm just trying to remember everything." Jacob pressed his fingers over his temples.

"Remembering what?"

Jacob recounted every detail to Killian as Karen drove them back to Mrs. Peterson's house. When they pulled into the driveway, Killian had a mess of questions.

"So this Archon has been chained up in that place since the flood? Like the Biblical flood; Noah and all that?" Killian asked, as Jacob nodded. "That means Enochian is the language of angels?"

"It appears that way, or maybe demons," Jacob suggested. "Or both, I guess."

"So, mom was studying the languages of angels and demons?" Killian stared out the window, dumbfounded.

"No, not exactly. I don't think she knew whose language it was. She had a theory, and that's what they teach at the university, but maybe she was wrong. Maybe the Annunaki learned their language from angels or demons or Archons."

"But who's this prophet he was talking about?" Killian turned to face his dad.

"I have no idea. I can't imagine what Amazarak thinks is coming, but if that being is released, it could be devastating to the world. I've got to call Mark and tell him about this. Karen, call Dr. Abrecrombie." Jacob pressed a green button unlocking all the doors.

He watched Killian, who was staring out the window as a ringing came over the speakers. "Killian, take the lads inside. Give them anything they can find to eat."

Jacob glanced in the backseat as the ringing sounded for the second time. "You guys did amazing, stellar, phenomenal. I'm so proud of you. As soon as I find some Guinness, it's all yours."

Little cheers of triumph burst into the air.

Killian opened the rear door, shuffling the leprechauns into the duffel bag.

"Mark Abercrombie here," a voice answered.

"Mark, it's Jacob."

***

Killian, pulling his phone from his pocket, checked the time. It was nearing midnight, and his stomach growled. He quietly opened the door,

37

peeking down the hall. There was no sign of Mrs. Peterson or any of the cats. Tiptoeing around the antique furniture, he made his way into the kitchen, unzipping the duffel bag.

"You guys get whatever you want to eat and put it in the bag. I'll be back in two minutes to take you down to the cellar."

"Can't we eat with you tonight?" Freckles asked. They gazed up at him, pleading with puppy dog eyes and pouting lips.

"All right, I'll take you upstairs for a bit, but no fighting with Duncan and Crocker."

They promised, spitting on the ground, raising their hands in the air, and spinning around three times.

Killian crossed the hall to the bathroom, shutting the door.

The leprechauns went through every cabinet, drawer, and shelf in a matter of minutes. When Killian returned, the duffel bag was overflowing with food.

"Seriously," Killian said, picking up the large satchel, straining with every muscle.

"Onward, peasant." Murphy jumped on top of the bag. One hand held the duffel strap as the other shaded his eyes. He looked like a seafaring captain searching for land. The others marched behind Killian, up the stairs, and into the bedroom. Killian tossed the duffel on the floor, and the leprechauns dove in the bag. Wrappers flew in every direction as a plate of deviled eggs was passed around. There were also several bags of chips, four dozen cookies, two loaves of bread, and a bag of apples.

Killian grabbed a pair of apples and said, "Duncan, Crocker, where are you guys?"

The sound of bottles falling to the floor echoed from the bathroom. Going inside, he found two froth-covered brownies playing in a bubble bath with Wendy perched on the soap dish. Killian shook his head, laughing as he did.

Holding the apples up, he said, "You guys want some lunch or what?"

The two brownies evaporated into thin air, reappearing on his shoulder, squeaky clean and dry. He handed each one an apple.

"Wendy, do you want to come and see your choices?" Killian asked.

The little mermaid held her palm out graciously for him to take. Scooping her up, he escorted her into the room, where the replete leprechauns were singing a merry archaic song:

Oh morning sweet, Oh morning bright,
Come feed us rainbows with your light.
If the path be strange and the road be wrong,
Oh, morning, feed us all day long.
When the rains come down upon my crown,
Let clovers spring up from the ground.
If trees then whisper, "Here comes the moon,"
I pray, this day, we've made it through.
And jolly, trolley, we'll carry on,
With the morning, sweet and breakfast gone.
Into the night, with stars so bright,
Let supper come up with delight.
A fire cooking something sweet,
And on this hearth, may we then meet.

Claps rang out from everyone. The leprechauns bowed one to another as was their custom after a meal and a song.

"That was excellent lads, really beautiful," Killian said as Wendy pinched his finger, pointing to a piece of bread she desired.

Slowly, Killian's door began to open as his dad trudged in.

"You okay?" Killian asked, handing Wendy her slice of bread, and setting her atop the aquarium.

"Yeah, I'm good, I'm just exhausted, and we forgot to do Havdalah tonight." Jacob sat in a nearby sofa chair.

Killian waited a few seconds then said, "What did Dr. Abercrombie say?"

"Mark said they're not too happy about the hillside collapsing. I told them there was nothing we could do. They're going to announce a cover-up in the morning. Tell the state department there were some unstable seismic anomalies throughout the New England region last night, or something like that."

"That makes sense." Killian opened a brownie and tossed his dad a Star-crunch. "This lady has the best snack cupboard I've ever seen," he commented through a mouthful of chocolate.

"You know, lads, there's something else we forgot in all this savage business." Murphy wiped deviled egg from his white goatee.

"What's that?" they asked.

"We never figured out what happened to Smirk, Pixel, and Pixley."

4: ICE CREAM AND DEMONS

Maria snapped her fingers viciously towards her twin daughters, sitting next to her in the pew. Pandora closed her book, turning towards her mother. The harshest pair of chestnut eyes in Pennsylvania glared at her. Pandora elbowed her sister in the ribs. Andromeda flashed her eyes at her sister but caught her mother's contemptuous scowl instead. Slowly, Andromeda removed the earbuds and folded her hands.

Using sign language, Maria said, "Pay attention, or there will be severe consequences after the service."

They nodded as Maria turned her attention back to the chorus, beginning to sing. As their mother sat back, they noticed two unfriendly eyes peeking around her shoulder. It was Orion, their younger brother, sneering at them with a sense of justice in his eyes.

"You traitor," Pandora signed.

Andromeda signed, "I'm going to set all of your toys on fire when we get home."

Orion smiled a devious smile and sunk back into the pew. Pandora tapped her fingers across her book, peering around at the beautifully sculptured statues of saints placed within the tiny cathedral. Sixteen years had passed since she'd been christened here, and everything was still the same. The stained glass windows brought vivid colors to boring pasty brown walls, and Jesus hung from his cross at the center of the sanctuary as he always did. *I like Catholicism if only for the art,* she thought.

An older lady, Miss Susan, walked up to the ambo. A giant bible, called the Lectionary, awaited her arrival with a bookmark specifying the particular passage intended for the congregation. Her earrings shimmered in the lighting as she placed her jeweled fingers upon the open pages. Finding her mark, she began to read.

"A reading from Genesis: 3:1-5, 'Now the serpent was more crafty than any of the wild animals the Lord God had made. And he said to the woman, "Has God indeed said, 'You shall not eat of every tree of the garden?' And the woman said to the serpent, "We may eat of the fruit of the trees of the garden; but of the fruit of the tree which is in the midst of the garden, God has said, 'You shall not eat it, nor shall you touch it, lest you die'." The serpent said to the woman, 'You will not surely die. For God knows that in the day that you eat of it, your eyes will be opened, and you will be like God, knowing good and evil."

Pandora listened as Miss Susan's sing-song voice finished the scripture. She'd heard this passage a hundred times before, but today a strange thought crossed her mind. *If the snake was Satan and God made the snake, then God made Satan? And if Satan is the embodiment of evil, then God created evil? Why would an evil being be allowed in the garden with two helpless humans? Why was it allowed to talk to the woman? Was it her fault than that they sinned?*

While she pondered these problems, her eyes wandered the congregation and, unfortunately, landed upon the admiring gaze of Mickey Brown. Maneuvering away from this calamity, she folded her hands gently upon her book, hiding the title from curious eyes.

Her attention returned to the ambo, where an older man was climbing the stairs. It was Mr. James, who everyone loved because he always handed out lollipops. His gigantic mustache laid heavily upon the microphone as he began to read.

"A reading from the letter of St. Paul to the Ephesians: 6:12-13, 'For we do not wrestle against flesh and blood, but against principalities, against powers, against the rulers of the darkness of this age, against spiritual hosts of wickedness in heavenly places. Therefore take up the whole armor of God, that you may be able to withstand in the evil day, and having done all, to stand.'"

Sitting straight up, intrigued by this new piece of scripture, her mind began a new set of analyses. *What exactly was this scripture saying? We don't fight against each other? Meaning what, humans aren't fighting humans they're fighting something else? What are we fighting? Are we fighting angels and demons? What was a principality, anyways?*

While she chewed on these questions, the congregation rose. The procession of the Holy Gospel made its way down to the platform. A chorus of Alleluia rang out across the sanctuary. Father White, a tall man with broad shoulders and a booming voice, held the Gospel above his head and said:

"A reading from the Holy Gospel, according to St. Matthew: 4:5-11, 'Then the devil took him up into the holy city, and set him on the pinnacle of the temple, and said to Him, 'If you are the son of God, throw yourself down. For it is written: 'He will give His angels charge over you' and 'In their hands, they shall bear you up, Lest you dash your foot against a stone.' Jesus said to him, "It is written again, 'You shall not tempt the Lord your God.' Again, the devil took him up on an exceedingly high mountain, and showed him all the kingdoms of the world and their glory. And he said to him, "All these things I will give you if you will fall down and worship me." Then Jesus said to him, "Away with you, Satan! For it is written, 'You shall worship the Lord your God, and him only shall you serve.' Then the devil left him, and behold, angels came and ministered to him.'"

Pandora froze. *What was this? All this stuff was in the Bible? Jesus had dealings with Satan? Satan owns all the kingdoms of the world? Satan offered these kingdoms to Jesus?* Her interest was piqued at an all-time high. She had never been so interested, in all her years of going to Mass, to listen to the homily.

The elderly priest in his kelly-green robes lifted his hands, projecting them out to the people, saying, "The Lord be with you,"

The congregation responded, "And with your spirit."

Pandora was on the edge of her seat, eagerly awaiting explanations for the scriptures read. *How did they correlate? What were the answers to these riddles? What insight did the Holy Catholic church have locked in their vaults of ancient wisdom?*

Watching from the corner of her eye, Maria smiled at her daughter, listening with such enthusiasm.

The priest cleared his throat and said, "In these times of trouble. In these times of confusion. In these times of heartache, mistrust, chaos, murder, and death, we must remember one thing that sets us apart from all others who breathe the air of this world. One thing that makes us unique in a world full of woes. We know that there is an evil in this world. This evil roams around like a lion seeking whom he may devour. In this world, you shall have trouble, but ask yourself, where does this trouble come from? Is it your fellow man, is it your neighbor, is it your spouse, is it a sibling or a loved one, or is it something else? Something wicked, something supernatural, something demonic?"

Pandora receded into the pew, resting her back on the velvet padding. These were the most profound words she'd ever heard from a priest. Instantly, her mind went to the most obvious questions. *Was the devil really real? Were angels really real? Was there more to this world than just flesh and blood?* She sat there for a minute, maybe twenty minutes as these new revelations brought her to only one conclusion. *What did any of this have to do with her?*

Returning to her book, she opened the pages and began to read. "Before Alice arrived in Wonderland, she had to fall, fall, fall." Pandora lifted her head, avoiding Mickey's continuous gaze. *What an intriguing statement,* she thought. *What is with today and all these crazy enigmas?*

Pandora turned to her sister, whose eyes were closed. She started to tap Andromeda's shoulder, but clearly, her earbuds had been reinstated, and she was lost in her own world. Then, the congregation stood, and the twins rapidly followed suit, glancing over at their mother, who nodded at them. The crowd exited the pews making their way to a bowl and a cup that was offered to them freely. They partook with their family and friends and then headed straight for the parking lot.

***

The doors unlocked, and they navigated inside each to their traditional spot.

"Girls, what do you want to eat?" their dad asked. "That includes you, too, darling," he said, looking at his wife passionately.

"Robert, you are the absolute worst," she laughed, hitting him with her wallet.

"Seriously, we're all holy for about another twenty minutes before we do something wrong, so let's do something horrible first like eat desserts for dinner. What do you say, girls?"

"Fine," Pandora said, buckling her seat belt.

"Whatever, Dad," Andromeda replied, shuffling to the next song.

Robert looked at them with a dismal stare, then signed to his son Orion, "Do you want sundaes for dinner?"

Orion nodded, signing back, "Thanks, Dad, you're the best."

"I am the best," Robert boasted, glancing at Maria.

"The best at being devious and deceiving, I know what you're thinking," Maria grinned.

"I'm thinking two thousand calories in assorted ice creams, loaded with fudge, sounds exactly like what this family needs to bring us a little unity."

"Uh, huh, well, you can drop me off at the house before this two thousand calorie smorgasbord begins because these thighs want no part in your evil doings," Maria demanded.

"Babe, seriously, your thighs are like my fourth favorite part of your body, and they need these two thousand calories, come on, come with us."

"You can go through the drive-thru, but I'm not touching a single thing," she gibed.

Fifteen minutes later, Robert was sucking down a hand-spun chocolate milkshake. Orion had a sundae with five different types of fudge draped across it. Pandora was biting into a slice of frozen Oreo cake while Andromeda dipped a spoon into a cherry-flavored gelato. Maria glared at Robert contemptuously, raising a spork towards an amazingly triumphant banana split covered in nuts.

"Do not ask for anything from me later because I will be on the couch watching Potter in a comatose state," Maria sniggered.

"And I'll be sitting right there with you, my love. What do you think tonight, Order, Goblet, Hallows?"

"Let Orion decide," she proposed, looking in the backseat.

Unfortunately, but not to her surprise, syrup and ice cream covered his face and hands. Glancing up from his trophy sundae, he smiled. Smiling back, she turned to Robert, "I'll ask him after he takes a shower."

Robert moved the rear-view mirror so he could see the twins. "Girls, do you want to watch Potter tonight?" he asked.

Andromeda's earbuds were in again, although they were hard to see from her jet-black hair draped over them, but her spacious stare out the window made it clear.

Robert glanced at Pandora and said, "Honey, Potter?" but no response came as she tied her blonde hair up into a ponytail, engrossed with the book in her lap.

Maria turned around, shouting, "Girls, your father is speaking to you."

Andromeda pulled out an earbud. "What?"

Pandora looked up from her book. "Yea, Dad?"

"Do you girls want to watch Potter with us tonight?" he asked.

A simultaneous, "No!" rang out as they resumed their personal interests.

Robert looked at Maria, disappointed. "They used to watch Potter with us all the time. You couldn't get them to stop. Now we can't get them to do much of anything."

Maria filled with admiration for her family-oriented husband. "They're seventeen, honey, Annie only cares about music, and Pan only cares about books. There are worse things in the world."

"Yea, boys," Robert grumbled.

Maria laughed, "I meant drugs and alcohol, but yea, there are boys, too."

The garage door rose, and within two minutes, the family had scattered throughout the house. Orion ran to the shower, Robert worked the Blue-Ray player, and Maria changed clothes. The twins were in their room on opposite sides, not speaking. Pandora rolled across her bed, thumbing to the final chapter in her book as Andromeda scrolled through her phone.

Although they were twins and shared a room, each of their sides was very different. Andromeda's love of music shouted from the walls as her poster collection took up every inch of her side. There were pictures of Paramore, Muse, Queen, of Monsters and Men, Michael Jackson, Sublime, Taylor Swift, and of course, the Beatles.

Pandora, in contrast, had layered her wall with book covers from all her favorite books. There was *Harry Potter, Twilight, Hunger Games, Dracula, Frankenstein, Sherlock Holmes, Wicked, Lord of the Rings,* and The *Hobbit,* to name a few. She had two bookshelves so full they couldn't hold a magazine if she needed them to.

Andromeda landed on the song she'd had stuck in her head for days: "Who Wants To Live Forever," by Queen. The music began, and she sucked in the notes like a glass of water. Each word and each beat brought happiness to her like nothing else in the world. When the song concluded, she smiled, took out one earbud, and threw a pillow at her sister, knocking the book from her hands.

"What the frick?" Pandora exclaimed, glaring at her sister.

Andromeda unwrapped a piece of strawberry-flavored gum, placing it in her mouth and offered some to her sister.

Pandora pulled out a box of mint-flavored tic-tacs with an unthankful sneer across her face for her sister's rude interruption of her reading.

"I saw Mickey undressing you with his eyes again today. It's only a matter of time before you fall prey to his muscular jock form and his many bountiful accolades."

"No, thanks, Annie," Pandora said, thumbing back through her book. "Of course, we could always dye your hair blonde, and he wouldn't know the difference," she suggested.

"But there are still those baby blue eyes of yours, and I'm not wearing contacts so that you can get some guy off your radar," Andromeda popped a giant bubble of gum.

"Do you find him attractive? He's more your type, don't you think?" Pandora coaxed.

"Pan, seriously, have you lost your mind? With that shaved head, brand new Mustang, money oozing from every orifice. There's nothing there that interests me." Andromeda grinned, her typical sarcastic smile.

"That, to me, makes it sound like you're very interested in what you see. Or at a minimum, the accolades you would acquire." Pandora corrected, sliding the bookmark in its place. She rose and walked over to their vanity, grabbing a brush, and stared out the window.

Andromeda watched her sister upside down, her head hanging off the bed, "I mean sure, I guess I could date him. Then manipulate him into letting me have his Mustang to drive to school. I could cut out from being seen with him at lunch, then make excuses in the afternoon for band practice. I'd have to see him on the weekend, but at least I could get out of here for a while and maybe see his sister."

Pandora examined Andromeda through the reflection in the mirror. She appeared lost in thought, planning out this elaborate scheme.

"You're not serious, are you?" she asked a look of disgust on her face.

Andromeda shrugged. "I suppose it all depends on if I wanted to dye my hair blonde and wear blue contacts."

"I mean, his sister, Annie, what would you want to see that snobbish prig for?"

47

"Eye candy, a break from cavemen, I don't know." Andromeda rolled over, straightening herself on the bed as the blood rushed out of her head. "Anyways, she has a boyfriend, who she's attached to at the hip, and he's a moron."

Pandora shook her head. "I think Jimmy is the sane one of the two of them if you ask me."

"I'm not asking you," Andromeda snapped, placing the earbud back in and staring at her phone.

Pandora put down her brush and glanced back out the window. A boy was climbing over Mrs. Peterson's fence and walking into their backyard. He was holding something strange in his hands.

"Annie, come look at this," she called.

Andromeda didn't respond. Pandora grabbed one of her pink scrunchies and flung it at Andromeda's face.

Andromeda's emerald green eyes flashed at Pandora.

Pandora pointed out the window urgently.

Andromeda slowly rolled off the bed and stared out the window. Her eyes immediately found the strange boy.

"Who is that?" Andromeda asked, removing both earbuds. "What is he doing in our yard?"

"I don't know, but he looks kind of cute from here. Don't you think?" Pandora smiled.

Andromeda rolled her eyes. "The only boy you finally think is cute is some weirdo breaking into our yard. Who cares how he looks? What's with the grass swaying behind him like that?"

Pandora looked closely. A wake in the weeds swayed behind him. "Not just that, where did all of the lightning bugs come from?"

They followed a horde of lightning bugs hovering all around the strange boy.

"Where in the world is he going?" Andromeda wondered, as the boy jumped their fence and headed towards the forest.

"Do you want to follow him?" Pandora suggested, a devilish grin upon her face.

"Should we? We both know where your curiosity always leads us," Andromeda said with a sideways grin.

"Oh, come on, it'll be fun. We know these woods like the back of our hands," Pandora directed, grabbing her chucks and tossing Andromeda's boots to her. Within moments, they were around the back of the house, heading into the forest, following the mysterious boy.

5: A DISTURBANCE IN THE WOODS

Killian stumbled over various roots and branches making his way deep into the thicket of trees. A monotone beep rang out every thirty seconds from the tracker he carried. Typical signs of life blipped on the radar: squirrels, rabbits, a deer here and there. Flipping the radar to stealth, he detected small trace readings of paranormal energy binging erratically. *Typical faeries,* he thought, *but still, it could be Smirk, Pixel, or Pixley.*

A humming sound vibrated around him. He glanced around, appreciating the escort of lightning bugs chauffeuring him through the wood.

"You got anything there, sir?" Murphy asked, swatting at a low-flying cricket.

"You better have something soon. Jeanie-Mac! What if that thing from last night broke free? I don't fancy seeing it out in the open like this," Lil McMan punched a buttercup, square in the center, spewing pollen into the air.

"No feck Killian, that thing was deadly, and this place is sketchy," Freckles added, brushing pollen off her nose.

Killian didn't respond; he was busy tracking a violet-colored dot on the screen, checking its frequency. "I think …, maybe …"

The leprechauns glanced uneasily at one another.

Killian donned his aviator glasses, transforming the scenery from an ordinary sunset to an array of digital code. Types and sizes of trees in the vicinity scrolled down the lens, along with temperature readings, air quality analysis, and radiation levels. The forest seemed normal enough.

They trekked on for half an hour, discovering an unusual clearing in the woods. A central tree stood like a watchman overlooking the forest. Bushels of amber flowers spread across its canopy.

Killian surveyed the area. A circle of weeping willows surrounded the grove with thousands of lightning bugs flying all around. Killian rechecked the tracker. He was standing exactly where the entity should have been. Adjusting the gauge on his glasses, he changed the frequency settings, but still, nothing was visible.

Cornedbeef and Lil McMan held down Squeezie while Cabbage tried to stuff lightning bugs down his pants. Clover and Freckles ignored the boys, turning their attention to the blooming bouquets surrounding them. They gathered dandelion stems and lemon-colored petals, weaving them into floral crowns as they walked.

A twig snapped behind them, startling the party. Everyone turned to investigate, but nothing was there. Killian switched the tracker from stealth to physical. Two humans were hiding behind an oak tree several feet away.

Pressing their frequency signature, he read:

Two Homo-sapiens:
Gender Analysis: Female
Female A: Sixteen Years, Eleven Months, Eight Days
Female B: Sixteen Years, Eleven Months, Seven Days.

Killian breathed a sigh of relief. It was just two girls. *They must have followed me here from the neighborhood.*

He snapped his fingers twice, and the leprechauns vanished in every direction. He wasn't sure if the girls had seen them in the twilight, but it was best not to have to answer unwanted questions. Immediately, he stuffed all his devices into his backpack, smelling his breath as the bag zipped shut.

Figures, he thought, *should have grabbed a mint after Mrs. Peterson's lasagna.* By the time he stood up, the girls were standing right behind him.

Shocked, he stumbled backward over a large tree root.

"I'm sorry," Pandora bent down. "We didn't mean to startle you. We're curious as to what you're doing out here?" She reached out her hand and begrudgingly, so did Andromeda.

They helped Killian to his feet. He stood there, speechless, staring at the two fascinating girls. The angrier one had dark hair and a tattered Metallica shirt on with torn jeans. The anxious one had blonde hair and was wearing a pink dress with baby-blue chucks.

"Um, earth to the new guy," Andromeda signed as she talked.

Killian watched her hands, shocked that she knew sign language, and thought she might be deaf, or maybe she thought he was deaf. As he was about to speak, he stopped realizing the girls were twins. They had the same round dimpled cheeks and pouting lips bitten slightly by pearly white teeth. Their arms folded across their stomachs as they tapped their feet on the ground. He went to speak, but his thoughts were muddled.

"Pan ... clearly, he doesn't want to talk to us, and while the scenery here is amazing, mom and dad are probably freaking out, wondering where we are. Let's go," Andromeda demanded.

Her enchanting jet-black hair whipped in the air as she turned around back in the direction they'd came. Pandora frowned at Killian, noticing the strangest necklace she'd ever seen on his neck, but turned in agreement with her sister, to head back home.

"No, wait, wait a second," Killian croaked, clearing his throat. "I'm sorry, I'm sorry, I ...you just startled me, that's all."

The girls stopped, turning their heads slightly and glared at him.

Andromeda spoke first, her tone accusatory. "Just who are you? Why were you in our backyard? What in the world are you doing out here in the middle of the forest? And what is that atrocious thing hanging around your neck?"

Killian touched the seashell necklace he had forgotten to put in the bag. "This is an old family heirloom."

His answer was less than satisfactory, and they turned back around to leave.

"W-w-wait," he stammered.

They stopped, arms still folded, refusing to turn around.

Killian hesitated then blurted out, "To be honest, this is an electronic device for transportation into another dimension." He froze, astounded at what he had said.

Andromeda turned around so fast that Killian almost fell over again. She glowered at him, her emerald eyes flashing with malice as if he was the dumbest guy on the planet.

Pandora stared at him, confused.

Killian didn't know what to do, he couldn't lie, and he couldn't tell the truth.

Pandora unfolded her arms and placed them on her hips. "Well, since you don't want to tell us about your necklace, will you tell us who you are and what you're doing out here?"

Andromeda gaped at her, annoyed.

"Who am I? My name is Killian, and uh, me and my dad, we're staying with Mrs. Peterson. You must live next door. Sorry about crossing over like that. I'm looking for something. I mean someone, something, yeah." Killian's heart raced in his chest as a knot tightened in his stomach. His first real interaction with a girl, a gorgeous girl, no, two beautiful girls, and it was an interrogation that couldn't be going worse.

"Well, which is it? Someone or something?" Pandora asked, her sapphire eyes piercing his.

"It's more of a pet. Kind of like a pet. Yeah, a pet, it's a pet, like a pet." Killian's gaze fell to the ground, and he shuffled his feet.

"Come on, Pan. He's an idiot, let's go. I don't have time for this." Andromeda reached for her sister's wrist.

A sudden gust of wind blew across the wood, and upon that wind, a voice whispered, "Andromeda, you must stay."

Everyone froze.

"What was that? Was that you?" she pointed at Killian. "How do you know my name?"

Killian gawked at her. "That wasn't me. I don't even know your name. I mean, I guess now I know your name, but I didn't before, It's pretty."

Andromeda rolled her eyes.

Another gust of wind wandered through their midst, and upon the air, a soft voice breathed, "Pandora, I need your help."

She looked around apprehensively, "Killian, what's going on? Where's this voice coming from?"

Killian dove into his backpack, pulling out the tracker and the gilgameter. The large violet dot on the tracker had transitioned to red, pulsating right where they stood. Immediately, he flipped on the gilgameter, but the needles were bouncing all over the place like the night before. His heart pounded with fear. *Was the Archon back?*

A tempest furiously blew through the limbs above, shaking branches to the ground while flowers fluttered everywhere like snow. A voice rang in Killian's ears, begging for help, and he looked around frantically for the source.

"Where are you," he screamed, but the breeze caught his words, throwing them into the howling storm that pressed down upon them. Lightning flashed in every direction, illuminating the tree above, like a many-fingered god.

"Grab something quick," Pandora shrieked, clinging to a massive root jutting from the ground.

"Is it a tornado?" Andromeda screamed, but Pandora couldn't hear her. Large pieces of sod flew off the roots before them swirling into the air. Killian's backpack slid from his fist, soaring into the sky. Their grip on the bark slipped as the wind suddenly ceased. They fell hard to the ground. Killian jumped to his feet and rushed over to Pandora, helping her up.

"Thank you," she muttered, catching her breath.

"Don't worry about me. I got this." Andromeda said, standing to her feet and massaging her neck.

"I've never experienced anything like that in my life," Pandora said, staring around.

"Me, neither," Killian agreed.

"What's that?" Andromeda whispered, pointing to a spot about thirty yards away. A bright green glow pulsated from the ground. Killian swiftly peered around, looking for his backpack, but it was nowhere.

"Should we go over there?" Pandora murmured.

Killian surveyed the light, then glanced at Pandora, who was shivering. "I-I'll go check it out. You two stay here," he moved forward.

"Absolutely not! I want to see what this is just as bad as you do. I'm going, too," Andromeda chided, immediately tramping through the fresh soil toward the mysterious glow.

Pandora folded her arms, watching the two of them walk away. She sprinted forward to join them. "Well, I'm not staying there by myself, obviously," she panted.

The hike was more complicated than they had anticipated as the roots had grown to the size of tree trunks, crisscrossing above the ground like a wild maze.

"Maybe it's a spaceship?" Andromeda announced as the glow grew more luminous.

"Maybe it's a hole to Wonderland?" Pandora suggested.

Killian glanced at her, surprised. "I love Carroll."

Pandora smiled.

"Leave it to you to be talking about books when we're about to discover aliens." Andromeda sneered.

"I seriously doubt it's aliens," Killian said.

"Oh, you know it's not aliens, huh? Well, if you know what it is, don't leave us hanging. In fact, why'd you come out here, to begin with? What do you know?" Andromeda interrogated.

"Yea, Killian, what were you doing out here? And what was that thing you were carrying?" Pandora asked.

Before Killian could answer, they jumped an enormous root and discovered that they were standing right before the green glow. Each of them squinted as they peered down at the object. The twins gasped as a woman laced in emerald leaves with silver veins lay before them, confined by a large root. The jade glow was emanating from her being, and a strange pair of lifeless wings lay beneath her.

"Are you hurt? How can I help?" Killian asked, unfazed by her appearance. He tried to maneuver down to her on the root, but she screamed in pain.

"Killian," she moaned, and he recognized her tone as the disembodied voice. She reached towards him, but then faded out of consciousness.

"Um, guys, Killian, look quick," Andromeda stammered.

Killian looked up as a pack of giant black wolves crossed into the circle of willows. Giant paws stepped over chaotic mounds of roots. Drool dripped from their gaping jaws. Pandora grabbed Killian's arm, shaking nervously. He held her behind his back as Andromeda stood beside him.

"Do you have a plan?" Andromeda asked, feeling a rush of adrenaline pour into her system, making her heart thump like a pounding drum.

"Only one," he gulped. He took a deep breath and yelled, "Cornedbeef, Cabbage, McMan, Murphy, Clover, Freckles, Squeezie, where are you?"

"What in the frick? Who in the world are you calling?" Andromeda hissed as the wolves drew closer, snapping their jaws and snarling.

"Lucky charms, lucky charms," Killian screamed, but there was no reply.

"What a psycho," Andromeda grumbled.

"How are there wolves in Pennsylvania?" Pandora whispered, ignoring Killian's strange verbiage. "Wolves haven't been in this state in over one hundred years."

"How do you know that?" Killian asked, twisting to look at her.

"Because I read," she snapped.

Killian turned back around and analyzed the pack. They had massive shoulders the size of grizzly bears' that rotated masses of muscles over long husky bodies. Their eyes burned as white as stars as their razor-sharp teeth sparkled in the moonlight.

"Oh, God." Killian shuddered.

"What, what is it?" the twins asked.

"These aren't wolves at all. They're lycans," Killian wiped off the sweat beading on his forehead.

"What does that mean?" Andromeda fumed.

"It means grab something to defend yourself. A log, a branch, anything!"

Andromeda gazed around the ground, trying to find a weapon. Pandora stood there, shaking. Andromeda looked at her in disgust.

"Why do you always have to be so curious, huh? Do you see where it gets us? Every time," Andromeda shouted, picking up a large branch.

"I'm sorry," Pandora mumbled, spotting a small log she could throw.

"They must be after the dryad," Killian warned. "We have to protect her. They don't feed on humans. They prey on fantanimals, um, spirit creatures, like her." Killian nodded towards the unconscious being pinned under the root.

Andromeda looked down as a pit of roots circled the lifeless being like a den of snakes. Suddenly, a song came to mind, and the lyrics poured through her body. "Touch my world with your fingertips, And we can have forever, Our forever is today!" This being before her was touching her world and calling in desperation to be saved. She needed her.

"You're saying they want to eat her and not us?" Andromeda asked, turning her attention back to Killian.

"Basically," Killian gripped two sticks tightly as if they were katanas.

"How would you know that?" Pandora asked.

"I'll explain later, but—" a sudden blast of howls broke out across the meadow. Fear nearly crippled the trio as the blood-curdling noise painfully reverberated in their ears.

Andromeda felt a burning within. Stronger than anything she'd ever felt before. Courage coursed through her veins like fire in her blood. The howling only made her angrier and more sure of what she needed to do.

She screamed at the wolves, her voice amplified with authority, "You want her? Come on then. I'll kill you if you touch her!" She held up her branch like a bat prepared for the worst.

"They'll have to get through the three of us," Pandora said softly, standing between them, shaking, but holding the small log.

"Watch the right-side Killian, Pan the left," Andromeda advised.

The wolves bolted towards them. Everyone braced for impact, branches held defensively.

"Stop!" a voice commanded, and the wolves froze like ice. The enormous root beside them rose into the air, swaying like a charmed serpent. The sound of branches cracking like toothpicks echoed all around them as the jade woman fluttered out of the gorge. Immediately, the wolves bowed as the entity floated by them.

The glowing emerald dryad radiated with power and centered herself in front of the trio. Upon her head was a small silver crown, and her wings sparkled like diamonds. She held in her hand a small wand with something like a star at the end. She bowed lavishly before the trio.

Killian motioned for them to bow before her, and they did so awkwardly.

"My heroes, hmm. Welcome to Judea Glade. My name is Karaleine Keyleaf, Queen of the Dryads. Forgive me for this test, but all who wander here must be assessed. Of course, your coming to me was by no accident. Everything happens in threes, you see. So it always has been, so it always will be. Time comes to us in the past, present, and future. The world is presented to us in gasses, solids, and liquids. The bodies you inhabit are blood, flesh, and bone. Therefore, it is only right that the saviors of the new world should come to me in three: Killian, Andromeda, and Pandora, hmm."

None of them said a word. They just stared at the dazzling being, dropping their weapons to the ground.

"Follow me," she invited. The roots and branches of the grove wiggled and writhed, forming pathways towards the heart of the center tree. Queen Karaleine waved her wand, and an emerald gateway appeared in the heart of the poinciana tree. She flew right through the gates, beckoning them on with her sing-song voice.

The trio glanced at one another as they climbed the wooded path into another dimension.

6: THE QUEEN'S NEST

Killian, Pandora, and Andromeda stepped through the emerald gates of the poinciana tree, crossing the veil into another world. The gateway closed rapidly behind them. There was no sky — only a dazzling ceiling of flowers and stars entwined by silver branches.

They found themselves in the middle of a bustling kingdom ripe with activity.

Killian watched a parade of pixies carrying silver plates of food, making his stomach growl.

Andromeda spied tiny groups of faeries cleaning platinum roots extending up the walls. The little beings worked with intense ferocity making the pathways of trees sparkle like polished silverware.

Pandora giggled as a group of sprites splashed playfully in a massive fountain full of crystal clear water.

They followed the Queen, drawn by her power, but rarely noticed her fluttering before them. She waved and greeted the beings coming and going through her halls with outstretched hands as if she was leading a parade.

Pandora felt as though she had wandered into a dream, that here, life itself seemed fabricated.

Killian's mouth hung open as the journey brought them through halls of gold and past translucent waterfalls with ivory fish swimming upstream.

Andromeda ran her fingers over astounding varieties of plants, mesmerized by their greenery growing wildly along the corridors.

Soon they were passing over small bridges made of sapphires, rubies, and amethyst. Andromeda gasped as singing emanated from the petals of ivy filling the gateway. High hoops and arches gave way to courtyards and gardens overflowing with flowers and greenery of all kinds.

Pandora and Andromeda knelt on the ground, petting a herd of unicorns, no bigger than rabbits, running freely over the lush meadow.

"Follow me, young ones," the Queen implored with a wave of her wand.

The trio obeyed, finding themselves ushered into a massive basilica domed a hundred feet above them. Trumpets and harps echoed across the sanctuary as they stepped slowly upon the pearl floor. Three tiny beings delivered three emerald chairs to the center of the room, and Killian couldn't believe his eyes.

"Smirk, Pixel, Pixley, what are you doing here?" he asked, as the three tiny beings made their way before them.

"I summoned them, of course, hmm," the Queen chirped floating by. "And they would not refuse their Queen, even for a great friend such as yourself, Killian Gold."

Smirk flew toward him, bowing low, his saffron eyes humble and his smile proud. Pixel lifted the hand of Pandora as Pixley grabbed

Andromeda's hand. They kissed them softly, allowing a tear to fall upon their palm. A sparkle of stars burst over the twins' hands then disappeared.

The Queen held out her starry wand. Smirk, Pixel, and Pixley flew to the Ivory Throne, kissed Queen Karaleine on the cheek then sped off down an archway. It was then Killian understood that they were no longer his but were now in the service of their Queen.

"Sit," the Queen ordered, perching upon her mighty pearl throne observing her guests.

They sat, still mesmerized by the majesty of the basilica filled with silver trees blooming with purple fruits.

"Questions?" the Queen asked, holding her wand to her chin.

Killian studied the chamber, enthralled by his surroundings. His first thoughts were of Rivendell or Lothlorien, Asgard, and Valhalla, but none of these places seemed to compare to this. He wanted to say something, but the words wouldn't come.

Music filled Andromeda's ears with the most heavenly chords she had ever heard. A fantastic blend of stringed instruments coupled with soprano voices impregnated the basilica. She seemed to be able to see the music pouring over the atmosphere in bursts of golden dust evaporating like fireworks. Her mouth opened, she began to speak, but she closed it again before the words came out.

Pandora's eyes felt as if they would pop. She couldn't remember the last time she'd blinked, for when she did, her eyes burned. But the pain in her eyes was quickly erased by the smell emanating around the chamber. Fresh baked cookies and cinnamon rolls permeated the atmosphere as her mind attempted to comprehend the grandeur she was experiencing. She felt as if she had jumped into one of her books. Was she in Neverland, Wonderland, Narnia, or Oz? She had no idea, but this world was fascinating beyond anything she had ever dreamed of.

Queen Karaleine smiled at her astonished guests. "Quite remarkable, is it not? Maybe, more answers first, then questions, hmm. Let's see, no mortal man or woman of Gaia has passed into this realm, and no one ever will again. Your faces have shown me that you appreciate the majesty of my nest even if you cannot find the words."

The Queen waved her wand, summoning two ruby sprites. They flew to her, carrying tiny vessels filled to the brim with golden nectar. She snapped her fingers, and the three guests were each handed a crystal glass. They drank the warm elixir and immediately felt joyous like pure happiness was coursing through their veins.

The Queen stood from her throne, raising her arms high into the air, "This is my home, in your tongue, it is called the Covenant Chamber, and I have guarded this place for over twenty-five hundred years. Hmm. A very long time indeed for this moment to arrive. A king and his queens or queens and their king, hmm," she beamed, but in her eyes, a curiosity lingered.

The Queen's gaze released them, and their bodies relaxed in their chairs. Killian peered around the room, noticing they were alone. He raised his hand with a slight tremble.

"Yes, my dear, go on," the Queen encouraged.

"Your majesty, where are we exactly? I mean, I understand this is your home, but what dimension are we in?"

"Excellent question, Killian. Yes, that is the primary enigma. What dimension, indeed?" The Queen sipped her chalice and placed it within the center of a bent sunflower.

"The world, as you know it, is only half of a whole." She flew high into the air and picked a small fruit that hung from one of the many protruding branches of the domed ceiling. She returned softly to her throne, brandishing the purple sphere for all to see.

"This plum represents Earth," she split the plum in two. "My world, this dimension, is the land we call Pangea, and you may think of it as the meat within this fruit. My people call your world, your dimension, Gaia, and that dimension covers everything like the skin of this plum. But in truth, we are all children of Mother Earth. It's quite simple. We are but separated by a veil." Her voice trailed off as they sat for a few moments pondering her words.

"Why has no one seen you before? Or why don't you show yourselves?" Pandora asked.

"Why? How? When? Oh, my dear, that is a long and tedious discussion we do not have the time for in this hour, sadly. However, I believe you will find the answers you seek when you walk your path of

64

destiny. Surely, this will provoke more questions than there are answers for, but it is enough to say this. The destruction of the great prism has left both of our dimensions shattered. Now fate has brought you to me and from you shall spring the healing of the Earth. A great King once said, 'A kingdom divided cannot stand.' That, in essence, is our dilemma, hmm."

"But why are we here, and how can we save anyone?" Andromeda asked.

"Simple acts of kindness and feats of courage can alleviate wars or save a trapped Queen. A touch of love can dispel hate and move masses. In the end, the purging of temptation can save much, if not all."

"I'm not good at riddles," Killian whispered, finishing the nectar in his glass.

"Me either," Andromeda sighed.

The Queen studied them intently then waved her wand as a rainbow appeared over their heads. "All the wise men have searched for us and found us not, let the children take the stage, and the past forgot. Hmm. Verses from an old rhyme I'm afraid, a grand prophecy in our world. You see my young ones. The black death has come. We do not understand it. We cannot fix it. We cannot heal it. For all the magic, splendor, and wonder in our world, we have found no cure for this disease. As it was foretold, 'a trio of gold shall break the mold and heal the blistering wind. When our time has chose, what worlds will know, the prism will be healed.' You three are the trio of gold our prophecies speak of. Now, it is time for me, Karaleine Keyleaf, Guardian of the Ark and Queen of the Dryads, to bestow upon you the powers I have been assigned to give, hmm."

With these words, an ancient chest was escorted into the basilica by hundreds of faeries. Trumpets blared throughout the chamber as every sprite stood at attention. The faeries placed the giant ark carefully upon a marble platform directly before them. Three angelic statues sat on top of the lid made of solid gold. The trio gazed at it in awe. They could feel a strange power resonating from within it as the hairs stood up on their neck and arms.

Pandora was captivated by the beautiful images. The angel's eyes swirled like a galaxy of stars staring back at her, mesmerizing and compelling. Bells tolled as cracks ran down the divine statues. Blinding light poured from the fissures causing the trio to shield their eyes. A rumbling earthquake shook the room as the bells tolled louder and louder. A wind swept over the place, purifying the air with the scent of rain. The floor began to rest, and the light ceased its blinding assault. They opened their eyes to find the angelic figures of the lid transformed before them into glorious living beings: hands cuffed, wings spread, fiery eyes peering down upon them.

The first angel's silver hair flowed gracefully with his long pearly beard, standing before Killian. In his arms were two ancient stone tablets. Killian received the tablets, but the weight of them caused him to falter. He strained, noticing many strange etchings upon them. "Killian Benjamin Gold, from the bloodline of Adam, to you, I bestow the inheritance of the Earth. May it serve you well in the dawning of the new age." The angel vanished from sight. Killian placed one tablet beside his chair, tracing the mysterious script with his fingers as bells rang in the distance.

The second angel's skin glowed like polished brass, and he wore a robe of onyx. He stood before Pandora, presenting her with a golden bowl full of wafers. She inhaled the scent of freshly baked bread, the smell alone satiating her mind and body. "Pandora Lilly Aster-Konig, from the bloodline of Eve, to you, I bestow the bread of life. May death flee before thee in this coming age." Pandora held the bowl in her hand, gazing at the alabaster wafers. The bells chimed louder as the angel before her evaporated.

The third angel had a halo floating mysteriously above his head. He stood before Andromeda, holding out a long wooden rod flowering at one end. He handed it to Andromeda. She gripped the rod, running her fingers down its rough edges. She brought the flowering end close to her nose, smelling the sweet aroma of lilies and roses. "Andromeda Rose Aster-Konig, from the bloodline of Enoch, and the bloodline of Lilith, take the scepter of prophecy. May the future bring unity and life in this new age." She examined the rod as the angel dematerialized before her eyes.

The chiming of the bells came to an end. The Queen moved from her Ivory Throne and levitated before them.

"Hmm. Three tools I have guarded for centuries are now yours. You have been chosen to undo what has been done and to create what has not been envisioned. Trust your hearts, your minds, and especially each other. For your success is dependent upon your honor, faith, and haste, or I am afraid we shall all perish in the coming night. Do not look for help when there is none. You yourselves, must pave a way and create the answers. Now, we must sleep as the world turns thrice."

The silver-leaved chairs transformed into massive emerald petals soft as silk. Branches grew out of the ground, raising the trio high into the air, encircling them within a lavish silver nest. Killian held onto the stone tablets like two fluffy pillows. Pandora's bowl of wafers spilled all around her engulfing her within them. Andromeda clenched tightly to her rod as the rough wooden texture turned to scales wrapping her in a serpent's grasp. The trio sunk, as if under a spell, into the nest's magical embrace falling instantly asleep.

7: THE VANISHED

Killian awoke to a cold breeze numbing his body. The nest that had encompassed him was nothing more than ash as he laid upon a mass of decaying soil. A putrid smell filled his nostrils as he arose, examining the room.

Pandora and Andromeda began to stir, the foul stench making them queasy. Killian peered around in horror, the glorious kingdom of Queen Karaleine resembled a graveyard of decay. The brilliant glow and abundance of life had transformed into rotting roots and drooping, putrid plants.

Pandora plugged her nostrils, stood, and walked over to Killian. "Where are we? What happened?"

Killian cocked one eyebrow to the side as his perplexed eyes stared around. He was bothered that he didn't know the answer to her question. He was anxious that he didn't know how to get out of here, but he was mainly worried about not looking concerned and foolish.

Pandora smiled at him, seeming to understand how little he knew. She examined the lines of his brow, the stormy grey color of his eyes, and his disheveled chestnut hair. He was handsome, not gorgeous, but refined somehow and mysterious. The next second she recoiled, taking a step back with a jolt.

"What, what is it?" he said, puzzled by the sudden look of shock on her face.

She pointed towards his torso, mouth gaping.

Killian panicked, patting down his shirt and jeans as if a creature were crawling up them.

She reached out, grabbed both of his hands, and flipped them over.

Killian's eyes widened. The letters engraved into the stone tablets were now etched into his skin, running up his arms. They were black as ink with spots of blood accenting the characters. He stared at them for a long time, feeling the slightly raised abrasions, until Andromeda's squeal broke his concentration.

"Oh my God, my first tattoo," she screamed, tracing an uncanny resemblance of the rod running up her left arm.

Pandora ran to her, grabbed her arm, and surveyed the imprint of roots from her fingertips to her shoulder.

Andromeda beamed with pride as her sister examined the mysterious markings with apprehension.

Pandora dropped her sister's arm and explored her own for some newly inscribed symbology. She breathed in a sigh of relief, finding nothing peculiar imprinted upon her.

Andromeda grabbed her sister's arms to check for herself. She folded back the white collar of her sister's pink polo dress, searching around her neck and shoulders.

"I'm still innocent," Pandora teased as Andromeda ran her hands down Pandora's arms. Then, with immediate satisfaction, Andromeda flipped Pandora's palms over, revealing two hidden symbols. It was a sideways eight, splashed with blue flames.

"Aww, Pan, it's so you," Andromeda said.

Pandora stared at the inscriptions for a long time, and her concentration was only broken by Killian's low, smoky voice saying, "Those are beautiful."

Pandora shut her hands quickly, placing them behind her back.

Killian watched her blue eyes waver as they stared into his.

"What's wrong?" he asked.

"I've ...I've been branded, tainted, disgraced." Tears rolled down her dimpled cheeks. She shut her eyes and looked away from him.

Killian stood there, wanting to say something smart, something comforting, something that would help, but the words wouldn't come.

"Those letters are fascinating." Andromeda seized Killian's arm and scratched the letters gently.

"Thanks, those roots slithering up yours is bad-ass," he replied.

"I know!" she said with an uncharacteristic smile.

"'Pan, it's not that bad. Let me see them again." Andromeda said, causing her sister to turn around and face them.

Andromeda wiped a tear from her eye and tried to smile.

"They kind of look like ..." Killian trailed off.

Pandora watched him intently and said, "Go on."

"Well, I mean, it looks like the symbol for infinity, somewhat. I've just never seen it illuminated with flames before. It's beautiful. I mean, your

70

hands are beautiful. I mean, you know together, it looks nice." Killian rubbed the back of his neck, his nerves on end.

"I love it. It's so you, delicate, but fiery." Andromeda smirked.

"You think I'm fiery?" Pandora said with her hands on her hip.

"I mean, you're not a cannon, but you can get snippy," Andromeda said.

"Thanks, Annie. Let's have another look at yours." Pandora reached for her sister's arm and traced the coiling staff up to her shoulder. The flowers bloomed white and red. She placed her nose close to her skin and smelled. She could detect the concoction of roses and lilies coming from her shoulder. "Yours couldn't be more perfect, Annie. All dark with a touch of flowers."

"But guys, where are the gifts the angels gave us? Or did I dream all of that? Do you remember angels standing here giving us gifts?" Killian asked.

"Absolutely," they responded.

"And the Queen, where is she?" Pandora questioned.

They looked up the steps to where the Ivory Throne once stood, but only dust remained.

"I don't understand any of this. What's happened here? Why are we surrounded by death and decay? Where are the silver trees and purple fruits? Where are the unicorns and the pixies? Why do we have these markings? I didn't ask to be branded. I don't want to be branded. How are we going to get home? I—" Pandora began gasping for air as Andromeda immediately held her tightly.

"Calm down, it's just like we've practiced. Breathe in through your nose and out through your mouth. In and out, in and out, that's it. We're going to be fine. Everything's going to be fine. Nothing to get worked up about," Andromeda reassured her, rubbing Pandora's back as she took deep breaths.

"Anxiety," Andromeda mouthed silently to Killian.

"I can't read lips," he responded, looking at Pandora with uncertainty.

"Saying it out loud just makes it worse," Andromeda said.

"Talking about it, as if I didn't know what you were talking about, still makes it worse," Pandora wheezed, trying desperately to calm her breathing.

"Come, my children. Come to me," a familiar yet aged voice echoed over the pavilion.

They turned rapidly to see the Queen, ancient and brittle, sitting beside a small puddle left over from the fountain. They rushed to her side, wincing at the state of the once dazzling dryad.

"Queen Karaleine, what happened to you? What happened to this place?" Andromeda reached out to help her.

"Don't touch me, for I am in transition. Nothing can stop that now," the Queen whispered. "My purpose has been fulfilled, and all my days have rushed upon me at once and my kingdom. The power has passed on to you now. Each one of you." She pointed to the markings upon their bodies. "Be wise, be strong, and unite our worlds."

Slowly, the Queen cupped the remaining handful of water from the puddle and drank from it. For a moment, a jade glow flowed back over her broken body, revealing a shadow of what she once was. She raised her tiny wand and allowed the tip to consume the remaining drops of the fountain. A faint glimmer twinkled from the end. She rose and stood tall, pointing the wand towards the canopy above, shouting an ancient incantation.

"Lefatuakh et Hadelatot!"

The ceiling above cracked and peeled, transforming into a parted emerald gate.

"Our fate rests in your hands. Go now, and may you find divine favor in all your endeavors. Farewell, my golden trio," the Queen moaned, falling to her knees.

A terrible wind blew through the room as Killian grabbed the twins' hands, pulling them from the Queen towards the gate.

"Hurry," the Queen screamed as the trio ran up silver roots decomposing beneath their feet, falling away in chunks. They leaped from branch to branch, hoping the Queen's magic would sustain them for a few moments longer. Through the gates, they could see the poinciana tree of the glade and the willows that circled around it. They could see the Pennsylvania night sky and the clouds rolling in. With a final lunge,

72

they dove through the opening, landing on the sod just before the gateway closed.

They laid on the ground, panting and breathing in the fresh air.

"Killian, is that you, sir?" a voice asked.

"It's Killian!" shouted others, as a chorus of voices rose from the shrubs. Immediately, seven ecstatic leprechauns tackled him to the ground.

"Guys, guys, guys," he groaned, trying to free his hands so he could stand.

The twins were already up, wiping grass and dust from their eyes. They watched the small creatures attacking Killian and began to laugh.

"Aw, they're adorable," Pandora smiled as the leprechauns became aware of them.

"Lads, pull yourselves together. There be witches about," Murphy barked, eyeing the girls suspiciously.

"Shut up Murphy, you old moron. These were the girls tailing us three nights ago. They ain't witches," Cornedbeef rebuked.

"Of course, they're not witches. More like goddesses if you ask me," Lil McMan reached for Andromeda's hand, kissing it softly. "What's your name? Queen Maeve?" he purred, with the suavest undertones he could muster.

Andromeda slid her hand from him slowly but winked so as not to offend the knee-high creature. "Goddess will be fine," she answered.

"Back off, lads, give them some room," Killian said, getting between them and the twins.

"Oh, you spend three days with these floozies, and now you want to get all territorial, do ya?" Clover cursed, her arms folded, and blood boiling.

"We've been out here for days, waiting. No edibles, no goodies, no bangers and mash, and he's been doing nothing but flirting with these hussies," Freckles bellowed, turning her back to Killian.

The other leprechauns cheered for Killian, high-fiving each other excitedly.

"Who are you calling hussies and floozies, you little red-headed shrimps!" Andromeda said, balling up her fist.

"Shrimps? How would you like your hair seared to a crisp? Jezebel!" Clover retorted, her eyes glowing a radioactive green.

"Calm down everybody before I get angry. You guys know what happens when I get angry," Killian yelled.

Everyone stared at Killian.

Pandora was taken aback, but Andromeda looked as though she could spit fire.

The leprechauns gaped at his sudden macho change of demeanor. Then they burst out laughing, rolling around on the ground and slapping their knees. The twins watched the comical escapade explode into mocked reenactments of Killian trying to be angry. Squeezie did the primary impersonation with a nasal voice and a wagging finger.

"Now you fellas listen here. If you don't stop acting like fools, I'm gonna tell my daddy," Squeezie mocked.

Even the twins began to roar with laughter while Killian stood there, slightly embarrassed.

"Okay, okay, I don't sound like that. Knock it off," Killian said.

All the leprechauns imitated him together with high-pitched shrill voices, "Okay, okay, I don't sound like that," they mimicked, laughing harder and harder until they couldn't breathe. The twins bent over laughing so hard their stomachs hurt. Squeezie ran by, giving them a high-five, whooping like a cowboy.

"That's right, laugh it up, you bunch of rascals. We'll see who gets Spaghetti O's when we get back to the house," Killian threatened.

Silence swept over the leprechauns instantaneously as the twins continued laughing.

"Let's not get crazy, lad. Be reasonable," Murphy pleaded.

"Don't be a toss-pot mate. We're just having a little fun. No harm done, really," Lil McMan implored.

"Yeah, thems was just jokes," Cabbage added.

"Please, please, please don't take the food away," Cornedbeef sniffled.

Killian folded his arms, unimpressed.

A chorus of "We're sorry, we're sorry, we're very, very sorry, we couldn't see it, we can't believe it, we up and ruined your party," rang out over the group. They repeated this many times, sounding sadder and sadder each time.

"All right already. Quit your singing," Killian said.

The leprechauns folded their hands behind their backs but continued swaying back and forth in a uniformed manner, big pouting lips sticking out from underneath their beards.

Killian glanced over at the twins, who were smiling at him, though he felt like an idiot.

"What were we talking about before all this nonsense started?" Killian asked.

The twins shrugged.

Killian racked his brain, trying to remember, his thumb rubbing his chin.

"Oh yeah, how long have you been out here again?" Killian asked, glaring at the group of leprechauns.

"Three moons, genius! Where've you been?" Clover snapped, still annoyed. "And I mean that quite literally, like, where have you been?"

"Three days." Andromeda gasped. "Oh my God, mom, and dad are going to kill us." She pulled out her phone, checking the reception; Pandora did the same. Both of their batteries were dead.

"We gotta get back right now, Killian," Pandora said, putting her phone back in her pocket.

Killian didn't hesitate, knowing his dad would be just as worried, and motioned to the leprechauns. "You lads heard the goddesses. Let's go."

But the leprechauns didn't move as they grumbled amongst themselves.

"What is it? Guys, come on. Don't be like that," Killian urged. "I'm just kidding. We'll get some food when we get back."

"No appreciation, that's all I'm saying. No appreciation at all," Cornedbeef mumbled.

"Mmm," Clover and Freckles glowered.

"Aye, aye, aye, "the others agreed.

"I appreciate you waiting for me. I do. I was scared senseless when I couldn't find you. Come to think of it, where were you the other night when those wolves surrounded us?"

They all blushed and glanced around, somewhat ashamed. Then Cornedbeef spoke up, saying, "We wanted to help ya lad, but we just couldn't free ourselves to get to ya."

"Aye, aye, aye," the others chanted.

"What do you mean you couldn't free yourselves?"

"We couldn't move. Honestly, for hours, we couldn't move, and then these bells started ringing. The sound was everywhere, and then they stopped, and we were finally free."

"Killian," the twins shouted, and they were already across the glade, entering the thicket of the forest.

He held up a finger and turned his attention back to the leprechauns.

"Come on, guys. It wasn't your fault. I'm sure you were just under the Queen's spell. She had her reasons for holding you back, I'm sure. But that's over now, and we have to go."

"But Killian, don't you want your backpack?" Clover asked, her tiny arms still folded in frustration.

"Yes, please, where is it?"

All seven of them pointed to a nearby tree, where they had hung it on a low hanging branch.

"Oh my God, thank you so much, Clover. You are the absolute best," he said. "And most beautiful," he whispered.

He grabbed the bag and slung it across his back. Clover beamed and rallied her fellow kin to keep up with Killian. Within minutes, they had caught up with the girls and were making stellar time.

Killian felt a tug on his jeans and looked down. It was Murphy; he looked frightened.

"Sir, I'm not sure what has happened, but something is definitely wrong."

"It's okay, Murph, we were just in Pangea with like a thousand fairies. It's okay for the girls to see you."

"That's not what I'm concerned about," Murphy stammered, gnawing on his nails.

Killian picked up the leprechaun and placed him on his shoulder. "What is it? What's going on?" he whispered.

"Major things, sir. Something in the atmosphere. Something in these woods. Something, something everywhere."

"Okay, Murph, stay calm. My dad will know what's going on. I'm sure everything is fine."

"If you say so, sir," he stuttered, frantically looking around.

They passed through the woods swiftly, ending at a trail of bushes just to the back of the twins' house.

"What is it?" Killian asked, looking around.

The twins glanced at one another with fear in their eyes.

"I've never seen our house so dark," Andromeda muttered.

"What do you mean? Maybe everyone is just asleep," Killian suggested.

"Uh, no, my brother sleeps with a light on, and the back porch has a solar light that's always on. Our house has never been this dark," Andromeda stated.

"Well, maybe one time, remember, during that blizzard, when we lost power," Pandora said.

Andromeda glared at her. "That's pretty much the point, Pan. Why is the power out? It's August. There hasn't been a blizzard. It's ninety degrees outside."

"What about that storm the other day before we went to Pangea?" Pandora proposed.

"Wait a minute." Killian pulled out the tracker from his backpack, flipping it on. The only readings were the three of them.

"That's strange," he said.

"What, what is it?" Andromeda asked, trying to look at the contraption.

"Well, this device can trace any living being within a five-mile radius, but there's no one here except us."

"I told you something was wrong." Murphy tugged at Killian's pants.

"Hold on, let me extend the radius out to ten miles, that's the most I can do." Adjusting the settings, he gulped, his palms sweating and his heart racing. "There's not one single person in this town."

"Why? What do you think has happened?" Pandora grabbed her chest, breathing in deep gulps of air.

"Stay calm, Pan," Andromeda said. "What are you saying, Killian?"

"I'm saying that neither your family nor my dad nor anyone else in this neighborhood is here; everyone is gone." They continued kneeling for a few moments behind a large mulberry bush, considering their situation.

Killian broke the silence, holding up the tracker again. "Let me ..." he switched the device to the paranormal setting. He stared at it, his heart pounding instantly.

"What is it?" Pandora asked.

He turned the device so they could see. Six yellow dots were moving across the screen, and seven blue dots were clustered around them.

"What does that mean? Someone is out there?" Andromeda asked.

"Yes, but they're not people," Killian answered.

"Not people? You mean animals are wandering around?" Pandora asked.

Killian glanced at her. "This tracker has two settings: physical for human life; and paranormal for beings like the leprechauns and the Queen and faeries and other creatures."

"So, thirteen fairies are flying around out there?" Andromeda asked, rolling her eyes.

"Not hardly, the tracker works like a rainbow. The higher up on the spectrum, the more powerful the entity. These blue dots are the 'chauns, and these six yellow dots are something else."

"Like what, Big Foot?" Andromeda jabbed.

"Maybe," Killian responded, touching the dots on the tracker.

A message flashed across the screen: "Out of Range For Analysis."

"Of course they are," Killian spat.

Pandora and Andromeda looked at each other, confused. "You mean there is a Big Foot?" Pandora gasped.

"Of course, but no one calls them Big Foot. We call them Chewies." Killian chuckled. The girls didn't laugh.

"Oh, come on. You know, like in Star Wars? As in Chewbacca?" Killian raised his hands in exasperation.

The girls raised their eyebrows with an awkward grin, obviously meaning, *you're so weird*.

Killian turned his attention to his backpack, reaching in and pulling out a small, black-faced phone. "Anyways, whatever they are, I have this."

"A cell phone?" Andromeda rolled her eyes.

"And it does what, exactly?" Pandora asked.

"Well, it freezes time, basically, kind of."

"And you probably have a magical whistle in there that summons a pack of eagles to come and rescue us." Andromeda ranted.

"I wish," Killian responded.

"That's it! I can't take this anymore," Andromeda growled, staring at the house. "We need to see if mom and dad are in there." She grabbed her sister's hand.

"But I just told you there's no one in there," Killian pleaded.

"Yea, and now yellow dots are closing in on us, and we're doing nothing. What if they're in trouble or worse, dead?" Andromeda's voice broke with fear, and she sprinted forward, pulling Pandora behind her.

Killian stood there, watching them run. Immediately, he checked the radar. Whatever it was, it was a few streets over. He reviewed the Charleston. The battery bar read two percent. He would only have one good bubble, and that's it. *I need more equipment*, he thought. Turning around, he looked down at the leprechauns.

"Cornedbeef, Cabbage, Lil McMan, and Squeezie, go help the girls and bring them back once they're sure the house is empty. Don't let them linger. The rest of you come with me."

"Aye, aye, aye," they saluted, and the party split.

Killian was in Mrs. Peterson's home within seconds, jumping over the broken front door. The house looked utterly ransacked. Every area looked as if a tornado had hit it. He ran to his dad's room, keeping the tracker open, watching the dots maneuver through the streets. Seeing his dad's things scattered across the room brought a sudden rush of pain and a flash of tears into his eyes. *Where was he? What had happened here? Have I now lost my mother and father?*

He didn't have time for emotion. He grabbed his dad's suitcase, opening the hidden compartment, grabbing every spare piece of equipment he saw. He ran to his room, instantly catching fur in his face as the brownies tried to kiss him all over his cheeks.

"Guys, no time, jump in the duffel," Killian commanded.

The bag was lying on the floor, and Clover and Freckles were shoving snack cakes into it. Killian ran downstairs, grabbing a water bottle, then ran straight back to the room. Wendy waved at him from her aquarium, and he lifted the lid, motioning for her to jump in.

"Come on, Wendy, we gotta go," he insisted as she cautiously swam into the water bottle. He fastened the lid tightly, placing it in the duffel bag. *One last thing,* he thought, he grabbed the picture of his mom and her beaded necklace off the dresser drawer. He zipped up the duffel and checked the tracker. One of the dots had snuck up close to the twins' house, and the power cell was blinking red.

He ran down the stairs; Clover, Freckles, and Murphy followed. Looking out the window, he saw a massive being with the head of a bull and the body of a man. It stared at the twins' house smoke issuing from its two ringed nostrils. It must have been ten feet tall with muscles bulging over its hairy body. *A Minotaur? Seriously?* He thought.

"This is not good. This is not good. This is not good."

Priming the Charleston, he reached into the duffel bag and grabbed two of the seashell necklaces and two golden rings. He handed them to Murphy.

"You have to get these to the girls. Tell them to put them on immediately."

The leprechauns zoomed out in a flash. Killian checked his necklace and ring to be confident he had it. He rechecked the tracker, but it was dead. He sighed, took a deep breath, and stepped over the broken door.

The minotaur had disappeared. Killian hurried to the van, hiding behind it, surveying the area. There were no sounds to be heard. The atmosphere was eerie, as if the air had a weight pressing down upon him. Looking through the windows, he saw the parents' SUV. He ran towards the vehicle. Nothing else moved. He glanced up at the front door, noticing it was busted in as well.

He sprinted inside but stopped abruptly; the deep darkness of the house surprised him. "Pandora, Andromeda," he whispered. "Where are you?"

Screams burst out from the second floor above as a crash of glass reverberated throughout the house. Killian ran from room to room, trying to make it to a back door. The shrieks were moving out of earshot and headed towards the forest. Finally, he found a sliding glass door, but it was locked. Killian looked around and saw nothing but a dining room set. He picked up one of the heavy metal chairs and threw it through the sliding glass window. The sound of glass shattering made the monster stop.

Killian stepped into the backyard, anger bursting through his body at the sight of the minotaur's grotesque arms wrapped around Andromeda and Pandora. Rage boiled in his veins at their faces consumed with terror.

"Hey, you piece of shit, I'm going to kill you for touching them!"

The minotaur smiled, showing its mangled teeth. "I'll be back for you, not to worry," it snarled, with a deep gravelly voice, and headed back into the forest.

Killian panicked, looking for anything to stop the creature from moving. He grabbed the closest thing he could find, rocks from the flower bed, and hurled them at the beast, hitting it in the head twice. A ferocious growl came from the monster. It threw the girls to the ground, then turned and planted its feet.

"You want death, boy? I'll give it to you."

Killian, white-knuckled, held the Charleston behind him, his finger hovering over the execution button. The minotaur charged. Large chunks of soil flew in the air from its thundering hooves. Killian had never seen such power before. He looked around for Murphy, Clover, and Freckles, hoping they'd gotten to the girls in time.

Out of nowhere, red, orange, and yellow beams of light hit the minotaur in the face, torso, and legs. The creature slowed for a moment, and Killian saw Cabbage, Cornedbeef, and Lil McMan pressing in. He maneuvered to the right, trying to get a glance of the twins, but the minotaur's roar knocked everyone off their feet. Killian rolled over, scrambling towards the Charleston, reaching for it as the minotaur closed in. The monster dove at Killian as he pressed the execution button.

A force field, resembling a giant white bubble, enclosed the area. The minotaur was frozen in time, blood suspended on its face. Killian stood, staring at the beams of light shooting from the three enraged leprechauns. He ran out of the bubble, finding the twins holding each other and weeping.

"Are you okay?" he asked, looking over their shoulders. Their tears turned to wails as Killian saw the small, lifeless body upon the grass. He bit his fist, holding back a scream of terror as he looked at the hollow, dead eyes of Squeezie.

Clover, Freckles, and Murphy were kneeling beside him, sobbing.

A roar sounded in the distance, and Killian knew they didn't have much time. He examined the girls' necks. They had the necklaces on, and upon their fingers were each a golden ring.

"The force field won't hold much longer, we have to go," Killian muttered, tears trickling down his face.

The girls stood and buried their faces in the crooks of his arms.

"I'm so sorry, Killian, there was nothing we could do. The creature was on top of us before we knew it. The little one tried to fight it off, but the monster stepped on him," Andromeda cried. "It's my fault. I should have listened to you. No one was even in the house."

Killian felt their tears running down his arms, and he knew they were not just for Squeezie. Their parents were gone, their little brother was gone, everything they thought they knew had been turned upside down.

Tears streamed from Killian's eyes, despite him wanting to look strong and brave for the twins.

"He died a hero, a brave little leprechaun, but he will have died in vain when that force field breaks. All my equipment is dead. Everything must be charged if we are going to fight whatever is coming after us. We must leave. We have to go somewhere where there's power," Killian urged.

Andromeda stared at him, and her emerald eyes glistened with a vulnerability he'd yet to see from her. "What if there's no power anywhere? What if we can't find them?" Andromeda wiped the tears from her cheek.

"We have to try, but I don't know the area. Where can we go?" Killian asked.

"There's Reading," Pandora suggested, drying her eyes with Killian's shirt.

"How far?" Killian asked.

"Way too far, what about Fleetwood?" Andromeda suggested, regaining her composure.

"Maybe," Pandora shuddered, focusing on her breathing and desperately fighting off another panic attack.

"How far away are these places? Killian pressed.

"Fleetwood is like ten minutes from here. I mean driving. Are we driving? We're not walking, are we?" Andromeda stammered.

Three booming howls sounded in the night. Killian looked at the twins with fear in his eyes. "Whatever else is out there, I don't have lots of weapons for, except this," he touched the seashell necklace. They looked at him with puzzled expressions, feeling the ones around their neck.

"This necklace takes you into the void, the veil between worlds. My dad made it. This is our only protection from what is coming, but I've never been in there longer than five minutes. It's incredibly draining, but we'll be safe and can get away from this place. Which way is Fleetwood?"

The twins looked at each other, as Andromeda indicated, "To the right."

"You mean west?" Killian asked.

They nodded uncertainly.

"Come on," he motioned for the leprechauns to follow.

Clover screamed out, "We're just going to leave him here? And what about them?" She pointed to the frozen leprechauns in the Charleston bubble.

"Clover, we're running out of options. It's not the best, it's not ideal, but we have to," Killian said.

Tears rushed down her cheeks as she blew a kiss to Squeezie. Murphy saluted Cabbage, Cornedbeef, and Lil McMan as they passed by.

"We'll never be a rainbow again," Freckles sobbed over and over.

A shudder ran through the bubble, showing that it was weakening. The Minotaur's eyes followed them as they ran by.

"Time's almost up. We have to hurry. The field is about to break." Killian ushered them quickly through the bubble and to the side of the house.

They peeked around the corner. Nothing was there.

"Does anyone have the keys to your car?" Killian asked.

"Dad keeps one of those magnetic key boxes under the SUV in case we ever get locked out."

"He does?" Pandora asked, surprised.

They ran swiftly to the vehicle. Underneath, the box was lying on the concrete. "That's strange?" Andromeda questioned.

"No, that explains a lot actually, it's lost its magnetism." Killian grabbed the key and unlocked the door. He slid the key into the ignition, but nothing happened. "Just what I thought."

"What?" the twins asked.

"EMP, that probably knocked everything out. Nothing is going to work here, maybe not even this equipment." Killian threw the bag to the ground.

"But, these work, right?" Pandora asked, pointing to the necklace.

"Yea, well, I hope so." He kicked the front tire enraged.

"Does this mean we're walking?" Andromeda gasped.

Pandora screamed as three frightful minotaurs stood in the driveway.

"Go, we'll hold them off," Murphy shouted, as a blue beam shot from his eyes, piercing the minotaur on the left.

Killian grabbed the duffel bag and reached for Pandora, who was already holding Andromeda's hand. The trio placed their fingers on the seashell necklace. Clover and Freckles shot beams of indigo and green light, trying to protect them.

"Now," Killian screamed.

Instantly, the trio was transported into the veil. They gazed around at the colorless, displaced world they were in, panting and shaking.

The elements of the veil began to work on them immediately. Frigid air circulated around them, freezing the sweat, beading upon their foreheads. The shell necklaces were glowing with blue highlights curving around the shell.

Andromeda chuckled.

"What's funny?" Killian asked, shocked at this sudden outburst.

"It's nothing, it's nothing, really," she giggled again then laughed uncontrollably.

Pandora laughed at her sister's unexpected hysteria, tears clinging to the creases of her eyes, but Killian was slightly concerned.

"Are you going to let me in on your little joke or what?" he asked.

"It's just …." she laughed again. "Okay, okay, it's just that, of the two things you told us about this necklace, the story about it being a family heirloom was the lie and the part about it being a transportation device into another dimension was the truth." She burst out laughing again.

This explanation caused them all to laugh, and it was a deep, hearty, healing laugh that lasted for several minutes.

Then silence fell over the trio, and they stood contemplating all that had transpired. Pandora wiped more tears from her eyes as Killian hiked the duffel bag up onto his shoulders.

"So, west, right?" he asked. The twins nodded solemnly, and together they set out through the milky fog of the veil.

8: AREA 51

Jacob's eyes burned as he stared at the bright white wall before him, his hands shielding them from the relentless fluorescent bulbs. He writhed uncomfortably in the rigid chair as his teeth chattered from the freezing temperature. He'd lost all track of time. He couldn't understand why he'd been dragged here in the first place and why none of his demands were being answered. *Had Mark forgotten about him? Had he plotted something against him? Where was Killian?*

He returned to his meditation. Reciting the words he held so dear in his heart. "*Shema Israel Adonai Eloheinu Adonai Echad.*"

The door opened slowly as a broad-shouldered, bald man entered. His square-cut jaw forged a smile across his face as his muscles strained against his tight-fitting uniform. He seated himself stiffly upon the chair, staring at Jacob with evident disgust. Jacob stared back. The smell of old tobacco emanating from the General almost made him gag.

He tossed a small black device onto the table. Jacob looked at it, recognizing the Charleston device. He shot up out of his chair, excitement taking over his body.

"Did you find Killian? Where is he? Why can't I see him?"

General Marx motioned for him to sit down, pulling out a long Cuban cigar.

"You haven't seen your son, Dr. Gold because we don't have him." His voice was raspy and perturbed. "I will, however, inform you that your son attacked one of our special agents with this," referencing the device on the table with a nod. "Now, you tell me what I'm supposed to think?" Marx crossed his arms, stretching the fabric to the brink.

"I'm not sure what you mean, General." Jacob banged his fist onto the table. "I didn't know agents were being sent for my son in a way that would make him feel he would need to use a device like this."

The General lit his massive cigar and filled the room with an exhale of smoke. "You see, this is why I have a distaste for our science department. The lab rats think they're smarter than the men in the white coats, but you're in my maze and if you don't start explaining why your son had a classified, government-issued, Charleston P-22, well, let's just say, a very different sort of agent will be sent after your boy and the Konig girls."

Jacob shivered, from anger or cold, he couldn't tell. "Marx, my son, has done nothing wrong. The Charleston device is mine, government-issued by this facility, or have you forgotten that I work here?"

"Oh, I'm very aware that you worked here, Mr. Gold. I don't think you know who you worked for, and I don't think you fully understand the gravity of this situation. And I sure as hell know, you are making your son's chances of surviving this situation, unlikely." The General blew another drag of tobacco into the air.

Jacob coughed, grabbing the Charleston. "Why did my son have this device? Is that what you want to know?"

General Marx nodded, biceps bulging.

"Since I lost my wife fifteen years ago, my son has spent every day with me out in the field. I know it wasn't safe. I do realize this was against protocol, but if you had a son who'd just lost his mother, what do you think you would have done?"

The General didn't answer, appearing uninterested. He merely glared at Jacob over his smoking cigar.

"Oh, I forgot you're a heartless bastard who doesn't care about a single person other than himself and the almighty dollar. I know my son would have only used this weapon if he felt threatened. That means my son didn't trust your men, and that means I don't trust you. Not that I ever have."

General Marx rapped his fingers across the table as if bored. Smoke continued to fill the room as he stood slowly from his chair, towering over Jacob.

"Trust, loyalty, honesty, are these things that concern you, Doctor?" the General asked.

Jacob was taken aback. His mind filled with anger and confusion.

"Come this way." The General walked out of the room as two armed guards entered, pushing Jacob from behind, forcing him to follow.

The hall was gray, like most everything in Area 51. Stone walls, stone floors, stone ceilings, metal doors, alloy bathrooms. He'd never been impressed with this facility; of course, he'd never actually been here before either. All his interactions with Dr. Mark Abercrombie were arranged through data-feeds or video chats. All he ever knew of this place was what he saw in the background of the screens.

They walked down one long hall, then another, and another, until Jacob began to think when the General said, "his maze," he was speaking literally. They stopped at a large elevator shaft with roll-away doors. Marx placed a finger upon a keypad and waited for the doors to open. A cloud of smoke followed him inside like a black cloud of arrogance and pomp. Jacob repeatedly coughed from the intake of smoke.

The guards jabbed Jacob in the back, and he stumbled into the lift. He could see that they were on the fifth floor as the General pressed the highlighted button, blinking basement twenty. Down they plummeted, and a sudden rush of claustrophobia consumed Jacob. The event at the cave still weighed heavy on his mind, and this descent into the abyss triggered his nausea.

Finally, the doors opened, and Jacob shuffled out, breathing in the open air. His hands were on his knees as he tried to cease his head from spinning.

"Not a fan of elevators, doctor?" rasped Marx as he walked out into the strange environment.

Jacob straightened up and surveyed the area, realizing they were in a train station of sorts in a hollowed-out cave. Several tracks ran through multiple tunnels, leading in three separate directions. The trains themselves were stopped at various docks as military men loaded and unloaded huge pallets from the cargo platforms.

So this is where the silver-bullets were located, Jacob thought.

The armed guards nudged Jacob on, and he stumbled forward into a corridor through another set of winding hallways. Eventually, they entered an expansive room, causing Jacob to gulp. Laser-like burns spread across the floor, walls, and ceiling. The remains of scattered pieces of heavy machinery lay decimated across the room.

"Look familiar to you?" Marx taunted.

"You guys played laser tag in here with real guns," Jacob suggested, the nausea resurfacing.

The General moved forward until his nose was nearly touching Jacob's. "You don't care much for authority, do you, Dr. Gold?"

The General spat on the floor, returning his fierce gaze.

"My men didn't do this, but you do have one thing right. It does involve lasers. We're just not sure how they work yet." He slowly smiled an awkward evil grin. "Follow me."

They walked back into the hall and down a few more rooms to a laboratory. The guards shoved Jacob inside, and his body went rigid. He surveyed seven small beings tied to individual tables with metal goggles clasped over their eyes.

"I'm assuming you know these creatures?" Marx grinned, releasing another gray cloud of smoke.

"How? Why? What are they doing here?" Jacob stammered.

"These pathetic reprobates were with your son and attacked my agents so he and the girls could escape. It was quite the battle I hear."

"Battle?" Jacob gasped. "What are you talking about?"

"Yes, battle, Dr. Gold. These little scoundrels pack quite a punch. There was a bit of resistance when we finally got them here, but as you can see, they're sedated now."

Jacob shook his head, rage, and despair, filling his chest.

The General took one last drag of his cigar, extinguishing it upon the table, even though it was only halfway done. "You see Doctor, just like this cigar, all things come to an end of their usefulness, sometimes sooner than expected. So, back to trust, loyalty, honesty. Please attempt to explain to me why I was never notified that you had seven level-six, paranormal entities in your possession and that you were using them as your own personal bodyguards?"

Jacob peered at the bodies, saying nothing. Rage filled his soul at the sight of his tiny friends imprisoned because they had fought for his son. His son, who was on the run from government agents and for what. *What could he have possibly done?*

"I'm waiting," Marx growled, but Jacob didn't respond.

"I see. Slipped your mind, maybe, very well. I can overlook that. Sure, a simple mistake. What I can't seem to get over is the fact that you were directly told to grab every mechanism and weapon you were issued from that house and to bring it back here to this base?" The General slammed his hand against the wall next to Jacob. "And yet, your son was running around with a P-22 and a pack of rats that can shoot laser beams from their eyes."

"I must have overlooked that," Jacob replied, with as much sarcasm as he could muster.

The General laughed, then punched Jacob hard on the jaw. He fell to the ground, blood pouring from his mouth. Marx kicked him violently in the ribs, and Jacob keeled over.

"You're pathetic," Marx spat. "But now that you're where you belong, sniveling on the floor, I have my final question, and I hope you have an answer for it."

Jacob winced with pain as his breath came back to him. The taste of blood slid down his throat as he stared blankly at General Marx's black leather boots.

"My agents reported that your son and the Konig girls vanished into thin air, right before their eyes. Now," the General drew in a deep breath and placed a boot upon Jacob's open hand, pressing down gradually, "exactly, how did they do that, Doctor?"

So that's how they got away, Jacob thought, *through the veil*. The pressure on his hand was tremendous, and he screamed in pain.

"How were they able to disappear?" the General asked again, but Jacob could only scream, refusing to give in to the General's demands.

"Obviously, you want your son to die," Marx chastised as his phone began to vibrate. He kicked Jacob one more time and walked away to answer it.

"Marx here," he yelled, pacing before the guards. The General gave a significant number of grunts and sighs, but finally, one word slipped from his crooked smile. "Excellent!"

Walking towards the door, the General ordered, "Bring him," and the soldiers immediately lifted Jacob from the ground, yanking him up by his arms. They were back in the hallway, walking down the corridor, as Jacob's boots dragged against the floor.

After a few moments, Jacob uttered, "I can walk," standing to his feet, shaking off the soldiers. Walking increased the pain in his side, and at times he used the wall to prop himself up. When he did this, the soldiers buffeted him with the heel of their rifles, right in the spine, and Jacob nearly tumbled over from the spasm of pain.

His mind could only think of Killian. *Where was he? What had happened to him? How did these girls get involved? Why was a secret covert division of the U.S. Government so desperate to find him that they would kidnap an entire town*? Jacob's thoughts stopped as they passed back by the mysterious trains and into the elevator.

"Where are we going?" he asked, watching the General press the button reading "Atmosphere."

Marx took out another cigar, lighting the end. "There's a special delivery headed this way, and you're the guest of honor." Marx grinned, blowing a cloud of smoke in Jacob's face.

9: OUT OF THE VEIL

Killian didn't think he could take another step through the milky-white fog.

Andromeda fell to the ground behind him, coughing up clumps of phlegm.

Pandora leaned over, holding her stomach, breathing in heavily.

"How much farther?" Killian asked.

Andromeda looked up, her face as pale as a ghost, and her eyes bloodshot. She rubbed them fiercely. "I told you, I don't know, I can't tell anything in here. The trees don't look like trees. There's no sky, and the ground looks like one big black puddle. We may have completely missed it."

"We've been here for hours, Killian, don't you think we should check and see where we are?" Pandora panted.

Killian thought hard. If he was honest with himself, he was scared to come out of the veil. *What would be waiting for them on the other side? What if the minotaurs had joined forces with other paranormal beings? He had nothing, no gilgameter, no tracker, no Charleston. Everything was dead. There were no defenses. But he knew one thing for sure. They would die if they stayed in here much longer.*

"All right, we're getting out of here, but if something is off when we go back, press the shell immediately. At least here, we can stay hidden."

The twins nodded in agreement.

Killian took a deep breath, holding the duffel bag tightly.

"Ready?" he asked. They nodded again, fingers touching their seashell necklaces.

"One, two, three."

Instantly, they were teleported into the blackness of the Pennsylvania night, under the cover of a dense forest. They looked around for any sign of the minotaurs or any other beings. Nothing moved, and there was silence everywhere.

"I guess we're alone," Killian said. He swung the duffel bag from his shoulder, unzipping the seam. Two round, horned balls of fur came flying out.

Pandora screamed as Andromeda grabbed a nearby tree branch. The two brownies shrieked and rushed behind Killian.

"It's okay. It's okay. Come on out guys, it's fine," Killian coaxed, easing them out from behind him. "These are my friends." He motioned towards the twins.

The brownies eyed the girls suspiciously, and the twins returned their gaze. Killian stood up, wrapping his arms around the brownies, and a low purring seeped out of them. He took Pandora's hand and laid it gently upon Duncan's soft, snow-white fur. The brownie looked up at her with flamingo-pink eyes. Killian placed Andromeda's hand between Crocker's golden horns. She ran her fingers through his black hair, cautiously avoiding his mouth. Both brownies resumed their purring-hum, then suddenly jumped into the girls' arms, nestling within the crook of their necks." It was love at first touch.

"Well, that was quick," Killian grinned, returning to his duffel bag.

The girls snuggled the little tricksters as their complexions began to normalize.

"What's with the socks?" Pandora asked, attempting to take one-off.

"No," Killian shouted.

Pandora froze.

"I'm sorry, they-they hate to have their paws sock-less, it makes them crazy-mad," Killian said.

"It's cute either way," Andromeda laughed, tickling Crocker's gold patch between his horns.

Killian rustled through the bag, finding multiple snack cakes. He tossed one to each of them as the sound of crinkling plastic filled the air.

After the last Twinkie, Killian checked every piece of equipment, but nothing worked. His hand brushed the beaded necklace his mother had given him. His fist clenched around its smooth, familiar touch. Oddly, it made him think of his father. He had no idea where he was, just like he had no idea what had happened to his mother. At least he had this reminder of her, but what did he have from his dad? Nothing physical, only memories, but he would take that any day. He pulled the beads out, placing them around his neck.

He looked at Wendy, still floating in the water bottle, arms crossed, and sneering. Undoing the cap, she climbed up to the top, her tiny head sticking out and examining the terrain.

"Is that—" Andromeda began.

"A mermaid?" Pandora finished. The twins moved in closer, but Wendy scowled at them, returning to the inside of the bottle.

"Her name's Wendy." Killian lifted the bottle to eye level. "Come on, Wendy, come out and say hi to my new friends."

Wendy shook her head grumpily and folded her arms as Andromeda and Pandora leaned their faces in to see her. In a flash, she burst up to the top, spitting water in the twins' faces.

"Wendy," Killian yelled, putting the cap back on.

Wendy smiled innocently from within the bottle with her hands behind her head.

The twins wiped their cheeks with their sleeves as the brownies giggled, vanishing from the girls' shoulders then reappearing in each other's place. The twins were startled but began to laugh.

"So, what do we do now?" Andromeda asked, looking around.

They surveyed their surroundings. Massive trees climbed into the sky, blocking out the stars. The terrain before them was unfamiliar. At this point, Killian didn't have a clue which way was west anymore.

"I'm assuming no one's phones are working?" Killian asked.

They all checked, but each one was dead.

"I guess we just walk until we find civilization," Pandora suggested.

"Point the way," Killian replied.

The girls looked at each other, just as lost as Killian.

"I think we were headed in this direction." Andromeda pointed towards a clump of trees to their left.

"Are you sure?" Pandora asked as Duncan nestled in her hair.

"I think so, but I'm not positive."

Killian crossed the duffel over his shoulder. "Let's go anyway, your first hunch is always the best, my dad always said."

They began the hike, jumping with every stick and twig that snapped. No one spoke for a long time, until Pandora's silvery voice broke the silence.

"So, you're Catholic?"

Killian glanced over at her, jumping a small log. "What do you mean?"

"The rosary you're wearing. Aren't you, Catholic?" Pandora asked.

"Oh, this," Killian slid out the beaded necklace from within his shirt. "No, not really, my mom was. She got me this when I was born. She's been gone a long time, so this is one of the only things I have from her." He tucked the beads back in and stared off into the darkness of the forest.

Pandora wanted to say she was sorry, but the words never came.

"What about your father, and these creatures, and these gadgets? What is all this about?" Andromeda asked, jumping onto a large tree stump.

Killian swallowed, thinking about what he could and couldn't say as his dad had taught him, but then he realized what they had gone through together. They'd been in the kingdom of a Dryad Queen. They'd seen his

96

leprechauns, brownies, and mermaid. Minotaurs had almost kidnaped them. If ever he was going to be able to talk to someone about his secret life, these would be the two people he could.

With a long drawn out breath Killian began to explain. "Well, my dad works for a part of the government that does paranormal research and rescue. Most of the time, it's just some form of tricksters like a brownie or a sprite, but sometimes it can be a rather menacing entity."

"Like what?" Pandora asked.

"Like those minotaurs, or worse."

"Worse than those things?" Andromeda said in disbelief.

"Well yeah. I mean, that thing in crystal cave was much worse."

"Which cave?" Pandora asked.

"Crystal Cave, that's the whole reason dad and I were here in New Jerusalem. There was a monster or a demon or something in that Cave."

"A monster or a demon," Andromeda scoffed.

"Oh my god. Did you hear it collapsed the other night? Our dad was devastated; he works there," Pandora blurted out.

"He used to work there," Andromeda corrected.

Pandora nodded. "True."

"Your dad worked at Crystal Cave?" Killian asked, thinking this was too much of a coincidence.

"Yeah," Andromeda answered. "He was the major historian, tour guide, manager, cashier, you know, everything. They don't have many employees."

"That's strange," Killian said, placing his hands in his pockets.

"Why?" the twins answered.

Killian glanced sideways at the girls. "Well, I mean the collapse, that was kind of …." Killian couldn't quite figure out how to say that he and his dad were slightly involved in the destruction of their father's business.

"Are you trying to say you were there when it collapsed?" Pandora asked, amazed.

"Are you why it collapsed?" Andromeda accused.

Killian swallowed. "Seriously, it wasn't us. It was that being imprisoned in the cave."

"Oh my God, that thing was real?" Pandora shook her hands wildly as if they had slime on them that she was trying to throw off.

"Yeah, it was. What do you know about it?" Killian asked.

"Dad always went on and on about the spooky things that happened at the cave. The gemstones would glow, and sometimes he could hear grunting or groaning early in the morning or late at night," Andromeda said.

"Or like the ghosts, people always said they could see them when All Hallows Eve was near," Pandora added.

"Then, there was that one time when the whole cave smelled like rotting corpses and spoiled milk for a week," Andromeda recalled.

Both twins gagged, recalling the smell of that memory.

Killian watched them, amused. "Well, yeah, there was something imprisoned there, but it was in the veil, you couldn't see it. My dad crossed over, and it nearly killed him."

"What was it?" the twins asked, regaining their composure.

"Something called an Archon," Killian said, stepping through a large pile of brush.

"And that's what?" Andromeda asked.

"Well, I didn't see it since dad royally pissed it off and the cave began to collapse, but he told me about it. It was like an angel or a demon that had been there for thousands of years, and it was waiting on a prophet, or something, to come let it out."

"An angel or a demon?" Pandora asked.

"Yeah, I guess. Dad said it had four wings and horns, and it must have been super powerful to take down that entire hillside."

"That's, that's so weird," Pandora whispered.

"Yeah, it was," Killian answered.

"No, not that." Pandora turned her head towards her sister. "Annie, do you remember Sunday during the scripture readings when—"

"No," Andromeda interrupted. "I have no idea. My earbuds were back in before they started talking."

Pandora rolled her eyes.

"Anyways," she turned back to Killian. "The scripture readings that day were all about angels and demons, and Satan and Jesus. It was the strangest conglomeration of scriptures I'd ever heard."

"Hmmm," Killian narrowed his eyes, removing his hands from his pockets and running them through his hair.

"You don't get it. The first scripture was about the snake in the garden, which was Satan, but then the next scripture was about people shouldn't fight against each other. We're supposed to be fighting against principalities and other things, like demons and stuff."

"That's in the Bible?" Andromeda asked, rolling her eyes.

Pandora nodded. "Yeah, and don't you think it's quite the coincidence? I mean, now that we have seen angels ourselves, and Killian's dad saw, well, maybe it was a demon."

They pondered this for a while. They hadn't had much time to contemplate what had happened. The chest with the gifts. Angels standing before them. The minotaurs attempting to kidnap them and how all of this changed their world view.

"Did your dad ever talk about angels and demons with his work stuff, Killian?" Andromeda asked.

"No, never. We only ran into what people usually consider fairy tale or mythological creatures. Most of the time, we just called them fantanimals, but never anything biblical like that." Killian kicked several pinecones out of the way.

"Do you think it's all connected?" Pandora asked. "Like the paranormal creatures you find. Do you think they come from a place where the angels and demons come from as well?"

Killian thought for a few moments. "I suppose. I mean Queen Karaleine was working with or protecting those angels that came from the chest, so maybe their worlds are all interconnected. To be honest, I don't have a clue."

They walked in silence, thinking, contemplating, as trees swayed above them. Andromeda played with the golden ring Murphy had given her when they were escaping the minotaur. The deep blue moonstone in the center shimmered as she examined it.

"What is this?" she asked.

Killian glanced over at the ring as Pandora inspected hers. "Oh, that's part of the Charleston mechanism. The gold acts as a conduit powered by the heat of your body, just like the necklaces my dad made. Inside, the ring projects a frequency that blocks out the Charleston. So, if you're wearing one of these rings, the Charleston doesn't affect you while everything else in the bubble freezes. That's how we got away."

"Oh," Andromeda said, raising the ring to her eye until the moonlight bounced off the stone.

"What about these?" Pandora asked, touching her seashell necklace.

"Well, first, and I'm sorry if this sounds super geeky, but I love science," he said as the girls nodded.

"You see, everything in this world has a frequency, and once you find that frequency, you can manipulate it. You can make things fly. You can change its anatomical mass. You can maneuver electrons to rearrange its center of gravity, all kinds of stuff. Sometimes frequencies can even manipulate space and time. My dad theorized that black holes are merely a trapped frequency, stuck in consumption, like a whirlpool or a tornado unable to dissipate."

"What grade are you in?" Pandora asked.

"Um, maybe the basic version," Andromeda added.

Killian smiled, noticing he was out of breath from excitement. "Okay, sorry, I know it's a bit heavy. Um, you know how you can hold a seashell to your ear and hear the ocean?"

The girls nodded.

"Well, it's not the ocean at all. It's the veil."

"The what?" the girls asked.

"The veil, that we were just in, with the fog and everything."

"Oh yeah, right, I forgot you called it that." Andromeda nodded.

"My dad figured out the frequency of the veil from the echo in the seashell. Then he started experimenting with it and figured out how to transport things in and out of the veil by projecting dark matter at the frequency's primary wavelength."

The girls chewed on this new information while Duncan chewed on Pandora's earring. Shaking him off, she said, "So, this is where you got these guys right, from the veil?" pointing at Duncan.

"No, that's the strangest part. These guys, and all the paranormal creatures, from what we understand, come from another dimension. I'm guessing that dimension is Pangea. The veil is a place in between our world and theirs. They don't or can't go in there as far as dad and I can tell."

"You mean like the void in *Lord of the Rings*?" Pandora asked.

Killian looked at her, amazed. "Yes, um, very much like that."

Andromeda rolled her eyes. "Okay, I think I understand about the veil and everything, but how did you get these little guys? I mean, how do these things come into our world?"

"Well, the theory is that there are rips in space that happen all the time. The rips last for a few moments or days and then heal themselves. So, at some point when the tear is open, creatures from that dimension wander over into our world."

Andromeda shivered as another cool breeze passed over them. "Do people from our world wander through these rips into their world?"

"It's possible," Killian answered. "Dad thinks this might happen all the time. Some people disappear without a trace. The tears in space may be the culprit."

A loud snap rippled through the air. Killian and Andromeda froze.

"Sorry, that was me," Pandora said, stepping off a large broken branch.

They blew a sigh of relief.

"Well, then how many people know about this stuff?" Andromeda asked.

"I don't know. It's hard to say. There's my dad's special division. Probably Russia, China, Germany, a handful of other countries. Maybe a handful of other people, I don't know." Killian adjusted the duffel bag as the wind began to blow harder against them. It was a strange wind for August. They shivered from the sudden burst of cold.

"I've never actually gotten to talk to anyone about any of this before." Killian smiled. "It's exhilarating to be able to share all this with you two."

The twins smiled back and then looked away. Pandora tucked her blonde bangs behind her ear as Andromeda straightened her black shirt, glancing sideways at her sister.

They hiked on for a while longer, each one contemplating the strange happenings of the past few days. Feathers flapped overhead, making everyone pause. Hardly breathing, they listened for more motion. An owl landed on a tree a few feet away.

"Just an owl," Andromeda sighed. "That's a relief."

Pandora nodded, examining the marks inscribed upon her hands. "What do you think we're supposed to do?" she asked, glancing at her sister.

Andromeda inspected her inscription, touching the black roots running from her left wrist to her fingertips.

Killian glanced at the strange letters on his forearms, contemplating their origin and meaning. "There must be a reason we were given those gifts from the angels. And there must be a reason why they, I don't know, melted into us," Killian said.

"So, what is it?" Pandora asked.

"The Queen said we had a path to walk, and we would learn things as we went, right?" Killian pondered aloud.

"I guess so. I mean, it was all so muddled down with riddles," Pandora answered.

"She said something about unity, right?" Killian asked. "Bring unity to our worlds. Unify what, Pangea and Gaia?"

Pandora shrugged her shoulders. "What do you think, Annie?"

Andromeda was a few steps behind them, lost in her thoughts, saying, "We come back, back to our world and my parents and little brother are gone. Mrs. Peterson is gone. The whole town is gone, and minotaurs are walking around. I mean, what the frick?" Her voice quivered with anger.

Killian glanced briefly at Pandora who grimaced at the sound of her sister's thoughts.

The trees thinned as they walked to the top of a steep hill looking out upon the landscape. City lights bloomed in the distance surrounded by patches of dense Pennsylvania forests.

"That looks way too big to be Fleetwood," Andromeda pointed out, her voice rough and moody.

"Well, we'll figure it out when we get down there, I guess," Pandora said.

"Okay, guys, back into the bag." Killian motioned to Duncan and Crocker. Both brownies folded their sock-covered arms and shook their heads.

"The sun will be out soon, and there are hundreds of people down there. You don't have a choice. Now come on," Killian demanded.

The brownies looked at the girls with small pink eyes full of tears.

"I'm sorry, little ones, but Killian says this is what's best for you. We'll get you back out as soon as it's dark and we're someplace quiet, okay?" Pandora handed Duncan to Killian.

Andromeda lifted Crocker off her shoulder, hanging like a rag doll in her arms, until Killian placed him in the bag.

He zipped up the duffel and peered down at the lights. His shoulder ached from carrying the load for so long, and he was glad to see some rest in sight.

"Everyone ready?" he asked.

The twins nodded.

Within an hour, they had entered a Wawa gas station and were sitting at an empty table near the charging stations. A bing rang out as their phones powered on; it was just after seven in the morning. Killian opened his duffel bag slightly and grabbed the charging station for the Charleston. He handed Andromeda the gilgameter and a special plugin adapter.

"Here, plug this in your port." He motioned, holding up the brick size metal machine. She scrutinized it, plugging in the three pieces.

"Does anyone have any money?" Pandora asked.

"I think I have a twenty." Killian handed his wallet to her. Immediately, she was off ordering food and drinks.

"I'm going to the bathroom," Andromeda said, heading in the opposite direction of her sister.

Killian peered around, wondering if bringing out the gilgameter and trying to charge it would be too suspicious. He watched the bustle of traffic steadily moving in and out of the gas station. People grabbed coffee, donuts, Danishes, and then raced off to work. Killian thought it was strange. *Did no one here know what had happened just one town over?*

"Here," Pandora said, handing him a large cappuccino. "I hope you like it. The smoothie machine is out." She sipped her cappuccino and placed a strawberry Frappuccino with three Tastycake Cheese Danishes on the table.

Killian grabbed one thankfully, tearing into it immediately.

"Oh, thank God!" Andromeda gushed, returning to the table and scooping up the Frappuccino.

"Bathroom." Pandora jetted off around the sandwich station.

Killian tried the cappuccino. It was surprisingly good. He scooped up the change and put it in his pocket, then took another bite of his Danish, savoring every mouthful. When Pandora returned, Killian's Danish was gone, and he was busy enjoying the strange taste of his cappuccino.

Sitting down, she opened her Danish and took two large bites.

"This drink is excellent. What did you call it again?" Killian asked, removing the lid and mixing the brown liquid with a little black straw.

Pandora's mouth was full of Danish. Raising a finger to Killian, she swallowed and mumbled, "It's a cappuccino."

"Cappuccino." Killian took another sip.

"Hey, turn that up," a man hollered behind them, pointing at the flat-screen television on the wall. A nearby worker grabbed a remote as Killian, Pandora, and Andromeda turned around to see the news.

They sat there barely able to move as headline after headline rolled across the bottom of the screen.

. . . Unidentified Flying Objects unhinged.
The world watches as unexplained aerial phenomena enter the atmosphere.
Loch Ness Monster captured in Scotland.
U.S. Naval ships on high alert after disturbances around the Atlantic and Pacific coasts.
In New Zealand, hundreds of mysterious fairy colonies exposed.
Volcanic activity exploding around the Pacific Rim.
Bells heard around the world . . .

"World's coming to an end," the man shouted, getting up from his seat. "I knew it, I knew it all along, people say I'm crazy, but I knew it." The man made eye contact with their table, and they all looked away. He stumbled by them, heading towards the doors.

They glanced at each other, considering the broadcasts. Something had changed. It wasn't just the small town of New Jerusalem that had been hit by strange events; the world had. Maybe they weren't the epicenter, perhaps only a byproduct of something much more significant.

"Do you think the bells were the same bells we heard?" Pandora asked, grabbing Killian's attention.

"Maybe," he replied, scratching his head.

"What does all of this mean?" Andromeda asked, glancing around nervously.

"I don't know, things have changed, like Murphy said." Killian stared back at the television. "My hidden world, that I was never allowed to talk about has been revealed for everyone to see."

"Should we call someone?" Pandora suggested.

"Who?" Andromeda scoffed. "Mom, dad, do you think they have their phones on them? Look at the last time they tried to call us. It was on Sunday. They can't call, or our phones would be blowing up with messages. Something has happened to them and Orion."

"I have some text messages," Pandora said, turning her phone towards Andromeda.

"Yeah, I have the same ones, but they stop on Monday."

"What about the police?" Pandora suggested. "Should we report them missing? Should we report the whole town missing?"

"Don't you think they know?" Killian whispered. "I mean stuff is happening everywhere, what's local law enforcement going to do?"

"We need to talk to someone about something. We can't just walk around wondering what to do. Where are our parents and our little brother? Where's your dad?" Andromeda demanded.

"Hey, I don't know, I've been with y'all for three days, I don't know anything more than you do," Killian snapped.

A panic began outside. People screamed and pointed at the sky. All three of them pressed their faces against the glass, looking out past the roof of the gas station. A silver disc hung in the atmosphere, descending slowly. The wind blew everywhere as people ran for their cars. Killian threw all their electronics into the duffel bag as the UFO drew closer.

"What are you doing?" Andromeda shouted. "Do you think that thing is coming for us?"

"In all my time working with my dad, he always taught me to act first, think later." He zipped up the bags, throwing them over his shoulders.

"That sounds extremely backwards," Pandora yelled as the screams intensified.

"Yeah, well, when you're dealing with things smarter than you, more powerful than you, with greater technology or weapons than you, it's always better to be safe than sorry," Killian said.

Pandora nodded as Andromeda watched the UFO with an awed expression across her face.

The disc hovered twenty feet above the gas station. Small doors opened from the craft as a group of beings glided down upon an electric-blue light. They wore chalky-white suits with helmets like astronauts. When their feet touched the ground, Killian noticed that they were no bigger than a child.

The beings pointed inside the gas station. Killian grabbed Pandora's hand. She looked at him, fear mounting on her face, her breathing rapid. He grabbed Andromeda. "We have to go. We can't stay here to find out if they're good or bad." The twins nodded, touching their seashell necklace and entered the veil.

10: THE TALISMAN

Killian glanced across the street at a pair of tall, brick steeples. Strangely, no lights were illuminating the facility. Andromeda scanned the road multiple times until she was satisfied that there was no living thing in the vicinity. Pandora watched the skies with a fear she had never known before, wondering what was out there and why in the world it wanted the three of them.

"See, it says St. Mary's, I told you it was over here," Andromeda said.

"I see that I was thinking of St. Peter's down the street," Pandora replied.

"How many Catholic churches are in this town?" Killian asked.

"A lot," Andromeda replied.

"St. Margaret's, St. Paul's, St. Joseph's, St. Catherine's, St. Stephen's," Pandora added.

"Wow," Killian marveled. "This is like a little Vatican."

"Yep, Reading, Pennsylvania, famous for pretzels and Catholics," Andromeda joked.

"And who doesn't love pretzels?" Killian grinned, holding up a humongous salted pretzel.

"We really shouldn't have stolen these," Pandora said, taking a bite of her own.

"We'll pay them back later, or I'll just go to confession." Andromeda chewed her last bite.

"Are you sure it will be unlocked?" Killian surveyed the area once more.

"Yes, how many times do I have to tell you?" Andromeda snapped. "The sanctuary is always open for prayer. There should be candles to give us some light, and what's safer than a church?"

"And they have those awesome padded pews we can sleep on," Pandora added.

"All right," Killian yielded, "Let's go."

Swift and silent, they crept across the road to the front door of the church. Killian reached out and pulled on the looped handle, shocked that it was unlocked.

"Told you," Andromeda quipped as they snuck inside, shutting the door behind them.

Killian had never seen anything quite like the inside of this building. The floors were a beautiful, gray wood. Vaulted ceilings soared fifty feet above, held aloft by four massive marble columns that stood like sentinels at the altar. Elaborate religious paintings decorated the walls between magnificent stained glass windows. Rows of blonde birchwood pews lined the floor like a giant domino set.

"Do all Catholic churches look like this?" Killian asked, staring at the infrastructure.

"Um, some of them just depends." Pandora touched a small dish full of holy water and crossed herself.

"And you're sure no one is here?" Killian confirmed, laying down his duffel bag slowly as if someone would hear.

"Aliens just chased us, and you're worried about a priest?" Andromeda asked, glaring at him incredulously.

"The priest usually lives on the grounds somewhere, but we should be fine in here until morning," Pandora explained.

Andromeda walked down to the last pew in front of the altar and bowed.

Killian watched her, surprised at her pious behavior.

"She always does that," Pandora whispered. "Her own little ritual," she explained, moving further into the sanctuary.

"Just seems a little out of character for her." Killian gulped, realizing he had said this out loud.

Pandora chuckled. "Yeah, doesn't seem the religious type, does she? Don't be fooled, though. Her faith is essential to her. She just doesn't like authority and rules and people." Pandora laughed again, walking towards a specific corner of the sanctuary.

Killian followed as dim lights from random candles cast shadows along the walls. A statue of Mary stood before them, and Pandora reached out, grabbing one lonely stick from a small box of sand. Methodically, she began lighting all the candles around the statue.

Killian watched her in the orange glow of the candlelight. Her beauty was magnified a thousand times by the holiness and decorum of the sanctuary. She was a living statue carved to perfection, performing the holy rituals of a forgotten queen.

Andromeda walked up behind them, following Killian's gaze as he surveyed her sister. Surprisingly, she was jealous, but she didn't know why. His eyes were not like Mickey Brown, full of lust and arrogance. Killian's were tender and mysterious. At first, she thought he was an idiot, wandering in the woods alone, searching for God knows what. Now, because of him, a world she could have never imagined was opened to her.

Andromeda cleared her throat, and Killian shook, startled that he hadn't recognized her standing right beside him.

Pandora turned, looking curiously at her sister's perplexed expression.

Killian stepped over to the duffel and unzipped it completely. Crocker burst out and into Andromeda's hands as Duncan raced towards Pandora. They squeezed and hugged them as Killian got out Wendy. She was not at all pleased with her current predicament, but Killian's pretzel peace offering appeased her.

Pandora stared at the tiny mermaid with her beautiful purple hair munching the soft bread. "Killian, I have an idea." She waved her hand, and he followed her to a small, stone baptistery full of water. "Do you think she'd like to go for a swim?"

Wendy swan dived out of the water bottle before Killian could respond. Her emerald fin moved so fast that it was nearly impossible to see her swimming around. It was like watching a hummingbird zoom around a bush of flowers.

"Thank you, that was ingenious," Killian said. Pandora smiled as they walked back to the statue where Andromeda was holding Crocker.

"Are everyone's phones still dead?" Killian asked.

Andromeda checked her phone one more time, but Pandora didn't bother. Andromeda sighed. "Yea, why do you think that is?"

"I think it's the veil," Killian stated. "I think for some reason when we're in there; it zaps the power out of electrical equipment."

"And people," Pandora yawned, walking to a pew to lie down as Duncan appeared on her shoulder. Killian followed her with his eyes but stopped abruptly as Andromeda's suspicious gaze came into view.

"We need to have a serious talk," she demanded, grabbing him by the sleeve.

Andromeda walked out of earshot of Pandora, pulling Killian with her.

She turned on him with a pointed finger directed at his nose. "First off, what's your deal with my sister?"

Killian almost panicked, wiping his sweating palms on his jeans. "Um, I don't have a deal, that I'm aware of," he replied.

"You know what I mean," Andromeda hissed.

"Well, she's beautiful and—"

"You only like her because of how she looks?" Andromeda whispered with a fierce tone.

"No, I mean, well—"

"So, you don't like the way she looks?" Andromeda scolded.

"Of course, I like the way she looks."

"Don't I look just like her?" Andromeda's arms folded across her stomach.

Killian's mouth hung open as he searched for words to say.

"I don't want to hear it," Andromeda fumed. "Secondly, what is it that you know that you're not telling us?"

"Nothing, I've told you what I know, why would I lie, I have no reason to lie," Killian answered.

"You say you have no reason to lie, but I don't know that. How can I know you're telling the truth? Ever since we've met you, things have gone wrong. We get sucked into some fairy's tree. We pass out for three days. We come back with no parents. Monsters almost kidnap us, and then we're chased by UFOs."

Crocker jumped off Andromeda's shoulder and slid past Killian, gliding along the floor like he was ice skating.

"So, I'll ask you again, what are you not telling us? Why is this happening? None of this started until we met you and now look." She gestured to her left arm. "I have a tattoo slithering up my arm, of a rod some angel from a fairy kingdom gave me. Doesn't that seem strange to you?"

110

Killian shrugged. What could he say? He knew this was all strange to them, but for him, it was kind of normal. His thoughts were interrupted as Andromeda's voice broke in again.

"Anyways, more importantly, what would a UFO want with us? Why couldn't we trust it? Maybe they knew where our parents were."

"Or maybe they took our parents," Killian suggested.

Andromeda's fists balled up with anger. She stared at him, furious with this entanglement of questions she couldn't get answered. Now he's suggesting aliens kidnapped her parents and her little brother. A vision of Orion bound in chains by green Martian men popped into her head, and her anger broke as tears swelled in her eyes.

She spoke, her voice trembling, and her eyes downcast. "I'm sorry, Killian, but I need more answers than that. I can't deal with maybes and probably. I need to know how to protect my sister. I need to know how to find my little brother, my mom, and my dad. I don't know anyone who knows more about this stuff than you do, so I need you to give me more information about what could have happened. What is going to happen? What are we going to do?"

Killian glanced down at his arms and the row of symbols leading up them. He thought hard about what to say. What could comfort her? What could ease her pain? Suddenly, he thought of his mother and how he felt when he lost her.

"My mom disappeared when I was two," he began. "She worked for a university as an archaeologist and a linguist. They sent her to the Red Sea to find something. They say a bad storm came up, capsized her boat, and everyone drowned."

Tears flowed down Andromeda's face as she listened intently. He wasn't looking at her. He was looking at the flames flickering in the air from the candles surrounding Mary.

"My dad, he believes she's in the other dimension where these creatures come from, the place where Queen Karaleine lives—well, I guess lived. I told him I couldn't hold onto that hope anymore, because she's been gone for so long. I couldn't keep going back and forth between hope and disappointment hanging on my dad's only wish to find her."

He looked at her, and her emerald eyes sparkled with fresh tears. The cement walls she had built around her soul were momentarily erased, revealing a soft fertile ground eager to be explored.

"I know it hurts, not knowing where they are. I know it's frustrating not being able to do anything. I know that anger of wanting to rescue a loved one but being powerless to do so. Nothing is more infuriating than the feeling of helplessness. Nothing hurts more than losing hope. When that hope is lost, it's like you lose a piece of yourself in the process." Killian reached for her hand, and she didn't pull away.

"I don't want you to lose that hope. I want you to find your parents and your brother. I will do anything I can to make that happen. I will never keep anything from you or Pandora, okay?" Killian squeezed her hand, and she squeezed back.

"It's Pan," Andromeda sniffled.

"What?" Killian asked.

"Pandora. We call her Pan, and you can call me Annie." Andromeda dried the tears from her eyes.

"Thank you, Annie," Killian said as their hands parted.

Andromeda straightened her shirt and tied back her hair with a black band she had on her wrist. "Okay, enough of being emotional, now it's time to be productive."

Killian smiled at her, getting somewhat used to her drastic mood changes. "What are you going to do?"

"I'm going to go search every drawer in this facility until I can find a charger for our phones. If I find one, maybe we can research some of this stuff. Like what's going on around the world and how it ties back into here. Maybe we can find some clues about where our families went."

"That's a great plan," Killian said.

"Are you surprised," she asked.

"No." Killian grinned.

"Stay here with her. I'll be right back." She walked away, heading towards the foyer.

Killian gathered all the pieces of equipment he had brought from his dad's house. There were two gilgameters, four Charlestons, six pairs of glasses, and a charger for each one. He set the first three up and got them charging.

There were two pretzels left. Killian grabbed one, splitting it in half. He walked over to Pandora, who wasn't asleep. She was staring at the ceiling.

"May I join you?" he asked.

She nodded, moving her legs over as Duncan purred on her belly. He handed her half of the pretzel, and she took it. She sat up, her long blonde hair falling on her shoulders.

"What are you thinking about?" he asked, admiring her eloquence in the simplest of things.

"I don't know. Lots, I guess," she said.

"Like what? We're not going anywhere. You could tell me." He offered with a smile.

Pandora peered over at him, gazing into his big grey eyes, noticing every strand of messy chestnut hair gloriously out of place, considering his proposal.

She sighed and swallowed. Duncan moved angrily beside her, pulling his socks up as he did. "Why all of this? Why now? What can we do? We're just kids," she explained.

"Sometimes kids make the best conduits of power," Killian suggested, surprising himself.

Pandora looked at him, curiously. "Is that a quote from a book?"

"No, that was just me," Killian answered, raising his eyebrows innocently.

Pandora pondered his words for a few moments twirling her champagne-colored hair with her fingers. "Hmm, that was a good thought," she finally admitted.

"It happens," he replied. "Not frequently, but it happens."

"Queen Karaleine said something about a Black Death and that she couldn't figure it out. What are we going to do about it?" she asked.

Killian thought for a few moments, scanning the sanctuary. *What could the Black Death be? How could they stop something they didn't even know about?* Killian examined the remarkable craftsmanship of the sanctuary chewing on her question.

"Killian," Pandora whispered.

"I'm sorry, yeah." He stared at her, not sure what to say. "I guess, first, we need to find out what the Black Death is. Then we go from there."

Pandora turned away from him.

He felt like a failure. Both of them were looking to him for answers, but he couldn't figure this out.

"What if-what if," she stammered. "What if the Black Death killed our parents and we didn't do anything to save them? What if the Black Death makes you disappear, and that's why the whole town is gone? What if it killed my little brother?" She couldn't fight the tears back anymore and allowed them to flow like rain.

Killian reached across the pew and wrapped his arm around her. She buried her face in his shoulder, shuddering as the tears fell. Killian thought about her theory. *What if she was right? What if something called the Black Death had taken the whole town? What if his dad had been killed? What if the Black Death was what killed his mother?*

He fought back the tears running to his eyes. "Surely, Queen Karaleine didn't give us our powers before it was too late."

Pandora sat up and faced him. Tears stained her rosy cheeks. "What powers? We have tattoos etched in our skin. That's not power. We can't do anything I wasn't able to do before I was defiled by, by this." She stared at the infinity symbols on her palms, then clenched her fists.

"We don't know what this is all about right now, but trust me, it'll work itself out. I've worked with my dad for years. So many times, things have happened, and they didn't make any sense, but in the end, it did. To the point where I had to stop analyzing every minute detail thrown at me. Sometimes we have to flow with the current, you know?"

Pandora's lips curled as she wiped away her tears. "Like what?"

"What do you mean like what?"

"I mean, give me an example of when something weird happened, and it turned out okay in the end."

"Okay, um, just let me think for a second." Killian racked his brain, trying to think of the best example, but of course, his mind would go blank at a time like this. Pandora waited, her face changing from curious to frustrated almost instantly.

"Okay, well, one example would be when dad and I rescued the leprechauns from a Pooka Puk."

"A what?" Pandora asked, her eyes widening.

"A Pooka Puk. It's like a shape-shifting nature spirit that is extremely territorial and loves sharp objects."

"Okay, I've never heard of that, but go on."

"Well, we flew into Dublin to investigate some strange happenings on the neighboring city of Ashtown. Entire flocks of fallow deer were being slaughtered and mutilated near a place called Phoenix Park. The Pooka Puk had taken up residence there, sacrificing the large game and painting blood-murals on walls, houses, city buildings, you get the point. One night, there was a battle between the leprechauns and the Pooka Puk. It destroyed some of the major monuments of the town."

Pandora scooted closer, propping up her arms on the pew and resting her head in her hands.

Killian continued, thrilled because he had never been allowed to tell this story. "Now, when I was ten, five years before Dublin, I had met a Keshali in Transylvania who gave me a silver talisman. I loved it. It was two triangles hooked together with a sapphire stone. She told me to always keep it with me, to protect me, and to protect others, that it was an ancient symbol of something. I don't remember what it was, but she said it was super important."

Pandora shifted in her seat, beckoning Killian to continue his story.

"Okay, so, a few nights later, after investigating Ashtown, we camped out on a hillside by this old castle in a sheep pasture. It was brutally cold that night, but the constellations were blazing like fire; I'll never forget that. It seemed like you could reach out and grab a handful of stars if you wanted.

"Then suddenly, the sheep went crazy, bleating, and running chaotically over the field. Beams of light ripped through the air from the leprechauns shooting at the Pooka Puk, but it was way too strong for them. By the time we got down to the field, the sheep were dead, and only Murphy was left fighting. The others were injured or unconscious, lying on the ground.

"When the Pooka Puk saw me, it froze, and I froze, too. It looked like a bear with a lion's head. My dad had the Charleston in his hand, but he didn't use it. He just waited, staring at the creature. Then for no reason at all, it transformed before us into a little girl.

"I gasped, but dad walked right up to it like he'd known this creature all of his life. Within minutes he signaled for me to come over. I approached cautiously, but the little girl smiled, and I felt like everything would be okay. My dad said, 'This is Puk, and she is looking for something very important, and we've been very kind to have brought it to her.'

"I had no idea what dad was talking about, but he reached around my neck and took off the talisman. When the little girl saw the object, her eyes glowed orange like a sun. I didn't want to give it to her, but dad said, if I did, that Puk had agreed to take this form forever and to return to her home in the hidden hills. I looked around at the devastation the creature had caused, and the little bleeding leprechauns lying on the field. I agreed and handed dad the talisman. He placed it in Puk's small hand, and she disappeared. We never saw her again."

Pandora stared at him, amazed at the story, but confused at the same time.

"The point is," Killian continued, "I didn't know what the talisman was for, but I knew it protected me that night. I knew it protected the leprechauns as well. Puk would have easily killed them all and us next, but she didn't. I had what Puk was looking for by chance, coincidence, destiny, fate I don't know. The talisman had a purpose much more significant than I could have imagined, and it saved a bunch of lives.

"I don't know what these are or what they do." Killian held out Pandora's hands, and she unclenched her palms. "This is here for a reason. We don't know what the reason is yet, but we will. Tomorrow, a year from now, someday the three of us will know, and it could change our lives forever. It could change the lives of millions. We have to wait and see and do what we can for our families until then."

Killian finally relaxed, breathing in and sitting back against the pew. Pandora continued looking at her palms and then up to Killian.

"I wish the ring had never come to me. I wish none of this would have happened," Pandora quoted in a whisper.

Killian gazed at her in fresh amazement. His heart thumped deep within his chest. "So do all who live to see such times, but that is not for them to decide. All we have to decide is what to do with the time given to us." Killian finished her quote.

"Tolkien," Pandora smiled.

"Tye Maia Vala," Killian whispered.

"What is that?" Pandora asked, her face bright with wonder.

"It's called Quenya, the elvish language Tolkien created. My dad taught it to me when I was younger. We use it now and then." Killian explained, gazing into her deep blue eyes.

"What does it mean?"

Killian hesitated, shifting the beaded necklace around his neck. "One day, I'll tell you."

Pandora blushed. "You've seen some amazing things, Killian. Things I've only dreamed of after reading my books. I always wanted to find that rabbit hole and follow Alice right down into Wonderland or open a wardrobe leading straight into Narnia and never come back. Still, it looks like all those stories have come rushing into our world at the cost of my family and friends."

Killian smiled, gazing into Pandora's sapphire eyes. "But there's still hope, Pan."

Her eyes widened at the sound of her name, and she smirked, blushing.

"There will always be hope for people like us." Killian cupped her hands together and slid his away.

Just then, Andromeda entered the sanctuary, saying, "Hey, bring your phones. I found some chargers."

11: ENOCHIAN

Thunder rolled over the heavens as the three teenagers made their way down the dark hallway and into the priest's office. Killian shielded his eyes from the bright fluorescent light above. He hadn't realized it, but he'd become accustomed to the candlelight in the sanctuary.

He repeatedly blinked, waiting for his eyes to settle, peering around the room. A crucifix hung above a black leather chair pushed in behind a large oak desk. Two brown suede chairs sat in the front of the office and a conglomeration of portraits of popes from the last two centuries hung upon the wood-paneled walls.

"Over here," Andromeda directed, holding out three plugs.

"You found one for each of us?" Killian asked, still wincing.

"Yea, the secretary, had two in her desk, and the priest had one," Andromeda replied.

Thunder shook the walls of the office as the lights flickered all around them. With hesitant looks, they plugged in their devices as the lights blinked again.

Bing, chimed in everyone's ear as their phones turned on.

"All right, what do we need to look up first," Andromeda asked.

Killian fiddled with his phone, pulling up a browser. He scratched the back of his head as they all took a seat around the priest's desk. The twins followed suit, pulling up browsers on their phones, staring at him with anticipation.

"Well, what do we want to know first?" he asked.

The girls eyed him with irritation, then stared at each other.

"I think we need to know what has happened since we've been gone," Andromeda proposed to her sister.

Pandora nodded, "We also need to know more about these tattoos. What is the symbology? Is there anything connected between these images and religious lore? Or even like ancient mythology."

"Facts," Andromeda agreed, fist-bumping her sister.

The twins glanced over at Killian who was checking his Facebook account out of habit. He looked up, feeling their eyes beating down upon him.

"What are you going to research?" the twins asked.

Killian shuffled in his seat. "So, you're going to research current events?"

Andromeda nodded.

He looked to Pandora. "And you're going to research the symbology of our tattoos, right?"

Pandora raised her eyebrows and slowly nodded.

"Yes, the question is, what are you going to do?" Andromeda asked.

Killian tilted his head back, staring at the ceiling. Thunder rumbled through the halls. He stared at his reflection in the mirrored medallion encircling the fan. His hands were behind his head, and he noticed the symbols running down his forearms. He glanced back down to the twins. "I think I'm going to try to find out what these letters are."

"Uh, I'm doing symbology, thank you very much, get your own topic," Pandora said.

"I'm sure you'll find the answers before me being the genius that you are. I'm just going to give it a try." Killian winked.

Andromeda pretended to throw up and began scrolling on her phone. Silence filled the room as they each intensely researched their topics. Andromeda grabbed a batch of sticky notes from the priest's desk and began notating different events that had happened over the past several days. Pandora walked over to the printer, grabbing a few pieces of blank paper from within as Killian continued scrolling, from one website to another.

Suddenly, the sound of music burst into the air. Pandora and Killian looked up from their phones. Andromeda's head was nodding back and forth with the beat of the music. "We are the champions, we are the champions," echoed from the phone.

"Queen, seriously," Pandora said.

"I haven't heard music in like five days, leave me alone," Andromeda sneered, without looking up.

Pandora shook her head and returned to her phone. Song after song saturated the air as everyone's feet tapped to the beat.

Pandora was the first to speak, and Andromeda paused her song.

"I can't find anything about three angels giving gifts in any biblical texts. Gabriel visits Mary, that's just one angel. Raphael visits Tobit, and an angel wrestles with Jacob, and another angel lets Peter out of prison. There's, like, nowhere where angels give anybody gifts much less three angels." She stared at her phone as the others grunted, continuing their search.

Andromeda glanced up; a pile of sticky notes surrounded her on top of the desk. She placed her hands to her temples, massaging them thoroughly. "There's so much that has happened. I guess the most interesting thing is that 'The Bells Heard Around the World' was literally heard all around the world. China, Australia, Canada, Brazil, everywhere. Even more mysterious is that everyone heard them at the exact same time. Which, if my math is correct, which it usually is, I say, puts that time at the same time we were standing before the angels receiving our gifts. Now how could bells be chiming in both dimensions, Pangea and Gaia?"

This question caused Killian to pause glancing up from his phone. "That is weird," he said, "an excellent point, Annie."

Andromeda rolled her eyes, but the slightest hint of a smile curved around her lips. "Have you found anything, Killian?"

He scanned his phone again and then held it up for them to see. The twins huddled in close, putting their heads together. Their eyes widened at the sight of the images.

"That's it," they shouted, staring at Killian, amazed.

"How did you find it?" Pandora asked.

"Well, I searched for stone tablets with writing on them and found the Ten Commandments which have Hebrew written on them. Which does not look anything like this."

"Obviously," the twins stated.

"Then I thought about my dad seeing that angel in the crystal cave, and the language he was speaking was Enochian. Which my mother was researching. I thought that's an odd coincidence. I Googled Enochian script, and there it was. I even looked up my mom's university and saw the article she wrote on 'The Ancient Sumerian Texts of the Lost World and Why They Are Important Today.'"

Pandora placed her hand on Killian's shoulder. "That's a great find."

"You didn't say your mom was studying angelic languages," Andromeda said.

"Well, it's like my dad said, she didn't know they were angelic. She thought they were ancient Mesopotamian, belonging to a tribal people before the Egyptians, but she didn't know this. She didn't know what we know. Maybe if she had maybe …." His voice trailed off for a moment as another peal of thunder roared overhead.

Pandora immediately grabbed his phone. Killian looked at her in surprise. She snatched her pencil and a sheet of paper and began tracing the letters with their corresponding sounds. "Annie, look for a pen or a marker."

"For what?" Andromeda asked.

Pandora looked at her sister, like she had three heads. "Start labeling the letters on Killian. It might be a message."

122

Andromeda hit the top of her forehead and dove into the desk searching for a pen.

"Bingo," she yelled, holding up a black Sharpie.

"Let me see your arm, Killian," Andromeda demanded.

Killian stuck out his left arm, where three of the symbols lay etched in his skin. Pandora and Andromeda matched up the letters immediately: B, K, L. They wrote these letters under the tattoo of each identified marking. Killian stretched out his right arm, and the twins matched: T, S, M. They sat back, aggravated.

"There's no way that spells anything," Andromeda complained.

Pandora stared at the words trying to come up with something, but she couldn't unscramble it. "If only there were more letters," she whispered to herself. The twins looked at each other and turned to Killian. "Take off your shirt."

"What?" Killian said, a bit surprised by the request.

"You might have more letters under there?" Pandora said, reaching out to help him.

Killian stood up and backed away, his hands shaking.

"Don't be scared, I've seen lots of men's chests," Andromeda said with a smirk.

"You have," Killian muttered, frozen, as the girls approached him.

"Well, let's go, take it off," Pandora said with a huge grin. They each grabbed a sleeve and began stripping Killian of his shirt.

Killian winced as they stood back. He glanced down, shocked to see his skin speckled with markings all over his chest, abs, rib cage, and shoulders.

"Turn around," Andromeda said.

Killian spun around awkwardly. The girls gasped. Several more appeared across his back and shoulders.

"I wonder if that's his blood," Andromeda whispered to Pandora.

"What blood?" Killian yelped, trying to look at his back. Andromeda held him still, pointing out the blood sprinkled spots surrounding each letter.

"Oh," he said, scratching them absentmindedly, as if they would rub off. "I guess it's all part of the tattoo, like Pan's flames and your flowers." He looked up, catching Pandora's eyes and was glad to see she was not grossed out by his torso. In fact, she looked pleased, and he didn't quite know what to say.

Andromeda snapped two fingers in front of her sister's face. "Pan, let's get these markings identified, come on."

"Yes, you're right," Pandora agreed, fumbling with the phone and paper.

Within minutes they had identified every marking, ninety-eight in all. Pandora checked each one off the Enochian alphabet she had made, realizing Killian's skin contained every single one. She thought, holding the pencil to her chin.

"Do you have any more in any other places, perhaps?" Pandora asked.

"I …." A look of panic shot across Killian's face. "I-I can go check." He shot out of the room and down the hall to the bathrooms in the foyer. A few moments later, he returned and threw on his red three-quarter sleeve shirt. "Nope, nothing down there," he said. Then he began to stammer, "I mean there's plenty there, I mean, it's just the way it's supposed to be." His face was as red as a lobster.

The twins could not help but laugh. Killian sat back down in the chair, exhausted from embarrassment.

"So, I have the Enochian alphabet etched onto my body, what good does that do?" Killian asked.

The twins corralled their laughing as they sat down.

"Yeah, I don't know, that's weird," Andromeda stated.

"Thanks," Killian replied sarcastically.

"I mean, it's weird, like, what do you need a foreign language on your body for? Not that you look weird, I mean, you look great." This compliment slipped out faster than Andromeda had expected, and now it was her turn to blush.

"You do look great. Are you a swimmer?" Pandora asked, piggybacking off Andromeda's remark.

"I can swim. What do you mean, a swimmer?" Killian asked, confused.

"Oh, nothing." Pandora smiled dreamily.

124

They sat in silence for a few minutes as the sound of heavy rain beat upon the roof. Killian's mind raced with topics to bring up to divert the conversation from himself.

"Did you happen to find anything about the UFOs?" Killian asked.

"Oh yeah, plenty, why?" she responded.

"Did you find anything to explain why they were coming after us at the gas station. Or where they're from? Or who they are?" Killian asked.

"Um, no," Andromeda said as she grabbed her phone and began scrolling back through some of the articles she had clicked. "It doesn't appear that there has been any official disclosure or anything. They're flying around day and night all over the world," Andromeda clarified.

"Does it say where the highest concentration of sightings has been?" Killian pressed.

"I don't know, why don't you look it up yourself if you're so interested?" Andromeda said.

"Annie," Pandora moaned.

"What?" Andromeda huffed, glaring at her sister.

"We're all trying to figure this out. Watch your temper," Pandora insisted.

"It's okay, Pan," Killian said. "I'm just wondering now why that gas station was important, or I guess, why we're important?"

"Why was the little town of New Jerusalem, Pennsylvania, important?" Pandora added.

"And how did they find us at the gas station in the first place?" Andromeda finished.

They stared at each other for a few moments as a realization seemed to be brewing in the air. The answer was on the tip of their tongues.

"How were they able to find us?" Killian asked, working it out. "What did we do to draw them in?"

The twins watched him, hanging on the edge of their seat. They were almost there, almost to the answer.

"We came out of the veil. We went to the gas station and we …."

At once, they all looked at their phones.

"Shut them off," Andromeda screamed. They pulled the cords out of the phones and pressed the power buttons. The phones powered down in seconds, but a jolt of lightning ran through the building, knocking out the power. Thunder roared overhead as the old building shook. The darkness was thick as pitch in the windowless office.

Killian felt a hand reach for him, and he knew it was Pandora.

"Annie, take my hand," Pandora whispered. Through the darkness, her twin's right hand reached out and grasped tightly upon hers.

They rose and crept towards the door. Killian opened it, but the passageway wasn't much brighter. A faint orange glow lit the end of the hall, but in their current state of terror, it appeared to be the opening to the gates of hell.

Together they stepped into the hallway, barely breathing, attempting not to make a sound. They made it to the foyer as lightning flashed past the massive windows of the church.

"We get our stuff, and we get out of here," Killian commanded.

The twins nodded, hands trembling. They passed into the sanctuary, moving quickly to the statue of Mary where they'd left the equipment, the brownies, and Wendy. They froze, staring at the area. There was nothing there. They heard the squeaking of a door behind them and turned rapidly.

Three tiny figures in white suits with astronaut helmets stared at them. The small beings held weapons in their hands, and they were pointed directly at the trio.

"Shells," Killian yelled. They moved their hands slowly towards their necks, but it was too late. Beams of red light overtook them, and they were frozen stiff. They could only breathe and see. Not a single muscle in their body would respond to a command.

The beings walked towards them—the red glow from their guns illuminating the sanctuary. Killian watched in utter terror as the child-sized entities moved towards them. The shields of their helmets reflecting the light of the candles. The beings maneuvered in front of them until Killian could see his reflection in their visors.

Sweat slid down his cheekbone as his nerves trembled with fear. In the reflective visor, he could see his own terrified eyes. The screen flipped up, and Killian stared into a pair of large black almond eyes. They were inhuman, insect-like, but he could still sense malice behind them. A high-pitched clicking language sounded between the aliens in an apparent form of communication.

126

Without warning, the trio were lifted into the air, levitating above the pews as they floated through the foyer doors. The beings walked beneath them, holding their weapons locked in place. The front doors of the church opened, and lightning burst throughout the sky. In the branches of light, Killian could see the enormous, silver, disc-shaped craft floating above the rooftops, and in utter terror, they floated up towards the opening in its hull.

12: THE POWERS THAT BE

Killian's eyes peered around the inside of the craft. A metallic blue shimmer coated the walls of the angular dome. In the middle was a large, metal column, burning red and vibrating fast. He glanced down over himself, surprised to find nothing strapping him in. He wasn't even touching the seat but suspended inches above it and unable to move.

Next to him hovered Pandora, in a chair of her own, still unconscious as Andromeda on his left began to blink. He tried to open his mouth to whisper, but his lips wouldn't come apart. He tried to jerk or move in any direction possible, but it was useless.

Trapped by aliens, he thought, *what are the odds*. Despite his attempt to sneak a peek at his captors, he couldn't see around the blazing cylinder. He studied the structure of the craft.

For advanced technology, it seems rather basic, he thought, *no knobs, no blinking buttons, no fancy screens*. He glanced back over to Andromeda, who stared at him helplessly. She obviously couldn't move her mouth either, but her eyes spoke volumes: *I'm terrified*.

The gusting winds striking the sides of the ship slowed to a low hum, indicating a shift in direction and speed. The lack of g-force nausea was astonishing to Killian since he assumed they were landing. He'd flown hundreds of times around the world. One time, he'd even flown in an F-15 Eagle, and the force of the speed made him sick. This craft was nothing like either of them. To say the trip was smooth would be a grave understatement. It was flawless.

Killian watched nervously as the three beings made their way around the pillar across the metal platform. Within seconds the red rays were pointed at them again, and they were lifted from their seats. The morning sun broke in as the hull door opened. The beings levitated them through the opening and out into the world. The light outside stung his eyes. He repeatedly blinked from the dryness but being unable to rub them was pure torture.

Every thought possible raced through Killian's mind. *How long have I been unconscious? Are we on a different planet? Are we on Mars? Will we become food for some alien race?* His stomach was in knots, and he felt as if he would throw up at any moment.

His eyes slowly adjusted as he began to take in the scenery around them. They were floating above asphalt runways where military aircraft were parked in hangers. Camouflaged vehicles passed by, the drivers seemingly unconcerned with a UFO parked in their midst, and three teenagers being escorted by alien dwarves. Killian watched in amazement as groups of soldiers walked by, saluting the tiny monsters imprisoning them.

I can't believe it. We're still on Earth, and these aliens are working with our military, he thought.

The aliens guided them with weapons raised around aircraft carriers and past two F-16 Falcons. Killian stared at the jets longingly as he floated beside them. He'd always wanted to fly in one of those. When they were finally out of sight, a small building came into view. Killian grew more apprehensive the closer they got, like walking from the waiting room at the dentist's office to the actual chair for a root canal. The building was large but dwarfed in comparison to the surrounding hangers. As they approached the entrance, Killian realized the building was just the top of an elevator shaft and saw a familiar face standing outside of it.

"Dad!" his mind screamed, but his body couldn't respond. There he was, surrounded by guards and a massive bald man smoking a cigar. Killian wanted to scream, he wanted to tear apart these beings before him, but he couldn't do anything. His dad tried to run to him, but two guards hit him in the head, back, and chest with the stock of their rifles, making him fall to the ground.

The elevator door opened, and the three small beings lowered them to the ground and inside the compartment. Killian watched his dad from the corner of his eye. Blood dripped onto the concrete as Jacob wiped his lip. The elevator doors shut, and Killian stared at the panel. The elevator had ten times the number of buttons and gadgets the UFO had. The light for level six came on, and the lift began to move. Killian glanced over at Pandora, whose eyes were shedding tears onto the floor. He tried to give her a reassuring look but wasn't sure she got the message with him being unable to move his face.

When the doors opened, the aliens guided them out into a crowd of men in hazmat suits. The laser-beams that suspended them vanished, and they fell to the floor. Killian's muscles ached like never before. He shut his eyes and rubbed them fiercely. Ten or more hands grabbed him in every direction and forced him up and forward.

"Pan, Annie," he screamed, but all he heard was Pandora's screeches and Andromeda's curses, as he was whisked away.

Killian watched stone walls pass him by as he was pushed and shoved forward. Red lights flashed above a pair of doors, and he was directed inside. The men in yellow suits tossed him up on a table. Black leather straps coiled around every limb, pinning him down. One of the yellow suits reached around his neck, unfastening his necklace, and holding it up in the light.

"Where are we? Who are you? What do you want?" he hollered, but no one responded.

He watched in horror as one of the yellow suits in the corner raised a long silver blade with handles. The black visor glanced in his direction, and the scissors separated. The being in the yellow suit walked towards him, light-reflecting menacingly from the shears. The other yellow suits backed away as the one with scissors bent down.

Killian bent his head forward as far as it would go, screaming at the top of his lungs. "No, no, no!"

He heard something rip and tear away from his body as pairs of black rubber gloves poured a thick gooey substance down his legs. Cold chills spread from his head to his feet. He immediately felt nauseous and claustrophobic. Anxiety crawled over his skin, making every muscle in his body tense. He cringed as the last cut brushed his chest. Within seconds, they stripped him of all his clothing, his shell necklace, and his golden ring. The table was flipped perpendicular to the floor, so he appeared as if he were standing.

Killian glanced up, his naked reflection staring back at him from the mirrored walls. An oily film glistened over his body with an aromatic smell like frankincense and cinnamon. His head fell to his chest as exhaustion overcame him.

The suits stared at him through their black visors. Uniformly, they filed out and left him there, naked and freezing. He looked around the room. *Is this a lab?*

He thought for a moment putting all the clues together. There were soldiers and jets, aliens and UFOs, scientists and labs. Every bit of information came together in one screaming answer. He was at Area 51. This was his dad's home base, his corporate office, his employer. *Why am I stripped naked and strapped to a table? Why are they doing this to dad and me?*

He glanced around the room again. It was a typical military facility with stone grey walls, metal shelving, beakers, test tubes, and cabinets full of devices. He shivered as the freezing temperatures nipped at his naked body.

The sliding door opened, and a being walked in. It was at least ten feet tall and had the broadest shoulders Killian had ever seen with bulges protruding behind his back. They were bizarre large humps reaching up to its head. It wore a jet-black suit of armor and a large helmet. When it stepped forward, Killian's table shook. Giant gloved hands reached up and removed the helmet from its head.

Killian gasped. He'd seen beings like this before. He had the face of a man, but every feature was abnormally perfect. He had a chiseled square jaw with high cheekbones and smooth, flawless skin. Blonde hair plunged down his shoulders, braided in thick strands. The eyes were crystal clear without a trace of white in them, except for a sparkling pupil. In those eyes, his suspicions were confirmed; this was an angel.

He walked up to Killian and examined his body. He sniffed the air as if something repulsive had died in the ceiling.

"I hate pigs. They never use enough oil to get rid of the stench," the angel said. The voice was baritone, almost musical, but the words were coated with malice.

Removing a black leather gauntlet from his enormous hand, he traced one of the markings on Killian's chest. The eyes gazed into Killian's as if his very soul was under inspection.

"Leave us," his deep voice boomed.

A half a dozen of the small aliens bustled out the door. Killian was so enthralled by the angel he hadn't seen them come in following in his wake. The angel stepped back, continuing to examine his body as if his features were incorrect in some way. Killian couldn't muster up a single word.

"How did this happen?" the angel demanded.

Killian stared at the being, even though he understood his meaning completely. Still, he couldn't help but say, "What do you mean?"

"Humans, the dumbest pigs in the universe," the angel muttered. "How did these markings appear on your body? Where are the tablets?"

Killian was speechless. Should he tell him? Did he have a choice? Could he use it as a bargaining chip?

"Nowhere," he replied.

The angel's eyes changed, blazing like burning sapphires. "Who gave them to you?"

"Nobody." Even Killian was shocked at his own gall.

"Listen, pig. I can get answers by going to the other rooms and torturing the little female piglets for as long as I need to. Should I start with the dark-haired one?" There was no emotion in his voice, just absolute evil.

Killian glared at his vicious eyes, gritting his teeth, his jugular vein throbbing.

"No. I'll tell you. Just leave the twins alone," Killian said.

"Begin," the angel commanded, balling his hands into fists.

"There was a dryad queen and a box. The lid had three statues of angels on it, but they transformed into real ones. They gave me some stone tablets, and I fell asleep. When I woke up, they were gone, and these things were all over me."

The angel clenched his jaw and bent down, examining the markings in disbelief. He stepped back and paced for a moment, muttering things in a language Killian didn't understand.

The angel turned towards Killian and stuck out his hand. "Repeat this word, *Anav*."

Killian looked at the angel's hand and then back at his terrifying eyes. "Say what?"

"*A-nav, ANAV!*" the angel demanded.

Killian swallowed, hesitated, and said, "*Anav.*"

Several of the markings upon Killian's body flashed from black to gold, and a small grape appeared in the angel's hand. Anger like Killian had never seen before swept across the angel's face.

"Say the word *Anavim*," the angel demanded.

Killian breathed, staring at the purple ball in the angel's hand. "*Anavim*."

A pile of grapes flowed over the angel's hands and fell to the floor. The angel crushed the remaining grapes, splattering purple liquid everywhere, and walked out of the room.

Killian looked down at the grapes scattered over the floor. *What had happened? Was he able to create things out of thin air? Was that the gift he'd been given? But how did it work?*

His thoughts were interrupted by the yellow suits barging in again. They flipped him back ninety degrees until he was level and staring at the ceiling. The lights beamed down upon him as a syringe appeared before his eyes.

"No, wait," he said, his eyes bulging from the size of the needle. But it was too late as a stabbing pain shot through his arm plunging deep into his skin. In seconds, his eyelids shut, and he fell fast asleep.

***

Pandora shivered as the yellow suits left the room. The black straps cut into her wrists, and her voice was hoarse from screaming. The lab lights were super bright, burning her scalp where her hair parted down the middle. Her bare chest heaved up and down as she gulped large portions of air.

"Stay calm, stay calm," she told herself.

Her whole body shook from fear and cold. Sweat prickled across her skin as her anxiety tipped to boiling point.

"Slow your breathing, through your nose and out your mouth," she said aloud.

The door opened, and a massive man walked in with black leather boots and muscles bulging from every area of his body. Six aliens dressed in their white suits followed behind him. His face had high cheekbones and a square jaw, but his eyes were sparkling with a star shining in the middle. Pandora gasped as she realized what this being was.

The angel searched her body. Her skin cringed as his breath fell upon her. His fingers prodded her legs, arms, and stomach. His eyes widened as he located his item of interest. The angel tore away the bandages encircling her forearms. He raised her palms and stared at the symbols.

Pandora closed her eyes and breathed slowly, controlling her emotions, and drumming up courage she didn't know she had. Her voice returned, and her hysteria dissipated enough for her to say, "What do you want? Just tell me what you want."

The angel let her arms drop to her side and stepped back, his eyes investigating her body and contemplating something.

"Where is the manna?" the angel snapped.

"The manna. What manna?"

"The bowl of manna from the Ark. Give it to me," the angel commanded, holding out his hand.

Pandora shook with confusion.

The angel's jaw clenched. "Give me the animal."

Pandora thought he was talking to her, but the aliens shuffled around him, producing a small kitten from a crate. The angel held the kitten up. It was a calico no more than three months old. It purred at the sight of Pandora. The angel lifted his other hand and ran it over the small furry body. The kitten's big blue eyes shut as it stretched its back. The angel gripped the kitten tightly around its neck and snapped it. The kitten lay lifeless in his hand.

A cry burst out of Pandora. "You monster! Why?" she shouted.

"Silence, pig, hold this thing in your hands," the angel demanded, holding the lifeless animal before her.

She cupped her hands, and the angel allowed the kitten to fall within them. An unknown power seemed to surge from within her as a blue light hovered over the animal. The kitten rose and meowed. Pandora's mouth hung open as she stared in disbelief at the kitten gazing up at her.

The angel snatched it from her and tossed it to one of the small aliens. In seconds, the angel and the aliens were gone, and the yellow suits moved in.

***

Andromeda had never been so mad in her life. She'd punched one of the yellow suits, bitten another, and cursed more than she'd ever cursed in her whole life. Her chest heaved up and down as every muscle attempted to free her from her bonds. She'd never felt such rage. For the first time in her life, she thought she could kill someone if she got her hands on them.

The door swung open as six small aliens shuffled in, guiding a little boy no older than eight. Behind them was a massive being wearing all black. His stature made her anger dissipate, and fear crept over her at the sound of his roaring voice.

"Bring the piglet over here," he commanded.

The small aliens pushed the little boy over to Andromeda's side. The child whimpered and shivered in fear, his tiny eyes darting back and forth across the room. This only brought her anger back to the surface.

"If I get out of here, I am going to kill every single one of you," she hissed.

The aliens paid no attention to her as the man in black examined Andromeda's arm. She struggled, flexing her muscles, trying to rip the belts off. The man helped her, ripping the strands quickly from their attachment. It was then that she looked into his sparkling eyes.

The angel held her forearm in his grasp. He traced every line of the coiling tattoo from her fingers to her shoulder. Slamming her arm back against the table, he turned towards the aliens.

"Give me the piglet," he demanded.

The aliens pushed the little boy forward.

"Place your hand in hers," the angel directed.

The boy looked terrified and shook uncontrollably.

"Do it now, or I will go back into that room and kill both of your parents."

The boy looked up at the angel, tears pouring down his face.

"It's fine, I won't hurt you," Andromeda whispered, trying to comfort the boy. She held out her hand. The boy couldn't look at her, and Andromeda suddenly remembered that she was utterly naked, realizing the boy was ashamed.

The angel placed the boy's hand in Andromeda's and stepped back. Andromeda's head tensed and then relaxed. Her eyes fluttered rapidly and then stopped. The rose on her shoulder began to glow a faint red. A crimson root ran down from the flower over her arm into her hand.

Andromeda's voice rang out, and it was monotone and clear. "Bryce Brenden Lee, the bloodline of Eve, you will be a tiger among wolves when your time arrives."

Andromeda's hand fell to the table.

A black fist punched a hole in the stone wall. "Bring the piglet," the angel ordered, walking out of the sliding doors.

13: BREAKFAST AND LIES

Robert sat huddled together with his wife, Maria, and their young son, Orion. He couldn't decide if this room was an air-hanger, a banquet hall, an auditorium, or a theater, but it was massive. There was an enormous stage in the western part of the room with seats provided for everyone from the town. *If there's room for seven hundred people, maybe this is more like a civic center,* he thought.

"Honey," Maria whispered, getting his attention.

Robert glanced over at her tear-stained cheeks, blood-shot eyes, and messy black hair flowing around her olive skin. Her eyes shot a glance towards a husky man walking their way.

"It's John, see if he's found out anything," she said.

"You don't think it could be about—"

"Don't," Maria looked away.

Robert stood up and met the man halfway.

"Good morning," Robert said, shaking the man's calloused hand.

"Is it?" John replied, his bushy grey eyebrows furrowed with his wrinkled forehead.

"I think so. I mean, they just served plates of scrambled eggs and oatmeal an hour ago. I assume it's morning, but who knows at this point," Robert said with a shrug.

"Bloody Russians," John spat.

"Do you think they're Russians doing this?" Robert whispered. "You don't think these are actual aliens?"

"Nah, I'm pretty positive that disc they flew us here in had U.S.S.R. on the side of the ship. They've had these machines since the forties. Only the Russians would enslave children, dress them up like astronauts, and make them serve an entire town they just kidnapped."

John's eyes followed a pack of short white-suited beings moving through the crowd. They had a little boy in the middle of their huddle shaking as if he had just seen a ghost.

Both men shook their heads at the sight of the pale kid.

Robert cleared his throat and scratched through his salt and pepper hair. "Okay, but if it was the Russians or the Chinese, how did any of them get to New Jerusalem. Our Coast Guard, Air Force, Navy, you name it would have intercepted them? I mean practically every branch of the U.S. military would have seen a fleet that size coming in." Robert rubbed his scruffy jaw with his uncut fingernails.

"Wormholes, son, wormholes." John winked.

"You mean like wormholes out of the ground?"

John's eyes rolled, and he slapped Robert on the shoulder. "No, all that space stuff like them hydrogen-colliding, black-magic-matter, holographic portal stuff. Holes in time and everything. Like Star Trek. You never watched Star Trek?"

Robert shook his head. "Nah, I'm more of a fantasy kind of guy. Never really liked Sci-Fi."

"Well, we livin' in a Sci-Fi world, boy. You best start believing."

Robert chuckled, but John looked very serious. Robert raised his eyebrows and sighed, sticking his hands in his pockets.

"Has anyone found anything out?" Robert whispered, moving closer to John. "You know the girls are still missing, and these blasted astronaut-midgets running around here won't tell me anything."

"I know, Rob, but I haven't heard anything about the twins." John squeezed Robert's shoulder tight as their heads hung low. "Come on. We're having an old-fashioned council meeting over here, and you're invited. Just have to get Bob and Terry. The rest of the group is waiting over yonder." John began walking back through the crowd, and Robert followed glancing back at Maria, who waved him on.

Bob was a hefty man who owned the local grocery store, and Terry was a science teacher at the high school. The men shook hands, and Terry asked, "No word on Pan and Annie?"

Robert shook his head.

"These low life sons of—" but Bob's words were drowned out by a heated argument next to them. The words, "Idiot, government, lazy, traitor, and I'll kill ya," were all that could be heard.

The men dodged a chaotic sway of the crowd, like being in the center of a mosh pit, and headed to the northern wall where twenty other prominent residents of New Jerusalem waited. Robert recognized each person in the circle. A lawyer, two doctors, three principals, a few schoolteachers, and a handful of other distinguished individuals of the community were waiting.

The mayor walked into the center of the circle, his black ten-gallon hat looking absurdly out of place with his plaid pajamas. The mayor lifted the black rim for a moment, sliding his broad scarred hand through his snow-white hair. He placed the hat back on his head as his gruff voice began to sound.

"Ladies and gentlemen, I've brought you together to brainstorm about our town's current predicament. I don't have any answers myself, only questions just like the rest of you all. One of those little people scurrying around here gave me this letter at breakfast. It says an announcement will be made shortly, explaining why we were taken from our homes in the middle of the night and when we will be able to return. My question is, can we trust whoever has done this and what they have to say?"

Muttering cycled around the group, drowned out by the background noise of seven-hundred people having similar conversations in similar circles all over the arena.

Robert raised his hand first, and everyone turned towards him with anxious expressions. "Maria and I have been talking, and we think all of this may have something to do with what really happened at Crystal Cave."

This seemed to be a popular opinion, and heads nodded in agreement with Robert's assessment.

A small lady in the back who was a school librarian and a historian of sorts said, "That was the most tragic thing ever to hit New Jerusalem. Yet, the next day, something even stranger occurred. Little monsters kidnapped our town. I believe these events are unprecedented. There must be a correlation."

A tall, thin man interrupted the librarian. He was one of the lawyers from Jersey who had moved to the town a few years back. "It was all over the news, Betty. A tectonic shift in a bunch of plates under Massachusetts. It sent ripples down New England. That old cave was due to go anytime. This doesn't have anything to do with that. This is a political move, and we're caught in the controversy."

"What!" several people sneered. Others scowled and shook their heads.

The mayor chimed in, calming the group. "Thanks, Rosen, for that intelligent analysis. But this does bring up a point of interest. Who's responsible for this breach of liberties? We're surrounded by some of the most brilliant minds in Pennsylvania. So, what have you all come up with?"

A big, bald man spoke up, raising his hand, "I suppose the only ones who know the truth at this point are the Waterson brothers and the Taylors."

A few chuckles sounded around the circle.

"Them boys were always so hot-headed it would be a miracle if they aren't dead by now," the mayor said.

"Okay, then the question is who killed them and who is holding us here?" A short, stocky woman retorted in a high-pitched, demanding voice.

John raised his hand and began to speak. He started with his foremost theory on the Russians.

Robert rolled his eyes but made sure to look at the ground so no one would see him. When John finished, many others put in their opinions as well. A handful thought it was the U.S. government. A handful thought it was indeed actual aliens, and a handful agreed with John.

Just as the group seemed to be getting out of control, an elderly lady holding two black cats, stepped into the middle of the group. "I have a theory," she exclaimed.

Robert could not believe his eyes. It was Mrs. Peterson, his next-door neighbor.

"Yes, Mrs. Peterson, what is it?" the mayor asked with a drawn voice.

Her poofy blue hair bounced around as she centered herself in the circle. Rolling eyes glared at her with little enthusiasm. "Well, you all know I have visitors from time to time come to my house."

Several people nodded, and several more yawned.

"Well, this past weekend, I had some travelers stay with me. They were a brilliant duo. A father and son. The son was a brilliant young boy already in college and not even eighteen yet."

Several people sighed loudly. John went to stop her and bring her back outside the circle, but Robert motioned for him to wait.

"Anyways, they had the most peculiar sleep schedule I've ever seen. Slept all day and went out at night. The gentleman, now, what was his name again?" She thought for a few seconds and dropped one of the cats.

"Oh, that's right, Dr. Gold, Jacob Gold was his name. I never asked him what he was a doctor of, but he was interested in Crystal Cave. He even told me he was going out there the night it exploded."

Suddenly, everyone was a bit more interested in Mrs. Peterson's story, and ears perked up, especially Robert's.

"That's right," she continued, enjoying the center spotlight. "And I'll have you know they brought all kinds of species of creatures in my house. I know they did. I don't tell the visitors when they come, but the whole house is wired with cameras. I can see everything from my little ole bedroom." She said all this as if she was whispering to the librarian, but everyone heard her just fine.

"The boy had a live mermaid in a fishbowl, two furry little creatures that made a muck of my bedroom, and seven leprechauns he stashed in the basement."

Mouths hung open, and eyes stared at her in disbelief.

"Well, it's true," she said, in response to their gawking faces.

"Okay, okay, Mrs. Peterson, that's a wonderful story, and I would love to hear some more if we ever get the chance," the mayor said, ushering her back off to the side. Robert rushed over to Mrs. Peterson, grabbing her by the arm.

"Oh," she said startled. "Oh, it's you, Robby, oh dear, I'd wondered where you and Maria had gone off to. Where are the girls and little Orion?"

"Mrs. Peterson, I'm so sorry I didn't look for you sooner. Could you come over to where Maria is and tell her about this man and his son?"

"Well, certainly, dear." She bent down and picked up the cat meowing at her feet and followed Robert.

They were halfway to Maria when the intercom turned on. The high-pitched feedback caused everyone to cover their ears, except Orion. Silence spread over the arena as the crowd began to settle.

"Testing, testing, is this thing on?" a deep croaky voice asked.

A faint voice trickled out of the speaker in reply, "Yes."

"Hello, citizens of New Jerusalem, Pennsylvania. My name is General Marx of the United States Military. I do apologize for the inconvenience this has caused so many of you. Rest, assure your time here is coming to an end."

A few people clapped, and some hollered.

"That's right. The earthquake, which happened this past weekend, unfortunately was not from any ordinary fault line shifts. A nuclear bomb was discovered outside the city limits of New Jerusalem inside of Crystal Cave. The bomb was detonated, causing a rippling effect throughout the New England area."

Gasps echoed across the room with muttering spreading like wildfire.

"Unfortunately, no one will be allowed to return to their homes as the fallout of radiation has contaminated the forest and homes of your city. Our gracious government has arranged complete monetary reimbursement for the losses of property and items at five times their current value. Our agents will be along shortly, and you will all be filed into alphabetical lines to give an account of your property address and personal belongings lost in this tragedy."

The muttering grew louder.

"Furthermore, each of you will be submitted for a radiation analysis to check your contamination levels. When your name is called, please make your way to the east auditorium doors. I want to thank all of you for your complete submission and compliance with these demands."

At that moment, doors opened in several directions across the assembly hall—military men dressed in desert camouflage filed in like a stream of ants. Tables were set up and lines drawn for filing people in designated areas. Pushing and shoving started in every direction when the feedback sounded again over the speakers.

"Our first family to begin the radiation analysis is Robert and Maria Konig with their son Orion. Please make your way to the east wing doors where you will be escorted to the testing facility."

The voice of the General faded out. Robert ran to Maria as fast as he could. There would be no time for discussion now. Some people recognized Robert and moved generously out of the way while others screamed at the guards filing into the building.

144

What did they expect? Robert thought, as the civil unrest broke into a full-on riot.

When he saw Maria, her hands were moving faster than he'd ever seen as she attempted to explain everything she'd heard to Orion. He caught her gaze as she lifted her head. He ran to her and embraced them both.

"Are you okay?" he asked.

"We're fine, we're fine," Maria assured him although her hair was disheveled, and she was shaking like a leaf.

"Can you believe this utter nonsense?" Robert asked.

"I don't know, could it be possible?" Maria replied.

"No one put a nuclear bomb in Crystal Cave, Maria. That didn't happen."

"What if there were terrorists and they needed a place to hide it, and they snuck it in there without you seeing it and …" her voice trailed off as Robert shook his head.

"Didn't happen. I'm telling you; this is a lie. Do you seriously think our government would give us money because a bomb went off? Do you think they care about a small town like New Jerusalem?"

Maria shook her head, trembling.

"And we're not being taken for radiation evaluation, that's for damn sure. There's some other reason they're sectioning us off. They're separating us."

"Why? What do they want?" Maria wept, tears streaming down her cheeks. "Do you think they're looking for …?" She paused, raising her eyebrows.

"Maybe, but how they figured that out, I'll never guess. But maybe they know where the twins are. Maybe that's why we're first. We must pretend we're okay with everything. We have to pretend like we're going along with their game until we find the girls. But don't let your guard down for a second and don't tell them anything about the spear, understand?" Robert shook Maria's shoulders, gazing desperately into her eyes.

She nodded, understanding what they must do. They both reached down and grabbed hold of one of Orion's hands. They walked towards the east wing shielding Orion from the mass of chaos erupting in every direction. People were throwing tables and chairs at the soldiers who were tasing and beating citizens in return.

When they burst through the end of the crowded maze, they saw six individuals in hazmat suits, with black visors and black gloves waiting to receive them.

A soldier with a long list of names scrolled down a tablet until he found the name, Konig. "Please place your hand on the screen," he instructed.

Robert went first, laying his palm on the blue screen. The tablet identified his name, social security, address, blood type, marital status, and a list of other classifying documentation.

"Next," the yellow suit said.

Maria placed her palm across the device, followed by Orion.

"Identification protocol is now complete. Please, follow the soldiers," the yellow suit instructed.

Robert, Maria, and Orion stepped between the concrete barriers and into a long stone hallway. The six yellow suits followed on either side. Soldiers with rifles stood in front and behind, leading them down a stone hallway to a large elevator. The elevator doors parted, and the group filed inside.

Robert was amazed at the size of the elevator. There were at least fifteen people inside, and still room for twenty more. A soldier clicked the yellow button to level six, and the doors shut. When the doors reopened the place before them was nearly identical to the one they'd left. Stone walls rose twenty feet in the air with a hallway fifty-foot wide. The group filed out following the silent, armed guards.

Robert eyed the soldiers and examined the men in yellow suits. One against twelve; those were impossible odds. Robert glanced up at the lights beaming down upon them. They were like flashlights in the ceiling covering small areas down the hallway. They walked for several hundred feet in-between light and darkness like roaming through a forest where sunbeams only randomly breakthrough.

Robert's blood went cold as they turned the final corner, and the bulkiest being he'd ever seen came into view. A man, or something like a man, dressed in black armor, stood next to a pair of metal double doors.

A muscular, bald man stood beside him, smoking a cigar. Robert's hand tightened. He looked down at Orion, trembling as they approached.

The being in black stood like a sentinel looking down upon them with his onyx helmet. The armor was so shiny Robert could see his reflection in the giant's torso. The man with the cigar grinned a hideous smile. It reminded Robert of the Grinch from Christmas stories.

"Ahh, the Konigs. How I've waited for this moment," the man with the cigar said. "My name is General Marx." He blew out a cloud of tobacco, and Robert and Maria coughed. "Now, what I have to show you may come as quite a surprise. I assure you that she is in no way in any form of pain."

"Pain, she, who are you talking about? What are you talking about? Do you have our daughters in there?" Robert screamed; his hands balled into fists.

"Boys," the general said, and in seconds the soldiers had Robert pinned to the floor, and Maria and Orion separated.

"Thank you, boys," the General said. "Now, as I was saying. She is not in any pain. She can be in pain if you are unable to follow directions, but she doesn't have to be." The General let out another long cloud of smoke as he considered his next words.

"Being the gracious individual that I am, I may even allow you to see your other daughter if you behave. Do you intend to behave?" the General asked.

Robert looked over at Maria. She nodded, and he followed suit.

The General grinned again and looked down at Orion. "Now I've been told that this little boy here is deaf, is that right?"

Robert and Maria nodded.

"Well, I don't know sign language. So, you're going to explain that he's to stay with my two soldiers at all times. He is not, under any circumstances, to make any movements towards his sister, do you understand?"

They nodded, and the soldiers released Maria from their grasp. She knelt beside Orion and signed the General's instructions. The boy's eyes swelled with tears, but he nodded in understanding.

"Let me reiterate to the two of you how detrimentally important it is that you follow every detailed instruction I give you. Do not deviate a single step. This is your only warning. When Andromeda has fulfilled her purpose to her government, she will be returned to you. Should you have any questions, I may be willing to answer them if you can follow my every instruction while we are in this room. Do we have an understanding?"

They nodded, tears pouring down Maria's face. Robert thought the veins in his head and neck would explode from anger.

"Well then, let's go see your daughter."

14: GENOCIDE

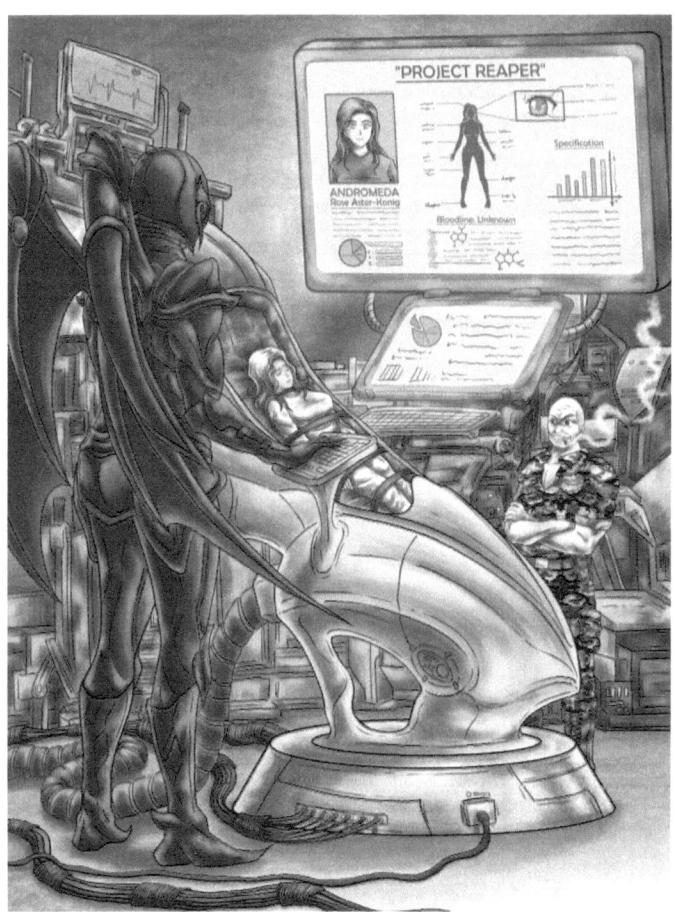

General Marx stared at the Konig family one last time, sucking in a drag of tobacco from his cigar. He turned toward the massive metal doors, linking his eyes with the facial recognition panel.

A robotic voice sounded overhead, "General Marx."

The metal doors slid apart, and the family was ushered inside by the soldiers and hazmat suits surrounding them.

Robert stared at the gigantic man in black walking before him, wondering what this massive creature could be. *Surely this thing is not human*, he thought. The giant's feet boomed with each step, shaking shelves filled with vials around the room. There was a hazy mist about the air, and the smell of flowers lingered everywhere. They walked into the center and were commanded to sit in three chrome chairs.

"Bring her," the General commanded.

Two of the yellow suits went through the mist as sounds of clanking and locks reverberated around the room. Within seconds, a female figure was guided forward in a wheelchair.

Maria gasped, and Robert tried to lunge forward towards his daughter, but the guard next to him pressed down on his shoulders, keeping him from moving. He couldn't understand it, but he had little strength to fight the guard.

"Don't worry," the General rasped. "She's in a sedative state of sorts, a special concoction from our research team. The mist above us is full of a potent narcotic. It causes drowsiness and muscle fatigue unless the antidote has been injected before exposure. I imagine you're probably beginning to feel the effects right about now."

Robert's hands tingled as he raised them to his face. They seemed unbearably heavy. He strained to lift his head and look at his daughter. There was something wrong with her. She was wearing all white scrubs, and her head hung heavy upon her chest. Her hair was no longer black like Maria's, but a conglomeration of scarlet and snow white. He tried to rub his eyes to get a better view, but when he raised his hand, he missed his face and almost fell out of his chair.

"All right, sweetheart," goaded the General. "Your family is here to see you. Let's show them what you can do? Starting with your brother."

The soldier next to Orion pressed a red oval button, and four wheels popped out of the chair legs. They rolled the small, black-haired boy beside his sister. A small table separated them. One of the yellow suits grabbed Andromeda's hand and placed it on the table palm up. Another took Orion's limp hand and placed it palm to palm with Andromeda's.

Everyone stared at the teenage girl whose heavy head rose slowly. Locks of hair dangled around her face in red and white strips. Her eyes were tightly closed as if she was in pain. Her pink lips parted, and a dead toneless voice began to sound.

"Orion Vega Konig, the bloodline of Eve, you shall be given a gift few mortals have ever received, but a cost must be paid, the cost of life for light." Andromeda's head lowered, and the yellow suits moved Orion to the left side of the room near a glass entryway.

"Lucky boy," General Marx said thickly. "Record that."

Another yellow suit stepped up with a large flat electronic device. Scrolling through names of the town's people, he landed upon "KONIG" and pressed the tab. The machine rang out, "Orion Konig, enter bloodline here." The yellow suit selected the tab for "EVE" and pressed continue.

"Do the mother next," the General ordered with a heavy cough.

The yellow suits wheeled Maria next to Andromeda, placing their hands together. Maria could barely move to see her daughter's face. Tears bloomed in her chestnut eyes as she took in the complexion of the ghostly figure next to her.

Andromeda's head rose as her words came out harsh and dead. "Maria Isabella Aster-Konig, the bloodline of Lilith, your labor of love will reduce the world to ash unless the prism is restored."

The yellow suit holding the pad selected, "LILITH" on the screen for Maria. A red light flashed, and they wheeled Maria to the right side of the room next to a grey set of doors. The man in black moved curiously next to Maria, looking down upon her like a snake ready to strike.

"Not so lucky, and the father." General Marx held out his hand, a cloud of smoke issuing from his mouth.

The soldiers wheeled Robert forward. The yellow suits placed his hand in his daughter's. He tried to move his head towards her, but he had little control over his limbs. He squeezed his daughter's hand, hoping she could understand how much he loved her.

Andromeda's head rose from her chest, strands of crimson and ivory covered her face. "Robert Wilhelm Konig, the bloodline of Eve, you must suffer greatly until the family heirloom is secured. Then you might find peace."

"Interesting," General Marx mumbled, staring at Robert.

The yellow suits pushed his chair next to Orion's on the opposite side of the room from Maria.

"Works like a charm," the General said, walking over to the tall black man.

The black helmet turned in the General's direction. The visor flipped open, and the starry gaze of the angel glared through them.

"Identify every pig from that town and notify me as soon as it's been completed. I will speak to the Supreme Commander about our predicament. All their gifts must be extracted."

"It will be done immediately," General Marx replied.

"Get this thing out of my sight." The angel seethed, closing his visor and gesturing towards Maria as if she was nothing more than a rodent.

The yellow-suits wheeled her through the double doors and down a stone hallway.

"Be quick, General, we have a whole world to reap." The angel stomped by, boots shaking the ground.

***

Killian's eyes opened, but he was still very dazed. The light of the room pressed down upon him, but he was able to shield his eyes with his hands. He looked around as his strength came back to him and sat up straight in the chair.

"How are you, son?" Jacob's voice sounded from behind him.

"Dad!" Killian tried to jump up, but his bare feet slipped on the floor.

Jacob caught him and placed him back in the chair, then sat at the table beside him.

"Take it easy, Killian, there's no rush. The drugs are starting to wear off, so take it easy for a few minutes."

Killian held his head with both hands. He felt like he was spinning. "Where am I? Where's Pan and Annie?"

Jacob winced and turned away, hoping Killian didn't see. "You're at Area 51. You know you always wanted to come here. I wish it hadn't been like this."

"Where are the twins? The ones I came here with?" Killian asked, attempting to stand again.

"Give it a minute, Killian. You won't be able to move for some time, so stop trying."

"Dad, what happened to them? Where are they?" Killian panicked and slammed his fist on the table.

"I don't know, son, I haven't seen them. They would only let me see you. Now calm down and explain to me how you got into this mess."

Killian stared at him, anger boiling inside of him. "I have to get to them. We have to get to them. We can't just sit here and do nothing."

"We can't go anywhere," Jacob yelled.

Killian was taken aback by this uncharacteristic change in his father.

Jacob ran his hands over his face and rubbed his temples. "Don't you think I've tried? We're prisoners here. There's nothing we can do about it. Now," Jacob sat for a moment, breathing heavily, "now, I've done a lot of things in the last twenty-four hours that one day I might sorely regret, but I did it so I could see you. So talk to me and tell me what this is all about." Jacob's hands writhed in his lap, balled into fists attempting to hold back a rage deep down inside of him.

Killian's hands gripped the seat, his knuckles turning white. He glared at his dad and closed his eyes. *Just breathe*, he told himself, *breathe like Annie told Pan, just breathe*. He opened his eyes, but his anger was too much.

"What did I do to get us into this, is that what you're saying? Is that what you want to know?" Killian asked, his hands trembling.

Jacob looked at him, confused. "I don't know who or what got us into this, but I haven't seen or spoken to you in almost a week. I need to know what has happened to you."

Killian closed his eyes again, gritting his teeth. "I'll tell you what happened. You sent me to find those damn pixies, and I ran into the twins, who followed me out into the woods. Then a tornado almost blew us to Kansas. A Dryad Queen took us into her kingdom. Then some angels popped off a box, and we woke up three days later to this." Killian stuck his arms out and pulled up the white sleeves of the scrubs.

Jacob peered over at the familiar markings. "Enochian, but how?"

Killian continued his rant, ignoring his dad. "We barely made it back to New Jerusalem. Then what do we find when we get there? A ghost town." Killian hit the table with his fist, feeling his strength returning full force. "No, wait, I take that back. Not a ghost town. You know why? Because there were minotaurs the size of bears roaming the streets trying to capture us. We made it out of there only to be hunted down by aliens the next day and end up here."

Killian reached up to touch the rosary his mom had given him, but it was gone.

"And they took mom's necklace," he screamed.

Killian's anger flared like never before, and he stood up, hobbled over to the door, and banged on it as hard as he could.

Jacob watched him, and his anger subsided completely. His poor son had been through so much in just one week, but he had survived it all. He had outsmarted military agents and aliens for days. Pride swelled up inside of Jacob, and he stood to his feet with tears in his eyes.

"I'm so proud of you, son," he said.

Killian turned his head, the rage in his eyes subsided. He stopped banging on the door and stared at his dad.

"I've never been so proud of you in my whole life," Jacob said. "Your brilliant mind, your tenacity, your quick wit, your survival instinct. You're just like your mother."

At the mention of his mother, Killian's anger broke, and he swelled with tears.

Jacob opened his arms, and Killian fell into them. He sobbed until every ounce of emotion was poured out.

"I'm sorry, Dad. I didn't know what to do. I had the twins. I had to take care of them. They depended on me to help them find their families, and I got us caught. Now, where are they? What are they going through? It's all my fault."

"No, son, no. You did an amazing job of protecting them. You rescued those girls, and you dodged military soldiers for days. No one could ask any more out of you than that." Jacob squeezed his son's shoulders, looking him straight in the eyes.

"I'm proud of you. So proud of you, and those girls' parents would be proud of you, too."

Killian nodded and put his hands over his eyes. "I'm sorry, I'm feeling a little woozy."

"Sit down, sit down. The drugs have to fully work their way out of your system before you do too much." Jacob placed Killian back in the chair and sat down himself.

Killian breathed in and out, hoping his head would stop spinning. "What happened to you? What happened to the town?"

Jacob rubbed the stubble of his jaw, wondering where to begin. "Well, when you hadn't returned after a few hours, I went out looking for you, but nothing came up on the tracker. I had no idea which way you'd gone. Then these bells rang in the sky. I've never experienced anything like it in my life. An hour later, maybe less, a silver disc hung over Mrs. Peterson's house. Then another and another until a whole fleet of UFO's were speckled across the city."

Jacob leaned forward, lowering his voice. Killian urged him on with his eyes.

"I had orders to bring all the government-issued equipment back to base. There was a planetary disturbance happening, and New Jerusalem, Pennsylvania, was one of the hot spots. I figured it had something to do with Amazarak, so I didn't question it at the time. I thought they were getting the town out to save everyone from that demon's wrath, but now …."

Jacob stared at his son and then reached over, grabbing one of his arms. He pulled up the sleeves, and his fingers traced the runes on his skin. He sighed and looked at Killian, shaking his head.

"Whatever happened to the three of you is extremely important to the Black Knight."

"The Black Knight? You mean that bastard angel with aliens following him around like little puppies?"

"Shhh," Jacob hissed. "Yes, that's what everyone calls him here. Few have ever seen him, but since the bells rang, he's been more, hands-on, shall we say."

"But what does he have to do with all of this?" Killian asked, leaning into his dad.

"I don't completely know," Jacob said, rubbing his temples. "He wants something. He wants something you and the girls have. Something to do with this." Jacob pointed at the letters on Killian's arms.

"I can't give him this," Killian exclaimed, pulling his arms away, horrified. "This is inside of me, whatever it is. I can't give it away."

Jacob shook his head. "Don't you think I know that? Which means they're going to try to figure out some way to use you so they can use it. And not just you either. Whatever the girls have is important, too. I don't know what to do." Jacob wrung his hands in his lap then nervously tapped the table with his fingers.

"Dad." Killian sat up. "Do you know any words in Enochian?"

Jacob looked at him, surprised. "No, why?"

"I think," Killian looked down at his arms, rubbing the tattooed symbols, "I think these things respond to words in Enochian. The Black Knight came in and had me say something. Oh, God, what was it?" Killian put his hand to his head, trying to think.

"What did it sound like?" Jacob asked.

"Ana, Enan, Anar, Ananim, no, that's not it. It's those drugs. I can't remember."

"Well, what happened when you said it?"

"A grape fell into his hand and then a whole pile of grapes."

"Grapes?" Jacob questioned.

"Yeah, like round purple grapes, the fruit, you eat them," Killian said with raised eyebrows.

"Yeah, I get it, then what happened?"

"Well, then he was super pissed and stormed out of the room, and those bastards in yellow suits came in and stuck a needle in me."

Jacob sat back, mumbling to himself. "How does that fit with any of this?"

Killian looked mystified. "I don't know?"

Jacob looked at Killian, his eyes wavering, his mouth opening then closing again.

"What, Dad? Spit it out."

"Look, I don't know where Andromeda or Pandora are, but I've heard some things."

Killian stared at his dad, his eyes strained and impatient. "Well …"

Jacob swallowed and took a deep breath. "Andromeda, or Annie, as you're calling her, has a gift that can tell a person's bloodline and their future."

Killian shook his head. "She was given a stick with some flowers on it, and then it melted into her arm like this did to me. I highly doubt a stick is going to tell the future. I mean, who would ever come up with that?"

Jacob looked around the room. He knew they were watching them, and at any moment they could snatch Killian from his arms. There was a secret, and if Killian needed to know anything, it was this. Jacob motioned for him to move closer. They leaned their heads together as Jacob began to whisper.

"Listen, years ago, and I mean a long time ago before your mom disappeared. I attended a meeting in Washington. The Black Knight was there. He had a proposition for the world leaders to solve World Hunger, Cancer, Alzheimer's, Diabetes, Overpopulation, Animal Extinction, Global Warming, you name it."

"Yeah, and what was that?" Killian asked.

Jacob licked his lips, appearing nervous, even to mention the thought. "It was like Adolph Hitler all over again except on a much larger scale."

"What does Hitler have to do with anything?" Killian asked with a rising voice.

"Shhh, not Hitler, but Hitler's idea, and not his idea alone, but maniacs throughout centuries of human history."

"So the Black Knight wants to eradicate the Jewish people?" Killian said, astounded.

"Not the Jewish people. Hitler blamed all the world's problems on the Jews, but the Black Knight blames a different group. It's not just one ethnicity, either. It's something in the blood, something about ancestry."

Killian shook his head, baffled by what his dad was saying.

"There's a bloodline," Jacob continued. "A cursed bloodline, the Black Knight says, that goes back to the creation of man. He said if we eradicate that bloodline, then all diseases will cease, and balance will be brought back to the world. It's like a virus in the genome of man."

"And he wanted the United Nations to find this bloodline or something?" Killian asked, completely bewildered.

"No, he wanted us to put our resources together to find a tool he needed from an ancient artifact."

"What kind of tool?" Killian asked.

"A staff from the Ark of the Covenant. The ancient Jewish resting place for God himself in the Holy of Holies."

Jacob and Killian stared at each other for a few moments as all these words sunk in.

"Of course, the union denied his proposals and banished him from ever speaking again in Washington. But Mark and I knew not every nation would deny him access for long. Look at Germany, Spain, Rome, Egypt. Human history is chock-full of dictators wanting world domination, so it's always just a matter of time before one of them bites."

"The ark of the covenant." Killian sat back, connecting the dots.

Jacob nodded.

"So one of us has the tool to ..." Killian hesitated.

"To pinpoint the cursed bloodline and eradicate it." Jacob finished. "The Black Knight wants a genocide."

Suddenly, shouting spread outside the room. Gunshots echoed down the hallway, accompanied by a cluster of yells and screams. Killian glanced at his dad. A deafening bang hit the white door. Then a red glow encircled the handle. It fell to the ground with a clang, and the door opened.

15: THE GREAT ESCAPE

Killian watched as the large white door fell to the ground with a bang.

"Feck, that was loud," a voice said.

Killian moved over and peered outside. Six leprechauns stared at him with massive smiles.

"How—" Killian muttered as two black and white furballs tackled his face in the blink of an eye.

Killian grabbed the furry creatures and squeezed them. They screamed at the force of his hug as the others laughed. He held the two brownies in front of him, staring at their cotton-candy pink eyes.

"You guys snuck on board that UFO, didn't you, you little devils?" Killian rustled their hair with his fingers.

The brownies giggled, popping in and out of visibility so fast Killian could hardly keep up with their shadows.

"I imagine you guys got here a more vicious way?" Killian asked, looking at the state of the leprechauns. They were bruised, cut, and had bandages around different appendages.

"Not without a battle, ain't that right, boys," Jacob chimed in, stepping beside Killian. "Marx took me to the lab where you were. You nearly destroyed everything in that room. I sure am proud of you saucy little ankle-biters."

Jacob and Killian bent down as the leprechauns huddled around them, hugging each other, and patting each other on the back.

"All right, lads, we best be heading out. There's trouble coming like you wouldn't believe," Murphy said, staring ominously down the hallway.

Sirens sounded in every direction. Red lights flashed down the corridor.

"We can leave as soon as we find Pan and Annie. Can you guys find them?" Killian asked, looking at the brownies. They nodded, sniffing the air, then took off out the doorway.

The leprechauns followed, pushing and shoving each other. Killian walked into the hall, covering his ears, trying to adjust to the piercing screech of the alarm. Red lights rotated on the ceiling, casting a bloody ambiance down the hall.

Killian and Jacob bent down, picking up AK47s and multiple handguns from the deceased soldiers surrounding their door. Killian looked away from their pale faces as crimson blood pooled around the bodies. He tiptoed around the puddles, nearly gagging at the smell of copper. They quickly exchanged magazines and reloaded the pistols.

"9mm Baby Eagles, not much different than the Smith and Wesson you taught me on," Killian said, tucking one in the back of his white pants.

160

"Yeah, but it's been a while since I shot an assault rifle. Let's hope we don't have to," Jacob replied, clutching his AK47.

"This way lads, they're way ahead of us," Cabbage bellowed, turning a corner up ahead.

Jacob and Killian sprinted towards the group. They ran down five separate stone hallways turning corner after corner catching up slowly to the 'chauns. The next intersection bloomed with red light as a pack of white-suited aliens came into view. Lasers from the leprechauns pierced their bodies before they ever had a chance to react. Seven aliens fell motionless to the ground.

Killian watched as black clouds floated out of the bodies. The clouds took form and shape, like a shadow with eyes. Killian pointed his assault rifle at the obscurity. The shadows moved by him as quick as the wind, sending a cold chill running over his body as they passed. He turned down the hallway to follow them, but they were gone.

He stepped over several small bodies without a drop of pity in his eyes. He'd suspected these beings were evil, and that encounter just put the nail in the coffin. He glared down at the floor, looking directly into the dead-black-almond-shaped eyes of the aliens. He kicked one of the familiar guns that had held him and the twins in a state of immobility. The memory of the girls contorted in the red rays of the alien weaponry boiled his blood.

"This doorway, hurry," Freckles shouted.

Jacob and Killian sprinted again, jumping over another busted-down door. Killian's eyes surveyed the room. It was set up exactly like his, blistering white and bare. A metal table and a set of chairs sat in the middle. That's when he spotted the platinum blonde hair of Pandora.

His heart dropped into his stomach as tears ran down her tired face and onto the same white scrubs Killian wore. He ran to her watching the leprechauns working furiously to burn off the straps, binding her to the large metal chair. The last belt unraveled around her ankle, and she stood up wobbling. Killian caught her, supporting her weight.

He tucked her hair behind her ear and gazed at her sapphire eyes. Pandora threw her arms around him, and he squeezed her as tight as he could, lifting her a foot off the ground. He held her helpless in his arms as he clutched onto her back, inhaling the scent of frankincense and cinnamon flowing from her body. He slowly let her feet touch the ground, but she did not back away out of his embrace.

"I can't believe you found me," she said. Immediately, Duncan and Crocker popped onto her shoulder, rubbing their bodies against her cheeks.

"Technically, they found you," Killian said, ruffling Duncan's white hair.

The brownies purred, and Pandora giggled as dimples formed on her cheeks. "Thank you, guys, so much," she said, squeezing them tightly.

Killian turned and noticed his dad staring at him with a massive smile on his face. Jacob winked, and Killian felt himself blush.

"Oh, Pan, this is my dad," Killian said as Jacob walked over to her.

"Oh," Pandora said, straightening her hair.

Jacob reached out his hand and shook Pandora's. "It's a pleasure to meet you. Now, let's go find your sister."

"Annie!" Pan shrieked, "Yes, let's go."

Crocker flew through the air, followed by Duncan. The leprechauns followed as Killian, Pandora, and Jacob jumped through the doorway. The brownies popped in and out of visibility so fast it was difficult to keep up. The stone hallways seemed never-ending as the company rounded several corners. Two military guards stood around the next bend. Lil McMan and Cornedbeef nailed them with yellow and red beams of light, sending them falling to the ground.

Killian ran by the smoldering corpses, holding Pandora's hand as she gagged from the smell of burnt flesh. They turned two more corners and stared down a long dark hallway illuminated by one flashing red siren in the center. The shrieking alarm pulsated in Killian's ears as he strained to see down the hall.

"Give us some light," Killian said, and a burst of colors flowed down the corridor from the leprechauns' eyes.

The Black Knight stood at the end of the corridor, deflecting the beams off his armor. Killian watched the brownies pop into the room directly under the flashing red light. He held up his AK47, aiming it toward the menacing angel, but his dad was the first to shoot, letting a barrage of bullets spray towards the Black Knight. The bullets bounced off the angel's armor-like bb's on glass with sounds of "Ping, ping, ping," echoing down the hall.

"That must be some armor," Pandora said.

Killian nodded, waiting for the next play to unfold.

The Black Knight darted towards the room. His booming steps reverberated over the sound of the sirens. The leprechauns took off as well with Killian, Pandora, and Jacob in the rear. A fiery array of beams twisted in the air like a contorted rainbow set ablaze, but the Knight's armor continued to deflect them. The angel cleared the entrance of the doorway first, knocking down the metal doors with one hammer of his fist.

Killian and the others made it around the door seconds later, but too late. The Black Knight held Andromeda by the throat. She hung in his grip, lifeless as her hair dangled down around her face in strands of red and white. Her white scrubs were flashing pink in the red strobe light of the alarm.

"Who is that?" Pandora shrieked. "Is that Annie?"

Killian stared at the motionless body, then glared at the Black Knight. "What have you done to her?" he shouted.

The ebony visor retracted, and the once starry stare of the angel's eyes had transformed into a raging red inferno. The leprechauns stepped back, grabbing the pant legs of Killian and Jacob. Pandora shuddered and grabbed Killian's elbow. Killian focused the AK47 on the angel's face.

"A whole herd of pigs, here to claim something that doesn't belong to them," the Black Knight growled.

Two balls of fur popped in and out of the air like fireworks moving across the room. Crocker and Duncan landed in between the Black Knight and the group, their socks flailing like little vipers trying to get the angel's attention. Killian stared at them, completely baffled at what they were doing.

The brownies glanced back at Killian. Pink tears filled their eyes. They slowly removed the socks from each one of their paws and turned towards one another. Eight socks littered the floor as their baby claws snapped and twitched. They moved closer together, and violet sparks flew out from their nails touching.

Pandora gasped as Killian watched in utter disbelief.

The brownies' front paws entwined together as their arms twisted and contorted wildly. The bottom claws interlocked, writhing together like an interchanging clockwork. A monstrous growl bellowed from the balls of fur. Within seconds the black and white hairball had grown and expanded into a massive entity with sparks of electricity flying across the room.

Killian watched in terror and amazement as Duncan and Crocker transformed into a singular, massive monster. Muscles protruded from every crevice of their body. The hands and feet were as large as tree trunks with claws like meat hooks. The small golden horns had grown three feet in length, resembling the antlers of a ram. The brownies stood up, revealing their full height. Together they were as large as a polar bear.

Jacob and Killian's mouths fell open. Pandora couldn't move. The leprechauns cheered in amazement.

"Jeanie-Mac," Murphy shouted.

"Yeah, not so smashing big now, are you, Mr. Red Eyes?" Lil McMan taunted.

"What in the bollocks of St. Patrick?" Clover gasped.

"Pan them out, lads, pan them out," Cornedbeef said, smashing his fists together.

"Give 'em a knuckle supper," screamed Freckles.

A roar sounded from the brownies shattering the glass throughout the room. The angel dropped Andromeda, who thudded to the floor. The brownies smashed their arms into the flooring between them, and the angel, shattering the concrete. The force of the blow sent Andromeda flying at the leprechauns.

Jacob dove to catch her, but her head hit the ground.

The Black Knight's humped shoulders burst away from his back to reveal gigantic silver wings. "She's mine," he screamed.

The brownies roared, in return, the sound echoing through the room. They looked back at Killian with large pink eyes full of rage. Killian nodded as the brownies lunged forward, attacking the angel.

Pandora tried to run to her sister, but Killian grabbed her hand. "We have to go now! This is our only chance."

Jacob scooped up Andromeda, her lifeless form sallow and heavy. The leprechauns bolted into the hallway as the rest followed.

"Is she alive?" Pandora shouted.

Jacob looked down at the sunken cheeks and saw the slightest breath of air being sucked in.

"Yes, she's alive, but we got to get her out of here."

"Where do we go, Dad?" Killian yelled.

"Uh," Jacob breathed heavily, thinking, running, trying to figure out what to do. "I think we need to get to an elevator or a staircase."

"Yeah, and go where?" Killian hollered over the sirens.

"Um . . . There are trains down below on the twentieth floor."

"Okay, trains, sure," Killian said as they passed the alien bodies that the leprechauns had fried.

"Wow, that smells rank for sure," Freckles yelled, jumping over a headless body.

The sirens blared louder and louder as the elevator shaft came into view.

"Dad, there's no way we're going to make it down there." Killian huffed.

"What are you talking about?" Jacob panted.

"There's no way. That elevator is going to be shut off. Even if it does work, the central command will be able to control it. We'll end up surrounded by soldiers either way."

"Okay, what's your plan?" Jacob asked, straining every muscle to run as Andromeda's head bobbled with his movement.

"We need to split up. We need a diversion," Killian mumbled. He looked down at the leprechauns' red-headed tops bouncing all over the place.

"Lads, I'm going to have to ask too much of you as always," Killian said.

"We're here to serve, laddie," Murphy responded.

"Whatever you need," Lil McMan gulped.

"I need you to destroy this level. I'll take Clover and Freckles with me. You four stay here and destroy everything near the elevator shaft," Killian ordered.

"Aye, we can do that," Cabbage and Cornedbeef shouted.

165

"Good, kill anything that comes down here and —"

Just then, the doors to the elevator opened, and thirty soldiers ran out. Lasers from all six of the leprechauns spread out instantly. Killian and Pandora dove into a nearby room as gunfire sprayed past.

Shouting echoed down the hall. Killian could hear Murphy giving out orders. "Two to the left, get the one inside, die, die, die."

Finally, the screams and gunshots ceased, and everything grew quiet. Killian stood up and peered around the doorway down the hall. The leprechauns were standing in the foyer and gave him a thumbs up that the coast was clear. He lifted Pandora to her feet, and they headed back down the hall.

Jacob crept out of another room carrying Andromeda. Her head hung low over his arm, and Pandora reached out, brushing the cold, wet hair off her forehead.

"I'm here, Annie. We're going to get you out of here. I promise."

They ran down the last piece of the corridor toward the opening to the elevators.

"Okay, so about this plan …." Jacob said.

"Yeah?" Killian asked.

"I don't think that's going to work, either."

"Well, I don't know what else to do. This is Area 51, not a department store," Killian yelled.

They crossed out of the hallway and into the domed foyer in front of the elevators. Killian stared at the doors attempting to go up. They were jammed from a laser that had sawed it in two. It hung in the doorway, blocking the elevator from moving.

"What if we broke the elevator?' Pandora asked.

Killian and Jacob turned to look at her. Her silvery voice sounded strange in the war-torn foyer with dead bodies everywhere.

"Why don't we destroy the cable to the elevator and have it drop to the bottom floor," Pandora said. "They'll never see that coming. Then they can't take the elevator here."

"Okay, but then they'll know we have to take the stairs," Killian glanced over at the flashing red exit sign. He shook his head. "We're trapped either way. What if we don't destroy the elevator until we're close to the bottom?"

"Do you mean leave someone here to cut the cable?" Jacob asked.

"Yeah, leave the lads. We take Clover and Freckles. Anyone coming from the top will have to deal with the rest of them, and they can still work on destroying this place. Anyone coming up from downstairs, we'll have to deal with them. Then in five minutes, you lads blast this elevator shaft and send it hurling down to the bottom."

Pandora looked at Killian and squeezed his hand, reassuring him in his decision.

Jacob shook his head. "I don't know, but we got to do something fast."

"Guys, you understand what to do, right?" Killian asked.

The leprechauns nodded, and Murphy began directing his party in strategic locations.

Killian turned towards the staircase. "Let's go."

They shoved the door open and filed into the stairwell. It wasn't a typical stairwell. The stairs were three times the size of a standard staircase with a ramp and massive metal rails. Killian and Pandora looked over the side. They could hear footsteps and chatter, but it seemed very far below.

"We only have five minutes to get down fourteen flights of stairs. Let's go," Jacob said, heaving Andromeda up onto his shoulder.

They made it down two flights, then four, and then ten. A door flew open above them, and they heard a rush of soldiers piling out and climbing to the upper levels. They stayed quiet, pinned up against the walls until the troop was out of earshot. They continued their way down to the twentieth floor.

"How long until the—" Pandora began, but a sound like an explosion echoed through the stairwell.

"That would be the elevator," Killian confirmed. "Now, what do we do?"

"I've been thinking," a small voice said, and Killian looked over to Freckles.

"I say me and Clover bust through these doors and kill every last one of them blood-sucking soldiers for Squeezie." Freckles straightened her bonnet.

"Wait a minute. Those gigantic bull-thingies killed Squeezie?" Clover corrected.

"Some people say shamrocks, and some people say clovers. I say, they're all working together, so let's kill them all." Freckles moved towards the door.

"Let's do it!" Clover grabbed Freckles' arm and ran through the door.

Killian stood half-dazed as a banter of yells and gunshots rang out on the other side of the wall. Within a minute, silence crept over the stairwell, and the door flung back open. Clover stood there, tears falling to the ground.

"Where's Freckles?" Killian asked.

Clover cried and ran to Killian's leg, holding on for dear life.

Pandora recognized that cry. It was the same ear-piercing heart-shattering cry she'd let out when Squeezie died. It was the same scream Pandora had let out when the Black Knight killed that kitten.

"Show me where she is," Pandora said.

Killian walked through the doorway as Clover pointed towards the busted elevator shaft. Rubble was piled in every direction and on a small slab of concrete laid Freckles.

Pandora walked over to her, stepping over several soldiers as she did. She turned the body over, and her little yellow dress was stained with blood.

"It's okay. It's going to be okay," Killian's voice broke as he hugged Clover.

Pandora took her hands and gazed at the infinity symbols etched into her palms. She moved them toward Freckles, and they began to glow blue as she moved them closer and closer to the lifeless body. She placed them over Freckles' wounds, and the bloodstains dissipated. Within seconds Freckles was coughing and sitting up.

"How in the ...." Killian mumbled as he stared at Pandora.

"That's her gift," Jacob said, wincing in pain from the weight of Andromeda.

Clover jumped into Pandora's arms, kissing her all over her face.

"What happened?" Freckles asked, rubbing her head.

"You got shot. You were dead. She brought you back to life." Clover pointed at Pandora.

"Oh," Freckles said.

"Oh?" Clover yelled and slapped Freckles in the back of the head. "What do you mean, 'Oh'?"

Freckles didn't respond but looked lackadaisical at Pandora.

"Guys, we have to get on a train and get out of here before more soldiers get down here," Jacob said.

"You guys find the others and help them. One day we'll see you again," Killian bent down and hugged Clover and Freckles kissing them on the cheeks. He stood up and grabbed Pandora's hand, lifting her to her feet. "Hey, are you okay?"

Pandora stared at Freckles, who was staring right back. "Yes-yes, let's leave."

Killian and Pandora caught up to Jacob, who maneuvered Andromeda over his arms again.

"Which train do we take?" Killian asked.

They examined the three trains. Each one was painted a bright silver with a distinctive line distinguishing one from another. There was a blue train, a red train, and a black train. Killian looked around for any identification of where these things could go.

"Just pick one, Killian. We gotta leave, and we gotta leave now," Jacob urged.

Killian glanced over at Pandora, and the blue sparkle of her eyes told him what he should do, but, for a moment, he hesitated.

"What is it?" Pandora asked, her eyebrows raised in curiosity.

Killian stared at her deep blue eyes and for the first time, noticed gold freckles within them.

He smiled and said, "Let's take the blue one."

Pandora smiled at him and blushed.

"Fine, I'll put Andromeda in the blue train. You two run to the other trains and get them started," Jacob said.

"What, I don't know how to start a train," Killian said.

"These are silver-bullets. Press the green button, and the train does the rest. Just get out before it starts moving," Jacob said, jogging to the blue train.

Pandora ran to the red train as Killian ran to the black.

Killian slid open the silver door to the locomotive. His dad was right. The control panel was one long flat metal podium with one button in the middle. Killian pressed it, and an automated voice sounded in the compartment.

"Thirty seconds until departure."

The metal door beside him slid shut. He ran to it as the engines fired up, vibrating the cabin. A red lever stuck out in the middle reading "Manual Exit." He pulled down on the bar, and the door opened. He slid through it and jumped away from the train. The silver door slid shut, and the train began to move.

Pandora ran up beside him. "Piece of cake," she said.

"Oh yeah, no problem at all," Killian replied, rubbing the back of his neck.

Together, they ran toward the blue train. Jacob motioned for them to hurry as he held the door ajar. Smoke scurried out from the exhaust pipes running along the railroad. Pandora jumped in the front compartment as Killian followed. The train moved forward as they sucked in gulps of air.

"Simple, right?" Jacob asked.

They nodded.

"Where are we going?" Killian asked.

"These trains are designated for interplanetary visitors as I understand it. One goes to Washington D.C., one to Anchorage, Alaska, and one to Yucatan, Mexico," Jacob explained.

"Which one is this?" Pandora asked, sitting beside her sister, who Jacob had laid on a black leather bench.

Jacob turned around and scratched his chin, "I don't know."

16: THE SILVER BULLET

Killian peered out into the darkness ahead, his hands resting on the control panel. The headlights of the train were dim, and all he could see was that they were in a rocky cave underground. The speedometer had peaked at two hundred miles an hour, but to where was the question.

He left the window and sat beside Pandora on the black leather bench. He watched her every movement as she gently arranged the hair on Andromeda's head strand by strand. The swirls of snow and fire streaming from her sister's crown were a beautiful contrast, but Andromeda's eyes remained shut, and her breathing labored.

"Why do you think … I mean … how do you think this happened?" Pandora asked.

Killian studied Pandora's face: the round ivory cheeks, the platinum blonde hair spiraling around her, a tiny chin and luscious pink lips. He heard her question but couldn't seem to focus on it at present.

Pandora didn't press him for an answer but wiped the sweat from Andromeda's forehead.

Jacob interrupted the tranquil silence, laying the assault rifle on the floor, and cocking the pistol in his hand. "I'm going to search the train and see if there's any food. I'm sure we all need to eat. I haven't eaten in days."

Killian heard the voice as if it were far away. He glanced up just in time to say, "Oh, Dad, I'll go with you."

Jacob turned briefly, holding the door open. The wind howled outside the metal walls. "No, you should stay here in case she wakes." Jacob winked.

Killian didn't argue and returned his attention to Pandora. She laid one hand on her sister's forehead, and the other stretched out to meet his. She didn' look up as he took her hand.

Her touch sent chills flowing over his body. His forefinger traced the veins running from her knuckles to her wrist. Her skin was as soft as silk, and he gently glided his fingers over the tiny bones connecting her fingers. He held her hand as if it was the most precious object on Earth, as though it could shatter if he let go.

He turned her hand over and studied her palm. He placed his finger upon the flames wrapping around the infinity symbol. *These hands can bring the dead back to life*, he thought. *What would that change? What would she do with such a gift with such power? She will be seen as a god. People all over the Earth will flock to her. They'll beg for a touch from her hand to save their loved ones. It'll never end. The need for her will be too great a burden for her to bear. She can't let people know what she can do, not yet?*

Andromeda coughed, and her eyes flew open. She shot up out of Pandora's lap, looking around frantically. Her sudden movements petrified Killian and Pandora.

"Where am I? What's going on? Why can't I see anything?"

Pandora shot a glance at Killian, fear filling her eyes.

"We're here, Annie, we're right here," Pandora said, reaching out to grasp Andromeda's hand.

Andromeda pulled back at the touch of Pandora's fingertips. "No. Don't touch me," she yelled frantically.

"Annie, it's okay," Killian said, "It's just us. We're safe. We escaped the military base. We're on a train heading far away from there."

Andromeda's head moved around as if she couldn't quite gauge who was speaking and where. She looked up to the ceiling and side to side, rubbing her eyes viciously.

"Why can't I see? Why can't I see," She screamed in shock.

Tears rippled down Pandora's cheeks as she watched her sister struggle. Killian placed his hand on Andromeda's back. Andromeda nearly punched him in the face as she writhed with fear. Pandora scooted beside her sister, wrapping her arms around her.

"Annie, breathe like you've always told me, breathe and let the fear and the anxiety wash over you and fade away. Let it be a breeze you can feel, flowing over you and passing by. We're right here beside you. Nothing can harm you here."

Andromeda breathed in and out, cupping her face with her hands.

"That's it. We're here for you. We're not going anywhere. No one is going to separate us again." Pandora sniffled, fighting back the tears that so easily poured from her heart.

They rocked back and forth with her holding her tighter and tighter as Andromeda's struggle finally ceased. She relaxed in her arms as tears poured down her olive cheeks. She cupped her hands over her face and cried until her white scrubs were spotted with tears.

"What happened? What's happened to me? What's happened to us?" Andromeda whispered.

Killian glanced over at Pandora, unsure of what to say.

He swallowed, and his voice cracked as he spoke. "The leprechauns and the brownies saved us. Duncan and Crocker snuck onto the UFO when we were captured. Somehow, they found the 'chauns and rescued my dad and me. Then we found the two of you and . . ." Killian looked at Pandora, uncertain of how much more to say.

"They saved us, Annie. Now, we're on this train far away from those bad men and that angel."

A tremor ran through Andromeda at the mention of the Black Knight. "Don't mention that thing," she snapped, shaking with fear.

"Okay, Annie, anything you need. We're right here." Pandora ran her hand through her sister's hair, glancing at Killian, who shook his head.

The door beside them slid back, and everyone jumped.

"Is everything okay, what's happening?" Jacob walked into the cabin.

"Annie, woke up, but . . ." Killian looked over at Pandora.

"But . . ." Pandora whimpered.

"But, I can't see anything," Andromeda cried.

Jacob laid his pistols down by the rifles and scratched his chin. He moved towards Andromeda, bending down in front of her.

"Andromeda, my name is Jacob Gold. I'm Killian's father. I want to look at your eyes if that's okay?"

Andromeda nodded and lifted her head toward the voice, opening her eyelids.

Jacob put his hands to his mouth, stifling a gasp. He examined her eyes and motioned for Killian to look. Killian leaned forward and couldn't help but gasp. Andromeda's iris had changed from emerald to blazing gold.

"Pan, look at this," Killian gulped.

"What, what is it?" Andromeda asked.

Pandora stood up to look at her sister thoroughly in the face. "Annie, your eyes . . . your eyes are gold."

"They're what?" Andromeda choked.

173

"They're gold, as gold as the sun. They're stunning," Pandora said.

"Yeah, well, I don't care how stunning they are if I can't use them," Andromeda growled.

"Andromeda, are you feeling any discomfort in your eyes? Any pressure around here?" Jacob touched her forehead and rubbed her temples with his thumbs.

"No, no, it all hurts here." Andromeda pointed towards the back of her head.

"That's interesting," Jacob said.

"What, Dad, what is it?"

"Well, as you know, you don't see with your eyes. You use—"

"The occipital lobe through the optic nerve," Killian finished. "Yeah and—"

"Well, that's right here." Jacob ran his fingers along the back of Andromeda's skull. "Is this where the pressure is?"

"Yes," Andromeda squealed.

"Hmmm. There's a massive knot back here. She may have a severe concussion from when her head hit the floor."

Pandora reached around, feeling the golf-ball-size knot on the back of Andromeda's head. She shuttered at the touch of the mass.

"Oh, Annie," Pandora said.

"What are you saying? That this is temporary?" Andromeda asked. The hopeful plea in her voice could not be missed.

"It's possible. Although, I've never heard of a person's eyes changing colors from a concussion. I don't know what he did to you, but the eye itself seems normal. I'd say once this swelling goes down, it's likely that your vision will return, but that's just a guess."

"Well, that's something," Andromeda sighed, relaxing on the bench. "Thank you."

"The good news is that I found some food and there's a freezer so we could put some ice on that knot. Do you guys feel like eating?"

A simultaneous, "Yes," was shouted from the trio.

"Come on, Annie, I'll help you up," Jacob said.

"Please, everyone, please do not touch my hands," Andromeda begged, trembling.

"Okay, Annie, no one is going to touch your hands," Pandora assured her. "Just wrap your arm in mine so I can lead you around."

Andromeda followed Pandora's instructions, and they walked through the exit door.

Pandora gazed around as they entered the next car. The floor was made of a swirling coffee-and-almond-colored marble. In the center was a massive bronze chandelier with three tiers, and along the sides of the car were purple clothed tables. The chairs were ornate with large exaggerated wooden carvings and velvet seating.

"I think we should eat in here," Killian suggested.

Pandora nodded, describing the room to Andromeda as they walked.

"Wish I could see it," Andromeda said as Pandora guided her around the full-size bar running through the center of the car.

"What's that smell?" Pandora asked, tilting her head toward the ceiling.

"I don't know, what do you smell?" Andromeda asked.

"I smell all kinds of things like caramel apples and spiced rum, steak and mashed potatoes, chocolate cherries, and mint."

Killian glanced around the room, wondering what she was talking about because he couldn't smell any of this. They exited the car and proceeded into the next one. Killian no longer wondered what Pandora had been smelling. The next car was a banquet hall piled with platters of food on double-decker tables lining the walls.

"I meant for this to be a surprise, but your sister has quite a nose there." Jacob laughed.

Pandora smiled, grabbing two silver plates large enough for a Thanksgiving turkey. She handed one to Andromeda to hold and began piling on the food. Killian and Jacob followed suit, diving in immediately. Killian selected two steaks from a tray that read *Filet Mignon*, three scoops of cheddar mashed potatoes, a grilled stalk of corn, and a piece of every cake on the dessert table.

"You guys ready?" he asked, motioning to the girls.

"Yep," Pandora answered, guiding Andromeda back to the dining car carefully.

They entered the car and selected a table. They ate in silence for a long time. Every bite of food was cold, but more delicious than anything

175

they had ever tasted. They chewed and chewed until their jaws were worn out. Andromeda struggled for a few bites, but quickly figured out a method of feeding herself blindly.

"Your hair looks amazing, Annie," Pandora said, filling a spoon full of mashed potatoes.

"My hair, what about my hair?" Andromeda asked, touching it gently with her fingers.

"Oh, you … you haven't seen it," Pandora stuttered.

"What is it, Pan? Spit it out."

"Well, it's all white and red like a candy cane kind of," Pandora explained.

"What?" Andromeda yelled.

"It looks amazing, Annie, like fire and snow. It's bad-ass," Killian said.

Andromeda continued massaging her scalp stroking her hair suspiciously.

"What about something to drink?" Pandora suggested.

"Excellent idea. I'll go see what there is," Killian jumped from his seat and headed to the bar.

"Killian, grab some ice for this knot on Annie's head."

"Absolutely," Killian replied, staring at a variety of liquor and wine. He opened several drawers finding silverware trays and shot glasses. He opened the tiny coolers under the bar and saw a conglomeration of craft beers. He grabbed several and took them to the table.

"I'm not drinking that," Pandora said.

"This is for her head until I find something else, genius," Killian replied.

"Oh." Pandora blushed and grabbed the bottle. "Annie, this is going to be a little cold."

Pandora lifted her sister's hair. She slowly pressed the bottle against the knot, and Andromeda shivered.

Killian returned to the bar resuming his search, roaming through racks of wine bottles in an array of colorful assortments and liquor bottles from around the world. He maneuvered the beers around in the freezers searching for some sodas but could only find two bottles of water. He took them to the girls, and they accepted them with cheeks full of chocolate and strawberry cake.

176

Jacob wiped his mouth with a shiny napkin and moseyed up to the bar to browse the selections. He stumbled upon a six-pack of Seagram's Ginger Ale and a liter glass bottle of Perrier.

"Killian, do you guys want these?" he asked, setting the six-pack on the top of the bar.

"Yeah, that's great," Killian said, jumping up from the table and snagging the drinks. He broke one-off for each of them and said, "Do you want one, Dad?"

"Uh, no thanks. I think something a little stronger after the week I've had," Jacob replied.

"Yeah, me, too," Killian said, returning the sodas and grabbing a bottle of Johnnie Walker.

"Yeah, I don't think so." Jacob snatched the bottle out of Killian's hand. "And you definitely don't begin your drinking career with scotch, son."

"Oh, is that what that was. I thought it was a type of syrup you add to ginger ale like grenadine." Killian grinned as he picked up the three sodas.

"Sure, you did." Jacob placed the scotch on the top shelf.

Killian returned to the table, and Pandora watched him unimpressed as he handed out the ginger ale.

"All this liquor, and you couldn't sneak one bottle past your old man," Pandora said.

"You said you didn't like alcohol," Killian replied.

"I don't like beer, but there's nothing wrong with some vodka and cranberry."

"Pan, you've never tasted anything stronger than root beer." Andromeda shook her head.

"Oh yes, I have," Pandora said. "I've had communion wine."

"That doesn't count." Andromeda opened her can of ale and chugged half of it down.

"Ahh, that's it," Jacob said from the bar.

"What?" Killian asked, turning his head.

"*Anavim Min HaErets*. A fine Cabernet Sauvignon from the Golan Heights." Jacob popped the cork and searched for a wine glass.

Killian's hands shook. "Dad, what did you say?"

"This is a Cabernet from Israel. Cabernets are like—"

"No, I mean the Hebrew, what was it again?" Killian ran to the bar.

Jacob turned the label so Killian could read it. "It says, '*Anavim Min HaErets*'. You know, 'Grapes from the Earth.'"

"That was the word the Black Knight had me say. That was the word that created all those grapes," Killian shouted.

Jacob turned the bottle over and reread the Hebrew. "*Anavim*, of course, so that means, possibly, maybe—"

"That Enochian is Hebrew just with a different script," Killian finished.

Killian and Jacob laughed and shouted, giving each other a high five.

"What's going on over there?" Andromeda hollered, looking vaguely in their direction.

Killian ran back to the table in a state of exhilaration. "Enochian is Hebrew. I mean, Hebrew is Enochian. Either way, they use different scripts, different letters, but the same verbiage."

"And that means what exactly?" Pandora drawled.

"Just watch," Killian said with excitement. He pointed to the table and said, "*Anavim*!" A pile of grapes appeared out of thin air in the center of the table.

Pandora gasped.

"What is it? What just happened?" Andromeda asked.

"Killian just made a pile of grapes appear out of thin air."

"Seriously?"

"Yeah, and watch this," Killian folded up the white sleeves of his scrubs so Pandora could see the etchings on his forearm.

"*Anavim*," he said, and the etchings bloomed gold and then faded as more grapes fell upon the table.

"This is unbelievable," Pandora said, rubbing the strange letters on his arm.

"Dad, tell me something else in Hebrew. Let me try to make something else appear," Killian shouted, barely able to contain his excitement.

"Well, I'm not fluent or anything," Jacob responded.

"What about something from Havdalah, something from the song?" Killian clapped his hands, staring at his dad.

178

"How about *Mayim,* that means—"

"*Mayim,*" Killian shouted, and a ball of water splashed onto the table.

Andromeda scooted back from the sudden flow of grapes and water splashing into her lap.

Pandora and Killian laughed.

"It's okay, Annie, it's just water and grapes," Pandora reassured her.

"That doesn't mean I want it all over me," Andromeda complained.

"Something else, Dad, something else," Killian jumped, elated with his gift. "What's that one part? *Baruk atah,* heytah *orah.*"

When Killian said, "*Orah*" a burst of light as bright as a star flashed in the cabin. The three of them shielded their eyes as the light lingered and then dissipated.

"What happened now?" Andromeda asked in response to their gasps.

"Nothing, Killian just summoned a star in the car. That's all." Pandora shot a fiery glance at Killian. "Do you want us all to go blind?" she asked, rubbing her eyes.

"You need to be more selective over the words you say, son," Jacob added, rubbing his as well.

"Yeah, yeah," Killian said, breathing heavily. "Sorry, I just ... I can't believe this. I can make things appear out of thin air. This is unbelievable, and Pan can bring people back to life."

"What?" Andromeda asked.

"Well," Pandora poked at a potato on her plate with her fork. "I mean technically I haven't brought a person back to life. Only a kitten and a leprechaun."

"Where in God's name did you find a dead kitten?" Andromeda asked.

"I didn't, that black devil posing as an angel killed one in front of me. Broke my heart, but then he put it in my hands, and it came back to life," Pandora explained.

"I guess the question remains then, what can Andromeda do?" Killian asked.

The three of them turned towards her. Even without her sight, Andromeda knew their eyes were staring at her. She scratched her head and fumbled with her hands.

"Well, are you all sitting down for this?"

"We are now," Killian said as he and Jacob tucked themselves into the table.

Andromeda swallowed as sweat prickled over her palms. She took in a deep breath. "When someone touches this hand," she raised her left arm, pulling back the white sleeve of the scrub, "I-I know things about that person. About their past, their present, and their future."

"What kind of things, Annie?" Pandora asked.

Andromeda pulled the sleeve back down and rubbed her hands together in her lap. "Mainly, I know where their DNA comes from."

"What does that mean?" Killian asked, scooting his chair up closer to the table.

"When my hand touches someone, I go into a kind of trance, and I see the person standing before me on an astrological plain. Galaxies swirl in the background as two great moons appear beside them. If the black moon turns red, then that person is a descendant of the first mother, Lilith. If the white moon turns blue, that person is a descendant of the second mother, Eve."

"Lilith. Who's Lilith?" Pandora asked.

"Lilith was made at the same time as Adam. She was his original wife," Jacob answered.

Killian and Pandora stared at him with mouths open.

"I thought Adam and Eve were the first two people created. How could Adam have a wife before her?" Pandora asked.

"It's complicated," Jacob said, running his fingers along his scruffy jawline. "Most people don't understand that there are two origin stories in the Bible. In Genesis, chapter one, there is a story about God creating the world in seven days, with the simultaneous creation of a male and female. That is the story of Adam and Lilith. In chapters two and three, there is a very different story about a woman created from Adam's ribs who eats the forbidden fruit. That is the story of Adam and Eve. Didn't you ever wonder why God made all the animals of the planet male and female and then supposedly stopped with humans?"

"No," the three of them answered.

"Exactly, people don't usually think about these things. In ancient mythology, God made Lilith as a wife for Adam, and they were created simultaneously. But Lilith rejected Adam as her husband and wandered out of the garden of Eden, taking their children with her."

"Are you sure?" Pandora asked, folding her arms with a scowl.

"This, of course, is the legend of Lilith. I'm not saying it's canonical theology of modern Christianity. You asked who Lilith was? I'm explaining," Jacob said softly.

Pandora shook her head in disbelief.

"It's true, Pan. I know things now, things I never knew before," Andromeda said, blinking rapidly.

Pandora turned her attention back to Andromeda, who was rubbing her eyes fiercely.

"What is it, Annie? Are your eyes okay?" Killian asked.

"Yeah, I think … I think I'm beginning to see something, but it's all blurry." She rubbed them again, looking up excitedly.

"Oh, thank God!" Pandora said.

Andromeda peered around slowly. "You guys look like a bunch of giant blobs."

"Well, that's comforting," Killian said with a smirk.

Andromeda laughed. "Sorry, it's a lot better than nothingness."

They laughed, and Killian reached for his ginger ale, chugging the rest.

"Andromeda, please continue telling us what you know about Lilith, if you don't mind," Jacob asked.

Andromeda wiped her eyes one more time and stretched them widely. "Well, Lilith and Adam had many children together, but in time she and her children became bored with Eden and wandered outside of the garden and into the world. They were curious." Andromeda emphasized the last word and glanced over at Pandora.

Pandora swallowed and swished the ginger ale around in her can, hiding her eyes with her hair.

"She became Queen of a land called Canaan and …" Andromeda rubbed her eyes some more.

"And what?" Jacob insisted.

"And she was the first woman to give birth to hybrids. Um, half-human and half angelic beings. She became the wife of a powerful angel called Haylel, and they ruled Canaan for centuries."

"Haylel," Jacob said, leaning back in his chair. "I've never heard of that angel before."

Andromeda closed her eyes and placed her hands on her temples. "I can see them together in my mind. He played a golden harp for her, and she danced for him like no woman has ever danced before. Their love was powerful and amazing, but their children were monsters."

"Hmmm, I wonder if they're the Nephilim," Jacob mumbled. "What else can you tell us, Andromeda?"

"Well, there's one other thing," Andromeda said, wiping a tear from her eye. "I had a vision. I guess it was a vision." More tears fell from her eyes.

"About what?" Pandora asked, leaning in towards her sister.

Andromeda breathed in, struggling to keep her composure. "There were angels, thousands of angels lined up in a black desert. Each one had a guillotine. I was standing on a huge rock, overlooking a herd of sheep and goats. An angel stood beside me. He commanded me to divide the herd. In my hand appeared the scepter of prophecy. It was no longer on my arm, but back in my hands, and I held it high above my head. The sheep moved away from the guillotines, but the goats walked towards them. When they were divided, the angels beheaded every goat. The blood ran over the desert, and crows feasted on their flesh."

Andromeda stopped and burst into tears. Pandora rubbed her back, looking confused.

Killian glanced over at his dad. Jacob ran his fingers through his hair, buried in contemplation.

"What does this mean?" Killian asked.

"This is what the Black Knight wants. The great genocide of humanity," Jacob said.

"Genocide?" Pandora shrieked.

"The Black Knight," Jacob explained, "wants to destroy the bloodline of Lilith. He thinks if this is accomplished, then God will return or something like that. He needed that staff. That was the tool. The prophetic tool he needed to complete his goal. Without it, you can't know who descended from who."

"What is it, Annie?" Pandora asked as Andromeda shivered violently.

182

"Mom," Andromeda moaned.

"Mom? What about Mom?" Pandora asked.

"Mom's bloodline is from Lilith. That demon intends to kill all the people in the town from that bloodline. I've already sorted them all." Tears poured down Andromeda's cheeks as she rocked back and forth.

"They're going to kill Mom?" Pandora screamed, her hands gripping her face.

Killian shook his head in disbelief then turned towards his dad. "Did you know they were going to do this?"

Jacob put his hands over his face. "I didn't know their parents had already been tested. I didn't know the timeline."

Killian stared at his dad. "We need to go back there now. We need to save them," Killian shouted.

"We can't go back," Jacob said.

"We have to. We can't let their parents die," Killian yelled.

"We can't go back," Jacob roared. "The train is automated. It goes from point A to point B. There's no stopping it. Besides that, we would get killed if we tried to go back there. This was the only way."

"There's always another way. There has to be a manual control somewhere," Killian yelled.

"Yeah, if you have the access codes," Jacob said.

They stared at each other, fists clenched, and jaws locked. Pandora stood up and lifted Andromeda with her. She turned and walked towards the front of the train.

"Where are you going?" Jacob asked.

"To look for myself," Pandora said, without turning around.

Andromeda held onto her shoulder as they passed through the door.

"Dad, I can't believe you allowed this to happen," Killian said, running his hands through his hair like a madman.

"What did you want to do? Take on Area 51? With what, a couple of rifles and some handguns?" Jacob said, standing up.

"We had the leprechauns, too, and the brownies," Killian said, shoving his chair against the table.

"Yeah, the leprechauns who got captured and the brownies who are dead now."

"You don't know that," Killian yelled as a tear formed in the crease of his eye.

"You don't know the Black Knight, Killian. He's lethal and hates everything on this planet. Duncan and Crocker sacrificed their lives, so we had a chance to escape. The 'chauns did the same. Area 51 is a gigantic maze. How lucky would we have had to have been to find their parents and not die trying?" Jacob moved towards him, but Killian held up his hand.

"Just don't, Dad," Killian said, and he walked out of the room and into the locomotive.

The silver door opened, and Killian stomped inside. Pandora was searching around the control deck for some type of manual override. Andromeda sat on the black leather seat with her face in her hands.

Killian didn't speak. He immediately began to search as well. He slid his hands around the upper panels hoping there were secret compartments full of wiring or hidden touch screens for overrides, but there was nothing. He scooted by Pandora and slid under the dashboard, feeling every crevice in the compartment, but it was solid as a rock. He stood back up and could hardly look at either of them in the face.

"Maybe there's another car, Annie," Pandora suggested. "Maybe there's a control system in the back of this thing, and we can throw it in reverse back to that prison."

Andromeda didn't move, and she didn't respond.

"Excellent idea. I'll help you," Killian said.

"No, I think your family has helped us enough," Pandora snapped.

Killian was taken aback. Pandora's eyes were like daggers in his chest. He turned away from her hurtful gaze and stared out the window. They were still underground, whirling past black rock at two hundred miles an hour. He placed his hand on his forehead, rubbing it until he felt like he was peeling the skin off his bone.

"Come on, Annie, get up, let's go, there's no time to lose," Pandora yelled, and she grabbed her sister by the arm.

"Stop," Andromeda commanded, throwing Pandora's hand off.

Pandora stared at her sister. Her fury now turned in her direction. Andromeda's gaze bore down upon her, the gold of her irises swirling around like molten lava.

184

"This was the only way, Pan. We can't go back." Andromeda said as the white of her knuckles blazed against her balled-up fists.

"What do you mean we can't go back? We have to go back. Are you just going to let Mom die?" Pandora shouted.

"She could already be dead, and how many thousands or millions more will die if they capture us and use me for the Black Knight's plan? He won't ever have me in his clutches again, ever," Andromeda screamed.

Pandora stared at her with teeth-gritting, and her jaw closed tight.

Andromeda turned away, walked over to the control panel, and stared out into the stony darkness.

Killian was suspended with fear and didn't dare speak his opinion in this sisters' quarrel.

Pandora walked to the silver door. It opened, and she walked through.

Killian stood there, not knowing what to do.

"She'll calm down. She has to. This was the only way," Andromeda muttered.

Killian watched tears fall onto the control panel as Andromeda hung her head low. He sat down on the bench and placed his hands over his eyes. He scratched his scalp, pulled his hair, punched the leather cushion, ground his teeth together, and then stopped.

"I hate being backed into a corner. I hate feeling helpless. I must do something. We need to do something," Killian said.

Andromeda twisted around; her golden eyes filled with tears. "We are doing something. We're getting me as far away from that demon as possible, and that will save the lives of millions."

Killian stared at her. The person before him was not the same person he'd met three days ago. Her hair, her eyes, and her demeanor had all transformed. Everything was changing.

"So we get you away from him, but where are we going? What train is this? Are we headed to Alaska, Mexico, or Washington, and when we get there, what will we find? We may not be able to go back, but we sure as hell can't go forward either." Killian focused intensely on Andromeda's gaze.

"Your eyes look so much like your mother's, storm-grey like the beginning of deluge," Andromeda said.

Killian squinted, and his brow furrowed. "Can you see again? You can see my eyes?"

Andromeda nodded.

"And my mother's eyes, how do you know what her eyes look like?"

"I told you. I know things now. I can see things," Andromeda turned around and stared out the window.

Killian looked up to the roof, stretching his neck as far as it would go. He scratched the linen of his white scrubs. Every muscle in his body tensed up.

"Is she alive?" Killian asked. "Is my mother alive, Annie?"

Andromeda nodded.

Killian gasped for air. He clenched his chest as his heart pounded. Tears formed in his eyes as his legs shook.

"Where is she? Do you know where she is? Can we find her? Is she okay?" Killian asked.

"Maybe," Andromeda whispered.

Killian shot up out of the chair. He wanted to hug Andromeda, but he didn't. His feet and body moved around uncontrollably from excitement. Then a realization hit him, and he stopped himself—his palms filled with sweat.

"Do you know if your mom is alive?" Killian asked.

Killian watched as Andromeda's head slumped to her chest. She was weak and shaking. He walked over to her, placing his hand in the middle of her back. She shivered from his touch, then collapsed into his arms. He pulled her to the black leather bench and laid her down.

He didn't have to ask her what the answer was.

17: FIRE AND DARKNESS

When Killian's eyes opened, he was still in the locomotive. Andromeda's head rested in his lap— sound asleep. Pandora sat in the corner with her knees pulled tightly to her chest and a scowl on her face. Killian glanced at her royal blue eyes and winced from the pain of her glare.

"How long have I been asleep?" Killian asked.

Pandora didn't respond but continued to glare at him. His question stirred Andromeda, and she shot up, frantically looking around.

"What happened? What's going on?" Andromeda asked, looking at Pandora and then to Killian.

"Why don't you tell me what's going on?" Pandora said.

Andromeda glanced over at Killian. He shook his head and shrugged.

"Were we asleep? How long have we been asleep? Where are we?" Andromeda shot off the bench and gazed out of the train.

The black cavern was gone, the sun was shining, and hemlocks and spruces spread out as far as the eye could see.

"Pan, have you seen this?" Andromeda asked. "Why didn't you wake me?"

Pandora didn't answer. She watched Killian as he moved beside Andromeda, gazing out the window.

"We must be in Canada, maybe even Alaska," Killian said.

"We're above ground now. Who knows how long until we get to that next base. What are we going to do?" Andromeda asked, glancing over at Killian.

Killian opened his mouth to speak but coughed, choked on his spit, and hit his chest with his fist. He looked up at the twins and motioned for them to continue while he caught his breath.

"Pan, what do you think?" Andromeda asked.

Pandora shot her a glance and looked away.

Andromeda cracked her neck and then her hands, trying to relieve the tension in her body.

The silver door behind them slid open, and they all turned around. Jacob walked in carrying military uniforms and wearing one himself. It was white with silver cords crisscrossing the front. He had on black dress pants tucked into military boots.

"Oh good, you're all awake. You'll need to put these on. Even in August, temperatures drop to the forties here," Jacob said.

He looked over the stash he had, handing the girls navy blue skirts with silver tops and matching blue blazers. He tossed the rest of the clothes to Killian. A black dress uniform with golden cords and an embroidered jacket with matching pants and boots.

"Sorry, I know this is not ideal, but it's better than those white scrubs," Jacob said in response to their expressions. "Girls, you'll need to find some shoes. I didn't know your sizes, but you're going to want boots if we plan on hiking," Jacob said.

"Hiking?" Pandora's face contorted with disgust. "The last time I went hiking, it didn't turn out so well." She shot a scornful glance at her sister and then towards Killian.

"I know you guys understand the risks we're all taking here. I'm sure we are getting close to the base now. I think Nevada to Alaska is roughly three thousand miles and we've been going two hundred miles an hour for about," Jacob turned his watch over, checking the time, "about fifteen hours."

"That means we're three thousand miles in right now," Killian said. "How long have we been asleep?"

"I'd say about thirteen hours, give or take," Jacob answered. "You can see why I'm in a rush. Our power naps have put us in a dangerous predicament. I think I have an idea, but first, you've got to change clothes. Then meet me in the last car."

"Isn't there something else to wear other than this?" Killian asked, holding up the black dress jacket.

"I've spent the last twenty minutes looking all over this train for supplies, weapons, and clothing. This is an ambassador train for General Marx to entertain guests as they visit the secret bases. So, no, this is all there is." Jacob turned and walked out of the room.

Killian looked at the twins studying the outfits they'd been given.

"I guess I'll go in here and change," Killian said.

The twins didn't respond as they held the clothing up to their bodies. Killian walked through the door and into the dining car. He knew there had to be a bathroom somewhere. He ventured into the next car and through a set of black double doors. A sign for men pointed to the left and women to the right.

He stepped into the men's room and undressed. He stared at his lean torso. Bruises lined his ribs, and there were mysterious scratches across his abdomen he didn't remember getting. He turned his neck to the side and saw a dark brown bruise running down the front. *Wow*, he thought, *I'm beat up.*

He unbuttoned the golden circlets of the black jacket, noticing the fine detail of golden swirls lacing the collar and shoulders. He set the coat

189

down and put on the cotton shirt that went underneath. He checked the size of the pants and was surprised at his dad getting it right. He slid on the slacks and the black belt with the golden clasp. The military boots shone with a black gloss so shiny that he could see his reflection.

He stood before the mirror and placed on the finishing touch. The jacket was surprisingly comfortable, and he twisted in the mirror, looking at himself in shock. He'd never been dressed so nicely. He pulled the sleeves down and folded the collar until it was straight. He walked out of the bathroom and back through the silver door into the dining car.

The twins were standing by the bar amidst an argument. They turned, and their mouths dropped at the sight of Killian. He smiled, taking in their beauty. Andromeda's hair was pulled up into a bun, and the silver blouse contrasted beautifully with her golden eyes. Pandora's long blonde hair fell around her face, and her eyes shone brilliantly against the navy uniform.

Pandora still looked mad. Andromeda looked perturbed but focused.

"Did you find the bathrooms, Killian?" Andromeda asked.

Killian nodded, "They're just through there."

He walked through the silver door into the next compartment, pointing towards the black double doors. He watched their bare feet leave hazy footprints on the grey tiled floor as they passed by. The smell of frankincense brushed by him as Pandora flung her hair in his direction. The girls disappeared behind the doors, and Killian stood there alone.

He looked around, clicking his tongue. He knocked his fist against his thigh and leaned against the wall. When the girls didn't return from the bathroom, he considered heading down the compartments alone. He twiddled his fingers for another moment when the silver sliding door opened.

"Killian, come on, I need your help," Jacob said.

Killian glanced back at the black double doors and pushed himself off the wall. He walked out through the next three cars. They were all remarkably similar, with private bedrooms lining the interior. Each room had a fancy chandelier hanging in the middle of the compartment, and wooden doors painted purple. The floor was burgundy and soft, with gold lining etching the floors.

The next two cars were lined with bars and smelled like aged tobacco. Pictures of the General entertaining guests from all around the world filled the wooden walls. There were popes and presidents, kings and queens, and a few individuals who looked like the Black Knight.

"Okay," Jacob said as the silver door slid open to the last car. "Look at this piece here."

Killian looked in the midway and saw one silver panel. Jacob lifted the panel, revealing the coupling that linked the last two cars together. He glanced at his dad.

"Here's my idea. If we all get in this last car, I'll try to break this piece apart. Then, while the train moves on to its destination, we can roll to a stop and get out and hike from there. Hopefully, we'll get somewhere before the search vehicles figure all of this out."

"You're going to break that with what exactly?" Killian asked.

Jacob pulled out a hammer. "I found this in an emergency tool kit under one of the bars."

Killian looked at his dad and shook his head. "I guess that will have to do."

"I've already packed backpacks of food and water to take with us. I put them in there and—"

"Dad," Killian interjected.

"Yeah," Jacob said, staring at the couplet.

"Thanks."

Jacob looked up at him. Killian looked away.

"I'm sorry I yelled at you," Killian said. "I get so angry now. Everything has me on edge, and I lose my temper. I'm trying to keep everyone alive and—"

"I know, Son," Jacob stood up, placing his hand on Killian's shoulder. "It's too much for a seventeen-year-old to bear."

Killian half smiled and looked down at the wobbling panel. The sliding door behind them opened, and the girls walked through. They each had a pair of military hiking boots on instead of the dress shoes Killian had.

"Where did you find those?" Killian asked, pointing at their boots.

"There were smaller pairs in one of those rooms with the purple doors. They might be made for aliens because they're too small for me, but they'll have to do," Andromeda answered.

Killian looked at his shoes, shining brilliantly, but knew they'd be painful after walking for hours in the woods.

"Okay, everyone into the next compartment and grab the backpacks of food," Jacob said.

The twins crossed over and found the bags, pulling the straps on. Killian stayed beside his dad and watched him pound the metal couplet over and over with the hammer. He'd created one dent.

"Dad, that's not working," Killian said.

Jacob sat down and laid the hammer beside him.

"Let me try for a minute," Killian said.

"Be my guest." Jacob handed him the hammer.

Killian bent down and slammed the hammer against the couplet. A massive dent imprinted the top. Jacob looked over at it.

"You must have hit the same spot I was working on." Jacob grinned.

Killian laughed. "Okay, Dad."

Killian hammered again and again. The couplet bent and twisted but wouldn't fall out. Killian gripped the hammer tighter and hit the couplet as hard as he could. Another dent formed, but it didn't fall.

"What the frick?" Killian said.

He threw the hammer down. Jacob peered over the lid, watching the ground fly by beneath them. The couplet was beaten up, but nowhere close to falling apart.

This thing needs to be melted, not beaten," Killian commented, looking over his dad's shoulder.

Jacob rubbed his chin. "That's a great idea." He stood up and stepped back. "Killian, scoot down close to the couplet and say the word, *Esh*."

"Why?" Killian asked.

"Your gift, try your gift," Jacob urged.

"Oh, yeah." Killian bent down until his head was beside the bobbling panel. He focused as hard as he could on the couplet and said, "*Esh*."

The couplet was caught in a brilliant blue flame swirling around it. The couplet dissolved into a black gooey substance and began to fall apart. The compartment shook, and Killian stood up.

"Get in here," Jacob yelled.

Killian jumped between the sliding door into the compartment. The girls watched out the window as blobs of green and brown took shape forming into giant spruces and hemlocks clustered together like living skyscrapers. The sunrays sprinkled threw the branches like pixie dust as their car slowed to a crawl.

"Here, throw this on." Jacob handed a backpack to Killian.

"Great, thanks, where are the guns?" Killian asked.

"The what?" Jacob said.

"The guns, you know shoot-shoot, bang-bang?"

The twins looked over at Jacob.

"Oh my God, I forgot the guns in the other compartment."

They stared out the side door, and the train was miles ahead of them as their car came to a standstill.

Jacob ran his fingers through his hair and punched the wall of the train. The twins stepped back.

"Dad, it's okay, we—"

"It's not okay, son, it's not okay. Do you have any idea what we could face in the next few hours, and now we have nothing to use for protection," Jacob kicked over a nearby chair.

Killian swallowed and looked at the twins. Their eyes were shaky, looking from him to his dad.

Killian bent over beside Jacob, who was sitting in a chair with his hands over his face. He placed his hand gently on his dad's shoulder.

"Dad, you got us food and water and off that train. We'll make it. Come on."

Killian grabbed his dad by the arm and lifted him up.

Jacob's eyes were bloodshot as he rubbed them intensely. "I'm sorry, guys. I've put us in a dangerous situation now. I'm so sorry."

"It's okay, Mr. Gold," Pandora said.

"Yeah, as long as we stay together, we'll be fine," Andromeda added.

They patted Jacob on the shoulder and stepped outside into the brisk air. The scent of evergreen engulfed them as the vibrance of the hunter green forest welcomed them into its midst.

"So, now what?" Pandora asked.

"Well, now we hike and hope nothing finds us," Jacob said.

"Hike to where?" Pandora asked, shivering from the cool breeze.

"There should be a river nearby. I remember Mark telling me about his trip to the Anchorage base. He said they passed a lot of rivers going up. If we find a river, we can follow it to a harbor somewhere. We may even find a boat and could hitch a ride. Either way, we need to get away from these tracks," Jacob pulled up his bag and headed out into the dense forest.

Killian glanced over at the twins. Pandora turned her head to look away from him, and Andromeda gave him half a smile as she followed behind his dad.

"Pan, I just wanted to say—"

"Don't talk to me, Killian," Pandora spouted off and followed behind her sister.

Killian kicked a rock the size of a chihuahua with his shoe hoping to send it flying, but, he only bruised his big toe. His anger flared, and he aimed for a smaller rock in retaliation, sending it flying by Andromeda.

Andromeda looked back at him with eyes flaring.

Killian huffed, stuck his hands in his pockets, turned, and followed the group.

They hiked for hours under the hemlock trees and spruces. They hadn't seen any wildlife so far other than a few bald eagles spooked by their traipsing through the woods. Jacob stopped and sat on a hundred-foot tall tree that had fallen. Its trunk rose four feet into the air, and the girls had to push themselves up several times to get a good position.

They opened the backpacks to survey the contents inside. Everyone opened their bottles of water first, drinking a hefty amount. Then the real search began as they opened small plastic bags. Killian unwrapped a small piece of cheesecake that had been smashed into a round cookie. Andromeda pulled out a piece of steak, and Pandora, a cluster of fried shrimp.

"Um, I'll trade you," Killian said softly.

Pandora eyed his round ball of cheesecake. "Only because I'm deathly allergic to shellfish," she answered, snatching the cheesecake from his hand.

Killian took the shrimp and began to chew.

"You know that's not kosher," Jacob said, biting into a large apple.

194

"I don't care," Killian said, shoving three in his mouth.

"I never thought I'd be hiking in a place like this, eating cold steak, and wearing a military uniform," Andromeda said, tearing off another tough bite.

"The greatest things in life happen unexpectedly. Someday we'll all look back on this as an amazing part of our life that we'll never want to forget," Jacob said, chewing his bit of apple.

Everyone rolled their eyes at his response.

"Do you think this is Alaska?" Pandora asked Jacob, turning away from the others.

"Could be Canada, could be the Yukon, I'm not sure yet," Jacob said. "At some point, we'll either hit a mountain range or a river, and then we can get a better gauge from there. Of course, we won't be positive until we get to some form of civilization."

"And when we hit civilization, then what?" Andromeda asked.

"You're the prophetic one. Why don't you tell us?" Pandora sassed.

"I've already told you what I think, so your attitude had better stop, real quick," Andromeda fired back.

Pandora turned her back to her sister and folded her arms.

Killian stood up and walked over to his dad. He unzipped his pack and fumbled around, looking sideways at Jacob.

"What is it, Killian?" Jacob asked.

Killian looked over his shoulder at Andromeda, who glanced at him. He picked up a plastic-wrapped brownie and unraveled the squashed chocolate. He looked back at his dad, who was looking at him, confused. Killian glanced back at Pandora, who was shuffling through her pack, but Killian knew she was listening intently.

"I wanted to ask if you knew any other Hebrew words that could help us if we get into trouble," Killian said.

"Oh," Jacob tossed his apple core. "Well, that's a good idea, I guess. Let me see." He rubbed his hands over his jawline, scratching like he had fleas. The length of his beard was becoming more and more uncomfortable.

"We already know fire. There's the word for stone."

"Yeah, what's that?" Killian asked.

"*Eben*," Jacob said.

195

Killian looked off in the distance and said, "*Eben.*" A stone fell about fifteen feet away. "Hmmm . . . not incredibly useful. What about a big stone?" Killian asked.

"That would be *Eben Gadolah*," Jacob answered.

Killian repeated this word, and a one-ton rock fell on top of the small stone, shaking the ground around them.

"Wow," Killian said.

The twins slid off the tree and walked over to the boulder, smacking the side of its dull gray surface.

"Hard as a rock," Andromeda said.

"Well, it is a rock, so," Pandora mumbled.

Andromeda rolled her eyes. "How about the word for missile?"

"Yeah, missile doesn't pop up that frequently in the liturgy, I'm afraid," Jacob said with a chuckle.

"Liturgy. You know it's getting close to twilight, Dad," Killian said. "Wasn't today, Shabbat?"

"Yeah, it was," Jacob said.

"Do you want to do Havdalah?" Killian asked.

"Well, I guess it'll be fine, even though we can't see the first three stars yet. Do you remember the words?" Jacob joked.

"Most of them," Killian said.

"Girls, do you mind?" Jacob asked.

"No, not at all," Andromeda said.

"Please go ahead," Pandora said with a smile.

Jacob cleared his throat. Killian blushed slightly, looking at the girls.

"Are you sure you're ready?" Jacob laughed.

"Yes, Dad, come on," Killian said.

Jacob put his arm around Killian and together they began to sing: "*Lai, lai, lai, lai, lai, lai, lai, Baruk atah Adonai Eloheinu Melech haolam, boray pri hagafen*, amen."

As these words floated into the air, balls of light sparkled all around them like twinkling stars with more colors than the rainbow. Pandora and Andromeda gazed around in amazement. Jacob and Killian glanced at one another in disbelief but didn't break the rhythm of the song.

"*Lai, lai, lai, lai, lai, lai, lai, Baruk atah Adonai Eloheinu melech haolam, boray minay vesamim, amen.*"

The sparkling stars encircling them burst into mini fireworks as this verse concluded, splashing all around them in a mystical dance. A sweet smell of spices spread across the wood as darkness fell outside their circle.

"*Lai, lai, lai, lai, lai, lai, lai, Baruk atah Adonai Eloheinu melech haolam, boray me'oray ha'aysh, amen.*"

The sparkling stars dissipated, engulfing them in darkness. A massive blaze burst upon the ground, immersing them in orange flames that spiraled up into the sky. Blue and yellow twists of fire danced around them, but they felt no heat. Jacob and Killian continued singing, coming up to the last verse.

"*Baruch atah Adonai Eloheinu Melech haolam. Hamavdil bayn Kodesh lechol bayn or lechoshech bayn Yisrael la'amim bayn yom hashevi'i leshayshet yemay hama'aseh. Baruch atah, Adonai, hamavdil bayn Kodesh lechol, amen.*"

Within the fire, the stars returned, swirling around like a tornado. The stars consumed the fire and erupted into a final waterfall of color and majesty. The four of them came together, hugging one another and crying in awe of the magnificent phenomenon that had just taken place.

The darkness slowly crept in all around them, but they were so full of joy they didn't notice.

"That was the most amazing thing I've ever witnessed," Andromeda said.

"I've never felt so alive in my life," Pandora added.

"I have no clue what just happened," Killian said, and they all laughed.

Pandora wrapped her arms around his torso, and he lifted her off the ground, squeezing her as hard as he could. Andromeda hugged Jacob, and he patted her on the back. Finally, the depth of the darkness pressed down upon them, and they stopped laughing, cheering, and hugging.

Pandora slid her hand into Killian's, and he gripped her palm tightly. Andromeda pulled her backpack on, waiting for the others to follow suit.

"I don't suggest we make camp just yet. It's probably best if we keep moving through the night. Is everyone up for that?" Jacob asked.

They nodded and followed Jacob as he resumed the hike.

Killian glanced over at Pandora, who was smiling her familiar beautiful smile. She leaned up to his ear and said, "I'm sorry."

Killian turned towards her and said, *"Tye Maia Vala,"* in a half-whisper.

"You never told me what that means." Pandora gripped his hand with both of hers.

"It means, you're a beautiful angel," Killian said, gazing into her eyes.

Andromeda gagged in the darkness and said, "Get a room, you two."

"What was that?" Jacob asked, and the others laughed.

They walked in the darkness for a while, not speaking. They stayed within a few feet of one another, still cautious of any wildlife in the area or anything darker.

"So, tell me more about yourself, Killian," Pandora said with her silvery voice.

"What do you want to know?"

"Well, what house are you for starters?" Pandora asked.

"What do you mean?"

"You know, what Hogwarts-house are you?" Pandora slid her arm around his.

"You tell me your house first?" he asked, bumping her with his hip.

"Oh, for God's sake, she's a Hufflepuff, can't you tell?" Andromeda blurted out ahead of them. A twig snapped somewhere in the distance, making them all look around.

Killian shrugged and kept moving. "I imagine you're a Slytherin?"

Killian could see Andromeda's smile in the tone of her voice, "As a matter of fact, I am. How'd you know?"

"Just a clever guess," Killian said, with a laugh.

"So what house are you, brainiac? Ravenclaw, I imagine," Andromeda kicked over a log and grabbed the straps of her backpack.

"That would be correct. The best house there is," Killian clarified.

Pandora pushed him in the side, separating herself from his grasp. "Hey," she said.

"What?" Killian pulled her back beside him. "I'm just saying Ravenclaw is the most important house."

An owl hooted in the distance, and something small seemed to shuffle in the woods beyond.

Killian looked around, but Pandora didn't notice and said, "I happen to think that all four houses have equal worth."

198

"Spoken like a true Hufflepuff," Andromeda said. "Everyone knows Slytherin is the superior house."

"Psh," Killian and Pandora said together.

Jacob cleared his throat, grabbing the trio's attention. "I don't think you can count Gryffindor out as being one of the most prestigious houses, if not the greatest. Personally, I look at the rare magical items left by the founders to define each one of the houses' positions of power. For instance, Hufflepuff's house gem is a cup from Helga. Ravenclaw has Rowena's diadem, and the Slytherin house has a locket. It's obvious then that Godric's sword makes Gryffindor the superior house."

There was silence for a few seconds, and then the trio burst out laughing.

"What?" Jacob said, turning around. "I think that's a very valid analysis."

"Okay, Dad," Killian laughed. "You just leave Potter to us professionals, and you stick with Lord of the Rings."

The laughter echoed throughout the wood as the darkness lurked back into their midst. They hiked several more miles until Andromeda's voice broke the silence.

"Hey, why don't you make yourself useful and conjure us up some grapes? I want to see if this stuff you create is edible."

"Mmm, that's a great idea," Killian said. He stuck out his hand and said, "*Anavim.*"

A cluster of grapes dropped in his hand. Pandora snatched it before he could pluck one for himself. She grabbed one of the purple fruits and tossed it in her mouth. She chewed and couldn't keep silent the sounds of pure delight.

"Don't be selfish, hand some over," Andromeda demanded.

"*Anavim,*" Killian said, and another cluster dropped in his hand. "Here, take this one."

Andromeda reached over and grabbed the bundle of grapes. She tossed three in her mouth, and as the juices hit her tongue, ecstasy rang from her lips with a hum.

"Those must be some amazing grapes," Jacob said.

"Here, Dad," Killian said, conjuring another cluster and tossing it over.

Killian created another batch, but Pandora stole it out of his palm.

"Hey," Killian said.

"Sorry, but I'm already out. They're delicious. You should try them," Pandora teased.

"I'm trying to," Killian said as he spoke the words again. He plucked a ripe violet grape from the cluster and tossed it in his mouth. The flavor was unlike anything he'd ever experienced. It was grape but intensified a thousand times with a crunchy skin and a creamy center. "This is amazing."

Jacob stopped everyone, motioning for them to be quiet. Their ears perked up, listening intently to their surroundings.

Killian could hear his heart pounding in his chest. "What is it, Dad?" he whispered.

"Just a minute," Jacob answered.

They listened, and Killian could vaguely hear something like static in the distance.

"Do you hear that?" Jacob asked.

"It sounds like water," Pandora said.

"Let's hope so. Keep quiet. Most kinds of wildlife stay close to bodies of water," Jacob said.

The party continued through the woods. Killian grabbed Pandora's hand, keeping her close beside him. Andromeda walked side by side with Jacob, looking intensely before her for any sign of a threat.

They drew closer to the sound of rushing water, and sighs of relief spread across the party. Their pace picked up as they passed between a cluster of bushes, but a howl in the dark froze them all.

The sound of rustling leaves sprang out in every direction. The group turned in a circle, pressing their backpacks together, peering through the darkness at the unforeseeable threat.

"What do we do, Dad?"

Jacob swallowed, scanning the bony trees. Two pairs of glowing yellow eyes stared at him. "Fire, we need fire."

Andromeda elbowed Killian in the side. "Make some fire now."

Killian looked out into the darkness, trying to find a target. He caught a glimpse of eyes rushing to his left.

He screamed, "*Esh!*"

One of the hemlock trees burst into flames, shooting a torch of fire thirty feet in the air. The forest blossomed with an orange glow, and red teeth munching on limbs and bark. A dozen grey wolves surrounded them, growling, with white-fangs bared.

"I think I've seen this before," Andromeda said.

"Yeah," Killian gulped. "Any branches around?"

Everyone looked closely at the forest floor beneath them, but they could only see two sticks in the vicinity.

"Here," Pandora shouted, shoving the stick in Killian's hand.

"*Esh!*" he shouted, igniting the end of the bark.

The wolves pressed in, steering clear of the blazing hemlock. Killian waved the burning stick in front of them, looking around for his next move.

"Killian, you're going to have to ignite a wildfire between them and us. Then we have to try and make it to the river," Jacob yelled.

Killian glanced over at his dad, who nodded confidently.

Killian turned back to the forest and set twenty trees burning like an inferno within seconds. The heat from the blaze almost knocked them over.

"Come on, to the river. Let's go," Jacob shouted.

They ran. Killian continued looking back and to the sides of them. He lit tree after tree ablaze as they approached the river's edge. Killian looked down. It was a thirty-foot plunge into the water, a hundred feet from the rapids. A howl sent them turning around. Five of the pack had gathered back together, pinning them up against the edge.

"We have to jump, there's no other choice," Jacob yelled.

Andromeda flew off the side, plunging into the river. Jacob leapt after her.

Killian grabbed Pandora's hand, and they looked for a moment at one another. Together they jumped from the ledge into the water.

18: WHITEHORSE

Killian opened his eyes to a bright blue sky. The ground beneath his back was pebbly, and the sound of a bubbling brook flowed by his feet. He shivered from the cold embracing him, and his soaking wet clothes felt as if they weighed a ton.

He turned his head to his right. Pandora lay next to him, but he could not see her face, only locks of matted yellow hair. Andromeda sat up on the other side of her, looking from side to side. Her navy blue jacket was almost black from the water it had absorbed, but her golden eyes were still penetrating and bright.

"You okay, Killian?" Andromeda asked, spotting him on the ground.

Killian leaned forward, his back aching. "Yeah, I think so. I think I hit a rock at some point down the rapids."

"I think I hit three of them," Pandora said, turning over to look at him.

Killian turned to her and brushed away a few specks of gravel clinging to her face. She reached up and ran her hand through his chestnut hair. They stared at each other for a few seconds, maybe a few minutes until the sound of gagging broke the silence. They turned to look at Andromeda.

"You two have lost it." Andromeda stood, stretching her back.

"Actually, I think we've found it," Killian said, gazing into Pandora's sparkling sapphire eyes.

"Oh my God, I'm literally going to be sick." Andromeda twisted, and her back cracked and popped multiple times. "Killian, where's your dad?"

Killian looked around, and then shot up off the ground. He searched the river and then the rocky embankment. He ran up to the forest line of spruces and hemlocks behind them. He scanned the gravel bank for any sign his dad had been there.

Pandora walked over to him, placing her hand on his back. "Maybe he went to look for firewood or something."

Killian surveyed the rocky bank again. "I don't see any footprints."

"Do you see that?" Andromeda asked, pointing to the south. A large black cloud was billowing in the air, spreading in every direction. "I'm guessing that is the inferno you unleashed."

Killian swallowed, turning away from the ominous smoke. "Right now, we have to find my dad. If that's the wildfire, we didn't have a choice. How else were we going to get out of there alive?"

"Oh, I totally agree. It's just, if that thing is blazing through the forest, it's going to push every wild animal in the countryside towards us." Andromeda brushed the gravel off her legs and tried to empty her boots.

Killian nodded. "Do we stay, or do we go? Is that what you're asking?"

Pandora slid her boot off, and a pile of tiny pebbles spilled out. "He could have washed up farther downstream," Pandora suggested, hitting the shoe with her hand to release the final bits of gravel.

Killian ran his hands through his hair. "What about the packs? Are there any left?"

They scanned the area, but not a single backpack had survived their escape in the river.

"Okay, so no packs, and we're missing Dad, okay," Killian said, turning away from Pandora and pacing. He rubbed the top of his forehead. "We don't know if he's gone beyond this point or is farther down." He stopped walking and took off the dress shoes, emptying the pebbles. "So, do we stay or go? What would Dad do? What would he want us to do?"

He peered around. Andromeda raised her eyebrows while Pandora bit her lip.

"If Dad had been here, he would have woken us up. He wouldn't have just left us," Killian said, emptying his other shoe.

"Maybe," Andromeda interjected, staring at Killian.

He turned and looked at the black smoke filling the air. "He would know we would have to continue down the river if he is behind us. So, he would need to catch up to us, and if he's farther down the river, we need to catch up to him."

Pandora bobbed her head from one side to the other, scrunching her nose.

Andromeda rearranged her hair in a bun. "We head down the river because that's the most logical thing your dad would think we would do, and we're supposing he would do the same, right?"

Killian nodded. "I think that makes sense, don't you?" He asked Pandora.

"I guess," she said, wiping the gravel off her skirt.

"Well then, there's no reason to stay around here." Killian grabbed Pandora's hand. She grasped his tightly, and they began to hike down the river.

Andromeda followed behind them, shaking her head. "Freaking love birds."

The hike was worse than before because their boots were waterlogged and extremely difficult to maneuver. Their clothes clung to them like leeches, sucking the energy from their bodies. The cool morning breeze sent tremors down their spines and aches deep into their bones.

With each step, Killian became more nervous. Every turn they made and every minute that passed placed doubt in his mind. He glanced behind them, but no one was there. Pandora squeezed his hand to tell him it would be all right, but he didn't look down into her gaze.

"How long have we been walking?" Andromeda held up her arm, shielding her face from the sun.

"Hours," Pandora answered, wiping off a bead of sweat rolling down her cheek.

"How about some of those grapes, Killian, before I starve and freeze to death?" Andromeda suggested.

"What?" Killian asked, feeling their gaze upon him.

"Grapes, make us some grapes," Andromeda said.

"Oh, yeah." Killian conjured up clusters for all of them. They chewed in silence as every drop of juice brought life to their joints and mood.

Within minutes, Andromeda had tossed her naked stem to the side and was licking her fingers.

"Not that I don't love these grapes," Andromeda said, "but I can't wait for you to learn the words for steak and lobster, clam chowder, macaroni and cheese—"

"Oh, yeah, and corndogs." Pandora smiled. "And chicken nuggets, and French fries, and funnel cakes. Oh, I would love to get a sugary fried pastry right about now."

Killian half-smiled at the two of them, "You girls and your stomachs," he shook his head.

"A girl's gotta eat," Andromeda said, "but all this talk about food is making me even more hungry."

"Yeah, me too," Killian said. "Maybe when we find civilization, I can finally get on a computer and find a Hebrew dictionary. Then I'll really be able to use this gift."

Silence crept over the group again as the gravel crunched underneath their feet. The sun moved up the skyline, but the breeze off the river continued chilling them to the bone.

"Did you hear that?" Pandora held up her hand for them to be quiet.

They stopped and perked up their ears. Instantly, they all turned to the east. Two cars drove through the trees.

"It's a road," Andromeda said with excitement.

She moved towards it, but stopped as Killian yelled, "Wait."

Andromeda turned and stared at him.

"What about my dad?"

Andromeda drew in a deep breath. Pandora clinched his hand with both of hers.

"What about him? What about my dad and my little brother?" Andromeda's eyes flashed at him. "They're stuck in some prison, and we're out here in a forest thousands of miles away, but do you see me whining about my dad?"

"Okay, Annie," Pan said.

"No, it's not okay, Pan." Andromeda stomped her foot on the ground, balling up her fists and turning her gaze back onto Killian. "What's the alternative? Do we stay out here walking this river until another pack of wolves spot us or worse? Do we wait to freeze to death tonight or start another inferno here?"

"Okay, Annie," Pandora yelled. "He gets it."

Killian cracked the bones in his neck and hands. "No, she's right. You're right, Annie. Dad would want us to get out of here either way. Hopefully, he can find his way to wherever we're going. I'm so sorry about your dad and your brother. I wish there was something we could do for them. Maybe we still can." Killian's head hung low, and he turned and looked down both sides of the river again.

Andromeda's anger subsided, and she shook her head, swaying slightly. She walked beside him and placed her hand on his shoulder. "I'm sorry, I don't know why I said all of that."

"You said it because it's the truth." He glanced at her golden eyes, and they were soft and understanding. "It's okay," Killian said. "He'll be fine. They'll all be fine. They're after us, remember. Let's see where this road takes us."

They turned towards the road and hiked up the bank.

"What's our story?" Pandora asked, looking up at Killian.

"What do you mean?" Killian asked.

"We're dressed in military garb, soaking wet, walking out of the forest, and have no idea where we are. If someone asks what we're doing, what are we going to tell them?" Pandora asked.

"That's a good point," Killian said, stepping over a root.

"How about, we're soldiers who crashed our Humvee in the forest, and we're running away from the fire?" Andromeda suggested.

"That makes it sound too much like we're responsible for the forest fire," Killian said.

"We are," Pandora added, shoving Killian playfully.

"I know, but that doesn't mean we have to tell people," Killian said. "Not to mention, we're too young to be soldiers."

"I think I could pass for a young marine just out of basics." Andromeda adjusted her coat jacket, drawing a sophisticated smile across her face.

"Yeah, but you're wearing the uniform of an officer or something higher," Killian pointed to the gold stripes on her arm.

Andromeda looked down and felt the embroidered patches. "God, okay, you figure it out, then," Andromeda said, stomping over a broken tree limb.

The road was getting closer as another car passed by.

Killian looked around the woods, trying to come up with some lie. "Shoot, nothing we say is going to explain what we look like."

Pandora wrapped her arm inside his. "Just going to have to wing it, I guess."

They stood on the edge of the black asphalt, relieved to see something familiar.

"This way?" Andromeda said, turning to the left.

Killian nodded, and they turned to follow Andromeda. It was another ten minutes before a car drove by. It was an older Volkswagen with a young family inside. The trio didn't wave at the vehicle as it passed by but watched the eyes of the driver, who swerved a little staring at the strange group.

"Should we try to hitch a ride with someone?" Andromeda asked.

Killian shrugged.

"We could get a lot of answers by riding with someone," Pandora said, "but they would also have a lot of questions. On the other hand, I'm sick of walking."

"Let's keep walking until we see a sign or something. There's a good amount of traffic. There has to be a town close by," Killian said.

In the next half hour, only two semi-trucks passed by them, and Killian had conjured up six more clusters of grapes. Andromeda had cursed fifteen times, and Pandora was getting a blister. Killian swept her off her feet and carried her for a bit.

Bushes rustled behind them, and they turned, hearts pumping in terror. Pandora slid off Killian's back, her breathing tightening. A herd of reindeer crossed over the road, diving into the cover of the forest.

"Wow, I thought I was going to have a heart attack," Pandora said, breathing tightly.

"Me too," Andromeda said.

A few moments later, a large, yellow Ford pick-up truck pulled by them. The vehicle slammed on its brakes, and the rear lights flashed to reverse. The truck zig-zagged on the side of the road until it was several feet from the trio. A tall man stepped out of the truck. He motioned for them to come over. They looked at one another and crossed the street, walking up to the man's vehicle.

He was a Yupik with a long black ponytail and a weather-worn face. His appearance was hard as nails, but his voice was soft and welcoming.

"Erm, you guys lost?" the man asked, tipping up his vanilla-colored, ten-gallon hat.

"You wouldn't believe," Pandora muttered.

"Hello sir, is there a town nearby?" Killian asked as dignified as he could muster.

"Yes," the man answered.

The trio looked around at one another as the stranger's gaze scrutinized each one of them. The smell of raw fish permeated the air around them, and Pandora slowly placed her collar over her nose.

"Thank you, sir, um, how much farther is it?" Andromeda asked sweetly.

Killian and Pandora looked over at her with eyebrows raised.

Until that point, Killian hadn't noticed anything in the stranger's hand, but as he moved his arm, Killian twitched in fear. A long brown stick of meat rose to the man's mouth, and he bit off a chunk with pearly-white teeth.

It's just jerky, Killian thought, breathing a sigh of relief.

"You're a pretty skittish lot, I can tell," the man said. "Must have been through a lot." The man looked at Killian with a nod and a small grin.

"We have, sir. We fell in the river a ways back. We've been freezing to death ever since. How far did you say the town is from here?" Andromeda asked again with a voice that sounded like honey.

"I didn't," the old man said, not turning to look at Andromeda. His gaze was fixed on Killian. "Got any weapons on you, young man?"

Killian was taken aback. *Was this a threat? Was he going to try and rob them? Was he going to try and kidnap the girls? What was this guy playing at?*

Killian didn't respond but stared back at the old Indian boldly. He scooted Pandora behind him. The man took another bite of his jerky.

"Sir, we need to get to a town for some supplies and a good night's rest. If you would be so kind as to point us in that direction, we can be on our way," Andromeda said gently.

Something moved inside the truck—a shadow within the windows. The trio stepped back, uncertain what was about to happen. A window rolled down, and a voice shouted, "Get in the truck."

The old man chuckled with a nasal laugh.

"Dad?" Killian said.

He ran up to the window. Jacob sat in the passenger seat, white as a ghost.

"Hey son, do you mind getting in before I bleed to death?"

Killian turned around to the girls. "It's my dad."

They half-smiled, still staring at the Indian suspiciously.

Killian held out his hand, and the older man reached for it.

"How did you ever find him?" Killian asked, shaking the man's hand wildly.

"'Bout twenty-five miles up on the river. Out catching this morning's crop when I saw him on the bank. Hop in. We've wasted enough time," the man said, opening the driver's door and climbing inside.

210

Killian opened the doors to the back seat, and a jackalope head stared at him. He cocked his head to the side. It was a wooden plaque with a rabbit's head and eight little antlers pointing out.

"Gonna have to jump on the other side, boy. I just got that back from the taxidermist," the old man said.

Killian shut the door and walked to the other side, peering into the bed of the truck. A net full of salmon rested on the bed. The twins followed him, pulling their silver blouses over their noses.

Andromeda pulled herself up to the door but hesitated to sit down. "You know we're all soaking wet, right?" Andromeda asked.

"Don't worry about it," the old man said, "this old beater seen worse than water in it."

Andromeda couldn't agree more. She was sure the black stains sprinkled across the floorboard were blood. She moved over to the middle of the seat, resting her arm on one of the Jackalope's antlers.

"You're going to have to sit in my lap," Killian said, turning around to Pandora.

Pandora pushed Killian up into the seat and hopped on top of him. She shut the door and rolled up the window.

"You ready back there, snowflakes?" the old man asked.

Three thumbs shot up, and the old man nodded in the rearview mirror. The engine fired up, and a cloud of black exhaust ripped through the air.

"Dad, are you okay?"

Jacob winced as he turned around. His white jacket was stained red and wrapped around his knee. "I'm okay, just need to stitch up this cut on my knee, that's all. How are you guys?"

"We're fine," Killian said, sliding his arms around Pandora, who was shaking with cold.

"Can you turn the heat on?" Pandora asked.

"Sure can," the old man answered, turning a knob on the dashboard.

"Guys, this is Jimmy. He's a fisherman here in the Yukon. He couldn't believe the story I told him about how you guys wanted to go do an old-time reenactment photoshoot in all this military garb for Killian's video contest."

"That's a pretty dumb idea," Jimmy cackled.

"It was, wasn't it?" Jacob said.

Three heads nodded as Killian let out an unsure, "Yeah."

"I bet Surprise Mountain was quite the surprise when that storm blew through," Jimmy said with a cough.

The trio nodded and looked at one another.

"Jimmy's already called his wife. They're going to let us stay the night and cook up some salmon while I let this leg heal. Doesn't that sound amazing?" Jacob asked.

"Yes," they said enthusiastically at the sound of real food.

"I don't think I ever want another grape again," Andromeda whispered.

They nodded in agreement.

The heat swept through the truck slowly, and the trio warmed their hands. A large wooden sign came into view. Two massive wooden horses stood on either side of the road. They were painted white with long flowing manes and front hooves bucking high into the air. Across the top, the wooden sign read, "Welcome to Whitehorse, Yukon."

Killian couldn't believe the beauty of the trees and the snow-capped mountains. He had been all over the world, but something about the north made his heart feel at home. A mailbox in the shape of a pink salmon marked Jimmy's driveway. The road cut through the forest, winding a half a mile off the main road. When they exited the wooded drive, they entered a large clearing in the middle of the spruce and hemlock woods.

In the center was a four-story log cabin. Killian had never seen anything like it. Each level had a deck running around the exterior of the building, like a log cabin hotel. The trio stared out the window in awe of the log mansion.

A woman opened the door as everyone exited the vehicle. Her long silver hair and beautiful high cheekbones reminded Killian of Pocahontas. She wore a rainbow-colored shawl over a dark chocolate gown.

"This is my wife, Rosalie," Jimmy said.

"It's been too long since we've entertained guests," Rosalie said, hugging each one of them as they approached the door. "And you're all soaking wet. Let's get inside and get some warm baths drawn."

Rosalie grabbed the twins by the arms and escorted them into the house. "My, aren't you two beautiful."

Jimmy motioned for the men to follow him. They walked up the broad wooden stairs of the patio deck and around to a sliding glass door. They entered the kitchen, and Jimmy grabbed two slices of deer jerky from the dehydrator. He handed one to each of them.

Killian smelled it, and a smoky-sweet flavor resonated on his taste buds. He took a bite and savored the molasses flavor covering the meat. Jacob held onto the bar for a moment as a shot of pain ran through his leg.

"Dad, are you alright?" Killian asked, setting down the jerky.

"Yeah, just give me a second," he replied with a grimace.

"Come on, we'll sew you up in here, and Killian can hop in the shower," Jimmy said.

Killian put his dad's arm over his shoulder and walked him into the bedroom. The yellow wood was amazingly vibrant, with reindeer heads decorating the walls. A large grizzly bear rug laid before the four-posted bed made of logs.

"Over here," Jimmy called.

Killian guided his dad into the bathroom. Wooden tiles blanketed the walls and floor. An antler chandelier hung down from the center of the room that ascended twenty feet high. Jimmy already had a first aid kit out with a needle and thread.

"Gonna need to see that wound, son," Jimmy said. "I've sewn plenty of these in my days. An employee of mine caught me right here in the cheek one time with a two-inch lure."

Killian raised his eyebrow staring at the white scar on Jimmy's cheek.

Jimmy looked up, "Oh, the other shower is through that walk-in closet. I'll bring you some clothes when we're done."

"Are you going to be okay?" Killian asked.

"I'm fine," Jacob said. "Go get a shower and clean up."

Jacob sat down on the toilet and placed his leg on the bathtub next to it. Jimmy cut the string with a pair of scissors and bent over the wound, unwrapping the maroon-stained jacket.

Killian walked back through the bedroom and into the walk-in closet. There were dresses and robes, wolf skins and mink coats, silk shawls, jeans, skirts, boots, and plenty more. The closet seemed more spacious than the bedroom as he came to a dead end with a large mirror. He stared at his reflection, and it was a horrible mess. He looked around the mirror for a handle. A brass knob hung to the right. He reached down and opened the door.

The room before him sparkled with salmon pink tiles and gold accents. Imprints of roses speckled the walls, and the scent of lavender filled the air. A crystal chandelier hung from the vaulted ceiling.

He stepped down three stairs onto the glistening pink marble. An enormous shower was positioned in the center of the room surrounded by an octagon of frosted glass. Large fluffy white towels dangled beside the marble counter with pearl sinks. A bouquet of plastic roses rested on each windowsill.

He peeled off the soggy uniform with excitement. He turned the golden handles, allowing the water to run hot until steam filled the room. He piled his clothes together and tossed them into an empty wicker basket. He stepped into the shower, smiling as the first drops hit his face. His entire body relaxed as he drenched himself in the water.

He lost track of time as the water cleared away his fear, anxiety, worry, frustration, and confusion. His mind wandered from Pandora to his dad, then from Pandora to her dad and little brother, then to the tattooed emblems on his body, back to her parents trapped in that godforsaken prison. Finally, as the water began to run cold, his thoughts were consumed by the Black Knight.

"Killian, have you turned into a fish or what?" Jacob called from the closet door.

"I'm almost done," Killian replied, quickly lathering himself.

"Almost? You've been in there thirty-five minutes, son. I laid some clothes here on these steps, hurry up."

"Yes sir," Killian said, saluting through the rain of water.

He washed his hair, rinsed, and turned off the water. He grabbed the fluffy white towel that seemed to absorb every droplet of water from him with one swipe. He walked across the marble and picked up the clothes.

There was a garnet-and-gold flannel shirt and a pair of light blue jeans. He tossed them aside and examined the brown leather belt, boxers, socks, and a pair of steel-toed khaki boots. They were all close to his size,

214

and as he put the items on, he glanced in the mirror. He felt like a lumberjack.

He walked out of the bedroom and into the living room which lay at the heart of the complex, complete with a fountain and a wrap-around aquarium on the bottom level. The ceiling rose forty feet to the top story. All the bedrooms centered on this room, with balconies outlining every floor.

His eyes caught Pandora's stunning champagne hair as she walked out of one of the upper rooms. Her appearance made him think of starlight falling around the face of the moon. She wore a long-sleeved black sweater, jeans, and boots. She rested her elbows on the balcony support and smiled at him affectionately. He motioned for her to come down, following her every step as she walked towards one of the spiral staircases.

"Are you hungry?" a voice asked behind him.

Killian turned to see Andromeda. Her hair was as white as snow with a flaming red ombre igniting the tips. Her golden eyes sparkled in contrast to her garnet minidress. Silver boots accented her black leggings as she leaned against one of the wooden beams.

"The guys are outside smoking some fish. They want us to join them," Andromeda said.

Killian nodded, catching his voice. "Uh, yeah, yeah, I'll be right over."

Andromeda turned and walked through the kitchen as Pandora came around the corner. Killian met her blue eyes, and his heart skipped a beat.

"You look like a mountain man," she said, running her fingers over his flannel. "I could get used to living like this." Her eyes scanned the majesty of the mansion.

"Yeah, this place is amazing," Killian said, taking her hand and walking with her to the oversized fireplace.

"What do you think this guy does to have all this money?" Pandora asked.

"I don't know. Maybe he won the Powerball or owns a fishing company or something."

Pandora held Killian's hands in hers as they sat on the couch, staring at the tremendous fire blazing before them. She drew circles over his palms with her gentle fingers, not looking into his eyes.

"I know this is silly to say," she began, turning his hand over and running her fingers down the imprints lining his palm.

"What is it?" Killian asked, and his stomach fluttered with a colony of butterflies.

"What is this?" Pandora asked, crossing her fingers into his.

"What's what?" Killian asked in a daze.

She looked up at him with vulnerable eyes, and her pink lips trembled. She reached out her hand and touched his chest. "This," she said, touching her heart, "What is this?"

Killian stared into her eyes, wondering what beautiful romantic words he could say to explain how he felt.

She waited, scrutinizing every movement that flashed across his face.

He smiled, thinking of exactly the words he wanted to say.

"*Melinyel, Orenya, Nienya, Tarinya.*"

Pandora blushed. "I don't know what that means. You know that."

Killian tucked her hair behind her ear and said, "It means —"

A harsh, deep cough echoed over the living room. They turned hurriedly to find Jacob standing there and smiling.

"Let's go, you two. It's time to eat," Jacob said.

They shot up off the couch, releasing each other's grasp. Killian felt as if they had been caught in some intimate act. Together, they moved around the furniture and walked past Jacob. Pandora held her head down low, not to make eye contact with him. Killian glanced at his dad, who winked approvingly.

They shuffled through another room and onto the back porch, where Rosalie and Andromeda were making drinks. A large firepit stood beside a decorative dining table adorned with an elaborate Indian headdress and small totem-pole seasoning shakers. Silver dining ware and plates lined the table. Andromeda handed them black goblets full of a peach-colored liquid.

"She said this is called *The Northern Lights*. I think it has alcohol in it," Andromeda whispered, sipping her own.

Killian and Pandora chuckled. They sat down at the table as Rosalie served up cranberry salad, slices of smoked salmon with herb dressing, and white bean hummus with roasted garlic.

"Dig in," Jimmy said, and they did just that.

Ten minutes later, they were all asking for seconds, and Rosalie was more than happy to oblige, throwing salmon steaks on their plates with a side of saskatoon berry pie. Fifteen minutes later, they were stuffed. Refills of the peach concoction went around again until everyone was struggling to keep their eyes open.

The sun settled, and the first stars appeared overhead. The firepit churned beside them, flicking red hot ashes into the air. Killian scooted his chair next to Pandora, and she leaned her head on his shoulder. Jacob and Jimmy were talking about current events as Andromeda swirled the cherry around in her drink.

"Look, look," Pandora shouted.

Everyone sat up, staring into the night. Swirling colors of lights snaked across the atmosphere, like an invisible hand brushing strokes of paint across the surface of the sky.

"Magnificent, isn't it?" Jimmy said, kicking back his chair and holding Rosalie's hand.

"Ah, yes, the northern lights. Many souls are being ushered through to the other side tonight," Rosalie said.

"What do you mean?" Killian asked.

"The legend of my people says that these are the lights of the torch bearers transporting souls from our world to the next," Rosalie answered.

Killian returned his gaze to the starry night, watching the colors dance as he chewed on Rosalie's comment. A cold wind blew over the table, extinguishing many of the candles.

"I think the mother wants us to go inside now," Rosalie said, patting Jimmy on the leg.

The trio grabbed their plates to bring inside, but Rosalie demanded they put them down.

"No guest in my house will lift a finger to do a chore. That's for the help to do," she said with a wink. She clapped three times, and a robotic maid came wheeling around the back porch.

"Yes, madam?" the robotic voice asked.

"Diana, be a dear and clean this up and the kitchen, too, when you're done," Rosalie said, passing by the robot.

217

Killian stared at the black-haired, silver-faced maid. He'd never seen one of the AI Class Four Chambermaids before. Andromeda stumbled behind him, carrying her black goblet, and high-fived the robot.

They filed into the living room, each one of them taking a place on a sofa. Jimmy threw another three logs in the fireplace and asked if anyone wanted coffee. Jacob raised his hand, and they headed for the kitchen. Andromeda sat sideways on a brown suede chair, letting her feet dangle over the armrest, setting her glass on the floor.

Pandora placed her head in Killian's lap as they relaxed on the couch. Killian ran his hands through her golden blonde hair. Within minutes she was asleep. He looked at her face, analyzing the unbelievable perfection of her beauty.

What would I do for her? What wouldn't I do for her? Suddenly, an image of the Black Knight popped into his head again. He thought of the brownies and how he couldn't protect them. How would he protect her?

He scooted himself out from under her and planted a pillow under her head. He walked into the kitchen where Jimmy and his dad were talking over their freshly brewed coffee.

"What is it, Killian?" Jacob asked.

"I was just wondering if there was a computer I could use?"

"Oh, it's kind of late. You're not tired?" Jimmy asked.

"No, not really."

"Well, sure, there's one over here in the office." Jimmy pointed down the hall with his coffee cup.

Killian followed Jimmy into an elegant room decorated with stuffed salmons on wooden plaques. His desk was solid glass, with a twenty-four-inch Apple touchscreen retracting from it.

"Manual override, deactivate securities," Jimmy said.

"Deactivating all security measures," the AI responded.

"There you go, browse away." Jimmy patted Killian on the shoulder and walked back to the kitchen.

Jacob stood in the doorway and stared at Killian over the top of his coffee cup. "Hebrew?" Jacob asked.

Killian nodded, sitting down in the rolling leather chair.

Jacob coughed and leaned against the door.

"Dad, are you feeling okay? You look red, and you're sweating."

218

"I think I'm going to go lie down. It must be the coffee." Jacob turned and began to walk down the hallway.

"*Melinyel Taryo*," Killian said.

Jacob turned and smiled. "*Melinyel Hildinya*."

Killian watched his dad limp down the hallway and place his cup on the kitchen counter. He returned his attention to the computer.

He typed in "English to Hebrew dictionary" and began consuming the massive log of vocabulary. He read through pages and pages of translations, memorizing everything like never before. The hours passed, but he pressed on, excited by his new ability and the possibilities these words would bring.

He paused and looked up from the screen, massaging his temples. He peered through the windows and down the hallway, but the only person he saw was Diana putting away plates. He closed the door to the office and sat down. He held out his hand and said, "*Zahav*." A bar of gold fell upon the floor. He picked it up and was surprised at how heavy it was. His reflection sparkled in the rectangle as he rested it on the desk.

He looked at the golden bar and said, "*Shoshanim*." A dozen roses fell on top of the bar. He lifted one of the roses from the pile and smelled. The scent was amazing. "Pandora will love these," he said.

He set the rose down and said, "*Eqedakhim, Rovim, Sakinim, Kharavot*." An array of weapons fell on the floor around him: guns, rifles, knives, and swords. He checked a few of the arms, but they weren't loaded. He thought for a moment, scanning the vocabulary whirling in his mind. He said, "*Eqedahkim Te'unim*," and more guns fell upon the floor. He picked one up and released the magazine. It was full of bullets. He nodded in satisfaction.

Something was happening to him; he was learning faster and understanding more than he ever had before. He learned five hundred words, then one thousand words, then two thousand words. The sun was beginning to come up, and the light flickered through the office windows. He wiped small beads of sweat from his brow as he pushed himself harder and harder to understand not only the words but also the grammar. He scrolled through site after site, memorizing pages of information.

Suddenly, the computer shut down, and the electricity went out. He pressed the power button to the network, but nothing happened. He walked over to the lamp, but it would not come on. He walked out into the kitchen and flipped the light switch, but nothing happened. Diana wasn't moving. She was frozen stiff in the middle of wiping a counter. He waved his hand in front of her face and patted her on the back. The sound was like rapping an empty tin can.

He said, *"Ner,"* and a large candle appeared in his hand. He concentrated on the wick and said, *"Esh."* A flame danced upon the candle as an orange glow flowed over him. He walked into the living room where Pandora and Andromeda were still asleep. He stared at the fireplace full of ash and said, *"Atze Hasaka."* A pile of firewood fell upon the ash. *"Esh!"* The logs burst into flame.

Killian sat down beside Pandora as she began to stir. The firelight swept over the room, and he blew out the candle, laying it on the center table. He looked down upon her and brushed away a few misplaced hairs. She rolled over, throwing her arms around him, and resting her head in his lap.

"How did you sleep?" Killian asked.

"Wonderfully," she said, squeezing his midsection. "How about you?"

"I haven't been to sleep yet," he admitted.

She sat up, "Why, are you okay?"

"Yeah, I'm fine. I was studying."

"Studying? Studying what?" Pandora yawned and wiped the sleep from her eyes.

"Hebrew, of course. Here, watch." He held out his hand and said, *"Vered Adom."* A red rose appeared in his hand, and he handed it to Pandora.

She breathed in the potent fragrance of the flower. "That's amazing."

"Watch this, *Sharsheret Hasafir.*" A golden necklace with a large sapphire pendant landed in his hand. He unlocked the clasp, and Pandora pulled her hair back, revealing her thin neckline. He reached around, fumbling to close the clasp. "There," he said as the pendant rested upon her chest.

"It's beautiful," Pandora said. "I've never seen a sapphire like this before. So you've been up all night studying Hebrew?"

"Yep," Killian said.

"How much have you learned?" Pandora asked, looking down at the sapphire pendant.

"A couple thousand words, I guess," Killian smiled, watching her admire the necklace.

Pandora looked up, "How'd you learn it all so fast?"

"I don't know. I think it's just part of these," Killian slid back his sleeve showing her the Enochian script. "I couldn't help myself. I just soaked it all up."

"Can you two be any louder?" Andromeda asked, straightening up in the chair. "Oh, my head."

"Annie, look at what Killian made." She lifted the pendant from her chest. The sapphire twinkled in the firelight.

"Wow," Andromeda said, squinting, her voice sounded genuine.

"And smell this." Pandora tossed her the rose.

"Yeah, I was wondering where the smell was coming from." Andromeda placed her nose on the center of the rose. "It's so sweet I feel like I could just eat this thing."

"Are you kiddos up already?" Rosalie asked, walking around the corner. "Where is that magnificent smell coming from?"

Andromeda held up the rose Killian had conjured.

"Where did you guys find roses?" Rosalie asked, taking the flower in her hand. "I've never seen a rose so full of petals."

The trio looked at each other for a moment while Rosalie examined the flower. Killian's eyes went from Andromeda's to Pandora's.

"We found it when we were hiking yesterday at Surprise Mountain," Andromeda said.

"Yeah, there was a massive bush there. You wouldn't believe how many blossoms there were, and bees everywhere," Pandora added.

"Wow," Rosalie said. "You'll have to take me there one day. I'd love to see that." Rosalie walked towards the kitchen. "Do you want me to put this in some water?"

"Yes, please," the twins rang out.

221

"I think a breaker tripped last night. Jimmy's going to check on it here in a minute," Rosalie said, turning the corner.

Killian looked at the girls, and his eyes were bulging. "Um, I may have created some other things that we may not be able to explain away so easily."

The girls looked at each other.

"Come on," Killian said.

They snuck to the office, and Killian stepped over the pile of weapons. The twins stood in the doorway, their mouths hanging open.

"What in the world were you thinking?" Pandora said.

"I was thinking, how do I use this power to create weapons to protect you, and voila."

"That's so sweet," Pandora purred.

Andromeda picked up one of the large rifles. "Wow, I've never held a machine gun before. Do you think they work?"

"Do the roses smell amazing? Were the grapes the best thing you've ever tasted?" Killian asked.

Andromeda nodded, "Touché."

"Check this out." He tossed Andromeda the bar of gold.

"Is this real?' she asked.

"Of course it's real," Pandora said, snatching it out of Andromeda's hand.

"Look, we gotta get these guns out of here before anyone sees them," Killian said, picking up handfuls.

The girls grabbed the rest, and they snuck out the side door. They walked down the porch steps and ran over to the bushes, tossing the weapons inside. The swords clanged against the rifles, sending the echoing sound of metal on metal reverberating across the woods. They walked around the back of the house and sat down by the empty fire pit.

Andromeda shivered from the morning cold and glanced over at the ash in the firepit. "A little help, Killian."

"What," Killian said, yawning.

"Can you light a fire?" Andromeda asked, emphasizing every word.

"Oh, yeah." Within seconds a pile of logs appeared in the hole and were set ablaze.

Pandora sat on Killian's lap as he rested his back upon the chair. Andromeda sat across from them, staring at the firelight. Killian felt his eyes becoming heavy as Pandora swirled her fingers through his hair.

"I wonder what else you can make?" Andromeda muttered.

"Yeah, I wonder if you can make, like, animals," Pandora said.

Killian yawned again. "I think I could. What would you like?"

"A kitten," Pandora said.

"A puppy," Andromeda added.

"*Khataltul,*" Killian said, and a snow-white kitten popped into Pandora's lap. The cat had golden eyes that strangely resembled Andromeda's.

Killian looked towards Andromeda and said, "*Klavlav.*" A small brown puppy appeared before her, and she scooped him up from the ground. The puppy's eyes were the same as the cat's.

The twins fawned over their new little pets. The kitten purred, and the puppy barked excitedly.

"This is the most amazing thing I've ever seen," Pandora said, turning to Killian, but he was fast asleep.

19: CABIN FEVER

"Killian, wake up," Pandora yelled, shaking his shoulders.

Killian's eyes slowly opened as he looked up from the patio into the midday sun. He shaded his eyes with his hands and sat up. Pandora's hand rubbed his back as a kitten meowed next to them.

"Killian, come on, your dad . . ." Pandora's voice broke.

"What about my dad?" Killian asked with a burst of adrenaline.

Pandora's eyes watered.

Killian jumped up and rushed inside with Pandora nipping at his heels. "Where is he, Pan?"

Pandora pointed towards a room on the second floor.

He bolted up the circular stairway and flung open the door. Jimmy stood over Jacob as Rosalie applied a wet cloth to his sweating forehead.

"He's taken a fever," Jimmy said, looking up at Killian. "A pretty bad one."

"Why?" Killian asked.

Rosalie pulled the satin covers back and revealed an oozing wound full of yellow puss with streaks of red running in every direction on Jacob's leg.

Killian gagged and put his hands to his mouth. His eyes teared up, and he fought back the urge to cry. "We need to get him to a hospital," his voice trembled.

"I know," Jimmy said, "but for some reason, the house has no electricity, and none of the vehicles are working."

"The cars aren't working?" Killian asked. "What's wrong with them?"

"I don't know," Jimmy said. "It's like the engine's been fried or the electric cables have been burned, or something."

Killian looked around the room and spotted Andromeda holding her puppy. Their eyes met, and she nodded. He turned around, finding Pandora in the doorway, biting her lip.

"Can I talk to you two really quick?" Killian asked, walking out of the room.

They ran downstairs and out the backdoor to the firepit.

"Are you thinking what I'm thinking?" Killian asked.

The twins nodded.

"It's just like New Jerusalem," Andromeda said.

"So, what are we going to do?" Pandora asked. "Your dad needs medicine; don't you know the word for antibiotics? Just make some."

"I didn't come across that word last night," Killian said, biting his thumbnail. "I could make a car, I think." He glanced at the puppy and kitten playing under the chairs.

"Even if you could make a car, do you think it's safe to move your dad?" Andromeda asked, running her fingers over the pup's head.

"And how are we going to explain a car magically appearing in the driveway?" Pandora added.

Killian paced back and forth. "If an EMP has been set off like last time, it's just a matter of time before those minotaurs are sent out again to find us."

"Or worse," Pandora added.

"How did they find us so quick?" Andromeda asked.

"They must have traced the tracks back to here, when they found the train car we dislodged," Killian suggested.

"So, now what?" Andromeda asked. "How are we going to defend ourselves from these monsters and take care of your dad at the same time?"

Killian sat in the chair, rocking back and forth. The twins sat on either side of him, resting their hands on his back. Andromeda suddenly went rigid as a cool breeze blew over the trio. Killian and Pandora looked over to see Andromeda's eyes turning white as a mist overtook them.

Andromeda opened her mouth and a dry dead voice spoke, "Killian Benjamin Gold, the bloodline of Eve, a new age rests on your lips, but the lion is seeking you. He won't rest until you're his." Andromeda shivered as the cold wind stopped.

Killian and Pandora stared at her with their mouths open.

Andromeda looked down at her hand where the roots were still glowing red. "I'm sorry, I . . . I forgot," she said, standing up and moving several chairs over. The puppy barked eagerly in her hands, and she set him down to run.

226

"That was amazing, Annie. Do me," Pandora said, reaching out her hand.

"No, Pan, I don't want to see you there. I can't see you there. Don't ask me to do that," Andromeda trembled.

"Does it hurt, Annie, when it happens?" Killian asked.

Andromeda glanced up, and her golden eyes stared at Killian. Then she turned away, looking back at the empty fire pit. "It hurts, but not my body, it hurts my soul."

Killian looked at Pandora, taking her hand in his. He shook his head at her, not to press Andromeda anymore. Whatever it was that Andromeda could see in her visions was dangerous to know and painful to see.

"So a lion is seeking me," Killian said, standing again. "That's the Black Knight, I imagine. Before we know it, UFOs will be flying all around this town, and a horde of monsters will be roaming the streets."

"Excuse me, guys, are you busy?" Jimmy walked out onto the porch.

"No, sir, please join us." Pandora stood up, pulling over a chair.

Jimmy walked down the stairs and sat in the wooden seat. He scratched his chest and tightened his brown leather boots. "Killian, I know this is hard, but I think we need to make a choice," Jimmy said, and his raspy, normally joyful voice, was sullen and low.

Killian sat down beside Pandora. She grabbed his hand and held it tight.

"Your dad's fever is very dangerous. Rosalie just checked it, and it's one-hundred and four. He needs antibiotics. Now I have some old bicycles in the barn. We could ride into town and go to the hospital. It's about twenty-five miles away. It shouldn't take but a couple of hours, and we could get a ride back from one of my friends. I'll probably rent a car for the week until we have time to figure out what's going on with these. Rosalie will take great care of him and the girls as well, I'm sure, while we're gone. What do you think?"

Killian looked at Pandora, and she nodded, squeezing his hand. He turned toward Andromeda, but she was staring into the forest.

"When can we leave?" Killian asked.

"Now." Jimmy got up and walked toward the barn.

Killian stared at Pandora. "Everything is going to be fine. We'll get the medicine and be right back."

Pandora reached up and brushed his cheek with her palm. "I don't want us to be separated, but if this will save your dad, then it's the right thing to do."

Killian took her hand from his cheek and kissed it softly. He stood and turned towards Andromeda, but she looked away.

Killian left the firepit and crossed the stone path towards the barn. Jimmy rolled out two Schwinn bicycles with flat tires. "Hold these for a second," Jimmy said. "Got to find that manual pump since the power is out."

Killian held the two bicycles, examining their durability. There was no rust on the body, and the chains looked reasonably decent. Jimmy was back in a flash and popped the needle onto the valve, pumping up the tires with his hands. "That should do it," Jimmy said, finishing the last tire. He stood up and tossed the pump back into the barn. "You ready?"

"Let's go." Killian hopped on the red bike and pedaled down the driveway.

Andromeda ran out, blocking his path, arms waving wildly. He stopped abruptly, skidding to avoid running into her. Jimmy pulled up beside them.

"Is everything okay?" Jimmy asked.

"Yes, I just need to tell Killian something before he goes," Andromeda said.

"Oh," Jimmy said, "I'll just check the mailbox real quick." He pedaled up ahead and around the trees.

"What is it, Annie?" Killian asked.

Andromeda bit her lip.

She looked just like Pandora when she did that. Her hair was flowing around her in the breeze, and she brushed it back gracefully. Her eyes refused to make contact with his.

"You can tell me, or you don't have to tell me. Either way," Killian said, placing his hand on her shoulder. "If it's too painful to say, don't say it."

She looked up at him, and her eyes were full of fear. "Something will happen; something is going to happen. I can't decide which thing yet. There are too many obstacles and variables in the path."

"What kind of things? What did you see?" Killian watched her eyes intently.

A tear escaped the crease in her eye and trickled down her cheek.

"What can I do about what you saw?" Killian asked.

"I don't know." Andromeda burst into tears. "You can't fight them alone, and we need you here, but your dad needs you as well, and it's all going to end . . ." She sobbed and threw her arms around his neck.

He hugged her tightly, and she let go, stepping back. She wiped her eyes with her sleeves.

"Every choice we make draws us closer to life or death, and you never know which is which until the end," Killian said.

"Make the right choices then," Andromeda said, and she turned around and ran back behind the house.

Killian watched her until she was out of sight. He placed his foot back on the pedal and pushed down.

Within minutes they were on the main road, headed toward downtown Whitehorse. Familiar hemlock trees lined the street as Killian pedaled harder and harder up the steep hill. They crossed the top and came into a clearing. The snow-capped mountains of Yukon decorated the horizon like a picture from a postcard.

"Beautiful isn't it?" Jimmy asked.

"Yeah, it is." Killian surveyed the skyline above the mountains, looking for anything that might be scanning the area. "How far did you say it was again?"

"A good two hours. Don't spend all your energy right now. We have a few big hills to cross on our way over. Slow and steady."

Killian pedaled and pedaled, passing groups of caribou, deer, and moose. He'd never seen moose before and was shocked to find they stood taller than a horse with gigantic antlers. An hour passed, and Killian still hadn't seen a town. His frustration was mounting.

Jimmy was surprisingly quiet, for which Killian was thankful. How many lies would he have to tell if Jimmy started asking questions? What if he wanted to know where they were from or how they all met? Jimmy coughed, and Killian felt a cold chill flow over him.

"Strange, we haven't seen a single car so far," Jimmy said.

This realization sent Killian's paranoia soaring as he looked around, peering through the trees and up into the clouds. "Yeah, that's strange."

"Your dad said you're already in college." Jimmy swerved out of the way of a fallen branch.

"Yeah, junior year," Killian answered. He dodged the branch and looked back at an eagle soaring high above.

"And you're only seventeen?"

"Yeah," Killian replied, wondering what question was coming next.

"I was sorry to hear about your mother."

Killian swallowed and wiped the sweat from his brow. "Yeah," was all he could say.

"We live in a broken world, don't we?"

Killian glanced over, but Jimmy was staring into the sky. He returned his focus to the road. *Mom's alive, and I haven't even told Dad*, he thought. *As soon as I get back, it's the first thing I'm going to do. That will help him fight this thing.*

The eagle dove down out of sight, and Killian searched the skies once more, looking for any trace of the alien presence.

"Have you ever seen a UFO in person?" Jimmy asked.

Killian's hand jerked the handlebars, and he fell off the bicycle, tumbling into the dirt. Jimmy slammed on his brakes and ran over to where he lay.

"You okay, boy? What in the world happened?"

Killian sat up, brushing the dirt off and checking his arm. His flannel shirt was ripped, and his elbow was bleeding. "Fantastic," he muttered.

Jimmy helped him to his feet.

"Thanks, sorry about that," Killian said. "It's been a long time since I rode a bicycle."

"It's okay. Are you okay?" Jimmy asked as his wheezy laugh returned.

"Yeah, let's get going." Killian jumped back on the bicycle.

They rode for a few minutes down a slope, then up another hill, passing trees on the right and a river way down the bank on his left.

"I imagine you've seen a UFO before, huh." Jimmy laughed. "I haven't seen someone wig out like that in a decade. You would've thought there was one right above us."

Killian searched the sky instinctively as if Jimmy had summoned one to their location. "Yes, I've seen one before. Have you?"

"Well, of course, I have," Jimmy replied.

"When?" Killian asked, his hairs standing on end.

"Been on the news all week. Most amazing thing to happen in my lifetime."

That's right, Killian thought, breathing a sigh of relief.

"Yeah, I meant, have you seen one in person yet?" Killian glanced over at Jimmy.

"I did actually, just the other day."

Killian gulped. They'd already been surveying this area. "What did it look like?"

"It was the one they call the cigar. Real long and silver, like a giant tube in the sky."

"A giant tube?" Killian asked. "I've never seen those before. I didn't know there were different kinds. I thought there were just the discs."

"Well, ever since last week, there have been three distinct kinds as far as I'm aware. The bell, the cigar, and the traditional disc. You're a bright young boy, do you think they're aliens?"

Killian raised his eyebrows and looked away. What could he say? He cleared his throat. "I don't know. I don't like all that space stuff," he lied.

"Oh, that's strange. Your dad said you wanted to be a scientist one day. I thought you'd be enamored with the new technology being disclosed."

Thanks, Dad, Killian thought. "Yeah, but I don't like thinking about beings from other worlds. It gives me the creeps."

"Well, I don't think they're aliens at all. They haven't even shown us a body yet. I want a full-blown interview with one of these creatures if they expect me to believe these are aliens."

"So, you don't believe they're aliens?" Killian's nerves relaxed as he pedaled hard up the next hill.

"I don't, but Rosalie does. She thinks they've been living inside of the Earth for over a millennium. Now they've run out of room down there and are venturing up to the surface to take over."

Killian thought about this for a minute. *Could that be possible?* He just thought they were minions in some rogue angel's army, but maybe they were a people who had consumed all their resources and were looking to take over humans.

They rode on, pedaling past rocky banks, strips of forest, then next to another run of rapids flowing like white horses down a stream. Killian kept his eyes on the sky, looking for the slightest glimmer or sparkle of a UFO.

They turned down the next bend, riding up to a large bridge with massive grey beams looping along the road. Killian thought the architecture looked like an AT-AT walker from Star Wars, and as they passed under the shafts, he glanced up, marveling at the passageway.

"How far now?" Killian asked.

"We're almost to the historic district. Then it's just a little way to the hospital."

They pedaled faster, noticing houses appearing on the left. To the right, the river was full in view, expanding as they ventured toward the downtown area. The highway spread out into six lanes, and abandoned cars were scattered in every direction.

"I've never seen this place so dead before," Jimmy said as his tone changed to a worried murmur.

Killian was afraid to explain to him what had happened and what was going to happen. They needed the medicine, and they needed to get out of this town as quickly as possible. Maybe he should tell Jimmy and explain the urgency they were under, but he was afraid of the questions he didn't have answers for.

They entered the downtown area. It was deserted. All the shops were closed, even the streetlamps weren't working. Killian was terrified to think this entire city had already been kidnapped and imprisoned.

"In twenty-three years I've never seen the town like this." Jimmy scanned the area as Killian followed close behind. "Let's stop here for a second." Jimmy pulled down a side street and up to a bait and tackle shop. The door was locked, and the lights were off. "Kevin never closes his store," Jimmy murmured.

"Jimmy, we need to get to the hospital and get back. This power outage must have sent everyone home."

Jimmy turned around and stared at him. "I thought the outage was just in the neighborhood. I didn't realize the whole area had been affected. What could have caused something like this?"

Killian didn't want to answer. He turned his bike back towards the main highway. "Let's get to the hospital. There's got to be people there. Maybe they can tell us what happened. Look the sun is already close to setting, we need to hurry."

Jimmy peered up at the sky. "This has taken longer than I thought," he whispered and turned his bike around. "We're going to have to ride these bikes all the way back."

Killian could hear the trepidation in his voice, but he had to get them moving. They pulled onto the street and down the road over another bridge. They turned onto Hospital Road as another forest of spruce trees scattered to their right and an elementary school to their left.

"The hospital is just up this hill," Jimmy panted.

Killian pedaled as hard as he could, sweat pouring down his brow. His elbow burned from the fall, but he didn't care, they were finally at their destination. The hospital came into view—a massive collage of buildings colored in blue and green. The parking lot was half full with an ambulance parked in the driveway.

They placed the bikes on the rack next to the entrance and walked through the open double doors. There were people everywhere inside. Nurses, doctors, and patients. Some were sitting, some were asleep, but most of them were walking around.

"Excuse me," Jimmy said, reaching out towards a lady in red scrubs. "We need some antibiotics for a bad wound a friend has. It might be going septic."

"Can you get him here?" the nurse said.

"No, we live on the other side of Mt. Lorne, and none of our vehicles are working."

"Wow, all the way out to Lorne, huh?" the nurse said, scratching her curly hair. "If it's septic, it may be too late. He would need to be brought here. You can start him on amoxicillin, but the pain is going to be excruciating, and he may not make it."

Killian's knees felt weak, and he grabbed Jimmy's shoulder.

"It'll be okay, son. We'll get it to him in time." When Jimmy looked back up, the nurse was gone. "What in the hell? Where did she go?"

They looked around, but she was nowhere to be seen. Killian kicked a nearby wall. A group of people looked up at him, but he didn't care.

"Come on." Jimmy walked down the hallway, trying to read the signs in the dim light. "There it is," he said, pointing to a black and white board. "The pharmacy is in the basement."

They took off toward the staircase and opened the door. It was pitch black with small beads of light moving around ominously.

Jimmy turned around, staring at Killian. "We need a flashlight or something to go down there. It's too dark."

"Stay right here. I'll find one," Killian said, running around the corner. He whispered, "*Ner*," and a candle popped into his hand. "*Esh*," and it was lit. Killian ran back to Jimmy, holding the candle.

"Wow, that was fast," Jimmy said.

"Yeah, they're just over there, no problem." Killian pointed aimlessly.

They ran down the staircase, passing several people carrying candles, lighting the stairwell with an eerie atmosphere. A sound of commotion could be heard from below as they reached the bottom floor. They opened the door to a dark room full of an orange haze. A mass of people was huddled around the pharmacy, demanding medicine, and arguing with one another.

"Joe," Jimmy screamed.

A bald man with a cane walked over. "Hey, Jimmy, you all right?"

"Yeah, I'm fine. We had some visitors, and this young man's dad got a pretty bad cut that's starting to turn. We need some antibiotics. What are you doing here?"

"Betty needs her insulin," Joe answered.

"How long have you been here?"

"A few hours. Vultures keep coming in, moving people out of line. The darkness is driving people crazy," Joe said.

234

Killian stared around at the hordes of people. The smell of sweat and body odor was horrendous. Candles were lit in every direction as people yelled and cursed at one another.

We don't have time to wait for this, Killian thought. Then an idea struck him. He snuck away from Jimmy and moved toward the center aisle. The pharmacy lab was about fifteen feet away. He glanced around for something to shield his eyes. An older gentleman was sitting on a bench with a pair of sunglasses hanging from his shirt.

Killian walked over to him. "Sir, could I borrow those glasses for a moment?"

The older adult looked up, squinting at Killian. "No," he said and placed his chin back on his chest.

"Why you …" Killian mumbled. He looked down at his pocket and whispered, *"Zahav."* He felt a lump of gold fill the emptiness. He pulled out the bar.

"Could I borrow the glasses for five minutes, and you can have this bar of gold?" Killian asked.

The old man looked up, squinting at the bar of gold, licking his lips, and said, "No."

What the frick is wrong with you? Killian thought. He looked back down at the older adult.

"Okay, what do you want in exchange for the glasses, sir?" Killian emphasized the last word loudly.

The old man looked up at him and smiled a toothless grin. "Coffee."

Killian put the bar of gold back in his pocket and walked away. A plastic bush was nearby, and he walked quickly towards it. He held out his hand and whispered, *"Kos."* A cup fell into his hand. He focused on the cup and said, *"Kafe."* The container filled with a thick brown liquid.

Killian walked back to the older adult. "Here, try this."

The man took the cup with a shaking hand. He placed the rim to his lips and sipped. His eyes widened as the flavor saturated his tongue. He took a gulp and licked his lips, splashing coffee all over his shirt. His wrinkled fingers wrapped around the glasses and handed them to Killian.

"I've never tasted anything like this before," the old man said.

"And you never will again," Killian mumbled, walking away.

He placed the solar shields on his face, feeling ridiculous. He moved back into the center of the aisle and whispered, "*HaOr HaGadol.*" It was as if the sun itself had filled the room. People screamed in every direction, ducking down and closing their eyes.

Killian stepped over ten people and hopped through the pharmacy window. He looked around for a label that said amoxicillin, but the light was dissipating. He whispered, "*HaOr HaGadol,*" reigniting the orb of light. In another ten seconds, he had the antibiotics in his hands, and he was climbing through the window.

He maneuvered past the people crying and yelling, stepping on several feet with his steel-toed boots. "Jimmy, follow me," Killian said, grabbing the man's arm and guiding him into the stairwell.

The light went out as the metal door rang shut. Killian took off the glasses and stuck them in his pocket. Jimmy rubbed his eyes and stared at Killian.

"What in the world happened in there?"

"I don't know. Maybe the power is trying to come back on?" Killian suggested.

"I've never seen anything like that before."

"Me, neither," Killian lied. "But I got the medicine, so let's get to Dad."

"How in the world did you get it?" Jimmy asked suspiciously, rubbing his eyes again.

"Some bottles were lying on the counter. I just grabbed them when the crowd separated."

They rushed up the stairs and out into the lobby. Killian thought there was no way to squeeze any more people into this building, but he was wrong. It was as if the whole town had gathered in this spot.

They went through the barred doors and out onto the driveway beside the ambulance. The bikes were gone, and darkness covered the streets.

"Where are the bikes?" Killian asked.

Jimmy looked around, frowning. "People do desperate things when shaken from their routine lives."

Killian threw his hands in the air. "What is wrong with this town? The nurse walks away, that moron won't give me his glasses, and now this. Has everyone lost their mind?"

Jimmy tried to pat Killian on the shoulders, but he was too mad and stomped away.

"Killian, my friend, I know many people in this town. They will help us out," Jimmy consoled him.

Killian shook his head. "How far away do they live?"

"Back in the historic area. We can be there in about fifteen minutes."

Killian looked around. Could he make a car? Would it run? How would he say it? He scanned the parking lot, analyzing the best vehicle to try. A bright blue Toyota Tacoma caught his eye.

"Why don't we check out these cars first and see if any of them work?" Killian asked.

"You want to steal a car?" Jimmy turned around with a disapproving look.

"Someone just stole our bikes. I don't want to steal a car, but I don't want my dad to die, either." Killian moved toward the parking lot.

"I understand," Jimmy said. "But I'm not stealing someone's car."

"We'll bring it back after we get the other ones working. It's just for now," Killian said, walking closer to the parking lot.

"You're a grown man, Killian. You do whatever you want, but I'll walk back before I step inside of someone else's vehicle." Jimmy turned and began walking down the road toward the highway.

Killian watched him for a moment, then ran over to the Tacoma. He examined the vehicle, memorizing every point of interest in his mind. He looked around, but no one was in the parking lot. *I hope some of the words in Hebrew match English.*

He took a deep breath and said, "Toyota Tacoma."

A replica of the truck popped onto the pavement, but it was about the size of a go-cart. Killian touched it. It was solid. He pushed it forward, and the wheels rolled. He looked inside, and there was a small set of keys. He twisted the ignition, and it purred like a kitten. *Hmmm, needs to be a bit bigger.*

He rolled the miniature Tacoma out of the parking spot and looked around again. There was no one in the vicinity. He said, "Toyota Tacoma

Gadolah." A Tacoma, twice the size of the original Tacoma, appeared before him. It was the size of a monster truck. Killian grinned from ear to ear. He grabbed ahold of the bar and pulled himself onto the step.

He opened the door and sat inside. The truck smelled like brand new leather. The key waited for him in the ignition, and he fired it up. He turned the lights on, lighting up the dark parking lot. The sound was like the roaring of a tiger. He grasped the wheel with both hands and threw the truck into drive. Within seconds, he pulled up beside Jimmy.

He rolled the window down and yelled, "Are you sure you don't want a lift?"

Jimmy gaped at the massive truck. "Where did you find this?"

"Just get in, and I'll explain everything."

20: CREATURES OF THE NIGHT

Andromeda stared at the dwindling fire, petting Jackson, her golden-eyed puppy, fast asleep at her feet. The coals breathed in with every breeze that passed by. She stood and walked over to the pile of firewood stacked neatly together. She threw several logs into the pit and stirred the ashes with an iron poker.

Flames reignited, licking the logs with garnet forked tongues. Andromeda sat back in her seat and looked up at the stars. They twinkled in the woodland oasis. She watched rows of colors pass overhead as the Northern Lights blossomed again.

A twig snapped in the distance, waking Jackson. Andromeda sat up as the puppy let out a bark that echoed through the wood. She picked up the assault rifle Killian had made and loaded the chamber while staring into the woods. The trees swayed with the wind like demonic black fingers reaching into the night.

Another twig snapped far to the left, and the puppy ran behind her feet. Andromeda pulled the rifle to her shoulder, scanning the darkness with her golden eyes. Sweat beaded on her palms, sliding against the black metal of the gun.

Three more twigs snapped, and a large hemlock tree bent to the side. Andromeda stepped back towards the porch and climbed the stairs. Jackson clawed at the glass door. Spruces turned in every direction as branches snapped and fell to the ground. A deep moan bellowed from inside the woods.

Andromeda scooped up Jackson and ran inside, locking the door. A golden tinge rested over the living room from the firelight. She tossed the puppy onto the sofa and checked the ground floor, locking every door and window. Another moan howled from the forest, shaking the windows, and the puppy whimpered on the couch. Andromeda dashed up the circular stairs, meeting Rosalie halfway.

"What was that sound?" Rosalie panted.

"I don't know. Something's out there. Something's coming," Andromeda said, her voice trembling with fear as she held the rifle.

Rosalie looked down at the weapon. "I've never seen a rifle like that before. Where did you get it?"

"Killian made it. I mean, he had it." Andromeda mumbled.

"It's nice," Rosalie said, raising her eyebrows. "Where were these sounds coming from?"

Andromeda motioned for her to follow and headed to the bottom floor. They jogged over to the glass doors and peered out into the forest.

"Behind the fire pit," Andromeda said, pointing towards the darkness.

The trees were still as stone. Andromeda's eyes surveyed the area, but nothing seemed out of the ordinary.

"What's that by the tree? That long, skinny thing?" Rosalie asked.

Andromeda peered in the direction Rosalie was staring. There was something there, but it was strange. It was like a blurred shadow standing between two spruces. A hemlock swayed to the right, and their eyes shot over to it.

Something like a shadow walked out from within the forest. It was twenty feet tall with arms hanging down to its knees. It stepped forward towards the fire pit and let out a booming moan like some freakish call.

Andromeda turned towards Rosalie, whose face was red with anger.

"Follow me," she said, her hands balling into fists.

They ran to the master bedroom, and Rosalie flung back the bearskin rug, revealing a trap door. She pulled it open, exposing a wooden staircase cascading down into a hidden cellar.

Andromeda followed her down into the basement. The room was solid concrete, with rows of gun racks lining the walls. She'd never seen so many weapons in her life. There were shotguns, pistols, rifles, machine guns, and revolvers, all waiting for their opportunity to be fired.

She glanced over at Rosalie, who had already thrown on a bandoleer with shotgun shells running across her chest. Rosalie grabbed a tactical belt and wrapped it around her waist. Two pistols hung from each side with six sets of clips. Then she snatched two shotguns from a shelf and a pair of binoculars.

"What are you waiting for? Put these on!" Rosalie threw a bandoleer to Andromeda and pointed to a tactical belt hanging on the wall.

Andromeda slid the strap over her shoulder and across her chest. She grabbed the tactical belt and buckled the snap. The belt was a bit too large and hung down low on her hip. Rosalie handed her a shotgun, clutching a black bag, and headed upstairs.

"They'll never take my house," Rosalie grumbled, loading six shells into the shotgun as they crossed through the living room.

Andromeda followed suit, watching Rosalie closely.

"You ever shot a slug before?" Rosalie asked, unlocking the back porch door.

"No," Andromeda answered.

"It's a heavy shot. Make sure the stock is on your shoulder. It's got quite the kick." Rosalie opened the door and stepped onto the back porch. She looked through the binoculars scanning the area.

"Here, take a look at our enemy." Rosalie handed the binoculars to Andromeda and steadied the shotgun against her shoulder.

Andromeda looked through the lenses. The goggles were night vision, lighting the scenery with a neon-green tinge. At least twelve beings were standing amidst the forest-line, like a pack of sentinels. They were lanky with long black claws and ghost-like bodies, but there was no face upon their heads, just a black hole.

Rosalie shot a single shell towards one of the monsters. Andromeda dropped the binoculars, covering her ringing ears.

"Check out that one to the left. Did I do any damage?" Rosalie asked.

Andromeda bent down and picked up the goggles, bringing them to her eyes. There was a hole in one of the creatures. It wailed and bent over as if it were in pain. Then the gap began to shrink as the gooey body reformed.

"You hit it, but it's healing itself somehow." Andromeda surveyed the area again.

"What!" Rosalie said, looking over at Andromeda.

"Yeah, and the others seem pretty pissed off," Andromeda added.

Several moans roared from the black figures as they began to move.

"Don't worry about the binoculars. Get your gun out and start firing," Rosalie demanded.

Andromeda dropped the goggles and lifted the shotgun to her shoulder.

"Pull the pump back to load the shell," Rosalie screamed, firing two shots.

Andromeda's hand slid the pump forward and back. She aimed for a black figure to the right. The gun was shaking slightly from her nerves, but she pulled the trigger anyways. The recoil plunged into her shoulder, and she screeched with pain.

"Use your pistols if that's too much," Rosalie shouted over another shot.

The black figures continued their approach, edging closer and closer to the cabin. Each shot momentarily wounded them. One of the biggest ones stepped across the firepit. The flames illuminated the shadow's body, unveiling black claws ready to rip and tear them apart.

Rosalie fired three shots into the being with one of her pistols, sending it trailing back behind the fire. Andromeda pointed her handgun at two more headed towards her. She fired ten shots as quickly as she could and landed three blows. The beings moaned again, shaking the windows behind them.

"Time to try something else," Rosalie said, diving into her bag.

"Is that a grenade?" Andromeda asked as Rosalie tossed a pin to the floor.

Rosalie nodded as she stepped down the steps and threw the grenade at the closest figure. An explosion rippled over the backyard. Andromeda fell to the ground beside the binoculars. She picked them up and peered at the being Rosalie had struck. There was a shriek of pain from the monster, and it collapsed to the ground.

"That should do the trick," Rosalie said, turning to Andromeda. "Bring the bag; let's kill these things."

Andromeda stood up, reached inside the bag, and grasped two grenades. She jumped over the steps and ran beside Rosalie, handing her the bag. They flung the explosives at the shadow monsters, blowing limbs and torsos to pieces.

Andromeda felt in the bag. They were out of grenades. She hoisted the shotgun to her shoulder and fired the last five rounds. Four of them sunk into the last creature, blowing away both legs. They walked towards the monster writhing on the ground. Rosalie reached behind her, drawing out a fifty-caliber desert eagle, and put two shots in its chest, silencing the creature.

They scanned the area with pistols in hand, searching for any survivors. Nothing was moving. The ground was full of gaping holes and steaming black puss.

Andromeda turned to Rosalie. "That was the most amazing thing I've ever done."

Rosalie smiled. "You caught on pretty fast. Might have to take you with us the next time we go Kodiak hunting."

"What's a Kodiak?" Andromeda said, placing the pistols back in her belt.

"Well, they're kind of like—"

A roar echoed through the woods. Rosalie stopped talking and looked towards the forest. Andromeda's hands shook with fear.

"What was that?" Rosalie whispered.

"We're going to need a lot more firepower," Andromeda said.

Rosalie nodded, and they ran back inside the cabin.

"What's happening?" Pandora yelled from Jacob's room.

"We're under attack, stay in there with Killian's dad," Andromeda yelled.

"I don't know what to do. He's burning up. His temperature is one-hundred and six degrees," Pandora shouted.

"Put cold towels all over him," Rosalie hollered, running into the master bedroom and back down into the cellar.

Pandora rushed over to the bathroom, grabbing several towels. She threw them in the bathtub turning on the cold water. Then she snatched all the washcloths and threw them in the sink.

She picked up the cold towels and placed them over Jacob's body. He thrashed and convulsed on the bed. She took the washcloths from the sink and stuck them around his face.

Looking up at the fan spinning around, she turned towards the window. A breeze was blowing through the trees. She flung open the window, letting in the cold drafts of air.

What else can I do? She thought. Mittens the kitten, rubbed against her ankles, making figure eights between her legs.

An idea struck her, and she ran out of the room and down the stairs. Andromeda and Rosalie ran by, looking like soldiers armed for war. Jackson barked at them from the sofa, but no one heard it. Pandora ran into the kitchen and flung open the cabinets, finding two large mixing bowls. She filled them with ice and ran back upstairs, pouring the ice over Jacob's body.

His complexion was as red as an apple. Pandora laid her hand upon his head, and the heat coming off his body was tremendous. She looked at her palms, staring at the etched symbols buried within them. She pressed both of them down upon his body, but nothing happened.

Several gunshots exploded outside the window, making Pandora jump. Jacob shuddered violently on the bed as the kitten jumped up in a chair, shivering. She pressed Jacob down into the mattress, hoping he wouldn't fall off. The vibrating stopped, and his body went rigid.

He wasn't breathing. Pandora felt for a pulse, but there was nothing there. She looked down at her hands as they began to glow. She held them over his body about an inch from his skin and floated them over him in a circular motion.

Nothing happened. Pandora pressed down upon his legs right next to the wound. She gripped as tight as she could, but nothing happened.

She threw the towels off him, scattering them upon the floor. She ripped open his flannel shirt, revealing his bare chest. She placed her hands upon his heart and closed her eyes. She felt the heat rising off him, and it burned her skin.

"Why can't I do this?" She screamed, kicking the side of the bed. "God, what do I have to do?" She threw her hands in the air, tears falling from her eyes.

She stepped back and stared at Jacob. His complexion was beginning to change, becoming paler and paler. A barrage of gunshots fired outside, and another roar shook the bedroom.

Maybe, I need to restart the brain, she thought. She walked up to Jacob's head and placed her hands over his temples. A blue glow shone through her fingers as she pressed harder and harder, but he laid there motionless. She let go and walked away.

She buried her face in her hands and cried, ignoring the screams and gunshots outside the window. *What is wrong with me? Why can't I do this? This is my gift. This is my power. Why can't I bring him back?*

She stared at Jacob's unmoving corpse, biting her lip.

Killian will be heartbroken. I can't let that happen. Not on my watch.

She stood up and walked back over to the bed. She crossed herself and prayed, "God, help me figure this out."

She ran her hands slowly back over Jacob. The blue glow underneath her palms began to shine. Sometimes the color faded, and sometimes it was stronger. She found the main artery in his leg and followed the intensifying glow up to his heart.

"This must be an important spot," she said. Her left hand remained on the heart as her right hand moved over his shoulders and neck. Her palm radiated blue as she followed the intensity up to his skull and over his brain. Her hands burst with energy.

Jacob's body blazed a cobalt blue as he rose off the bed. Pandora shut her eyes. The pain of her power coursed through her body like lava sifting through her veins. She screamed louder than she ever had before and fell to the floor.

Jacob's eyes opened. He coughed and heaved as the pounding of his heart settled. He tried to sit up, but his head was spinning. He spotted Pandora and a kitten beside her. He moved towards her, but his strength hadn't fully returned, sending him crashing to the floor. The kitten hissed.

He pulled himself up by the bedsheets, feeling the soaking wet comforter. Gunshots rang outside the window. Then a massive explosion shook the cabin. He covered his ears and limped towards the window, but the shots were coming from behind the house. He stumbled back across the room and knelt beside Pandora, attempting to pet the golden-eyed kitten. The small ball of fur eyed him suspiciously but allowed him to touch her. Jacob placed his other hand on Pandora's shoulder and shook her, but she didn't respond.

"Pandora, wake up," Jacob said.

She began to stir. "Mr. Gold, is that you?" Pandora asked, blinking rapidly, pushing herself up off the floor.

"Yes, it's me," he answered.

"Why can't I see anything?" she said, reaching out for him.

"You can't see?" Jacob asked, examining her face.

"No," she cried, rubbing her eyes.

"Let me see them," Jacob commanded.

Pandora straightened her face towards the sound of his voice, and her eyelids parted, revealing two golden irises.

"Well, your eyes have changed colors, just like your sister's did."

"What do you mean?" Pandora's hands shot up to her eyes, rubbing them intensely.

Jacob lifted Pandora and sat her in the chair next to the bed. "I think I was wrong about Andromeda's blindness. Whatever happened to her, I think, has happened to you. Your eyes are as gold as hers."

"They are?" Pandora asked, rubbing them again.

"Yeah," Jacob said, stretching his back and arms.

Another explosion shook the window as a vicious roar sounded outside.

"I recognize that sound. That's a minotaur," Jacob said. "What's happening out there?"

"I don't know. Something's been attacking the cabin for the last hour. I haven't been down there. I've been up here with you," Pandora said, as the kitten purred against her ankles. She reached down and picked up the snow-white ball of fluff.

"Where did this cat come from?" Jacob asked, staring at the little thing.

"Killian made it for me this morning." Pandora's voice cracked.

Glass shattered down below, and something thudded on the living room floor.

"I need to go down there. Killian will need my help." Jacob stumbled towards the door.

"Killian's not down there," Pandora cried, holding on tightly to the kitten.

"What do you mean? Where is he?" Jacob asked, grabbing her hand.

"He and Mr. Jimmy left hours ago to get you antibiotics, but they never returned. The power's been out, and none of the vehicles work. It's just like what happened back home." Pandora's tears fell across her cheeks.

246

Jacob looked out the window, and gunfire rang out again. "So who's down there? Rosalie and Andromeda?"

Pandora nodded, wiping her tears away with her sleeve.

"You stay right here," Jacob said, standing up quickly. "I'll be back as soon as this is over."

"No," Pandora screamed, reaching out for him. "You can't leave me here. I can't see anything. I won't know if something is coming to get me." Pandora's face shook with panic.

Jacob pulled her up off the chair and hugged her. "It'll be all right. They need me down there. You have this little kitten that will stay with you. I'll hide you in the closet and shut the doors. Then you'll be able to hear if anyone comes in." Jacob guided Pandora towards the closet.

Pandora's head shook in protest, holding the kitten in her arms.

"You'll be safe," Jacob said. "No one will even know you're in here." He sat her down in the walk-in closet as she shook, clutching the purring kitten. He shut the closet door and said, "I'll be back as soon as I can."

Jacob staggered towards the bedroom door and shut it. He climbed down the circular staircase to the ground floor. Shattered glass covered the ground. He gagged at the smell of death in the air and walked around the corner to see a minotaur lying dead upon a sofa he had demolished. He gazed out the window. Rosalie was firing an AK47 at a group of moving bushes. Andromeda was standing beside her, pounding out round after round from a twelve-gauge shotgun.

He looked around for a weapon. He wobbled and grasped onto the couch to steady himself. The stench from the minotaur was overpowering. He let go of the furniture and limped outside. Andromeda turned towards him with rage-filled eyes burning with madness.

Jacob threw his hands up in the air. Andromeda finally recognized him and turned back to the array of creatures attacking the cabin. Jacob peered around. Mutilated bodies were lying dead along the ground in every direction. There were minotaurs, steaming puddles of black ooze, giant wolf-like beings, and a troll.

Jacob ran to their side, seizing an SK that lay at their feet. It was empty. He picked up two shotguns, but there were no shells. He snatched up a large black bag, finding two Uzis inside. He slid in the clips and loaded the chamber. He turned his back to Rosalie and

Andromeda, creating a triangle and pointed the barrels at the foes running towards them.

A shrieking cry filled the air. Jacob looked up to see a half a dozen bat-like beings flying overhead with green faces, their bodies in the shape of a woman. The banshees came together in a triangular formation and howled in their direction. An invisible force knocked all three of them to the ground.

Jacob turned on his back and fired into the air, taking down two of the banshees. Three shotgun blasts sounded behind him, and he turned to the side. A werewolf fell to the dirt about five feet from where they laid. Jacob jumped up beside Rosalie, who threw down her rifle.

"I'm out," she shouted and reached for the bag.

Jacob turned and unloaded both clips at two minotaurs rushing towards them from around the back porch. Glass shattered everywhere as sprays of bullets passed by the ferocious monsters. Jacob panicked as one of the Uzis jammed. He threw it to the ground. Clutching the other, he aimed and fired.

One of the minotaurs fell through a window as the other jumped over the railing, landing right before him. Its monstrous arm reared back and slammed into his chest. Jacob flew fifteen feet through the air, landing on top of one of the dead werewolves.

A mighty roar echoed over the battlefield as three of the banshees pinned Rosalie to the ground. Andromeda turned around, but a hairy claw grasped her around the throat. Its nails sunk into her skin, piercing her flesh.

Silence swept over the field as a strange wind began to blow. The forest trees bent and broke in its wake. Jacob glanced up to the sky as a silver disc came fully into view. The craft spun in a counterclockwise rotation as the hull doors began to open. A blue beam of light shot to the ground.

The Black Knight dove out of the hull and into the night sky, his silver wings shining in the moonlight. He landed on the field with a giant ruby-red sword in his hand. A dozen white-suited aliens followed behind him, gliding down the blue stream.

His footsteps shook the ground as he approached Andromeda. Rosalie stabbed one of the banshees and lunged towards the Black

Knight. Without breaking stride, the angel swept his sword through the air, removing Rosalie's head from her body.

Andromeda screamed as the minotaur flung her to the ground. She landed with a thud before the armored boots of the Black Knight. She peered up into the angel's obsidian helmet, glistening in the firelight. The angel removed his mask and stared at her with a wicked grin.

"Hello, Piggy."

21: DRAKON

Killian put the Tacoma into drive and took off down the road. The headlights separated the eerie darkness as he glanced sideways at Jimmy.

"So, tell me how you got this truck?" Jimmy shuffled in his seat.

"Look, there's no easy way to explain this, I'm just going to have to show you." Killian lifted his hand and said, "*Zahav*."

A gold bar fell into his palm. Jimmy's hand shot to his chest as a look of shock spread over his face.

Killian smiled and offered it to Jimmy. "I can make things appear. I can create things. That's how I made this truck."

Jimmy took the bar in his hand, feeling the smooth, cubed edges. They turned down the hillside and approached a stop sign. Jimmy turned on the dome light and stared at his reflection in the gold.

"This is real?" Jimmy asked with his raspy voice.

Killian nodded as the truck came to a stop. The Yukon River stood before them, and a mysterious fog was rolling in across the overpass. Killian drove forward, peering through the mist suspiciously. He looked down into the pitch-black river. It made him think of a giant black anaconda snaking its way through the mountains. The steering wheel vibrated under his hands as he took the antibiotics out of his pocket and placed them on the seat.

Killian turned his attention back to the road as the fog cleared, revealing a gigantic creature standing right before him. He didn't have time to swerve as the minotaur drove both its fists into the grill of the Tacoma. The truck flew in the air over the monster and rolled against the pole of a traffic light.

Killian looked around, momentarily stunned. The truck was on its side. He glanced down to his right, but Jimmy was gone. He unbuckled his seatbelt and fell to the opposite side of the cab. *He must have flown out the window*, Killian thought as he stood up and pulled himself through the driver side window.

He stood on top of the Tacoma and peered around. A gruesome twelve-foot tall minotaur stood by the bridge ahead, smoke rising from its nostrils. Shock shimmered down Killian's spine as he realized that he recognized this monster. It was the same minotaur that had tried to kidnap the twins—the one who had killed Squeezie.

The minotaur dug its hooves into the ground, flexing its muscles and letting out a tremendous roar.

Killian surveyed the area, but he didn't see Jimmy anywhere. The buildings were dark, vacant, and nothing stood between him and this agent of the Black Knight.

"Don't have your magical ball this time, do you, kid?" The minotaur snarled.

Killian glanced back at the being and stretched out his hands. "No, I don't. I have something far worse in store for you."

Killian screamed, "*Sharshera'ot*," and a barrage of chains flew towards the minotaur, encircling him like a dozen chromed pythons on the attack. The creature writhed as the chains squeezed him, coiling around every limb. The minotaur sent out a deafening roar and broke the chains from his body.

"Now you've pissed me off, boy," the creature growled. "Orders are to bring you in unscathed," the minotaur spat a wad of blood to the concrete, "but I'm going to enjoy disobeying those orders." The beast's hooves took off, and the pavement shook. The monster bolted towards Killian with claws exposed, and teeth bared.

Killian pointed his hands at the creature and concentrated with all his might, screaming, "*Esh!*"

The minotaur burst into flames, falling to the ground and squirming in pain. The smell of burnt hair and flesh contaminated the air.

Killian's focus intensified as he watched the creature thrash around in agony.

One long roar echoed over the silence as the minotaur pushed himself onto his feet, ran onto the bridge, and jumped into the river

Killian stared down at his palms. "Well, that was easy." Killian smiled and hopped off the truck. A cough sounded a few feet away, and he ran behind the truck into an alley. Jimmy sat up, blood staining his pants and shirt.

"Are you okay?" Killian said, trying to help him up.

"What was that?" Jimmy gasped, wiping the blood from his brow.

"It was a minotaur, but it's gone now. We gotta get back to the cabin, come on." Killian tried to lift him to his feet.

Jimmy screamed in pain and fell back to the ground. Killian looked down at his splintered leg.

"Oh, man, that looks bad. Maybe we should get you back to the hospital," Killian suggested.

Several roars sounded coming from every direction. Jimmy shivered and grasped his leg.

"There's no time. Just stay here and keep out of sight," Killian ordered.

"What are you going to do?" Jimmy asked.

"I'm gonna kill me some monsters." Killian walked around the Tacoma and into the center of the intersection. The fog surrounding the Yukon River dissipated as a cold breeze ran across the street. Creatures of all types were marching towards the epicenter of the city.

Killian gulped, scanning the variety of enemies approaching. There were minotaurs and werewolves, trolls and gremlins, goblins, and shadow people called the faceless ones. Killian tried not to panic as he considered his options.

Could I set fire to all of them, he thought, but then the crowds separated, revealing three times the adversaries he'd thought there were. Killian scratched the back of his head as howls, barks, and growls echoed down the streets.

Nope, I can't do this by myself, he thought, stepping towards the Tacoma. A few of the werewolves barked at one another, seeing the fear wash over Killian. The barking made him stop, and an idea struck him.

He stood his ground, looking around at the multitude. Savage goblins picked at their spears while the gremlins ran their claws over the metal siding of the buildings. The werewolves howled once more as the moon shone down upon them. The minotaurs dug their hooves into the pavement and gripped their fists around their horns.

Killian licked his lips and held out his hands. Words of Enochian flew from his mouth like an array of arrows, creating an army of animals. Four massive lions with golden eyes crouched by his side—five gigantic black widows formed behind him with glistening gold orbs. Seven basilisks, ten jaguars, and fifteen gorillas filled the void around him, each one with a golden oculus.

He examined his creations, and for a moment, a terrible fear ran over him. The lion's jaws opened, roaring with intensity. The spiders' pincers clicked, and the gorillas beat their chests. Killian swallowed and held out his hand, motioning for them to bow. The creatures knelt before him and awaited his command.

The enemy's forces circled the intersection, staring menacingly at Killian and his troops. They hissed and spat, sending repulsive shrieks and cries of war into the air.

Killian surveyed the chaotic mass, determining what he would need to do to win this fight. One of the werewolves howled, sending a squad of minotaurs rushing forward. Killian bellowed his command, sending his pack of gorillas towards them.

The werewolf let out another howl echoing through the street. A separate battalion of trolls hurried at Killian from the left. Killian sent his basilisks slithering after them. Hordes of goblins and gremlins climbed the buildings, rushing towards the intersection.

Killian directed his enormous spiders, and they sped off spitting webs, attacking the green monsters. The jaguars lashed into the werewolves as the lions attacked the faceless men. Killian created giant eagles that swooped down from the sky, throwing trolls and minotaurs into the river. He created three more lions to stand by his side and waited for one of the monsters to break through his infantry.

A heavily spiked goblin spun its way out of one of the spider's webs and rushed towards him. The lions bent down in attack position, but Killian held up his hand. He waited for the goblin to get closer and shot out silver chains encircling it.

The gremlin writhed with pain as Killian lit the chains on fire. His fingers twisted and contorted as if he were controlling a puppet. He manipulated the chains and the intensity of the fire. The imp struggled, screamed, and then burst into a pile of green ooze.

Killian popped his knuckles and cracked his neck, looking for the next attack, but his soldiers had won the battle. Creatures were slaughtered in every direction as his creations made their way back to his side. He slid his hand across the lions' manes and over the basilisks' horns. He high fived the gorillas and scratched the jaguars' chins. The giant golden eagles bent down their heads, and he rubbed their beaks.

His victory was short-lived, as three cigar-shaped crafts hovered in the air. The animals stared into the sky as the UFOs circled the area. Killian stood in the center of his soldiers, glaring at the massive silver pipes.

Large hull doors opened, and red beams shot down from the crafts. Hundreds of creatures from each vessel floated to the ground, surrounding Killian and his troops. A resurgence of minotaurs, goblins, gremlins, werewolves, and trolls ventured out from the crafts.

Killian's animals encompassed him, facing the approaching enemies, ready for attack.

The cigar-shaped UFOs dropped off the remainder of their crews and shut the hull doors. They vanished in a flash as the streets shook with the mass of monsters approaching. The stench in the air was palpable like being next to the latrine of a slaughterhouse. Killian tried not to smell when he breathed.

He began muttering more Enochian under his breath, creating another horde of soldiers. Battalions of lions, elephants, tigers, polar bears, grizzly bears, gorillas, spiders, and scorpions joined his forces.

The monsters rushed in upon them armed with lasers, shooting down Killian's soldiers. He pointed in the direction of the minotaurs with guns and covered them in blocks of ice. Then he sent out his legions in three directions. They clashed with the monsters, tearing limbs and faces apart, ripping and shredding the flesh from the vicious green monstrosities. The slaughter was brutal, and half of Killian's soldiers had succumbed to their wounds. He created more and more animals to join the fight, but the enemy was strong.

A wind burst through the streets, and Killian raised his head to the sky. Six disc-shaped UFOs came into view. Bright yellow beams shot out from the sides of the craft, sending explosions erupting in every direction, wiping out animals and monsters.

An inferno blazed down the historic district. Killian blocked his face from the wave of heat. Three lions and six bears stood around him, growling at every blast. The balls of fire suddenly brought an idea to Killian's mind, and he reached his hands to the sky.

He screamed, *"Drakonim Gadolim!"*

The sky ignited with bursts of flame that transformed into seven gigantic dragons. Each one was the size of an aircraft carrier with wingspans a hundred feet wide. Two of them were black as coal, and two resembled a mixture of iron and sulfur, but the largest was an emerald green dragon with golden horns running down its back. Together, fourteen golden eyes glared at the UFOs.

The discs banked in opposite directions, and the dragons surged forward, chasing them with streams of fire. The UFOs dodged the reptiles, continuing their attack, blowing up building after building with yellow beams of light.

Killian focused on one of the crafts, assisting a dragon who was burying it with fire. Killian formed a bubble of lava encapsulating the UFO, and it crashed to the ground. Another UFO sped off behind him while the other four maneuvered through the dragon's fire.

Killian focused on the next disc, creating a ball of water to encompass it, and then froze it with ice. The craft swerved and bobbled in the air, crashing down to the ground. A dragon dove on top of it, tearing it to pieces.

"Three left," Killian said, focusing on the next UFO.

The hull doors of the remaining discs opened, and blue beams shot out from the bottom. Three angels flew out from the hull as each of the crafts were overtaken by the dragons.

Three angels garnished in white armor landed before him. Their wings were solid white, and upon their chests was an emblem of a scythe embellished with rubies. The lions and bears rallied to Killian's side. The angels' wings tucked into their backs as giant emerald swords rose from shimmering scabbards.

Killian thought, quickly looking around. He held out his hands and yelled, "Selaim." A cascade of boulders fell from the sky. Two of the angels dodged the onslaught of rock, but the other fell beneath the volley of stones. Three eagles dove upon the pile of rubble, picking apart the unconscious angel.

The other white knights didn't waste any time and struck out towards Killian. The lions rushed forward, but the angels slashed through them with ease, then flew into the air. The emerald dragon swooped by, grasping an angel in its claws. Two of the dragons joined him, ripping the angel limb from limb.

The last angel stared at Killian, his emerald sword gleaming in the firelight as he approached. Killian flung out his arms, sending a throng of flaming chains towards him. The angel's sword parried and destroyed the chains in one swipe. One of the basilisks reached up and dragged the angel down by its foot. A black dragon pounced upon the white-armored foe, clenching his torso in its grasp. The dragon squeezed, breaking the spine of the angel. Killian walked towards the last living enemy on the battlefield, picking up the emerald sword, examining its glass-like texture. He bent down and removed the helmet from the knight.

The angel's brilliance radiated from his body. The starry eyes turned milky white, and the angel coughed up a blue liquid.

"You'll never beat the Senate, boy," the angel muttered.

"I don't even know the Senate, but if they want me, I'll kill them, too," Killian said confidently.

The angel laughed as the blue blood trickled out of his mouth. "They'll find you soon enough, boy, but for now, the females are much more valuable." The angel's eyes closed, and a white mist floated through the air.

Killian looked up in horror. *The sixth ship must have gone after Pan and Annie.*

He ran to where Jimmy was, but the building had collapsed all around him. Killian screamed, and as he did, a burst of flame shot in the air from his anger. He looked down at his torso. His flannel shirt had turned to ash, and his bare chest sparkled in the night. Each Enochian symbol blazed like melted gold.

Killian held up his hands, and his surviving creatures surrounded him. Five of the dragons landed next to him, shaking the ground. The colossal green dragon lowered its head as its golden eyes followed Killian. He climbed on the back of its neck, and with his thought, he commanded the dragons to grasp all the remaining animals.

The dragons took flight, carrying tigers, lions, jaguars, and gorillas in their grasp. The basilisks wrapped their tails around the dragons' ankles, and the spiders crawled up the dragons' backs. The eagles picked up the few bears that remained and one giant scorpion.

Killian touched the side of his dragon, and its enormous wings spread out around him. The creature took flight as Killian stared into the darkness. "I'm coming, Pan!"

22: KILLIAN GOLD

Pandora trembled with fear as Mittens purred in her lap. A small trace of light ran under the door as she realized her vision was slowly coming back. She glanced down at the kitten. It resembled an oversized cotton ball.

The walls around her rattled, and she squeezed Mittens to her chest. Hangers bobbled off the rod as clumps of clothes hit her in the head. She screamed, terrified of what was coming. Her chest tightened, and her palms began to sweat. She focused on her breathing, closing her eyes, and trying to stay calm.

The vibration of the walls ceased, and silence filled the room.

She breathed in deep, looking down at Mittens, whose fur was sticking straight up. Pandora could see the two small golden eyes of her kitten in the darkness and realized her vision had wholly returned. She thought about standing, about walking downstairs, but the mere thought of movement paralyzed her.

The kitten meowed and jumped from her arms, running to the closet door. Her claws scraped the paint savagely as if she was trying to run away from something. Pandora moved towards the little animal, trying not to make a sound, but the kitten hissed and tried climbing the door.

"That's a bad kitty," she whispered, but the kitten didn't pay her any attention. It scratched harder and harder, pleading to get out.

Pandora placed her hand on the knob and turned. The kitten shot out of the closet and under the bed. Pandora listened for any other movements as she swallowed, her throat dry and rough.

She walked out, staring at the ominous room. One candle flickered by the bed, bouncing around like a warning signal, casting long shadows on the walls. The smell of something strange hung in the air as she crept towards the window to glance outside. The trees swayed but no other sign of life was visible. The silence made her skin crawl as her chest tightened with fear.

The flooring creaked outside the bedroom. Pandora turned around, clutching her mouth, stifling a scream.

The doorknob twisted and slowly opened. She held in her breath, her heart pounding in her ears. The door opened, and a small being in a white suit stood before her. The familiar astronaut helmet made her knees quiver. The smell of death wafted inside the room, slapping her in the face. It smelt like roadkill that had been baked in the noonday sun, and she gagged.

The alien raised the familiar grey gun with red rays and locked them onto her body.

Pandora shot out her hands and screamed, "No."

The alien retracted the ray.

"I'll … I can walk," she said.

The alien stepped aside, motioning for her to go downstairs. She inched towards the door, hardly breathing. She moved past the bed and thought of Mittens. *Would she be safe? Would she stay quiet?* The alien moved his gun, sending the red glow in her direction. She hopped toward the door frame in reaction to the beams.

Pandora crossed the threshold and pinched her nose. The smell had increased tenfold, stronger than rotting fish and sewage. She walked down the circular stairs, and a sudden commotion behind her made her turn. A high pitched, bug-like scream rang in the air as Mittens attacked the alien's leg.

Pandora bolted down the steps and into the living room. Broken glass lay everywhere as she stared out to the firepit. Rosalie's body was contorted upon the ground, and Andromeda was on her knees beside her with her hands behind her head. Jacob knelt in front of her, bleeding from one eye.

She turned towards the front of the house and spotted the dead minotaur draped across the couch. She realized now that was where the smell was coming from.

"There's no need to run, Pandora," a familiar silky voice said. "The perimeter is surrounded, and all I need is you."

Pandora turned and peered outside. The Black Knight smiled his sinister grin. She looked at the creatures surrounding her sister. They were women with a jade glow hovering inches above the ground, with long black shawls and no feet. Two minotaurs and three aliens stood around Jacob as a group of faceless shadows speckled the background. The belly of the silver disc could be seen hovering over the forest.

She glanced back around the room. A dozen alien soldiers pointed their guns at her, enveloping her body in red.

A shriek cried out from the staircase balcony. Pandora watched as Mitten's lifeless body flew over the rails and landed on top of the minotaur. Tears welled up inside her as she turned towards her captors. The Black Knight's hand beckoned her forward, and she headed outside, staring at her sister.

Andromeda's golden eyes wavered, conveying an intense reality. They had been captured again.

An alien nudged her in the back with his barrel, and she moved across the shattered back door.

"Slippery little pigs you human menaces are," the Black Knight said, sliding his fingers down his ruby blade. "Too bad your allies are dropping like sheep to the slaughter."

Pandora knelt beside her sister, and their golden eyes met for the first time. A bolt of lightning swept down from the heavens, knocking back the Black Knight. The twins stared at one another, unsure of what had just happened.

The banshees ran up, yanking the girl's hair back, sliding a knife to their throat. "What have you done?" one of them hissed.

The black eyes of the green women peered down upon their prey. Suddenly, they began screaming, backing away in terror. All three of them shouted, "They have the blood of God in their eyes, the blood of God."

The Black Knight stood up, shaking his head and catching his breath. "What is it, witches?" he muttered, walking towards the twins. The banshees pointed at the girls and covered their eyes. He stumbled towards them and held their faces up with his massive hands. The gold swirled within their irises like a tempest of holy fire. The Black Knight screamed, reared back his hand, and struck them both with one blow. The twins fell unconscious.

He spat on the floor and glanced up at the quivering banshees. "Blood can be drained you worthless wenches." He walked towards Jacob. "But there's no need for the extra pig on the ship." The ruby sword rose in the air and almost fell on top of him.

Jacob's face winced, and his eyes closed.

The Black Knight stared in bewilderment. The sword was encased in a thick block of stone.

"How in the Seven Chambers of the Holy of Holies …" the Black Knight's jaw tightened as a thundering sound grabbed his attention from above.

Four dragons plunged into his silver UFO sending it crashing into the woods. A deafening roar shook the forest as a giant emerald dragon landed on the roof of the cabin. Killian's eyes bore down upon them, meeting the Black Knight's as he clutched the scaly neck of his creation.

262

The dragon roared, and a stream of white lave emitted from its mouth. The Black Knight jumped back, his silver wings fully expanding. A stampede of animals with golden eyes rushed out of the forest, attacking the monstrous creatures surrounding the cabin. The eagles swooped down, aiming for the twins, but a dozen jagged blades expanded from the Black Knight's forearms. He sliced at the giant birds, taking them down with ease.

Killian stuck out his hands, and fire encompassed the angel. The Black Knight laughed as his armor consumed the flames, spitting them back at Killian. The green dragon dodged the bullet and dove into the air. Killian gathered the other four dragons in his wake and drove them towards the angel.

The Black Knight spread out his massive wings floating weightless in the air. Dozens of blades retracted on his shins and forearms as a pair of daggers emerged from his gauntlets.

The dragons circled the Black Knight and let out multiple streams of fire. The black armor soaked it in and spewed it back at the dragons. Three of the dragons fell into the forest with a thunderous crash shaking the cabin. The Black Knight grinned, and his eyes blazed like fire.

Killian directed his dragon around the angel, thinking desperately of what to do next. *If fire won't hurt him, how about ice. He* reached out his hands, and a ball of ice formed around the Black Knight. The angel plummeted to the ground, and the ice burst around him.

The angel turned around and threw a dagger directly at the emerald dragon, hitting it in the heart. The dragon roared and fell to the ground. Killian jumped from its back, rolling across its wings onto the dirt. The last dragon swooped in, but the Black Knight sent a volley of daggers into its ribs. The dragon crashed into the cabin destroying everything in its wake.

Killian stood up, staring at the Black Knight. The angel threw a shower of daggers towards him, and Killian forged a wall of ice, consuming the knives. He ran around the ice, sending a blast of chains towards the angel. The Black Knight cut through them with ease and sent more daggers at him. Killian threw up another ice wall, but one blade nearly made it through.

None of this is working, Killian thought as he waited a moment behind the ice. Suddenly, his dad's voice rang in his ears.

"Destroy him, destroy him," Jacob screamed.

Killian thought, *I can create life, but can I destroy it?*

The Black Knight flew over his head and landed on the other side of the wall. His wings spread out threateningly as his eyes burned with fire. His jet-black armor jeered at Killian with its impenetrable strength. Blades materialized from his forearms, and the angel took them in his hands.

"It was a good try, piggy, but now it's time for the slaughter." The Black Knight reached back to throw the daggers.

Killian peered over at the twins beginning to stir. He caught Pandora's eyes in his gaze, and they were trembling with fear.

"Yes, that's right, little piggy. When I'm finished with you here, she's next. The only one that truly matters is the prophet, and I'll drain her blood until her corpse is as white as snow." The Black Knight's hideous grin spread across his face as he reared back with daggers in hand.

Killian stretched out his arms as the inscriptions on his torso burst with a golden light. He screamed at the top of his lungs as every muscle in his body contracted with rage. Killian's hair and eyes burst into flames as his fingertips shot beams of light at the angel.

The Black Knight couldn't move and stared down at his pieces of armor, vibrating away from his body. His arms tightened as his neck went rigid. The silver feathers of the Black Knight's wings fell from his body scattering across the ground. The Black Knight shrieked a hellish wail as he tried once more to move.

Killian's powers burst from his body like a golden sun breaking through dawn. He screamed as the light burned through his eyes and veins. The Black Knight's body exploded like the supernova of a star, and a trillion pieces of light flew into the air.

Killian fell to the ground, unconscious.

Jacob ran to his side and tried to touch his hand, but Killian's naked torso was hot as lava.

The twins rushed beside him. Pandora reached out and stroked his face as Andromeda took his hand.

Killian gasped for air as the light within him retreated. His eyes blinked as he said, "Am I dead?"

The twins laughed as golden tears rolled down their cheeks.

"No, you're not dead, you idiot," Pandora cried, "but you're never leaving my side again."

"Pan, are you okay? I tried to save you. I tried to get here in time," Killian said.

Andromeda rubbed his knuckles with her right hand. "You saved all of us."

Killian's vision cleared, and he stared at them for the first time with his golden eyes. A bubble blossomed between the trio enveloping them. They floated off the ground as a thunderstorm swirled around them.

Killian blinked several times, confused at what he saw. "You have a crown on your head."

"I do," Pandora said, reaching up to feel, but her hands went right through the sparkling diamonds.

"I can see both of yours," Andromeda said, reaching out to touch her sister's, but she also missed.

"Yours is gorgeous, Annie." Pandora reached out for the assortment of pearls and rubies speckled across Andromeda's crown, but she couldn't touch them.

Killian looked around the bubble. "Where are we? What is this?"

Andromeda shrugged. "Let me touch your crown." She reached out trying to touch his, but instead patted him on the head.

"What does it look like?" Killian asked.

"It's solid gold with a large stone in the center shining like a star." Pandora kissed his hand.

"Wow, that sounds just like me." Killian grinned.

The twins laughed.

The light in their eyes faded, and so did their crowns. The bubble encompassing them floated to the ground as the storm scattered. Darkness swept over them as they returned to the backyard of the cabin. Killian stood up, peering around at the destruction. He locked eyes with his dad and jumped into his arms, hugging him tightly.

"You're okay," Killian said. "I went to get you medicine, but I ran into some trouble. Well, a lot of trouble."

"I'm okay, but Pandora may have some explaining to do," Jacob said with a smile.

Killian glanced towards her, and her eyes fell to the ground as she blushed.

"What happened?" Killian asked.

Pandora looked up, biting her lip. "Well, your dad ..." she paused, looking at Jacob. He nodded, and she continued. "Your dad may have died, just a little bit, but I brought him back to life, so no harm done."

Killian gazed at her in amazement. "You saved my dad's life."

Pandora blushed. "I also kind of let him die, so that was the least I could do."

Killian pulled her off the ground and threw her in the air, catching her around the waist. Their golden eyes swirled with love as their lips came together. Brilliant beams of light burst between them as they floated back to the ground. Their feet touched the rough grass, and their lips parted.

Killian ran his fingers over her dimpled cheek and whispered, *"Melinyel, Orenya, Nienya, Tarinya."*

Pandora's eyes widened as she gazed into his. "Now, will you tell me what that means?"

"Don't you know by now?" Killian asked, grinning ear to ear.

Pandora shook her head. "I need to hear it."

"It means I love you, my heart, my goddess, my queen."

Pandora threw her arms around his neck and pressed her lips into his. The starlight above brightened for a moment as vibrating colors flew overhead. They separated, but their hands remained together, joined as one.

Then a thought hit Killian, and he looked at his dad. "I promised myself I'd tell you something the next time we were together."

"What's that?" Jacob asked, standing in awe of what his son had become.

"Mom's alive," Killian shouted.

Jacob fell to the ground clutching his heart. The trio rushed to his side.

"How-how do you know?" Jacob stuttered.

Andromeda smiled, "Yes, she's alive. I saw her in my vision with Killian."

"Where is she?" Jacob asked, his heart pounding.

"She's on the other side, in Pangea," Andromeda explained.

"How do we get to her?" Jacob jumped up, looking around.

Andromeda glanced at Killian and her sister. "I don't know, all I saw was Anah, and she was riding a flaming bird."

"A flaming bird," Jacob muttered.

"Isn't this great, Dad? We know she's alive," Killian said, hugging Pandora.

Jacob nodded and turned towards Andromeda. He wrapped his arms around her as tears rippled down his cheek. "Thank you so much for this."

Andromeda nodded. Jacob let her go as he wiped the tears from his cheek.

"So, what do we do now?" Andromeda asked.

They stared at one another as a cool breeze blew. Killian shivered, and Pandora stroked his arm.

"What happened to your shirt?" Jacob asked, staring at his son's tattooed body.

"It kind of got incinerated earlier," Killian squeezed Pandora's hand. "A little burst of uncontrollable rage, you could say."

"Well, we need to get you some clothes," Pandora glanced towards the remains of the cabin. "I guess we won't be getting any in there."

"Oh, wait," Killian stood back and said, "*Beged*." A baby blue robe wrapped around his body with silver accents. "Better?"

Pandora nodded. "Do one for me that's beautiful!"

A silver robe draped over Pandora with baby blue lining swirling majestically around her.

Andromeda walked over to the crater where the Black Knight last stood. "Do you think we're safe now?"

Killian shook his head. "The Black Knight was just a pawn in this malicious game between good and evil. Something called the Senate is after us, and they were using him as their assassin or general or something, but they'll send more as soon as they find out what we've done."

267

"Then we need to move and soon," Jacob said.

Everyone nodded, staring around at the devastation.

Pandora's eyes landed upon the broken body of their host. "What about Mrs. Rosalie and Mr. Jimmy?"

Killian shook his head, looking over at her body. "They were two innocent victims in this battle of powers."

"I could bring her back, I think," Pandora suggested.

"What happened to Jimmy?" Jacob asked.

"A building fell on top of him during the battle I was in at Whitehorse," Killian said.

Jacob placed his hand on Pandora's shoulder. "I know you could heal Rosalie, there's not a doubt in my mind about that, but she and Jimmy crossed over together. If you brought her back and couldn't bring back Jimmy, her heart would be broken. I think it's best they left this life together."

"Look," Andromeda pointed to the sky, the aurora borealis spiraled above them with brilliant colors illuminating the darkness. "Who knows, maybe they're being ushered across right now?"

They stared up in a moment of silence, taking in the beauty of the spectacle above.

Pandora stared around at the death surrounding her. "What about all of these creatures Killian, did you make all of these?"

"Did you make these dragons?" Andromeda asked.

Killian nodded.

"Should I bring them back to life?" Pandora asked.

Killian glanced up to his dad, whose arms were folded in thought. Andromeda shrugged. Killian walked over to the emerald dragon and placed his hands on its hide. The reptiles stomach rose high above his head as the long sharp claws laid out beside him.

"A dragon would be helpful," Killian said.

Jacob and the twins walked over beside him, staring up at the massive beast.

"If this Senate is after us, whoever they are, we don't want them to find us. So, I don't think we can fly around with dragons," Andromeda said with a grimace.

"There's not just dragons here. There's lions, bears, jaguars, spiders, and gorillas," Pandora pointed out the fallen beings scattered across the landscape.

"Yeah, and none of them are common to this part of the world," Andromeda said.

"Well, the bears are," Pandora said.

Andromeda nodded in agreement.

"Where's the kitten and the puppy I made you?" Killian asked, looking around.

Andromeda shook her head, and so did Pandora as she stared back at the broken cabin.

Killian nodded without them saying a word. "We don't know where we're going or what we should do." Killian scratched the back of his head. "Having the protection would be great, but we also don't want to be seen. What do we do, Dad?"

Jacob rubbed his hands over his scruffy jawline. "These are casualties of war. These animals may be dependent upon you. I don't think we could release them into the wild, especially not the dragons."

Killian walked down the long-frozen body of the dragon, taking in the miracle he'd created. He made it to the dragon's head. It was the size of a small car with teeth like ivory spikes staggered down its closed jaws.

"Flying on this being was one of the most amazing things I've ever done." Killian bent down and rubbed the snout.

"They'll be another time, son, but for now, it's not safe for any of us."

Pandora stood beside Killian sliding her hand into his. "What about Mom, Dad, and Orion? Could we save them?"

Killian squeezed her hand and looked over at Andromeda.

Andromeda bit her lip and muttered, "Mom … Mom's …." Tears crawled down her cheek.

Pandora stared at her eyes, wanting to disbelieve the truth buried within them. She clung to Killian, burying her face in his chest. He rubbed her back, staring at Andromeda.

"Dad and Orion should be fine." Andromeda sniffled. "They're of the blood of Eve, but he killed Mom, and for what?" Andromeda kicked one of the dead banshees beside her.

Pandora's eyes swelled with tears.

"Why don't we look for her on the other side?" Jacob said suddenly, breaking up the silence.

"What do you mean?" Pandora asked, wiping her cheeks.

"Pangea is the spirit realm, the other realm, the realm behind the Veil, right?" Jacob said with his hands out.

The others nodded, looking around at one another.

"The spirits from our world go to Pangea. My wife and your mom are in Pangea. Let's go find them." Jacob couldn't contain his excitement; his face was glowing.

The trio glanced at one another. Smiles spread across their faces.

"You want to go save our moms?" Killian asked, glancing at the twins.

"You bet your life on it," Andromeda replied.

"More than anything," Pandora nodded, holding Killian's hand.

"Then, let's find the gate into Pangea."

ABOUT THE AUTHOR

J.R.R. Jones is one of the few Floridians who can claim that their birth originated in Florida. He has a Master's Degree in Ancient Languages and Theology as well as Business. His time is mainly spent filling the minds of students with wisdom and encouragement to enlighten the next generation. When he's not teaching, he's fathering, coaching, reading, or learning.

ALL THINGS THAT MATTER PRESS

FOR MORE INFORMATION ON TITLES AVAILABLE FROM
ALL THINGS THAT MATTER PRESS, GO TO
http://allthingsthatmatterpress.com
or contact us at
allthingsthatmatterpress@gmail.com

**If you enjoyed this book, please post a review on Amazon.com and
your favorite social media sites.
Thank you!**